BLOOD OF THE MANTIS

ALSO BY

ADRIAN TCHAIKOVSKY

SHADOWS OF THE APT 1

EMPIRE IN BLACK AND GOLD

SHADOWS OF THE APT 2

DRAGONFLY FALLING

SHADOWS OF THE APT 4

SALUTE THE DARK

BLOOD OF THE MANTIS

ADRIAN TCHAIKOVSKY

an imprint of Prometheus Books
Amherst, NY

Published 2010 by Pyr®, an imprint of Prometheus Books

Inquiries should be addressed to
Pyr
59 John Glenn Drive
Amherst, New York 14228–2119
VOICE: 716–691–0133
FAX: 716–691–0137
WWW.PYRSF.COM

14 13 12 11 10 5 4 3 2 1

Library of Congress Cataloging-in-Publication Data

Tchaikovsky, Adrian, 1972–
Blood of the mantis / by Adrian Tchaikovsky.
p. cm. — (Shadows of the apt; bk. 3)
Originally published: London : Tor, an imprint of Pan Macmillan Ltd., 2009.
ISBN 978–1–61614–199–8 (pbk.)
I. Title.

PR6120.C53B56 2010
823'.92—dc22

2010003560

Printed in the United States

To Annie, without whom many things would not have been possible

A Map of the Empire
and lands south, showing the Exalsee
Lake
Limnia
Jerez
Fort Raid
COMMONWEAL
Luscoa
Sa
Fort Watch
Liev
THE WASP
EMPIRE
Maynes
Ahn Je
Desollen
CAPITAS
Skiel
Szar
Myna
Darakyon
Forest
Tharn
Sonn
Slodan
Helleron
LOWLANDS
Asta
Vesserett
Akta
Tark
Dust Fort
Egel
Thord
Dryclaw Desert
Seldis
Iak
Everis
Mallen
Araketka
Shalk
Tyrshaan
Toek
Siennis
Solarno
Ostrander
Princep Exilla
The
Nem
Desert
Porta Mavralis
Mavralis
EXALSEE
Red Porphyris
Dirovashni
Chasme
Aleth
Silk Gate
Solorn
Porta Rabi
Stel
Forta
Tsovashni
SPIDERLANDS
Fort Taramis
HEMESH-ALLES

GLOSSARY

PEOPLE

STENWOLD MAKER—Beetle-kinden spymaster and statesman
CHEERWELL "CHE" MAKER—his niece
TISAMON—Mantis-kinden Weaponsmaster
TYNISA—his half-breed daughter, Weaponsmaster
ACHAEOS—Moth-kinden magician, Che's lover
NERO—Fly-kinden artist
ARIANNA—Spider-kinden, Stenwold's lover, former Rekef agent
BALKUS—Ant-kinden, agent of Stenwold, renegade from Sarn
SPERRA—Fly-kinden, agent of Stenwold
THALRIC—Wasp-kinden, former Rekef major, now renegade
TEORNIS OF THE ALDANRAEL—Spider-kinden Aristos
GAVED—Wasp-kinden mercenary
FELISE MIENN—Dragonfly-kinden duellist
DESTRACHIS—Spider-kinden doctor and companion of Felise Mienn
PAROPS—Tarkesh Ant-kinden soldier, now in exile
SALMA (PRINCE SALME DIEN)—Dragonfly-kinden nobleman
PRIZED OF DRAGONS—formerly Grief in Chains, Salma's Butterfly-kinden lover

ALVDAN II—the Wasp Emperor
SEDA—Alvdan's sister and one surviving relative
MAXIN—Wasp-kinden general in the Rekef
REINER—Wasp-kinden general in the Rekef
BRUGAN—Wasp-kinden general in the Rekef
MALKAN—Wasp-kinden, general of the Seventh Army (the "Winged Furies")
UCTEBRI THE SARCAD—Mosquito-kinden magician, Alvdan's slave
GJEGEVEY—Woodlouse-kinden, imperial advisor

DARIANDREPHOS ("DREPHOS")—half-breed artificer and imperial colonel
TOTHO—half-breed artificer in Drephos's cadre

KASZAAT—Bee-kinden artificer in Drephos's cadre
BIG GREYV—Mole Cricket-kinden artificer in Drephos's cadre

SCYLA—Spider-kinden spy, magician and thief
LINEO THADSPAR—Beetle-kinden Speaker for the Collegiate Assembly
PLIUS—foreign Ant-kinden in Sarn, Stenwold's agent
ODYSSA—Spider-kinden agent of the Rekef

PLACES

CAPITAS—capital city of the Wasp Empire
COLLEGIUM—Beetle-kinden city, home of the Great College
COMMONWEAL—the great Dragonfly state
THE DARAKYON—forest, formerly a Mantis hold, now haunted and avoided by all
FELYAL—Mantis-kinden hold
HELLERON—Beetle-kinden industrial city, conquered by the Empire
MYNA—Soldier Beetle-kinden city conquered by the Empire
SARN—Ant-kinden city allied to Collegium
SPIDERLANDS—Spider-kinden cities south of the Lowlands, believed rich and endless
SZAR—Bee-kinden city conquered by the Empire
TARK—Ant-kinden city conquered by the Empire
THARN—Moth-kinden hold near Helleron
VEK—Ant-kinden city-state hostile to Collegium

ORGANIZATIONS AND THINGS

THE ANCIENT LEAGUE—recent alliance of Moths and Mantids from the holds north of Sarn
ARCANUM—the Moth-kinden secret service
ASSEMBLY—the elected ruling body of Collegium, meeting in the Amphiophos
BATTLE OF THE RAILS—recent defeat of Sarnesh troops by the imperial Seventh Army
GREAT COLLEGE—in Collegium, the cultural heart of the Lowlands
MERCERS—Dragonfly-kinden order of knights errant
PROWESS FORUM—duelling society in Collegium
REKEF—the Wasp imperial secret service
SHADOW BOX—a mysterious artefact stolen from Collegium by Scyla

The Wasp Empire has commenced its great war against the Lowlands, capturing the cities of Tark and Helleron and defeating the Ant-kinden of Sarn in a pitched field battle. Now General Malkan's Seventh Army, the Winged Furies, waits for reinforcements before pressing on to Sarn itself. Malkan's victory over the Sarnesh was accomplished by a new weapon, the snapbow, devised by the former Lowlander Totho, now an apprentice of the Empire's foremost artificer.

The Wasp Emperor, however, is distracted by the promises of his slave Uctebri, who has pledged him eternal life in return for the blood of the Emperor's sister, Seda, and possession of the mysterious Shadow Box, a relic containing the power of a twisted ritual that turned the forest Darakyon into its current haunted and lifeless state.

Amongst the imperial agents sent to retrieve the box from Collegium were the Wasp mercenary Gaved and the face-changing Spider spy Scyla, the latter of whom has stolen the box and intends to sell it for her own profit.

Stenwold Maker, meanwhile, faces the task of attempting to unite the squabbling Lowlander cities against the Wasp menace before the imperial armies advance once again. His worries are increased by the loss of his niece, last seen fighting alongside the Sarnesh. Unbeknownst to him she has escaped her imperial captors, released by her former friend Totho, and carries with her the precious blueprints of the new snapbow.

ONE

Coasting at a hundred feet above the clear waters of the Exalsee, Taki threw the gears of her orthopter's engine into place with a tug of a stubborn lever. She listened for the rhythm of the two wings as they suddenly picked up pace from a mere thunderous beating to a steady buzz. Satisfied, she leant on the stick, throwing the *Esca Volenti* into a low, wide and, above all, swift turn that the fixed-wing giving chase could never match. She caught the brief glitter of bolts shot from its rotary piercer, but they were far off now, no more than specks above the glitter of the waters.

Below her the two ships were still locked together, but she had no chance to determine whether the crew of the *Ruinous* was still putting up any resistance, or whether the pirates had already begun their looting.

She flicked the smoked-glass lenses over her goggles and looked toward the sun. Sure enough, the little heliopter that was her other worry was trying to hide there, now a stark silhouette against the sun's muted sepia glare. She continued executing her turn, dragging the stick back to gain height. The fixed-wing craft in pursuit had cast itself across the waters too fast for its own good, and was making a ponderous business of turning itself around, arcing high over the distinctive white-walled retreat of the distant isle of Sparis.

The heliopter suddenly stooped on her, cutting its twin rotors altogether to drop like a stone and then, as she sped past, spinning the left blades a second before the right ones in order to sling the machine onto her tail in a remarkable piece of flying skill. A moment later she felt the *Esca Volenti* shudder under the impact, but the heliopter was a tiny thing, barely more than a seat and an engine, and she had to trust that whatever crossbow it had mounted before the stick would miss any vital part of her own craft.

Thinking of her flier, Taki became aware of an ominous clicking from the engine. *Running down again—always at the worst possible moment!* The fixed-wing was now coming back, fast, swooping low over the waters and then pulling up hard, trying to barrel in for her. She climbed and climbed, so that, with his rotary letting loose in a blaze of wasted ammunition, he passed in a blur below her. They had both left the heliopter well behind. Whilst it could balance and hover on a gnat's ball, as the saying went, it had nothing for speed.

She had to wrap this up quickly and then get back to the ships, but at the same time she had to do something about the warning noises her engines were making. *Time to do the usual.*

Taki yanked the stick back one-handed, so that for a second the *Esca* was pointing straight at the apex of the sky, and then she flipped the craft on its wing tip and turned into a steep dive. She saw the fixed wing flash past her again, unable to compete. After all, the *Esca Volenti* was one of the nimblest machines over the Exalsee and she could even give dragonfly riders a run for their money on the turns.

Releasing a catch, she felt the wood and canvas of the flier shudder as the parachute unfurled. This was her second, so if she didn't close matters here before the engine ran down again, then it would mean a forced landing at best. Taki listened anxiously, above the rushing of the wind, and heard the clockwork mechanism that sat immediately behind her screaming with spinning gears as the drag of the chute rewound it. Sometimes, not often, that failed to happen, and at that point she really would have had a problem, for the world before her eyes now was already a sheer expanse of sea.

She pulled the stick back again, putting all her weight on it, and heard the struts and frame of the *Esca* give all their familiar protests. Another catch flicked and the chute was gone, billowing away into the ether, and the *Esca Volenti* levelled out over the Exalsee, no more than ten feet over the wave tips, speeding past the jutting Nine Fingers crags.

The flash of piercer bolts zipping past told her the fixed-wing had found her again, and she led it sideways in a turn easy enough for it to manage, banking left and right erratically to avoid its aim, until, and too late for the fixed-wing to avoid it, they were heading straight for the wooden side of the pirate vessel. . . . And then the fixed-wing's rotary was punching holes in its own ally, both above and below the waterline.

She pulled up, dancing past the white sweep of the sails, and a glance over her shoulder told her that the fixed-wing had flown wide of the ship's stern. The *Esca* could turn like nothing else in the air. Most orthopters around the Exalsee had four wings, some had two, but she had her secret: two wings and a little pair of clockwork halteres—drumstick-shaped limbs whose metronomic beating kept the flier under her control in even the steepest of arcs.

And now she was following the fixed-wing, which had slowed down to match her speed to accomplish the turn. She lined the *Esca* up directly behind it, with one hand on the trigger of her rotary piercer, the weapon that had so revolutionized air fighting over the last ten years. Like an infantry piercer it had four powder-charged barrels with spearlike bolts, but these discharged one at a time, not all together, rotating as they did so while the feeding gears pulled through a strip of gummed canvas that fed new bolts into the machine. It possessed the speed and power of a repeating ballista fitted neatly below the nose of her craft.

Bang-bang-bang, and the fixed-wing faltered in the air. A moment later it was smoking, the mineral oil in its fuel engine catching fire. She pulled out from behind it, seeing it dip lopsidedly toward the waves.

The heliopter was right there, over the ships, puttering toward her, and she saw the repeating crossbow loose and loose again, its bolts falling short at first, and then flying wide. It was jinking sideways, trying to throw her aim off, and she missed with half a dozen shots before one, by sheer chance more than skill, struck near the left rotor, sending the wooden blades flying into pieces. The little craft spun wildly for a moment, and she saw the Fly-kinden pilot make a jump for it, darting off under his own power and doubtless hoping she would not follow him.

Behind her a plume of fierce black smoke began to rise from the waters where the fixed-wing had crashed.

She took the *Esca* right over the two ships, and noted that there was still fighting on board the grappled *Ruinous.* Slinging her machine into another tight turn, she opened up with the rotary again, punching holes down the length of the pirate's decks. She had been trying for the foremast and, as she pulled out of her strafing dive, she saw it sag slightly against the stays. Down below there was confusion, and then the pirates, with their aircraft downed and their ship damaged, were fleeing from the *Ruinous* under archery from the surviving defenders, cutting their grappling lines and trying to get underway.

If she had been more certain of her engine or her remaining ammunition, Taki would have dogged them all the way to the shore, but, as it was, she kept them under shot until they were committed to flight and the *Ruinous* had built up steam once again, and then she coasted the *Esca Volenti* back down, hoping for a landing on the vessel's foredeck. She fumbled between her legs for her string of flags, finally finding the right signal, but had to make three further passes before an answering flag granting permission was flying from the *Ruinous* and they had cleared the deck sufficiently for her to land.

The *Esca Volenti*, coming in slowly and pitching back, with its wings beating furiously against its descent, almost managed to hover. It was a sharp divide between almost and actually, however, and she had to throw the control stick every which way to stop overshooting the deck and ending up in the sea. The blast of her wings buffeted every loose thing on deck before her, scattering papers and hats and baskets and anything else light over the side. Then the spring-loaded legs she had now deployed were scraping the *Ruinous*'s wooden deck and she finally stilled the wings, letting the clockwork grind to a halt, as the *Esca* made its ponderous settling.

Taki unbuckled and hopped over the side of the cockpit, her wings fluttering a moment as she undertook the drop to the deck. A slight little thing, even for a Fly-kinden; her kind always made the best pilots, because of better reflexes and less weight to drag at their machines, though few of them ever wanted to engage in such a dangerous profession.

There was a big Soldier Beetle approaching who must have been master of the ship. "You, boy," he was shouting, "you took your sweet time!"

Boy, is it? Well, in her overalls and still wearing her helmet and goggles, why not? She hinged up the smoked glass, squinting under the sudden glare, and then pushed the goggles themselves up over her forehead.

"I came as soon as I saw the flare, Sieur. What losses?"

"Four crew dead," he grunted. He was rather old for this line of work, cropped hair just a greying speckle against his sandstone-coloured skin, and she reflected how it was odd that older ship's captains always drifted into the slave trade. "Two others wounded as won't work their way to Solarno now," he added.

"Then you'll have to limp along like the rest of us," she replied without sympathy, thinking how those men injured in defence of his ship would get scant sympathy from him. "Your . . . cargo?"

"Still below, where the bastards never reached," the ship's master said.

"Slaves?"

"Slaves from Porta Mavralis," he confirmed. "Plus five passengers, three of whom had the grace to come raise a blade in their own defence."

She nodded, fiddling with the buckle of her leather helm. "I suppose you'll be wanting my mark, Sieur."

His face darkened at that, and she smiled sweetly. *What, you thought I'd forgotten?*

"Give it here, then. Which mob are you with?"

"The Golden House of Destiavel wishes you a happy and prosperous journey to Solarno," she told him, handing him the token of her employers so that he would know who to pay the bounty to. "If it's any consolation, you can claw back a little for giving me and poor *Esca* here a float home."

"Having you on my ship all the way? Some consolation. You know they'll dock me my fee for this?"

"Take it up with your Domina. Take it up with your guild," she suggested. "Just don't take it up with me, for I don't rightly care that much, Sieur."

He scowled at her, four times her weight and almost three feet taller, and she armed with nothing but a knife because a pilot carried no more weight than need dictated. She just smiled at him, though, to let him know all the trouble he'd be in if he started down that course, and he stamped away to shout at his crew.

They were mostly Soldier Beetle-kinden too, that odd halfway house between Ants and Beetles, neither of whom had much influence in these parts. She knew Solarno was a strange kind of city—in fact all the cities of the Exalsee were strange. Those kinden who had lived here since long ago, since the Age of Lore, were not natural city builders. Some of them did not even know how to work metal. Instead, a peculiar crop of exiles and visitors from the north and the west and the east had come shouldering the original natives aside to found a scattering of communities about the shores of this vast and glittering lake.

She finally tugged the buckle of her chitin helm loose. *Passengers*, she recalled the master just mentioning. If she was going to be ferried home at a snail's pace by this tramp steamer then she could at least seek out better company than the master himself.

⁂

There was blood on Che's blade. From a mortal wound that she had inflicted? Impossible to be sure, but she doubted it. Her recollection of the sequence of events aboard ship was at best cloudy. She had decided that she did not like fighting very much.

That decision had come after watching a battle, an actual battle. She had read accounts of battles before, of course, but those came in two distinct flavours. The traditional romances painted them in vivid colours where great heroes reared up, surrounded by their foes, and slew tens on tens, or were slain heroically while holding a bridge or a pass just long enough for their fellows to prepare a defence. The second flavour was found in the history books, dry as chalk dust, stating how "Garael with her five hundred met the superior forces of Corion of Kes by laying ambush at the pass, triumphing by guile and surprise though losing most of her followers to the fray."

No mention, in either case, was made of all the blood. She had seen enough of that by now, both as she had performed her little best to assist the field surgeons, and then later when she was led along the rails, through that appalling litter of the dead and dying, with Wasp soldiers stalking amid them and finishing off those that still lived in a soldier's final mercy.

Cheerwell Maker, known mostly as Che, shuddered, and continued cleaning her blade. The pirates had outnumbered the crew by two to one and so she had brought her resisting sword from its sheath and cut and slashed, drawing its edge across arms and legs, thrusting its point into any part of the enemy that presented itself. The routine moves had come naturally enough, just like in those hours spent practising in the Prowess Forum. She had, in that brief moment, put her thoughts aside like a true swordswoman was supposed to.

Now she stood shaking slightly as one of the crew began to mop at the deck, swabbing the blood from it. Another man was heaving the bodies of slain pirates overboard, only five of them and one shot in the back. The dead crewmen were wrapped in canvas, gone from crew to silent passengers in a sharp moment.

"Well, damn me but look at *her*," said her companion, moving up beside her. He had fled to the top of the wheelhouse once the pirates had attacked, but had taken a few shots with his bow from that vantage point. He was Fly-kinden, but a particularly unsavoury specimen of one, bald and coarse featured and dressed in dark tunic and cloak like a stage-play assassin. Now he was staring at the approaching pilot whose aerobatics had apparently defeated the pirates' fliers.

The pilot was a female Fly even smaller than himself, clad in an all-in-one garment of waxed cloth strapped across with various belts and bandoliers. She seemed very young, with a round, tanned face and smiling eyes, and Che envied the light way she moved across the deck.

There were other passengers aboard, but only one had come up on deck to help them fight. He was a tall, severe-looking Spider-kinden man, who gave the pilot a little nod of acknowledgement as she approached.

"So," he said, with a bitter smile. "The Destiavel, is it?"

"My ever generous-hearted employers, Sieur," the pilot confirmed, grinning at him. "And you are Sieur Miyalis of the Praevrael Concord, unless I mistake a face. Your cargo still safe in the lower hold, is it? A shame for you if they'd been taken by pirates. Not so much shame for them, though. A slave in Princep Exilla or a slave in Solarno, I see no difference."

The Spider-kinden slaver narrowed his eyes. "Then I advise you not to meddle in the trade, little pilot," he snarled, and stalked away.

"Superb," the Fly pilot said vaguely, before gazing brightly at Che. "Let's see if I can piss you off too, just as quickly." She took a second look at the woman she was talking to. "You're a foreigner—in fact you both are, by your dress." She pulled the chitin helmet from her head, unleashing an improbable cascade of chestnut hair. There came a low whistle from beside Che and the pilot fixed the bald man with an arch stare. "What's wrong, Sieur? Is it your daughters I remind you of, or your granddaughters?"

"Nice, very nice," he replied sourly. "Well, lady aviatrix, my name is Nero, the artist." Che caught the moment's pause as Nero recalled just how far they now were from his usual haunts where his reputation might carry some weight. "And this is Cheerwell Maker, a scholar of Collegium."

"Collygum?" the pilot echoed, mangling the name somewhat. "Spider Satrapy, is that?"

"Not within the Spiderlands at all, Madam Destiavel," Che informed her, whereupon the pilot looked suddenly interested.

"You don't say? Look, I'm not Destiavel—they're just the house that pay my way so I can afford to keep my *Esca Volenti* in the air. The name's Taki, and you're well met. If you'll tell me more about where you come from, I'll stand you a drink on the Perambula when we touch land. Maybe even find you a place to stay. I take it you're on business?"

"Of a sort," Che admitted, conscious of how suspicious she sounded. Of course, their current business was not the sort to be discussed with just any stranger, but this Taki seemed their best chance of finding their feet quickly in Solarno, about which Che knew almost nothing.

"How comes you've got a boy's name then, Miss Taki?" Nero asked, still looking a little stung by her earlier comment. It was true though, Che decided: he was old enough to be the girl's father.

"Well, old man, strictly speaking it's te Schola Taki-Amre, but most people lose interest by the time I get through all that." She grinned, and Che had to admit that she was really very pretty.

"*Te* Schola, is it?" Nero replied, clearly nettled. "Well if it's noble blood, I can't compete with that."

She looked at him strangely, and then grinned once more. "Sieur, such a name's no rarity in Solarno. As for you, why, surely you can't merely be known as 'Nero' in whatever port you hail from? That would seem just dreadful." Her grin seemed to feed off his scowl. "When they came to Solarno, the ladies and lords of the Spider-kinden brought with them the chiefs of their servants to provide for them but, as we tell it, they had left their homes in more of a hurry than was wise, and so the chiefs were the only ones who made the journey. My grandmother assures me that we were all little ladies and lords of our own people back then, and only came with our own mistresses out of love. Take that how you will." Taki now leant on the rail, looking north to where a distant shadow on the horizon must surely be the coast of the Exalsee.

"Where I come from we're a bit choosier about who we give the honorifics to," Nero told her.

"And do *you* merit one, Sieur Nero?"

He glowered at her and remained silent.

"We have a lot to learn about Solarno," Che intervened. "In return you'd like to hear about my home, and Nero's?"

"Very much." Taki grinned up at her. "If you're proposing a deal, Bella Cheerwell, you have my hand on it."

Che took that hand, so much smaller than her own. "I must ask one thing first, though."

"Ask away."

"Have you . . . are you familiar with the Wasp-kinden, or their Empire?"

Something tugged briefly at Taki's expression. "Ah, them," she said, and there was suddenly a distance between her and Che. "I apologize but I hadn't realized you were one of theirs." The next words seemed almost forced out of her: "If you're an ambassador, I'll point you toward the Corta. They can deal with you."

Che chose her own words carefully. "I'm not 'one of theirs.' In fact . . ." It was the crucial moment, to trust or not to trust. "I am no friend of theirs at all."

In Taki's eyes the same caution was reflected. "Well then, Bella Cheerwell . . ." the Fly said slowly, "perhaps we have something in common after all."

TWO

Two months before.

⟨|⟩ ⟨|⟩ ⟨|⟩

Back in Collegium Stenwold Maker had left Lineo Thadspar and the rest of the Assembly to continue the rebuilding of the city and begin a muster in earnest. War had finally come to Collegium and, though the Vekken enemy was gone, war remained. Collegium was raising troops for the very first time in its history: not a militia but an *army*. All of the newly formed merchant companies had dispatched recruiters through the little road towns and satellite villages and these were now busy drumming up men and women willing to take the Assembly's coin and wear a uniform. The uniforms, however, were likely to be somewhat mismatched. The Assembly had officially adopted the sword and book of the Prowess Forum, in white and gold, and made it a proud badge for the new military, but much of the actual equipment was windfall, and most of the companies had their own ideas about uniformity. Collegium suddenly had inherited a vast number of discarded Vekken mail hauberks, short swords and crossbows that were barely used, and the Beetle-kinden were always a practical people.

Everyone realized that, come spring, all kinds of chaos would be breaking out, both north and east, and that was why this Sarnesh automotive was now out scouting the terrain. The passengers it carried were little more than an inconvenience.

Stenwold had certainly endured more comfortable journeys in his time, pressed in tight, as he was, between his two bodyguards and the automotive's crew. Even with Balkus half disappeared into the turret so as to man the repeating ballista, and Tynisa practically squeezed into his armpit, he was still trying to unfold his charts. He finally spread the map as best he could, forcing Tynisa to take one corner herself, while he tried to put in his mind a picture of the conflicting powers: his city's forces, his enemy and those he hoped would be his allies.

His pieces were all ranked ready for his move. Here was Tisamon, who had taken Stenwold aside and lectured him at length about the responsibility he had taken on: namely, the Dragonfly-kinden woman, Felise Mienn. That in turn meant Tisamon had to rub shoulders with her Spider-kinden doctor, which meant more friction as Tisamon and his whole race loathed the man's breed.

And it was more complicated yet, for Tisamon was the one person Stenwold could trust to look after the Wasp defector, Thalric, who was as murderous a piece of work as anyone could wish to have in custody. Then, on the other hand, Tisamon had no love of Arianna . . .

Arianna. Stenwold paused at the thought of her: a gem in a sky otherwise denuded of stars, but another defector. He sometimes recognized that look in Tisamon's eyes that said, *I am waiting to prove you wrong.*

My friends are driving me insane, thought Stenwold gloomily, and forced himself to concentrate on the map.

There was a Wasp army, or most of one, positioned several miles east of Sarn, but it had not moved since the battle that the Sarnesh had brought against it, and subsequently lost after the deployment of some new Wasp secret weapon. The Sarnesh had inflicted sufficient casualties to cause the Wasps to fortify their position and dig in, while awaiting reinforcements. Information Stenwold received from his contacts in Helleron suggested that those reinforcements would come with the spring—which was likely to see more of death than new life at this rate. He was only thankful that the winter they were on the verge of was forecast to be harsher than the Lowlands normally endured. Certainly it would not be suitable for the movement of massed armies. Even the Wasp Empire stopped for winter.

There had also been a Wasp army of 30,000 advancing on Merro and Egel, further down the coast, but it had been stalled by 200 men belonging to the Spider Aristos Teornis, and then destroyed by the Mantis-kinden of Felyal. Teornis was at Collegium still, wanting to discuss strategy and brimming over with great ideas about how other people's soldiers could be sent to their deaths, his own having mostly returned to their home ports. *Yet another Spider that Tisamon will have to be kept clear of*, Stenwold reflected glumly. Also at Collegium was Achaeos, lover of Stenwold's niece, still recovering from the wounds he took at the Battle of the Rails, together with the Fly-kinden Sperra, who was tending to him. That made up the tally of Stenwold's people, or so he had thought.

But the Fly-kinden messengers had changed all that: first Nero and then a sullen-faced girl called Chefre. On the strength of their news Stenwold was rushing north by east, as fast as a steam-engined automotive would take them.

⁂

Abruptly the automotive was slowing. Stenwold looked up from his charts, now crumpled and creased, almost indecipherable in the dim light inside the engine.

"What is it?"

"Men ahead, armed men," Balkus reported, from the turret, and Stenwold realized he must have mentally shared his visions and thoughts in silence with the Sarnesh driver, for all that Balkus was a renegade. "A camp, looks like."

"Imperial?"

"Nothing of that," Balkus reassured him. "Still, no small number, either. Got someone coming forward . . . now a pack of them, a dozen or so."

Trapped sightless as he was within the automotive's belly, Stenwold could only sit and fret until he heard the voice from outside.

"We've been watching you for some while," someone called out in a Helleren accent. "Don't think we ain't got the tools to crack one of these things wide open. Better you say who you are, now."

Stenwold pitched his voice to carry clearly. "It's Stenwold Maker from Collegium. And you must be Salma's people."

There was a pause and then: "That we are. Come on over, you're expected." The driver obediently followed them within the confines of the camp with the automotive, the tracks crunching and lurching over the uneven ground. Once the engine had stilled Stenwold reached up and unlatched the hatch, letting in a wash of glare from outside.

Tynisa stepped out first, hand ready on her rapier hilt, her movements as lithe and balanced as Mantis and Spider blood could make them. Stenwold followed at her nod of reassurance for, with Tisamon back home watching their prize defector, Tynisa had taken on responsibility for his safety as a trust of Mantis honour. Behind him he heard Balkus now twisting his bulky frame through the hatch, his nailbow clattering against armour plating.

The camp was a ragged, temporary affair, composed of rough tents and lean-tos without pattern or order. Stenwold guessed that, at the first word of an imperial force heading this way, they could be gone without trace into the surrounding wasteland. There were plenty of convenient gullies and canyons out here in the drylands east of Sarn and, if someone knew the land well enough, they could hide out forever. *And Salma would have followers here who knew every shrub and grain of sand.*

There were at least a hundred people in the camp, and Stenwold guessed that half that number again would currently be out scouting or hunting. They were a ragged mix, the lot of them: he spotted at least a dozen separate kinden and a fair crop of half-breeds. They were all well armed and wearing leather or shell armour, with a few suits of chain. He even saw repainted imperial banded mail amongst them, and plenty of Wasp-made swords. They had been busy, it seemed.

In passing his eyes across them, one familiar gaze met his.

Salma.

The youth had changed so much that Stenwold barely recognized him. He had been reshaped in fire and blood: drained and thinned by injury, toughened by rough living, given gravitas by responsibility. In place of the casual finery he had affected in Collegium he wore a hauberk of studded leather that fell to his knees but was slit into four to let him move freely. He had a helm, too, of Ant-kinden make, also an Ant-made short sword at his belt, and gripped an unstrung longbow in one hand like a staff. His face was gaunter, his eyes hollower, and there was dust powdered across his golden skin. On first sight he looked like a foreign warlord or brigand chief, savage and dangerous and exotic. So little about him recalled those College days.

"Salma," Stenwold greeted him, and then, "Prince Salme Dien."

"Just Salma," replied the Dragonfly noble. As he stepped forward, he clasped Stenwold's hand confidently, and like an equal and not a student. "It's been a while since Myna, Sten." His history since their parting was written on his face through bitter experience. His gaze passed on from Stenwold. "Tynisa," he said.

She was staring at him uncertainly. "Look at you," she said, "all grown up." She went to him, one hand held out as though she was not sure he was really there. A moment later her eyes flicked to the woman who stood just behind him, robed and hooded in dun cloth, yet whose skin shone through, whose face glittered with rainbows. An indefinable expression passed over Tynisa's face, and she looked away.

"Ah well," Stenwold heard her say very quietly.

Salma gazed at her for a moment, the silence dragging.

Stenwold opened his mouth a little, then closed it again. There was tension here he could not account for. He glanced at the rough-looking band of men and women that were the Dragonfly's followers. "Nero told me some of what you've been through," he managed eventually.

"He doesn't know the half of it," Salma told him. Something, some dark memory, caught in his voice as he said it.

Are we not grave men of state now, Stenwold thought. As he was about to reply, a woman's voice cried out in joy and Cheerwell was bundling between Salma's people, rushing up to Stenwold and throwing her arms about him, sabotaging the dignity of the solemn situation utterly. When Stenwold had finally managed to peel her off him he saw that Salma was smiling. It was not the easy grin of his youth, but it was a start.

"Uncle Sten, I've got something really, really important to show you," Che said excitedly.

"Best save it for Collegium," Stenwold told her. "We're close enough to the Wasp army here that I keep looking to the skies."

"You needn't worry," Salma told him. "I have scouts watching for them, and my people know the land better than they do."

"Even so," Stenwold said. "When you get to my age, you try not to rely too much on anyone else's information. Let's get quickly back to Collegium and then we can take stock."

There was a shuffling amongst Salma's followers and he said, "I won't be going to Collegium with you, Sten."

"No?" Stenwold watched him carefully.

"I'm not your agent any more, or your student. I have other responsibilities."

"Toward . . . ?"

"There is a nomad town of almost twenty-five hundred people out there that needs me," Salma told him. "Currently it's pitched up against the walls of Sarn, and the Sarnesh Queen is waiting for me to explain to her precisely why that is so, and what we want from her. More than that, I have almost a thousand fighting men who are gathered together only because of me."

"A thousand?" Stenwold frowned. "I hadn't heard . . . Who are they? What is this?"

"What it is, Sten, is an army," Salma said. "And who they are depends on who you ask. Deserters, brigands, farmhands, tinkers, lapsed Way Brothers, more and more all the time. The one thing they have in common is that the Wasp Empire is their enemy."

"Well, then, the Empire is all of our enemies," Stenwold pointed out. "I don't see . . ."

"Many of them were slaves," Salma explained, leaving a moment's pause for that statement to echo. "Many more are renegades. They trust me, and I am responsible for them. I have not gathered them just to hand them over to Sarn or Collegium as an expendable militia. They are my people, a people in their own right. I call them my New Mercers, but the name they see most often is the Lands-army. We will fight the Empire, Sten, but if the war is won, we will not just disband and return to burned-out farmhouses and servitude or punishment. That is what I will talk to the Queen of Sarn about, and what I will talk to you about, in due course, but . . . things are now different between us. No fault of yours, but events are in the way. I owe these people my service, just as a prince should."

"I understand," Stenwold said. "Perhaps I begin to, anyway. Your emissaries will always be welcome at Collegium." He glanced down at Che, who was looking suddenly unsure.

"Salma . . ." she began.

"I'm sorry, Che. You've seen a little of my work here. You must appreciate my position."

"But you could die, if the Wasps catch you. And they'll try, Salma."

"I know." He smiled, looking so much older than her. "When I was in Tark they killed me once, ran me straight through. If *she* had not come to me even as I hit the floor, that would have been the end of Salme Dien. After that experience, it's all borrowed time. I cannot turn from the right thing just because it may send me back to where I have already been."

"You're always doing this!" Che snapped at him. "Why . . . why can't you just come back with us? Salma, I've only just found you again, after all we went through. . . . Why does it have to be *you* that does this thing?"

"Because it needs to be done, Che, and no one else *will* do it," he told her. "And because a prince cannot abandon his people."

"Tell me one thing." Tynisa's voice cut across their words, and parted them neatly.

Salma met her gaze fearlessly. "Speak."

"Does she make you happy?" Tynisa's voice barely shook, but the effort needed to keep it steady was plain on her face. Her hand rested on her sword hilt as Stenwold looked from her to Salma nervously, and Che seemed equally surprised. He recalled that Tynisa and Salma had always been each other's confidants, but he had not supposed that they were. . . . Or perhaps it was because they had never come so close to one another, but that Tynisa had always hoped they would be, one day.

Stenwold risked a glance at Salma's people, a few of whom seemed to have picked up a scent of danger. The Butterfly-kinden woman's face remained serene.

"Yes," admitted Salma. "Yes she does."

A muscle twitched on Tynisa's face as her eyes sought the glowing face of the other woman. For a moment Tynisa's emotions were writ so plainly on her face that Stenwold had to look away: *For this?* she was obviously thinking, weighing her sword skill and her Weaponsmaster's badge and proud heritage. *You turn from me for this?*

"I hope you know what you're doing," Tynisa said to him flatly and turned away, her hand still clenching on the rapier's hilt.

Only Stenwold saw the faint glitter of tears.

"I'm making it up, a day at a time," Salma said, eyeing her back, "but who isn't?" His attention shifted. "Stenwold, I have something else for you." Then he beckoned. "Phalmes, let's have the prisoner."

A burly Mynan Soldier Beetle hauled up into view someone who had been hidden up until now behind Salma's warriors. It was a Wasp-kinden in a long coat, with his hands tied behind his back, palm to palm.

"His name's Gaved, he says. He caught Che as she fled the Wasp army, but we were in time to turn that around. We've questioned him and he claims he's not in their army, just some kind of freelancer." Salma tailed off, looking past Stenwold's shoulder to Balkus, who was pointing at the prisoner, jogging Stenwold's elbow. "What is it, Ant-kinden?"

"He was in that museum place," Balkus stated. "Doing the robbery."

Stenwold stared at the captive, unable to decide whether he recognized him or not. "If that's true, we have more to talk to him about than you might think," he advised Salma. "You're happy to hand him over to us?"

"One more mouth to feed is no good to us, and besides, he doesn't seem to know much about the Wasp Seventh that's camped northeast of here. He's all yours."

When they were ready to depart, Tynisa was the last to climb into the automotive. Even after Salma and his followers had returned to a camp already being packed up ready to move on, she stared after him, holding her face expresionless with all the craft and Art she had ever possessed.

⦶ ⦶ ⦶

"Yes," said Achaeos, "it was here." He looked about the room, once the centre of a rich man's pleasure, now dusty and untended with just empty cases and stands. The owner's family had taken everything of value, so only the house itself remained. Collegium's economy had not yet revived enough for buildings to be changing hands.

"We caught them in the act, really," Arianna explained, watching as the Moth himself, grey robed and like a dusty shadow, drifted from table to table, his free hand touching everything he encountered. "We came in from over there . . . then there was a Wasp that took a shot at us. Then we were fighting. It was all over very quickly." Behind her, at the door, Tisamon remained very still, but she sensed him like a nail in the back of her head. He was here purely to watch her, and she was sure he was just waiting for some perfidy—any excuse to do away with her. Oh, he would wait for the excuse, anything else he would call "dishonour," but there would be no turning back after that.

"Here." The Moth had settled by a small, delicate, wooden table. "Right here." He leant heavily on his cane, and she saw strain on his grey face that could be due to his injuries or something else. "Souls preserve us, how long was it sitting here?"

"What?" Tisamon demanded, stepping into the museum room. "*What* was here?"

"Don't you *feel* it? Tisamon?" Achaeos demanded. Arianna glanced back at the Mantis, and saw a disturbed expression on his face.

"Yes," Achaeos said, "you feel *something* at least, as well you should. In the last of the Days of Lore, Tisamon, when the world was being turned upside down, there was a ritual performed, a desperate, depraved spell of all spells, and when it went wrong, when it twisted from its makers' grip, it caused such anguish to the world as you and I and any of us here cannot imagine. Your people and mine, Tisamon, gone rogue from wiser counsel, determined to fight the tide of history by even the foulest means. And they failed, they failed so very badly, so that the unleashed tide of it destroyed the entire hold of Darakyon and bound the twisted souls of its people into the very trees. A taint five centuries old and still not shrinking."

Tisamon's jaw was now set, with a certain look in his eyes that Arianna realized was fear. "And this . . . thing?" he rasped harshly.

"The heart of the ritual. The very core of the Darakyon. And now it has been stolen," Achaeos confirmed.

"And the Darakyon wishes it . . . ?"

"Unclaimed. The Darakyon was happiest when it lay here, unknown and unsuspected, unused, surrounded by indomitable walls of disbelief, but now it is out in the world again." He looked from the Mantis to Arianna. "I do not need to dissemble or blur my words with you. You both know the power that magic can wield. This thing, and I cannot think otherwise, is the most potent relic to survive the Days of Lore, the greatest magic left in the world—and it is *dark*. You have seen the Darakyon, Tisamon, so you know what I speak of. In the hands of any who knew how to awaken it, its potential for harm would be unthinkable."

"Truly?" Arianna asked. "I've encountered magicians, and . . . they aren't the people our legends tell of: I've seen Manipuli turning people's opinions, tricks with dice, an image you think you see, that isn't there when next you look. And then some Beetle comes along and tells you it's all mass hysteria and done with mirrors. And now you're saying . . . well, in this day and age, I'm not sure I can see any great magic come to return us to the Days of Lore."

"The Days of Lore are gone," Achaeos agreed. "But to unleash the power contained within this—a box just so big, slightly too large to grip easily with one hand—would change the world. Your Beetles and the rest would not know it for magic, but it would touch and taint them: it would spread darkness in minds and hearts, breed madness, sour friendships and poison loves. And whoever made use of it would be, I'd wager, no more able to control it than its original creators."

"And some Spider-kinden now has it," Tisamon added, "who could be anywhere."

"Do you have so little faith in a seer's powers?" Achaeos asked him mildly. "I know who has it, because I have met with her before. I feel her echo here in this room."

"*I* saw a man," Arianna said.

"Yet she was a woman, nonetheless," Achaeos corrected, "the same that spied among us in Helleron, taking the face of that half-breed artificer."

"But you killed her!" Tisamon objected.

"I thought I had," Achaeos said. The rush of magic, in this city of all places, seemed to shake him. Standing in the shadow of the missing box, it was as though all the artifice and craft of the Beetles had never been. "I see now I was wrong, for she was here, in whatever guise, and she left with the Shadow Box of the Darakyon."

"For where?" Tisamon demanded. "For the Empire?"

"I will know," Achaeos said. "Within a day, or perhaps two. I am pressing with all the power I possess and I think that, even at this distance, the things of the Darakyon lend me more strength. They are desperate that the box should not be used, for its possessor would then command them. Soon I will be able to look upon a map and see it there, as plain as writing. Tisamon, will you go with me?"

"You're not fit to go anywhere," Arianna pointed out. Tisamon gave her an angry glare and she spread her hands. "What? He's injured. Stenwold would have a fit if he knew the Moth was even on his feet."

"Yet I must go," Achaeos insisted, "and I would have you with me, Tisamon—and your daughter too. A swift strike, wherever the box has gone to, to bring it back, safe from harm."

"For this I will go as far as the world can take me," Tisamon assured her. "Tynisa must make her own decisions, but *I* am with you."

Achaeos's blank eyes gave no clues. "Thank you, Servant of the Green," he said. "But we must arm ourselves in knowledge, first."

"What knowledge?" Arianna asked him. "Who knows more, of this? Doctor Nicrephos did, but he's dead. Surely he was the only one."

"There is one coming soon who also knows," Achaeos said. His words silenced them.

"How . . . ?" Arianna's voice petered out. She had spent a long time amongst the rational Beetle-kinden, but her roots lay with an older tradition. The Spider-kinden had their seers too. "You've seen . . . ?"

"Stenwold has snared a rare catch," Achaeos explained. "Fate's weave favours us."

"Achaeos." Tisamon's tone was flat, but Arianna detected the faint tremor there. "You were not . . . such a seer before, to have such gifted insights,"

"Save me your tact," the Moth said harshly. "Oh, I am no great seer, to foresee all things. "'Little Neophyte,' they once called me. But now I am led by the nose. *They* see this. They feed me whatever is needed so that I will dance to their steps. You know who I mean."

Tisamon flinched, a quick shudder passing through him. *Oh, he knows*, Arianna realized, and: *I want nothing to do with this. This is Mantis magic, and there is no place in it for me.*

"There is to be an interrogation," Achaeos continued. "I can all but hear the echoes of the questions. Tisamon, I would have you on hand. In case our man proves reluctant."

In any event it was a day's waiting before Stenwold could make the arrangements. The locusts of Collegiate bureaucracy had descended on him almost as soon as he reentered the city walls. When the message came it was at very short notice, Stenwold grabbing a free hour and an unused room, and assembling as many as possible to hear what was hopefully to be revealed.

They had Gaved seated at a table in what had once been some administrator's office. *This should be conducted in some place better than this*, Stenwold thought. *We should have oppressive interrogation rooms, perhaps.* But of course the worst Collegium could offer were the cells used by the militia, and rooms here within the College were more convenient. He and Che were sitting at the same table with the prisoner and would have looked like just off-duty academics except for Tisamon's brooding presence and Achaeos standing as chief prosecutor.

Also except for the fourth man sitting at the table, whom Stenwold was trying not to think about right now.

"You're not denying you were part of this theft?" Achaeos accused the prisoner.

The Wasp shook his head. "Your man spotted me right off," he shrugged, "so what can I say?"

"You can tell us exactly what you thought you were stealing."

"I have no idea what it was," Gaved replied. "I didn't even get a good look at it before your mob came piling in."

Achaeos glanced at Stenwold, who spread his hands cluelessly.

"Who wanted it?" Tisamon asked. "You must know that."

The Wasp shrugged. "We weren't told. You don't ask that in my line of work." So far as Stenwold could tell, he was not genuinely holding anything back. Gaved was simply a mercenary, a hunter of fugitives by preference. Stenwold, looking at him, saw a man who knew he was in serious trouble, but without that desperation he would expect of a captured enemy agent with Tisamon at his back. There was, so Stenwold guessed, no great secret that Gaved was holding close.

"I can tell you what *we* reckoned," the Wasp added, unexpectedly. "It makes no difference to me now. The Empire wanted this thing of yours for someone important. Someone really high up, like a general, perhaps, or someone in the Imperial Court. The fellow who gave us our marching orders said as much."

Achaeos bit his lip anxiously, leaning imperceptibly into Che, who sat very close to him. Their reunion had brought Stenwold more vicarious joy than almost anything else that had happened recently. It had been Che, too, who had unexpectedly spoken up for their captive, so that Gaved was sitting under guard but not bound.

"Where were you supposed to take the box?" the Moth asked.

"Back to Helleron," Gaved replied promptly. "Believe me when I say I wish I'd never taken on this job. Helleron's usually as far south as I make it, and I should have kept it that way. This was a fool's errand: Phin and the Fly dead, and I didn't even come away with the goods."

"Which brings us to your companion," Achaeos said carefully. He had already made his suspicions known to Che and Stenwold.

"Oh, Scylis?" Gaved said, in tones of disgust. "A treacherous bastard, he is. By now Scylis will be living it up in Helleron with all four helpings of our bounty money."

At which point the last man seated at the table said, "*Scylis?*"

It was the first thing he had said so far. He was similarly unbound, but Tisamon stood close behind him, wearing his clawed gauntlet, and with a stance that said he was looking forward to any attempt at escape.

"Thalric," Stenwold acknowledged his query. "The name means something to you?"

It had been an uncertain decision, whether to bring Thalric to this table, but, suspect as he was, he was their authority on imperial affairs, and they had a Wasp to interrogate. The initial reaction between the two men had been one of outright hostility. This was not Gaved hating the deserter but Thalric loathing the mercenary for, despite his turned coat, Thalric's mind was still black and gold.

"Oh, I once knew a Spider named Scylis," Thalric explained. "A very . . . able agent. Your niece, for one, should have cause to remember him."

"We all have good cause, Thalric," Stenwold informed him flatly, as Gaved merely looked on frowning. "We know something of what this Scylis is capable, and if anyone could walk out of Collegium in the middle of a siege and get all the way to Helleron . . ."

"I had wondered," Thalric said, with a tinge of mockery in his voice, "if you would finally start believing. It took me long enough, but I suppose your Moth there must have helped to persuade you. Sometimes being credulous can be an advantage. If you decide to go after Scylis, little Moth, I would suggest you take care. When he came limping in after catching your arrow, he was not pleased with you at all. If I had provoked Scylis's enmity I would not get within arm's reach of *anyone* else, ever again." He smiled until Tisamon shifted slightly, the metal of his claw scraping on the tabletop, and the smile instantly went sour.

"So Scylis will have passed the box once he got to Helleron?" Che clarified.

Gaved nodded. "That was the original plan."

"Then the plan failed," Achaeos informed them, "for the Shadow Box did not go to Helleron," He unrolled a somewhat tattered map across the table. Stenwold studied it but could see little there: the colours and shapes made no real match to places and lands that were familiar to him. It was an old map, he knew, prepared by Achaeos's own kinden when this city was still theirs. Just as Achaeos could not grasp how to fire a crossbow or turn a key in a lock, so Stenwold could not decipher the way the Moths represented distance and places on a page.

"I have charted the course of this Scylis, or whoever holds the box," Achaeos explained, although of his audience only Tisamon could follow his markings. "Not to Helleron, in fact, but some severe detour. A detour north and then east, here to Lake Limnia."

"Jerez," Gaved said instantly.

"You know it?"

"I've done good business there," the Wasp hunter replied. "That's Skater-kinden land: marsh and swamp, bandit and smuggler country. Imperial writ runs thin there and so that's where the fugitives go, hoping to get into the Commonweal, or even escape over the northern borders."

"So tell me," Achaeos said, "why take the box there? Nobody would go *into* the Empire just to get out again. Scylis could have gone straight north from here and found a pass into the Commonweal."

"The black market," Thalric suggested disdainfully. "Skater-kinden, degenerate creatures as they are, they thrive on it."

"He's right," Gaved confirmed. "You can buy almost anything around Jerez." He raised his eyebrows at Achaeos. "And sell anything, too."

"Then we have to go to Jerez," Achaeos decided. "Now. Today if we can."

"Achaeos, it's *inside* the Empire," Che reminded him.

"Just a few of us. Myself. Tisamon and Tynisa," he told her.

"Just for some box?"

"Che, I have never been more serious in my life," he said. "You were there in the Darakyon. You *saw*. I made you see. That is what this is about. You have to trust me."

"I do trust you but . . . you can't wander in and expect to find Scylis just . . . sitting there on this box, waiting to hand it over. I don't care how thin imperial law runs there, it's still the Empire."

"Then we shall take a guide," the Moth said simply.

Unwillingly, Che found her eyes being dragged down the length of the table toward Thalric. He and Gaved had both been her captors, and she had made her escape from each before they had truly had a chance to make her rue it. She saw the difference between them: Gaved had some quality in him, something that told her he might have handed her over to worse men but not touched her himself. Thalric had merely been putting off the moment when she would have screamed beneath his artificer's knife, but it would have come sooner or later. His iron sense of duty would have subjected her to such torture without remorse.

Stenwold opened his mouth to issue one of his usual blanket refusals, but it was clear in his face that he was unsure whether being in the Empire without a guide would be worse than being there with one.

"If he comes with us, I shall watch him," Tisamon supplied, "and he knows what I will do to him if he betrays us. There is nowhere in the Empire or beyond that will then shelter him."

"And I'll watch him too," Che added.

"No," Achaeos said, and she had been so ready for Stenwold to forbid her that it was her uncle she glared at before realizing whose voice had actually spoken.

"There is nobody I would rather have as my companion," the Moth told her, "as you know. But this is a task not fit for you. Stealth and secrecy, Che. A handful of us and no more, to find the box as swiftly as we may, then seize it without fail, and return. I would not involve you in this, as I would not bring along Stenwold or the Ant Balkus."

"But . . ." She looked half angry with him and half aggrieved.

"Your uncle will have other tasks for you, I am sure," he reassured her. "We *all* must play our parts. I am already taking from him two of his closest allies and, Master Maker, you cannot understand why I must do this, but I must. Tisamon has agreed, and Tynisa also, I am told. Will you allow us Thalric? He was a spymaster of the Empire, so he will have ways of hearing things, uncovering things, that we don't have."

Stenwold glanced at the ex-Rekef major whose face remained a watchful blank. "I am a fairly decent judge of people," he said. "Remember, I have been in the intelligence game for twenty years, almost: that gives me the right to say no more than that I am a decent enough judge. I do not trust you, Thalric, and I would almost rather have Tisamon kill you here and now than risk your betrayal. I know you will attempt one."

"Then you have more foreknowledge of my future than I do," Thalric said implacably. "What would you have me swear by? I seem to have lost most of the things I used to own."

"Gaved," Stenwold turned to the Wasp seated at the far end. "A word with you." He stepped away from the table, far enough that his low tones would be lost to those who waited for him. Gaved rose, his eyes fixed cautiously on Tisamon, and followed him. Stenwold looked him over once more, registering the long greatcoat made of tough leather that had seen patches added and tears stitched up in its time, and noting the burn scar on his face, the self-consciously unmilitary posture.

"So you're a mercenary, indeed?"

"I try to be."

"That can't be an easy resolution to keep, for a Wasp living inside the Empire."

Gaved studied him for a long moment, then lowered his eyes. "That's true, and I do work for Empire coin, on matters too shabby for the Rekef and too delicate for the army. But I work for others too, Master Maker, private work, for those that pay: tracing, hunting, finding."

"You value your freedom?"

"All the more for it being hard come by."

Stenwold shook his head. "I had not thought that a Wasp might be just as much a prisoner of the Empire as any of its slaves." He met Gaved's suspicious gaze again. "I have a commission for you."

"You want me to go after this box?"

Stenwold was watching him closely, watching every blink of his eyes. "I have the impression you know the country?"

"Better than any save the locals. My trade does well there."

"I will pay some now, some later, in good coin, if you would go with them, aid them in their task and, most especially, keep an eye on Thalric," Stenwold told him.

"So you trust me, do you?"

"More than him," Stenwold admitted. "Once the box is recovered, you can even make your own way home, if you want, although it will mean missing half of your money."

Gaved took a deep breath. "The Empire hired me to find that same trinket, Master Maker. That contract's dead to me, if you now hire me, but . . ." He shrugged, groping for the right words.

"But how can I know for sure that you won't sell us out?" Stenwold finished for him. "I had considered myself a fair judge of men of any kinden, and by asking that question you've confirmed my judgment."

Gaved looked away from him back to the group gathered around the table. "And your Mantis will kill me if I so much as look at him in a funny way?"

"Of course," Stenwold agreed.

Gaved smiled slightly. It tugged at the burn scar and did little to enhance his features. "You have a deal, then."

THREE

The war with Vek had made many names newly famous in Collegium, but none so comfortable with it as Teornis of the Aldanrael, Spider-kinden Aristos and Lord-Martial of Seldis, whose naval assault had broken the Vekken army, burning their ships and landing his mercenary soldiers along the beaches to drive the Ant-kinden from the city. He had been paraded through the streets in triumph and, though he had been in the company of a great many others, it had been Teornis that the men and women of Collegium had talked about afterward, especially the women. He was young and handsome and always impeccably dressed.

And of course it had not been long before rumour had whispered of his other victory against the Wasp Empire that threatened them even now. Why, he had held off an entire Wasp army for whole *tendays* with only 200 men . . .

For accommodation he had been given the best rooms in the guest wing of the Amphiophos, and he had not let them suffer beneath their somewhat overblown Beetle style, but had lavished them with draped silks and cushions —or rather his servants had. What matter that he would be staying there only a few days?

When Stenwold entered, Teornis was lounging on a couch, with two brightly clad Fly-kinden servants dancing attendance on him. *Servants or slaves?* Stenwold wondered. Slavery was outlawed in Collegium but was the cornerstone of Spiderlands society, and nobody was inclined to pose that question for fear of the reply. It helped, all the same, that there was not a manacle to be seen, and Teornis' staff were dressed as richly as Collegium's merchant magnates.

"Master Maker," the Spider greeted him in a pleasant, reassuring voice. Like the best of his kind he was the consummate socialite, all things to all audiences. "Thank you for accepting my invitation. Pray join me."

Stenwold cautiously moved to the couch facing him, accepting a goblet of wine from one servant, a honeyed locust from the other. Behind Teornis, a sultry Spider maiden reclined on her side amidst the cushions and watched Stenwold curiously, but the Beetle found himself thinking, *I have a sultry Spider maiden of my own*, and he smiled at that.

"War Master Maker, I should have said," Teornis added.

Stenwold swallowed the locust and held up a hand. "Please not that title, Lord-Martial. I have no stomach for it."

"Then I shall call you Stenwold, and you must call me Teornis."

"You are too kind."

"I am just kind enough," said the Spider. "You are now a hero to your people. I shall flatter you outrageously until you agree to my every demand." His smile was the whitest Stenwold had ever seen. "I always thought myself fond of titles, but even I find mine has begun to weigh on me. There seem to be ever more matters martial to deal with these days."

Stenwold nodded. "Someone in a hurry addressed me just 'War Maker' today."

"A hazard of a practical surname."

"It could be worse." Stenwold found himself smiling again. "When I was a student here, there was a fellow called Hiram Master who entered into the Assembly. Nobody had thought about it, but suddenly he was Master Master. He resigned a tenday later."

Teornis laughed politely. "Stenwold, are you currently in the right frame of mind to discuss Spiderland politics?"

"*Is* there ever a right frame of mind, for my people?"

"Nonetheless, there are matters we must discuss. I have been called back home. My mother and my sisters and my aunts have decided that my military skills, such as they are, are now required at Seldis. The Wasps are liable to take the annihilation of their Fourth Army rather badly. We will, of course, say that we have no control over those reckless Mantis savages and never have had. We have even sent messages of condolence, though I would not want to be one of those messengers."

"You think the Wasp Empire will attack the Spiderlands."

"The Empire will have to do something about Seldis, at any rate. Whether they will simply keep troops on hand to deploy against us, or whether they will actually seek to take the city, I cannot say, but they will do *something*." Teornis drained his wine and let a Fly servant refill it. "It is a strange thing, how the borders of our lands are intentionally blurred. On our maps, Merro and Egel are ours, and all the land to the edge of the Felyal. Some overly ambitious cartographers even place Tark and Kes within our borders. We like owning things, we Spiders. And yet, at the same time, living in Seldis gives one a strange perspective on life. For the Spiderlands proper it is a backwater, a place for the disgraced and the clumsy, but, playing our games there, and looking with amusement at our northern neighbours who cannot—forgive me for saying it—ever match us in our dances . . . well, we find that the borders are blurred both ways. That, strangely, we are Lowlanders even as you are. Lowlanders and Spiders both. This is why the Aldanrael, and several other families under our banner, have acted as they have.

You must allow that our disposition and actions will be important, in the months to come. We are no mere onlookers."

"You have proved that very ably, Teornis."

"Our army at Seldis grows, ready to repulse a Wasp invasion should matters become so dire, and we are seeking assistance from the cities south of us: Siennis and Everis-on-the-Isle. There is a complication, though, and this is where you can dabble in Spider politics, if you wish."

"I wish anything but," Stenwold told him, "but continue, please. What is your complication?"

"It is that we have another point of contact with the Empire. Over the last few years the Wasps have expanded along the eastern edge of the Dryclaw, until they have reached our own sphere of influence. If they were to put pressure on us there, then there would indeed be a complication. Military attention would be divided but, more importantly, so would political attention. Those with interests in that area might call for peace, even collusion. Self-interest, you understand, is a significant force in our culture."

"In all cultures," Stenwold agreed. "Where are we on the maps exactly, Teornis? The eastern edge of the Dryclaw is not well known to us, and the Scorpion-kinden discourage exploration." *As do your own people*, but that was a thought best kept silent.

"The desert is a triangle of sorts, broad at the northern edge, but narrow toward the Range of the Tail, as those unimaginative Scorpion fellows call it. South from there lies a large lake, and land that is my people's and yet not my people's, and a city named Solarno."

Stenwold nodded. "I've heard it mentioned."

"The Aldanrael has no interests or agents in Solarno, Stenwold, but I have heard that the Wasps have been seen there, speaking much of peace and trade and sizing up the local militia. Solarno is a renegade city, founded by those who had failed in the Spiderlands. Exiles and outcasts mainly, and officially we have no traffic with them. Unofficially, however, it is a thriving market, a stopping point for eastern-bound travellers, an oubliette for those who have slipped in the dance. The Spiderlands maintain Solarno's pretence of independence simply because it is useful, you understand?"

"And now the Wasps are there."

"And the rulers of Solarno, I'll wager, are not taking them seriously. They will instead play their games and try to use the Wasps against their local enemies. Solarno is the Spiderlands in miniature, if you will, for they are only one city but divided against themselves. If the Wasps catch them unawares, Solarno will turn from our plaything into the Wasps' own gateway into our lands. At that point any chance of aid such as we have recently rendered to Collegium will cease, because we will have our own worries to keep us busy."

"You want me to send some of my people to this Solarno?" Stenwold asked him.

"Spider-kinden agents would only be caught up in the dance," Teornis confirmed, "and worse, they would have their own agendas. At this juncture I trust your agents more than my own. Someone polite and diplomatic is called for, Master Maker, not swift to take offence nor quick to be deceived. Most certainly—mother preserve us!—not that Mantis. But I trust your choice in this."

⦶ ⦶ ⦶

Long journeys are soonest started was a Fly-kinden maxim. It seemed to Stenwold that his plans, for once, fell into place all too easily. A few days after his words with Teornis, and everyone seemed to be leaving except him.

There was only one Spider-kinden ship in Collegium's harbour now, but it was Teornis's personal vessel, the craft on which he had weathered out the sea battle, rather than on the great flagship that had been so prominent. Spiders always preferred guile and speed to strength. The sailors, too, were Spider-kinden mostly. Stenwold had never thought of them as a maritime breed but, then, the waters around Collegium were new to bloodshed. Eastward were to be found the longships of Felyal and the Kessen navy, giving the Spiderlands plenty of reason to man their fighting ships and protect their trade routes. Stenwold watched as the great grey sails of spun silk were hoisted slowly, billowing in the wind, strong as iron and yet light as air.

It had been easy enough, in the end, to choose who he would send off to Teornis' newly threatened land.

"I'm grateful to you for doing this," he said. "I know you're no agent, to be sent hither and thither as I choose."

"You know, I'm really rather looking forward to this," Nero told him. "I have been in every Lowlands city east of Collegium, and three or four in the Empire, too, but there's always somewhere new. Solarno is somewhere I always meant to pay a visit." He grinned broadly. "The world just goes on and on, doesn't it?"

"Just be careful," Stenwold warned him.

It was true, though, that Nero was the best travelled of any of them, and he had done his time in the Spiderlands too, been flavour of the month in Siennis one season, his daubs hung on everyone's walls. Stenwold glanced back in time to see Che hugging Achaeos tight. She, too, was attired for travelling: an artificer's leather coat and hard-wearing canvas breeches, and a big pack slung over her shoulder. She had insisted that she could not sit at home while Achaeos was off working for Collegium. Looking at her now, Stenwold still saw her as so very vulnerable, in a way that Salma and Tynisa were not. Was that just his wish to protect his own kin, or something truly powerless within her? *Still*, he forced himself to think. *Look at what she has come through. Look at what she has accomplished.* To deny her this chance and send some other simply because they were not blood kin would be hypocrisy on his part.

"You look after her well," he told Nero sternly.

"Sten, you couldn't have chosen a better unless you called up another Fly-kinden," Nero assured him, knowing that Sperra—Stenwold's other Fly agent—had adamantly refused to go anywhere near the Spiderlands. "Look at it this way," the Fly continued. "Me and a Beetle-kinden, it's perfect—you could go anywhere, two people like that. You could go into the Empire, even. I'd worry instead about the Moth-boy and his crew. They'll stand out just about anywhere they go."

"True enough." Stenwold sighed. "You know your route? You're sure enough of it?"

Nero nodded. "Ship to Seldis, overland south on the trade route to Siennis, Mavralis, and then by ship across the Sea of Exiles apparently, to Solarno. Fires your blood, doesn't it, hearing all those names?"

"Travel in the Spiderlands . . ."

"Isn't new to me, remember? And we'll have letters of introduction from your man the Lord-Martial there."

"Nero, he's not *my* man," Stenwold corrected. "He's nobody's but his family's and his own. Don't relax, and don't rely on him either. Cut loose from him as soon as possible and make your own decisions."

"Right," Nero confirmed, and grinned again. "I love the Spider-kinden. Never a dull moment."

One of the sailors called them, just then. They were ready to cast off, and the wind and tide were with them.

"Che," Stenwold called out.

"I know. Be careful. Look after Nero."

"That isn't quite—"

She came over and hugged him briefly. "We'll be all right, Uncle Sten."

"Just do whatever you can," he said, "but don't take risks."

His wings a blur, Nero was already touching down on deck. Che reached out to Achaeos, brushing fingers, and then she dashed after the Fly, thumping up the gangplank to turn briefly at the rail and wave down at them.

❖ ❖ ❖

For Achaeos the route was harder still: across the whole of the Lowlands, all the way to the borders of the Empire, and then further still. No ship, no rail could take him there, nor even a road untramped by imperial boots. This was where Jons Allanbridge entered the story.

Jons Allanbridge was an adventurer, a fortune hunter but, despite this, a good son of Collegium. He had fought in the air when the Vekken attacked, piloting his airship over their fleet to drop boxfuls of grenades—until the wind swept him too low and a catapult put a man's weight of metal scrap through the balloon.

Now, in return for a purse of gold and repairs to his craft, he would provide transportation for Achaeos and his companions. His airship, the *Buoyant Maiden*, would feel cramped with six aboard but she was a fleet little thing and Allanbridge had been flying her unnoticed over borders for years. Even a months-long jaunt like this was all part of the life of a merchant adventurer.

Like most Beetles, Allanbridge was squat and broad, a decade younger than Stenwold, with the hair already receding from his dark brow. He wore artificer's canvas, and a woollen robe over that, a long scarf bundled about his neck.

"These all of your lads, are they, Maker?" he asked. He was not one for titles, and Stenwold was grateful for that.

"All present," Stenwold agreed. About them the wind was up, tugging at the flags of the airfield, striking up a constant clatter of lines against the metal of scaffolds and flying machines. Stenwold turned to Tisamon and clasped hands with him, wrist to wrist.

"Sten, I must ask . . ." the Mantis began awkwardly.

Stenwold, who had noticed what company his friend had kept in the city, volunteered, "This is about the Dragonfly, Felise?"

"You must watch her," the Mantis warned.

"I'm surprised you didn't suggest taking her with you," Stenwold remarked, thinking of Felise's skills and the advantages of having a capable Dragonfly's sharp eyes and nimble wings.

"No." Tisamon's expression became opaque. "She is not ready yet. She would not . . . I do not think she would always remember our objectives." But then there was something more in his face, a sudden tug at its composure.

"Tisamon, what is it?"

"Nothing." Too quick an answer.

"Tisamon . . . ?"

The Mantis checked him with a look, eyes filled with an emotion outside Stenwold's experience. "I will go and she must stay. Do not ask me to take her—not yet. I will return to her. Remind her . . . I cannot . . . she . . ." The Mantis's breath caught. Uncomfortable truths were crawling just beneath the surface of his face.

"She would lose control, and then start killing Wasps indiscriminately," Stenwold finished for him.

"It seems likely," Tisamon agreed, in that instant burying everything that had been about to rise to the surface. "So you must find her a home here—and that Spider doctor of hers. He seems . . . able to help her."

Stenwold frowned. "In turn you must promise to watch Thalric."

"I'll consider it a wasted trip if I haven't killed him," growled the Mantis, on firmer ground here and without a hint of humour.

Tynisa, next, did not embrace Stenwold as Che had done, just clasped his hand in the manner of her father. *She has grown up now. She is no longer my ward.* The sword-and-circle badge of the Weaponsmasters glinted on her breast, a twin to Tisamon's own.

"This is important, Master Maker," Achaeos told him as his turn came. "I know you cannot see it, but I thank you for your trust." Of them all he wore no special cold-weather clothing, born to the mountains as he was.

"I learned a long time ago that there is more to this world than my eyes can see," Stenwold said. "Just you get the thing, whatever it is, and bring it back." Doctor Nicrephos had died for this box: another Moth who had been frantic about its importance. Stenwold noticed that Gaved had already gone aboard along with Allanbridge, gliding up onto the airship's deck with a flick of his wings. That left one man only.

Stenwold turned to him, a thousand warnings on his lips, but all withering in the face of that slight, mocking smile.

"What can you say to me, Master Maker?" Thalric asked him. "Why not stop me now if you are so very concerned?"

"I am only glad that my niece Che is not going with you," muttered Stenwold, at which Thalric smiled slightly.

"You mistake me Stenwold. I would not hurt her. If fate gave me the Mantis' life, well, that would be different, but in deeds done for my own sake, it would injure my honour to hurt such as her. I do not, however, expect you to believe me."

Stenwold was not sure he did, despite this apparent candour. "If you hurt any of these—Achaeos most of all, but any of them—you will hurt her. So consider that."

"Farewell, Master Maker." Thalric's own wings flared, taking him upward.

After it had slipped its moorings, Stenwold stood and watched the receding bulk of Allanbridge's airship. He could make out Tisamon at the stern, as a pale, green-clad figure staring back at him from the gondola

Be safe, old friend, Stenwold thought. *Be safe, Achaeos. Che will not forgive me if something bad befalls you. Be safe, Tynisa, and do not follow so much in your father's path that you cannot find the road back if you need to.*

On turning, he started, finding someone standing only a few paces behind him, up until now silent and unnoticed: Felise Mienn, unarmoured but with her sword gripped in both hands, point downward. She ignored him, for her eyes, sharper by far than his, were still fixed on the diminishing dot of the *Maiden*.

⦶ ⦶ ⦶

It was a long, cold trip for the passengers, and the routine aboard the airship quickly became one of silence and antipathy. They were such a mismatched crew that they had little to say to one another. Achaeos kept to himself, bundled in his thin robe and standing out in the open air in most weathers, staring at the horizon and fighting against the constant swell and sway of the gondola that unsettled his stomach. Tisamon watched the two Wasps suspiciously, always somewhere in sight of one or other of them, giving the impression that, had either of them tried to fly away, he would have leapt from the side to catch and kill them, for all that the fall would be his death too. Sheer fervent anticipation was writ large in his face for them to read. He spoke only with Tynisa, and they needed few enough words. Now they were underway on a venture once again they resumed a bond between them, a fighting bond. Wherever Tisamon did not watch, his daughter's gaze was liable to be found.

Allanbridge and Gaved were both used to a loner's life, each having had livelihoods that sent them off to many places in furtive solitude: the Wasp hunting and the Beetle shipping. By three days into the voyage Gaved had begun to regularly assist the aviator in small ways, with the ropes, with the mechanisms, even helping him cook on the airship's stove. An easy understanding had developed between the two of them—without need for speech since they thought alike. Save when Allanbridge brought the *Maiden* down for supplies or repairs, the company passed whole days in quiet routine.

Thalric leant on the rail, watching the Lowlands pass below him, wreathed in cloud, seeming so distant as to resemble nothing he had ever seen. He was a fair flier, for a Wasp, but he had never ventured so high, and it was so cold that he wore a greatcoat with two cloaks draped over it. Despite that, the odd freedom, the leisure of it here, in the upper reaches of the air, had all the appeal of the unfamiliar.

Earlier that day he had watched Jons Allanbridge rewind the *Buoyant Maiden*'s motor by releasing the great weight in the base of the gondola, the unreeling of its wire trace tensioning the spring of the airship's clockwork heart. Then Thalric, Gaved and Tisamon together had, simply by muscle power, hauled the weight back in. Allanbridge boasted that he could do it on his own with a crank, if he needed to, and Thalric supposed that must be right, even though his own muscles were still burning with the strain of it. The whole business had become a regular daily ritual for them, over the tendays they had been aloft.

Mind you, he was no longer as strong as he had been. The wound that Daklan had inflicted on him, during the Empire's attempt at executing him, still leached at him. Halfway through the winding process today he had seen spots before his eyes and had been forced to step away beneath Tisamon's contemptuous stare.

The gondola was mostly open to the elements, with a low, flat hold beneath it where Allanbridge would normally stow whatever contraband he was currently smuggling. Some of the passengers were sheltering below even now, but Achaeos remained at the stern, talking in a hushed voice to their captain, who was obviously unhappy with whatever he was being told to do. The Moth was another invalid at the moment, still walking with a stick, but he wore nothing but his usual grey and darned robe, whilst Thalric and the rest were swathed in every piece of cloth they could get their hands on. Up here the sun was bright but the air was icy cold: the harsh winter everyone had predicted was coming with a vengeance. Some days back, passing over the hilly terrain between Sarn and Helleron, Thalric had even seen snow falling, snow that must be descending like dust down around the Seventh Army, which was currently encamped somewhere below. The Lowlands seldom saw snow and most of the Wasp Empire was likewise blessed, but Thalric had his own memories, bitter for many reasons, of winters endured during the Twelve-Year War in the Commonweal with snow lying a foot deep and unprepared soldiers freezing to death by guttering camp fires.

Even thinking of those frozen days brought a great lump of loss into his throat, because all that was gone now. He was an outcast, a hunted man. First the Empire had betrayed him and now he was betraying it in return.

Or was he? This fool's treasure hunt the Moth had set them on hardly seemed a betrayal. A hunt for some trinket, some curio of a raided collection, and yet the Moth had decided it was the be-all of creation. But what did it matter, really, if some imperial courtier had decided to suborn the Rekef into acquiring for him a choice antique? Was that not the precise degree of rot that Thalric had uncovered at the heart of the Empire? Could he therefore not reinterpret this mission into something that was ostensibly even to the Empire's benefit? *Of course I can. You always can.* The Empire would not appreciate his help, though, and he suspected the others did not realize just what danger he might land in by going back there. Gaved was right about Jerez, though: if he could hide himself anywhere, it would be there: that shifting town was the bane of imperial bureaucrats, governors and tax collectors, a vast lawless pond of Skater-kinden who paid lip service to the Empire and then ambushed its tax caravans. Just the sort of place Scylis would run to, if he now had something to sell.

Would Scylis be aware of Thalric's disgrace? Having counted the days since, Thalric suspected not. It seemed mad that, on recognizing Thalric, Scylis might take him for the avenging hand of the Empire.

Or Scyl*a*. Achaeos swore that Thalric's old agent had been a woman all this time. The Wasp did not know what to think about that. *Or perhaps I do not want to admit I didn't know it.*

Complications, complications. He shook his head. Allanbridge was shouting at Achaeos now, claiming that something or other was too dangerous.

"You have me aboard," the Moth argued. "I shall shield you."

"And what if *his* lot are there?" the artificer demanded, pointing at Thalric. "Who shields us then?"

"Are they likely to be?" Achaeos turned to the Wasp. "Had the Empire taken Tharn, when last you heard?"

"Tharn?" It took a moment for Thalric to recall the name of the Moth-kinden mountain retreat that was situated just north of Helleron. "There were no plans afoot when last I heard," he admitted. "It will happen, though. I take it you wish to bid your home farewell while you still can."

"A farewell of sorts," Achaeos replied.

"If the Empire is there, you will see flying machines aplenty as we near the mountain," Thalric suggested.

"If we catch any sight of them, we'll instantly steer clear," Achaeos promised Allanbridge, who grumbled for a moment but acquiesced.

By the time they were in sight of the Tornos Range they were starting to make very heavy going. Allanbridge was wrestling with the engines to combat the force of the crosswind and the airship was slipping northward, so what had seemed a leisurely course toward a distant skyline became a battering progress that soon could see them dashed against the mountain peaks.

"I'm taking her lower!" Allanbridge announced with a shout. The airship's bag was filled with a gas he had called distillate of sphenotic, which could carry the ship's weight but would take them higher when it was heated. Now he was stifling the burner, that served as a stove on better days, and the airship began to descend through the layers of cloud even as it gusted toward the mountains.

The first they knew of company was an arrow that sang across the gondola's bows and lanced into the balloon.

Achaeos began waving his arms, a flick of his wings took him up onto the rail, then either the wind or his own volition whisked him off, and he was airborne. The shimmer of his wings ghosting from his back, he circled the gasbag, gesturing and shouting, while the rest clung to whatever they could find, waiting for their flying machine to begin its plummet to the ground.

Allanbridge laughed at them. "One arrow?" he called. "Even your worst ship can take a dozen before it falters, and Collegium kitted me with Spider-silk! See, arrows just stick in her!"

"But will they stick so happily in you?" Thalric yelled in return.

Then Achaeos was back, clinging to the rail doggedly until Tynisa helped him on board. Looking pale and exhausted even from that brief flight, he pointed toward the mountains.

"Mount Tornos," he announced. "Take us there."

"Your fellows going to shoot any more arrows at us?" Allanbridge asked. Beside him Gaved shrugged his sleeves back a little, freeing his hands for his stinging Art.

"I convinced them not to cut your machine open," Achaeos said. "No more than that for now. Bring us in, and I can talk to them further."

In the wind-whipped air they saw glimpses of several hooded grey figures, strung bows raised at the ready. It was impossible to say how many there were in all. Ahead, an entire mountainside seemed to have gone ragged. What had seemed sheer rockface at a distance was now revealed as intricately worked and carved, hundreds of hands over centuries cutting the face of the stone with statues and carvings, scripture and frescoes, story sequences of a thousand images telling the minutiae of the Moth-kinden mythology. Even Thalric, who had seen so much, took a moment to appreciate the vast scale and to realize how the carvings went on deeper into the mountain itself, leading to darkness that only the blank eyes of the carvers could penetrate. He wondered if he was the first Wasp ever to set eyes on these wonders.

He would not be the last, he knew. The Empire's hand had not yet risen against these carved rockfaces and these stepped slopes, but there were imperial armies in nearby Helleron, so this visit might prove his only chance to see Tharn as its makers had intended it.

It took a surprising time for Allanbridge to find a mooring he felt happy with, one that would not see his ship dashed against the mountainside by high winds. The city's makers had not foreseen such a need, of course.

When they were lashed securely, and had disembarked onto the perilous narrow walkways that were all the stone offered them, they finally met the Moth-kinden. The natives' greeting was delivered from the air, and comprised of pure hostility: a dozen grey-clad forms with arrows set to their bows, white eyes narrowed in anger. Achaeos took off into the air again, winging over toward them. Allanbridge and the others just waited, clinging precariously to the mountainside. If the Moths decided to make this intrusion a fatal one, then only the Wasps would have much chance of survival.

Still, Allanbridge began chuckling slightly, and when Gaved raised an eyebrow at him he said, "Waste me if I'm not the first Beetle aviator ever to tie up here. There's a story to earn me a drink or two."

"Not at all," Thalric snapped. "Beetles being what they are, I'll wager a dozen have already tried this trip. It's just that none of them were given the chance to return home and brag about it."

Allanbridge shot him a dark look, but then Achaeos was back with then, dropping into their midst and stumbling on his landing. Tynisa held him up, as he took a moment to catch his breath.

"They will let us in," he got out. "I can't vouch for the warmth of your welcome, but they say they will not kill you."

"Popular everywhere we go," Allanbridge muttered. "They realize, I hope, that I'm Collegium, not Helleron, right? I never went near a mineshaft in my life."

"Don't think that would make a difference, even under normal circumstances," Achaeos told him. "Our coming was foreseen, though. At least, *my* coming was foreseen. The Skryres are expecting to speak to me."

"Foreseen, expected, whatever," the Beetle muttered. "You just get your business done with, so we can be gone from here. Those lads with the bows aren't looking at me any nicer than before you went to speak with them."

There were rooms set aside especially for foreigners in Tharn, providing one comfort that the natives did not require, which was light. Heating was not part of the Tharn hospitality, it seemed, or at least the stone hearth remained conspicuously empty. As the light was by way of a stone wall carved into an intricate fretwork that let directly onto the icy air outside, they remained bundled in their thick clothes. The room was rich in elaborate engraving, poor in furniture, so they sat huddled about the walls and waited.

Achaeos himself had been given no chance to attend to their comforts. The moment that they had stepped in from the outside air there had been a messenger waiting for him, a girl of no more than thirteen.

"You are Achaeos," she stated flatly.

"I am."

Her blank stare was horrified yet fascinated. "The Skryres send for you, right away. You have to come with me, now.

◊ ◊ ◊

"You were ever a troublesome boy," the Skryre chided, as she drifted through her private study. Four carved stone lecterns supported open books and she paused at one to read a few idle words in the utter darkness. She turned her head sharply, catching Achaeos in the midst of shifting his footing. "By questioning what we did not wish, failing to question that which was given you to investigate, you always showed yourself a far from diligent student of the greater arts. Furthermore, clearly a man of poor judgment when it came to choosing his companions. Your tastes have changed, I see, and not for the better. For now, as well as the Hated Enemy, you bring us Wasps."

"Renegade Wasps," Achaeos explained.

Her expression remained disdainful. "The very kinden that you yourself warned us of, and now you bring them to spy out our halls. It must be some perversion of spirit that, every time you return home to us, you court banishment. Banishment at best is what you deserve."

"I require your aid," Achaeos persisted.

"You have no claim on it," she reprimanded him. "Your last crusade left many fools amongst our people dead, merely to cripple some single mechanism of the

Hated Enemy. Now the eastern Empire holds the city of our enemies, and raises a fleet of flying machines. Their soldiers are coming here, Achaeos."

"I . . ." Achaeos' mouth was suddenly dry. "I had not realized, so soon . . ."

"Oh, this is no great campaign for them," the Skryre said acidly. "This is a winter pastime for them, a mere diversion, to send a fleet of flying ships up here and install themselves as lords amongst the savage mountain people."

"But what will you do?"

"What we have always done: husband our knowledge against the storm, pry our minds into the cracks and shelter in the darkness. Do not measure us by your crooked standards, Achaeos. The Arcanum has a long reach, and we have found our path to survival."

"What is it? Tell me!"

"I tell you nothing," she snapped. "You have lost our trust, Achaeos—a son of Tharn and yet your allegiance hangs by a thread. When last you came here, you carried a taint; now you are utterly rotten with your embracing of the enemy."

He swallowed, hoping that to be just a poor choice of words on her part, but knowing it was not.

"Why have you come here, Achaeos?" she demanded.

"I must have your aid," he repeated. "No matter what you think of me, I must have it. You have to know that someone has found and freed the Shadow Box of Darakyon. Surely it cannot have escaped your notice."

"I have felt its passing," she admitted, seeming abruptly subdued, wrapping herself tighter in her robe.

"I shall retrieve it," he said simply. "It was stolen for the Wasps, but now it is loose, and I shall find it. And then . . ."

"And what?" Her words hung in the air as, eyes blazing in the darkness, she stalked toward him. "Where will you bring such a thing, Achaeos? Have you even considered that? Will you give it to the Hated Enemy and bid them build their confounded machines around it? Will you let the Empire have it, so as to teach them a cruelty even they do not yet possess? Perhaps instead you will lend it to the Spider ladies and lords to become a pawn in their endless games. Perhaps you shall reunite it with the Mantis-kinden, and thus destroy them with weeping over their lost family." She was standing only inches from him, glaring. "Or would you bring it here?"

"I . . . had thought . . ."

"You had not." Her skinny hand clutched at his collar. "Should we lock it here in darkness, Achaeos? Should it be our secret alone, that none may lay hands on such a vile and corrupted thing?" Her smile, when it came, cut him like ice. "And if you could track such a thing across the Lowlands, now that it is awake, which of our people would not hear it beating like a heart within the vaults of our mountain? Which neophyte or seer, or even Skryre, would not dream of the power that box contains, until they would have no free will or choice but they must seek it out. You would make us all into the very mad renegades that laid waste the Darakyon in the first place. You would infect us with their crazed ambition."

"But . . . it will fall into *some* hands."

"If the world is just, it will merely fall to some collector, like that man in Collegium, who will lock it away in some machine-haunted place where it may be lulled to sleep. Otherwise . . . at least, when the worst comes, it will not be of our doing again."

She pointed to the doorway. "Leave me now, Achaeos. And leave Tharn as soon as you can. Do not return here unless you keep better company than your present. Perhaps it would be best if you did not return at all."

The words left him feeling weak and sick inside. He had not realized how much strength Che had lent him, when they had last been here together. Through the malaise, something dark rose within him, something dark and barbed.

"And if I keep the box?"

She fell still, and he thought he saw a glint of caution on her lean face.

"You have assumed that I would pass it on to some other," he said, a little tremble in his voice. "What if I should open it myself?"

"Silence, boy!" she snapped at him. "You are rotted to the very heart. Best to slay you here and now, for who knows what doom you might call down upon your own people."

"I am at the bid of the Darakyon," he reminded her, "so slay the forest's messenger and who knows what it may do? I would fear to sleep for what dreams might visit me, if I had done such a thing. Yes, even if I were a Skryre of Tharn."

The Skryre bared her teeth. "You will be the end of us. May the Wasps destroy you and the wind scatter your dust! Go, Achaeos. Leave here, and if there is any kindness in fate then you will fail in your quest and be destroyed."

He turned from her, shaking inwardly with loss and fear, but also with a new anger.

When I have the box, we shall see who commands whom, came the thought, and only later did he pause to wonder where it had come from, for it had not been his own.

FOUR

The ruddy-skinned Ant, who had seemed on the defensive for the last few passes, suddenly came out with an explosive punch through the guard of his opponent, hammering into the man's jaw. The bone blade of his Art tore bloody gashes and his victim was spun to the ground, only to be up on his feet a moment later. The two of them, both Ant-kinden but of different cities, circled, and then closed again. As they both tired, more blows got through their defences, more blood was shed.

The crowd loved it. Not just any crowd, of course. This was an assembly of the great and the good: generals, high-placed mercantile officers from the Consortium, men of good family and great wealth. They stood and shook their fists and roared when the blood flew, howling and chanting and urging on the combatants, who needed no such encouragement.

There were only two islands of quiet in this bloodlust. Uctebri was one.

What a spectacle, he thought drily. *What wasted blood.* The scent of it was in the air, tweaking his senses in a way no other smell could. No Spider harlot's perfume could touch him like this. To his mind, the odour drowned out the crowd itself.

He sat behind the man who now believed himself Uctebri's master. They had taken Uctebri's old dark robe from him and given him another that was quartered, black and gold. It was to show that he was a better degree of slave than he had previously been: a *privileged* slave. He was valued enough to be finally allowed out of his cell. Or perhaps the Emperor just wanted to keep him close.

The Emperor himself was staring coldly at the fighting Ants. This fight, the whole series of brutal matches the evening had in store, was being thrown in his honour by some favour-seeking family. All around him the lucky invitees were baying for carnage and here sat the Emperor, not missing a moment, not enjoying a move. He never did, Uctebri knew. It was not that the spectacle was lost on him. He had no conscience to stain with the blood of these pugilists, nor high ideals that soared above them. He was a man on whose word 100,000 soldiers would butcher towns and villages. He could have his household slaves gutted before his eyes, his armies raze cities, his Rekef assassins slay monarchs and, knowing he could do all this without effort, he took no pleasure from it. Such ambitions were too petty to hold his interest, and so it was with all his pleasures. He lay with his concubines and ate his fine meals, ordered his subjects and counted his wealth, and it jaded him, day by day, whilst the burdens and fears of his state only preyed ever more on his mind.

Burdens such as the succession, of which there was none clear. An Emperor must have a successor, as Alvdan knew, and yet he took no wife, legitimized no offspring. Any child of his would inevitably become a threat, a tool for the power hungry. That threat was now contained in the form of his one surviving sibling, Seda, whose death warrant he daily considered. She lived only because, whilst she was under his control, so was that threat of overthrow. A son would change all that, of course. So it was that the Emperor of the Wasps, most powerful man in the world, lived in an agony of fear and suspicion, the food ashes in his mouth. Until, that is, a certain Mosquito-kinden was brought before him to make a remarkable, indeed impossible, offer. For if an Emperor were to live forever, why should issue, so to speak, continue to be an issue?

Such dangerous games we play. Uctebri, within the shadows of his cowl, permitted himself the shadow of a smile. Was he merely the prisoner and slave of the Wasps, or were they doing his bidding? It was a question worthy of a magician, because magic dealt in the gaps between certainties, and the truth of his status would only be resolved into fact once he tried to change it. Until then, he and the Emperor held to their opposite opinions. His were a scarce kinden, never numerous but now rare indeed, surviving as little more than the folktales of peasants warning their children: *Go to sleep or the Mosquito-kinden will come and drink your blood.* Sometimes, in remote places, they did.

Emperor Alvdan II had never quite asked what Uctebri intended to gain for himself from his planned ritual, though. He was so used to people offering him things in return for his favour.

The fight was apparently over, although Uctebri had not been watching it and had not noted which Ant had won. As people turned to talk to their neighbours, of sport or business or both, the Emperor leaned back. "Well, monster?" he asked. "Do you appreciate the honour we have bestowed on you?"

Uctebri sucked a deep breath in through his pointed nose, savouring the last of the shed blood. "Indeed, your Imperial Majesty."

"Displease us, creature, and we may yet see you too in the pits."

"I fear, your Imperial Majesty, that I would make a poor spectacle."

Alvdan snorted at that, and then turned to his left to relay the Mosquito's words to his neighbour. The man sitting there was the influential General Maxin, who thought he was using Uctebri to court the Emperor's further favour, just as Uctebri thought he himself had used Maxin to secure access to the Emperor.

Doubt and shadows, the very drink of magicians. Uctebri settled back, hearing someone above him say that the next fight would pitch a predatory beetle against a half dozen slaves, and would therefore be good sport and worth watching.

⦿ ⦿ ⦿

After the entertainment was done it was for Alvdan to rise first, which he did without even a glance at the night's anxious sponsors. The Wasp hegemony amused Uctebri. They set their Emperor up as inviolable and so far above them. Everyone else, officers in the army, scions of rich families or factors of the Consortium, all of them were within merely a pace of each other, and thus they jostled and fought for place. After the Emperor and his immediate retinue had gone, Uctebri knew there would be all kinds of elbow jogging over who should follow next.

He had cast several narrow glances meaningfully at General Maxin as they left, and now the burly, grey-haired Wasp dropped back a pace to walk beside him.

"You honour me with your attention, O General," said Uctebri with a sly smile.

"You forget your place, slave," Maxin told him coldly. "What do you want?"

"But you know what it is I want, General," Uctebri said humbly. "What I need, in fact, to bring his Great Majesty's plans to fruition."

"Your box," Maxin snarled contemptuously. "I have my men travelling to Jerez even as we speak. You'll soon have your trinket."

"However, General, so that I may be sure of it, I have asked a kinswoman of mine to attend at that place, and bend her own efforts to the same goal."

"You've had no chance to ask anything of anyone, slave," Maxin said, but there was no certainty in his voice.

"Nonetheless, such a request has been conveyed." Uctebri watched the man's face twitch uncomfortably. Was this not the most exquisite of pleasures? A general of the Rekef, whose spies and informers held the whole of the Imperial Army in terror for any question of their loyalty, and yet his heart trembled in facing a tired old slave. *You have your host of agents, General, yet you cannot guess at mine.*

"Your kinswoman had best stay out of the way," snapped Maxin, bluffing unconcern. "My men do not know to expect her, so she is likely to get hurt before she can properly introduce herself."

"Why, General," Uctebri said, "what makes you think that they will even notice she is there, unless she wishes it?"

⦿ ⦿ ⦿

The Emperor still convened with his regular advisors as tradition demanded, but a new elite had now arisen. *War* was the word that buzzed through the chambers of power in Capitas. War was the meat and drink of the Empire. It was war that made careers and secured futures, that greased the wheels of commerce and reaped wealth and power for those who could ride on its swelling tide.

The Lowlanders did not understand, and could never understand, that the invasion of Tark, the Battle of the Rails, none of this actually constituted *war*. Skirmishes and expansion comprised the day-to-day business of the Empire, but it took resistance, a line drawn that the Imperial Army had to cross, to make it count as truly war.

The Lowlanders had now drawn that line: it ran crookedly from Merro to Collegium, from Collegium to Sarn. The Empire had engulfed almost half of the Lowlands before it had even become a war worthy of the name.

The Emperor walked amongst his generals, viewing the great map they had commissioned, first from this side, then from the other. It was a piece of art, that map, carved by the most accurate slave craftsmen. The mountains and the ridges, the rivers and the forests, they had all been laid in veneers of coloured woods, while the cities were bronze medallions cast especially, embossed with the name and emblem of each. Wooden blocks and little parchment flags showed the disposition of known forces currently under arms across the Lowlands.

General Maxin watched Alvdan give the entire affair his blessing, pleased to see an expression of keen knowledge on the Emperor's face, which boosted morale. Standing respectfully back from the table, as the Emperor made his inspection, were the chief strategists of the Empire: two retired generals, a senior factor of the Consortium, a field colonel attached to the Eighth Army, which was currently in its barracks in Capitas awaiting assignment, a major in the Engineering Corps and yet another in the Slave Corps.

"This is our Winged Furies?" asked the Emperor, pointing at the army located on the silver thread representing the rail line between Helleron and Sarn.

"The Seventh Army, exactly, your Imperial Majesty," one of the old generals replied. "Here at Helleron is the Sixth, which is waiting for new troops before reinforcing General Malkan. Malkan himself is being resupplied and rearmed even as we speak."

"Rearmed? Is this the new master weapon we have been told of?"

"The so-called snapbow, your Imperial Majesty," the engineering major agreed. "Results in combat against the Sarnesh suggest that it is effective enough, but I fear reports may be greatly exaggerated—"

There was a look of mischief in Alvdan's eyes that the major missed. "Remind me again who is responsible for this new toy."

"It is the work of the outcast, Drephos the half-breed." The major's voice rang with disdain. "Amusing, no doubt, your Majesty, like all of his diversions, but no substitute for crossbow and automotive."

The Emperor smiled at him, and the retired general prudently stepped back, being wiser in the ways of rulers. "Major, we appreciate your professional opinion," continued Alvdan. "Therefore we have requested a sample of this new weapon to be brought to Capitas for our own amusement."

"I am sure that it will amuse you, Majesty."

"Excellent. Do you own a suit of armour, Major?"

"I fail to understand . . ."

"You dismiss this new thing so lightly, therefore you will surely stand by your own words." Alvdan was still smiling, as pleasantly as ever. "We shall therefore look forward to pitting the half-breed's craft against your professional opinion and, yes, Major, we do anticipate some amusement."

As the engineer stepped back, pale and shaken, Alvdan passed his gaze over the rest of them, and Maxin could almost read his mind: *It does them good to remember what "Emperor" means.*

"We are not pleased with progress in the Lowlands. We wish to spend the coming summer amongst our new subjects in Collegium. We trust this desire is clear."

There was a murmur and a nodding.

"Explain to us where our armies shall assault," Alvdan directed, picking out the Slave Corps major to reply. The man was an old campaigner who approached with the proper mix of deference and confidence. Few career soldiers stayed in the slavers to reach his rank, and he had long carved his niche in the human trade that war turned up.

"Your Imperial Majesty, we are facing a three-sided defence. You have been told, of course, that General Alder and the Fourth have been repulsed by the Lowlander savages along the coast. We have the Second Army marching to Tark from Asta, so as to set out along the coast once spring comes, thus making the best time overland. The Eighth is also listed to march to Asta, for deployment then where it is best thought fit. We plan to sweep down the coast as rapidly as possible, but at the same time we face the problem of the Spider-kinden."

"I have made my decision concerning the Spiders," Alvdan remarked. A frisson of interest passed through the assembled tacticians, for this was news. "We must assume that they have played a part in the destruction of the Fourth," the Emperor continued. "So I have instructed General Maxin here to have his agents destabilize the local cities of the Spiderlands. We intend to sow sufficient disruption at their borders to ensure that they shall not trouble our Lowlands campaign." He smiled at them. "The rest is a Rekef matter, and in General Maxin's capable hands, but no doubt the Second or Eighth can spare time to burn the Spiders' webs, if the Rekef so wish. Continue."

The slaver major gestured toward the map. "You have already heard how the

Sixth and Seventh Armies will be approaching the city of Sarn, but agents in the Rekef Inlander inform us that Sarn is currently allied with a number of lesser cities in that area, making any advance into contested territory dangerous." He glanced at Maxin. "General, perhaps I range into your territory now?"

Maxin stepped forward to the map, tapping the shining disc that represented Sarn. "The mixing of kinden that the Lowlanders are currently engaging in, in their attempts to find an alliance against us, allows our agents much more freedom to act than before. We are well placed to shatter this alliance of theirs by removing key figures and playing on their suspicion of each other. At that point, when the season turns, General Malkan will advance overland and by rail and destroy Sarn before heading north to mop up the primitives living there. Collegium will then fall either to the Seventh coming south from Sarn, or to the Second coming east along the coast, whichever seems most convenient at the time. So ends the war with the Lowlands."

"Not another Twelve-Year War then, we hope," said Alvdan.

"We cannot promise on our lives that your Imperial Majesty's flag shall fly over Collegium this summer," said one of the older generals, "but the Lowlands, though they have pockets of mechanical knowledge that matches our own, lack the unity and spirit of the Commonweal, or the reserves of manpower. We cannot but think that, by next summer at the very latest, all the Lowlands shall be yours."

⁂

"*The Lowlands shall be yours*," Uctebri murmured to himself derisively. He had not been present at the war council, but that was no barrier to him, for his mind gnawed through the fabric of this palace like a grub. Nothing ever escaped him, and meanwhile the Wasps remained so sure of their material world, so ignorant of the reality that moved invisibly behind it. He was back in his new chamber again, the one with the opening roof. He was allowed outside it only in the company of General Maxin or the Emperor, though he believed that, if need be, his own powers would secure his release. Again that blurring of boundaries and outlines, the hedging over questions of fact. Questions such as: *Do I do this for himself or for my kinden?*

Originally, of course, the secret masters amongst the Blooded Ones had set him on this path, yet now he had developed a personal stake, a chance to grasp power with his own hands rather than simply bow to the will of his betters. His kinden had never been a unified race. They were individualists one and all. It was why they were now so few.

He ordered his guard to winch the ceiling hatch open for, though it was a simple mechanical operation, he could not master it. The chill air fell into the room and made the fire tremble in the grate. Uctebri saw his own breath, and that of the guard, plume in the sudden cold.

There were no clouds blotting the heavens tonight, but he would not have cared if there were. He could read the clouds as easily as the stars hiding behind them.

He had dreamt long last night, seen many things. Now he stared up at the order of the heavens in order to help thresh through those visions and cast out the chaff of mere fancy.

There had been Mantis-kinden in his dream, and many others of the Lowlands peoples. A man who fought under the badge of the old Weaponsmasters . . . and a woman whose banner changed and changed, a spy in the way that the old races recognized that word. *She* was the holder of the Shadow Box.

Last night had been full of faces and blood. He had seen the figure of Emperor Alvdan II cast in gold, presiding over the beginning of a new world. Perhaps he should tell the man of that vision, and whet his ego still further.

The death of the mighty . . . that was something best left unsaid, but it had been clear last night, and was clear in the stars now. The fall of cities and armies marching. One did not have to be a seer to foresee such things in the future. The Empire had grown great, its borders overflowing with armed men. All the independent powers still left in this tract of world would be troubled by this next season of campaigning. He had seen last night the sails of the Spider-kinden; the white eyes of the Moths who had driven his own people into the wastes; a lame half-breed crushed stone in a hand of steel; a dead man arose to rule over the lost, with the sun as his queen. Uctebri made his notes and observations, but so much of what he had seen was still shrouded in darkness, even to his penetrating eyes.

He signalled to the guard and the shivering man gratefully winched the shutters closed. Even as he did so, Uctebri saw one last piece leap out at him. Blood, of course. Blood, which was the tide the world ebbed and flowed on, but blood particularly tonight.

He gave a thin and lipless smile just at the thought. There were many traditions of the old magic, Moth-kinden and Spider and more, old and lost and abandoned. Only the Mosquito-kinden understood the true value of blood, and when to reach deep into the minds of others and lay their hands on the knife.

⊕ ⊕ ⊕

Alvdan had spent the day unsatisfied. The mosquito slave constantly prevaricated and whined for his precious box. General Maxin counted over his agents and imagined that Alvdan did not notice the power games he played with the other two Rekef generals. He was getting ahead of himself, that one, taking imperial favour for granted. Perhaps it would soon be time for Maxin to discover, as so many others had, why the throne's benevolence should not be presumed on.

But if Maxin died, of course, his name could no longer be used to frighten Seda. Alvdan's sister had now lived in Maxin's shadow for eight years, after the general had disposed of all their other siblings. No, better to keep Maxin alive for now. Where else could such a convenient stick be found, to beat little Seda with?

And the military, his ingenious strategists! *I have an entire Empire to choose from, and this is what they give me!* True, the Slave Corps man had seemed fairly competent, but what true soldier had ambitions as low as commanding the slavers? Profiteers and brigands, the lot of them, though necessary, of course. The Empire would always need slaves, and it ground them up at such a rate that it seemed impossible there could always be more. There were always more, though: prisoners of battle, criminals and cullings from the provinces or raids against savage peoples living beyond the borders. The Slave Corps did a fine job, really, for all that it was inferior work for a soldier.

My generals just talk and talk. If there was no progress this spring then Alvdan would take his pleasure in devising torments for those men. For now he must take his pleasures elsewhere. He had eaten some small amount, drunk a little wine, his servants hovering around anxiously for his orders. Now he could at least slake his physical needs, though his mind would continue to worry and tug at all of his problems even then. With his entourage of guards and menials, he swept through the halls of his personal chambers and entered the rooms allotted to his concubines.

Only the Emperor kept concubines. Other Wasps might have their women, their slave girls, whoever took their fancy, and he knew that some foreign kinden such as the cursed Spiders delighted in great slave seraglios where one of their noble ladies might rut every night for a year and not see the same body beneath her twice, but the imperial concubines here were something different to that. The Emperor could call upon any woman within the Empire, of any kinden, of any station, slave or free, married or not, and yet here he kept a collection of women for his personal use only. That use was partly for the physical satisfaction, but more for political ends. They were all highly important to him, because they were hostages of a sort.

Most were Wasp-kinden, daughters of powerful families, governors, colonels; men whose loyalty to the Empire was paramount and yet not entirely guaranteed; men who commanded large armies out on the marches, beyond the close scrutiny of the throne, or Consortium merchant barons whose hands were often dipped in the imperial coffers—all had been required to contribute some close female blood kin to the Emperor's harem. It was a hard-edged honour but, still, the truly loyal gave without question, and for the rest there was always the fearsome spectre of the Rekef.

And, of course, General Maxin's own middle daughter was here. Alvdan had slept with her only once. In fact he slept with them all at least once. He knew Maxin was notoriously unsentimental but still he felt that, if it came to that, the death or disfigurement of his daughter might at least bruise the man's iron self-possession.

What am I in the mood for tonight? Alvdan asked himself. Something unusual, he decided.

"Bring me Tserinet," he instructed the Warden of the Concubines, an elderly woman who had served in the post since his father's time. There were no male servants allowed within the harem, and here, in their armour and with spears to the ready, were the only fighting women in the Empire, a dozen hand-picked female Wasp-kinden who were rumoured to be the equal of any elite duellist serving in the Imperial Army.

When the woman was brought out, Alvdan nearly reconsidered. She was no great beauty, Tserinet. Short and dark, with a flat face and a lean body, he had lain with her four times and each experience had been the same: passionless, without any sign of emotion from her. She had let him stamp himself upon her, and clearly willed it to be brief. Even when he had struck her in frustration she had not reacted.

Still, she now looked as forlorn as he could wish. When she met his gaze briefly there was something wretched and terrible in her eyes. Yes, she would do.

He owed it to his Empire, after all, to visit every part of it, at least vicariously. That accounted for all his concubines of other races: women of importance from the Empire's subject cities, serving as hostages to their families' good behaviour. At the moment, none was more important than Tserinet.

He wondered what news she had gleaned of her own city. The local governor worked them hard there, and work they did, each long day become a grind to produce food for the Empire, or armour and weapons and machines. Since its conquest, after the end of a long siege, Szar had become quite a pillar of the Wasp Empire, a city that practically ran itself for the Empire's good—and more loyal than the Emperor's own people because here was its queen: Tserinet, the ruler of Szar, adored of her subjects, queen of the Bee-kinden.

Yes, tonight he would stamp his rule upon Szar once again. Those Bees should be honoured by the attention.

⟨|⟩ ⟨|⟩ ⟨|⟩

He had been expecting the usual passionless and unresponsive coupling, but this was different. Tonight she met his attentions with a desperate fire, grappling with him like a real lover, locking her legs about him, moving with him as though she had a thirst only he could quench. He wondered at it, even as he thrust and gasped atop her, how this woman could have thus metamorphosed from the affectless creature he had known previously. When she grasped him now it was as though she was taking some great leap into an unknown and unplumbed void.

She left him quite spent and, when he rolled off her, she stared at the ceiling with tears in her eyes. He did not understand her at all but he had no urge to scry into the minds of all the subject peoples of his Empire. Well satisfied, he left her, still trembling, for his own bed.

⦶ ⦶ ⦶

It had been a farewell of sorts, that final act of hers, and not to the man she hated most in the world but to the world itself. For the next morning they found Tserinet dead. During the night, she had taken a broken shard of pottery and gashed at her own wrists, bleeding slowly to death. Tserinet, Queen of Szar and hostage for the obedience of her people, was no more.

FIVE

When Solarno came into sight it was as though a second sun had risen in the north. Che caught her breath and held onto the rail, seeing that field of white bloom and glow on the horizon, amongst the surrounding green hills.

So much else she had seen: the familiar streets of Collegium, where she had grown up; the avaricious energy with which Helleron's grime and vice trampled over its own poor; the stark simplicity of Myna, bitterly waiting for its revolution; the steadfast order of the Ants of Sarn. She had even seen the Spiderlands: the walled elegance of Seldis and the sprawling, unbounded luxury that was Siennis: its wood-framed spires and minarets defying the laws of architecture to soar into the sky, its bazaars roofed with a fortune in silks. Seeing this city for the first time, though, she decided that Solarno was the most beautiful place she had ever laid eyes on.

"I never grow tired of it." The Fly aviatrix, Taki, was at her elbow. "I've seen places, you know. I've travelled all about the Exalsee, and there's nowhere to match her."

The northern shore of the great lake was a gentle slope that plunged into the waters without beach or foreshore, and Solarno had been cut into it, tier upon tier, a broad but shallow band of the work of man extended against the rolling green of fields and pastures that rose steadily behind the city itself. Solarno was predominantly white stone with roofs of red and orange tiles, like surmounting flames, and it was brilliant wherever the sun struck it. Looking at it now, from the water, Che could discern its hierarchy at once: the great villas ranged closer toward the hills' crests and the commercial district lining the waterfront. She could see the sprawling west side of the city, where the houses were smaller and shone less brightly, and the compact east where rose the stacks of factories that hugged the waterfront along the lines of two rivers, turning the great waterwheels that drove the machines inside.

She saw domes rising above the roof line, supported on so many arcades of columns that some lofty buildings seemed to have no solid walls at all. The markets were all crowded into warrens of streets, the awnings of stalls forming a second roof layer, whilst the open spaces were parks or, on the higher tiers, airfields.

From the waterfront that ran the entire length of the city, a network of piers and promenades reached out onto the lake, and she now felt the ship's engine change pitch as it turned to move in on its dock. There were men there already waiting to receive them, more of the sandy-skinned Soldier Beetle-kinden, and also some Flies. Solarno was a Spider city, she had been told, but she saw precious few of their kind to begin with. She tried to remember what Stenwold had told her about the place, from what little information he had coaxed from Teornis. Solarno was not actually part of the Spiderlands, for only the western shore of the Exalsee had that honour. The rest of the littoral was split between the half dozen communities that ringed the great lake, each supposedly independent. And yet Solarno was intrinsically a Spider city.

"I'll meet you on dry land shortly, Bella Cheerwell," Taki told her. "Only, if I don't now send ahead for a hauler, then my poor *Esca*'ll sit on deck until morning, and we're due rain before then."

Che looked into the sky, seeing that there were indeed a few clouds gathering but nothing that would suggest a downpour. The winter chill of her journey eastward had been left behind, and the Exalsee seemed to be basking in last summer's warmth.

Taki's wings blurred into sight and she lifted from the deck with a nimble control Che could only envy, skimming across the water toward the city, almost low enough to touch the waves. A flurry of motion beside her told of the arrival of Nero.

"Keeping your distance?" Che asked him.

"She bites, that one," he grumbled. "Still, I'm not done with her, you'll see." He displayed a ragged piece of paper for Che's approval. It was a sketch, in charcoal and graphite, of none other than te Schola Taki-Amre, executed deftly and with the minimum of shading, and yet a match close enough that someone bearing only this picture could have picked out the pilot from a throng of other Fly-kinden.

"For her?" Che asked him, puzzled.

"Nuts to her. For me." Nero looked at the bustle of the approaching wharves, and past it to the citizens taking their ease on the promenade. "This place isn't quite what I guessed at, but I like it."

With the engine backing up, the trade ship ground to a halt, and the dockhands began to moor it. Nero flew over the rails to hover over the quay, feasting his eyes on these new surroundings. Che herself waited until the gangplank was lowered, and then again until the Spider slaver, Miyalis, had assumed his due precedence and strode down onto the dockside to find his factor and consign his cargo. It gave her a chance to study the crowd some more, to pick out the different faces and kinden.

Che was soon trying to decide what a typical Solarnese looked like, but the dock, as with docks anywhere, was a bustle of different races, so that was no easy task. The sand-coloured Soldier Beetle-kinden seemed most prevalent, resembling the people of Myna in feature, though so different in skin tone. They dressed mostly in white, from the plain sleeveless tunics of the dockers unloading ships to the dazzlingly clean loose shirts and trousers of the men and women strutting along the promenade with curved swords at their waists. A few wore dark armour and stood about in bands like mercenaries, with small crossbows hanging from straps at their belts. Others advertised the fact that they were of higher class by dressing in Spider-fashion coloured silks, though never quite pulling it off. For each of the natives she examined, though, there were two others awaiting her inspection. The few genuine Spider-kinden progressed like aristocracy through the crowd, but without the effortless detachment of their western kindred whose every step was smoothed for them by the sweat of a host of slaves they seemed barely to notice. There were Fly-kinden too, a multitude of the little people. In the Lowlands they dressed soberly, but here their garments were gaudy and bright, and phenomenally tasteless, each one a riot of silks and sashes.

And of course there were the others. The Dragonflies with patterned tattoos on their arms and cheeks could have been siblings to the pirates who had attacked them out on the lake. Here, too, they walked armed to the teeth, looking a far cry from her civilized Salma. Ants with greenish skin loped through the crowds, clad in shelly hides and paint, or just bare chested. There were kinden that she did not recognize at all.

She stopped and stared. There were Wasps. Not just any Wasps but soldiers of the Empire. A pair of them, standing right there on a street corner, watching the Solarnese throng just as she had been.

Teornis had been right in his assessment of the situation at Solarno, it seemed.

As she set foot onto the dock she saw her first blood shed in the city. Without any warning there were two men shouting at one another, standing almost face to face and bellowing, and yet the exchange had a formal quality, the insults extravagant and convoluted. For a moment she was unsure whether it was not some kind of play. Then the blades came out, thin, curved steel whisking from scabbards, and it seemed they would cut each other to pieces right there. They were two of the sand-coloured Solarnese, dressed in near-identical white tunics, save that one wore a flat hat with a red badge and the other had hair shaved close to the skull.

Then they had stopped, and taken a few wary paces backward, and the crowd was giving them what seemed to be a precise amount of room, retreating in a way that put Che right at the edge of this impromptu arena. The two men, who a moment ago had seemed incandescent with rage, brought their blades up to their shoulders and gave each other a stiff little bow, before assuming identical stances, offhand flung forward, sword held high and back a little. Che saw that they both wore heavy gloves, metal plated over leather, on their left hands.

A duelling society, she realized, and of course she was familiar with that. She herself had done her time in the Prowess Forum at Collegium. Still, those swords they carried were far from practice blades.

The two men circled, still crouched in their odd poses. Around Che there was money changing hands as a dozen opportunistic bookmakers gave odds. She soon gathered that the man in the hat was a narrow favourite.

Then they leapt forward, blades flashing, and were past each other, each having palmed off the other's sword with his armoured glove. Back to back, they glared at the crowd, and then spun on their heels and went back at each other. Che heard four separate clashes of the blades as they passed.

This time the man in the hat had a narrow wound across his right arm, and Che thought this would be the end of it, because she had accepted the violence as a formal duel, and in her experience those were not fatal.

In Solarno they fought by different rules, she now discovered. The men turned, and the first blood seemed to mark some milestone, because then they just went at each other, the shaven-headed man pressing his advantage, lashing at his enemy from all sides with swift, sweeping strokes that looked as though they would cut him into ribbons, driving him around the circle and shouting out wordless war cries as he did so. The cheering crowd was rapt, devouring the spectacle for all it was worth.

Then the shaven-headed protagonist missed a parry, his enemy's sword slicing across his forearm beyond the glove's edge and, as he flinched, the man in the hat continued his motion, spun all the way about, and drew the curve of his blade across the other man's throat.

There was a gasp from the crowd and then a great cacophony of whooping and yelling. Without warning there were armoured men pushing their way through the crowd, cuffing left and right with metal gauntlets to make room. They were more of the locals and they seized hold of the winning duellist, who seemed not a bit concerned, and also several members of the crowd, apparently at random. The newcomers wore hauberks of metal plates on a white leather backing, and flat-topped helms the same shape as the duellist's hat.

Their officer called out something like, "Who agitates?" which in retrospect Che realized might have been, "Who adjutates?" because she had heard the title "adjutant" used for the master of ceremonies in a duel. She had seen no one appointed, but a Spider-kinden came out of the crowd with a reassuring smile and, with a few words, put the soldiers at their ease. Satisfied, they let go of their prisoners and took a few respectful steps back. The winning duellist strutted over to the body and then looked around at the crowd, who were obviously waiting for something more. Che had a moment of horror when she thought he would mutilate the corpse, but then he pointed out two onlookers: a Solarnese woman, and Che herself.

Everyone was expecting her to do something and she had no idea what. Hands pushed at her from behind, thrusting her out into the ring. Her look of wild panic clearly passed them by and then the duellist had hold of her, taking her in a sweat-smelling embrace, before kissing her as close on the lips as he could manage.

Che shrieked and tried to struggle out of his arms, and then he had let her go anyway, so that she fell to the hard planks of the dock. He began kissing the other woman, who seemed more enthusiastic about it, then he grinned at the pair of them and, by his gesture, Che saw she was meant to take up the body.

Uncertainly she caught one arm and the Solarnese woman seized the other, and then they were lumping the bloody form out along a narrow pier that Che thought must be reserved for this purpose. It was a long strip of wood that extended further than the other jetties, and had no boats moored alongside. The duellist was coming behind them along with a couple of others who seemed to have some role in the ritualistic proceedings.

Someone passed her a ring of lead and a rope, which she accepted in a daze. She could not quite believe what was happening or understand what she had become involved in, but numbly she tied the rope about the dead man's ankle. The other woman meanwhile was assiduously looting, first slitting the victim's purse for a handful of silver coins, then taking a knife to pry a few opals from the man's scabbard. She held out the booty to Che, saying, "Take your slice."

Shaking her head, Che tried to back off, but the woman grabbed her hand and folded it over a few of the coins and a gem. "You want the sword?" she asked, her words fast in the strong local accent. Che shook her head even harder and the woman seemed satisfied. Then they pitched the body into the water, and the lead sank it out of sight.

Once back on the dockside Che saw the duellist pay both the adjutant and the man who had provided the lead weight. *Is that his entire livelihood?* she wondered. *Does he hang about in crowds with fistfuls of lead weights, waiting for people to die in formal brawl?* Che looked at her own unwilling gains and saw, head swimming with the strangeness, that, alongside the fingernail-sized opal, the silver coins were all Standards, minted locally but recognizably copies of the Helleron-stamped currency she was used to seeing all over the Lowlands.

She saw Nero approach, a thoughtful look on his face. The whole experience had served her as a pointed object lesson, she decided: she was now a long way from anywhere she was used to or understood.

Taki found them shortly afterward. When Che told her what had happened she merely shrugged, finding nothing remarkable in it.

"Let me take you somewhere more civilized," she suggested. "Even you, Sieur Nero. My employers'll put you up. They'll be delighted with you."

❖ ❖ ❖

"When the Spiders first came, you see, there was a war on," Taki explained. "The Solarnese were under attack from the ships of Princep Exilla, the Dragonflies. The Spiders were able to sort that all out—after they smoothed their way into the Prince's court and then did for him, easy as you like. After that, everyone was glad enough to give them the run of the place. And to us, too—to my ancestors."

The interior of the Destiavel Peace House was certainly Spider-kinden in style, a high-arched ceiling painted in blue and gold, decorated with delicate and intersecting arabesques, and the walls were scalloped with alcoves, each with its own casually displayed treasure. The ceiling was absurdly high, so that what Che had taken from outside for a four-storey building must have been only two, one rising behind the other in the ascending hillside.

"You're what, then? A servant, a slave?" Nero asked.

"What in the world do they teach you in your academies?" Taki asked him incredulously. The lofty ceiling made strange play with the acoustics, amplifying whispers, muffling raised voices.

"For a start, they don't even teach us the name of your backwater city, Miss te Taki," Nero told her huffily.

She grinned delightedly at him. "When you get angry, Sieur Nero, your face is more of a picture than anyone could ever paint. Yes, I suppose we're all too insignificant out here for you great foreign princes." Her gaze made a pointed contrast between their travel-stained clothing and the pristine surroundings. "When we first came here with our masters we were slaves, great Sieur, but we won out in the Day of the Three Concessions, as every child knows. Now I'm free to do whatever I feel like, but can you boast the same?"

"The Day of the . . . ?" Che shook her head. She had spent a decade learning history and now none of it was remotely useful. "But you work for the Spiders. And the Spiders rule Solarno?"

"Some of them do, some of the time. At the moment the Crystal Standard Party is in power, but that looks set to change even within the next few days."

There had been banners, Che recalled, on their way to this palatial residence. They had passed groups of malcontents who stood waving flags and ribbons, some red, some blue, some green and gold, but none of it had made any sense to her. Taki had done her best to ignore all of them. The local situation was clearly extremely complex.

"And where do the Wasps stand?" Che asked.

"Ah, well . . ."

But Taki cut the words off as a slave arrived. Slaves here, Che understood, had a metal band soldered about one arm, and this man was no exception. He was clearly a local, and Che wondered if he was a criminal or a debtor or simply unlucky. When he proffered a flute of wine to her she took it unhappily. Taki watched her reaction while sipping her own.

"You come here on a slave shipper, yet you don't feel comfortable with slaves."

"We just took the first ship out of Mavralis," Nero told her.

"Where I was born, there are no slaves," Che said, with no little pride. She expected another lesson in Solarno history, stressing the necessity of the slave trade, but Taki merely nodded thoughtfully.

"The Path of Jade Party are strongly against slaving," she said. "And more power to them, too, not that they'll get anywhere with that."

"Which party are you with, then?" Nero asked her.

Taki shook her head. "So long as they let me fly, I don't care about any of it. The Wasps, on the other hand . . ."

At that point a Spider-kinden woman burst in. Che took her as quite young at first but, as she rushed across the room to sweep Taki up into her arms, it became clearer that much of that youth was applied in front of the mirror.

"My clever girl!" she said. "Don't ever even think about another house! We'd simply fold without you. A purse from the Praedrael! Not that we really need their silver but it's the keeping score, my dear, sweet girl!"

Che and Nero stared in awe, because, in their experience, Spider-kinden were graceful, reserved and elegant creatures, and would never dream of behaving in such an effusive manner. Yet this Spider woman spun Taki about for a moment as though she were a child, and then released her, leaving the Fly to catch her balance in the air with her wings, before turning to the other visitors.

"And who are these?" she asked.

Che looked into the woman's face and saw a shrewd intelligence assessing her, despite the flamboyant show. *Spider-kinden*, she reminded herself. *You can never take them at face value.*

"Domina Genissa of the Destiavel," Taki introduced her. "These are Bella Cheerwell and Sieur Nero, who have come from far away. From beyond the Porta Mavralis. Beyond the Spiderlands, apparently."

"You are welcome, welcome," Genissa gushed. "We adore having new faces come to stay here at the Destiavel. Are you seeking employment?"

At her elbow, Taki gave a slight nod and Che just frowned at the gesture. Nero was quicker on the uptake. "Indeed I am, great lady. May I present myself as Master Nero of Egel, an artist of the first water."

"A foreign artist?" Genissa said. "How simply delightful. Have you tendered your services to any others since you arrived?"

"Lady, you are the first." Nero swept a creditable bow.

"Domina, shall I find Sieur Nero's assistant some lodging?" Taki interrupted, "while you take your ease with the great artist?"

"Yes, yes." Genissa replied with a dismissive wave, regarding Nero with a rather predatory expression.

Taki tugged at Che's arm to draw her out of the room, and out of earshot. "You have to be careful," she explained. "This business with the Wasps, well . . . I'm very fond of Domina Genissa, and she's always good to me, but her politics lie with the Satin Trail Party, just like all of the Destiavel, and recently the Wasps have started wooing them. There's no party line drawn out yet, but if the Reds fall into step with the Wasps, you'd soon hear about it the hard way if you were known to be an enemy of theirs."

"How do you know I'm an enemy—?"

"Give me some credit," Taki snorted. "I assumed at first you were an escaped slave, but then I realized you'd come in from the wrong point of the compass. But you've got some problem with the Wasps, I can see. Why not tell me about it, seeing as I've got plenty of my own reasons for not liking them."

Che stared at her, feeling that she was now on very unsteady ground, and with only this one small hand held out to her. But who else had she to trust, in this place, that might help her in her mission here?

"My people have the best reason of all to hate the Wasps," she said at last. "We're at war."

Outside, the promised rain, which she had not quite believed in, began to fall.

Odyssa could have taken ship if she had wanted. If she had wanted, she could have even taken passage on the same slaver as the Lowlander agents, and they would never have guessed. Still, Odyssa had travelled more than most and knew there were more efficient ways of getting from place to place than the uncertainties of the water. It had been easy enough, back in Porta Mavralis, to wait for a flier with space for one passenger.

She had changed into clothes more befitting a medium-rank Spider-kinden going travelling, clothes whose tailor had taken her figure into account. The Empire had no idea how to dress a woman, indeed how to do anything with women. In her opinion, women were the Empire's greatest unused resource.

She was a slender, attractive Spider woman, looking no more than in her late twenties after sufficient time before the glass. She had dyed her hair dark this season, against the fashion, since she felt it gave her a more sincere and serious look.

Although her Lowlander stooges had been given a long enough lead, the Solarnese pilot got her down before their slaver ship had even touched dock. Most of her kinden found flying uncomfortable but, after seven years serving the imperial Rekef Outlander, she was used to it. The Empire did not have so very many Spiders in its employ, so her services had been spread thin during these last few years in General Reiner's employ.

Ah well, we discard all our toys in time, she thought, *for the game changes, always.* It had been an enjoyable education, working amongst the Rekef, but *real* games were played for higher stakes—and by Spiders.

Odyssa had precise enough directions to lead her straight to her contact, but that was not how the game was played. Instead she spent several hours wandering the streets of Solarno, feigning interest at market stalls, delivering bland messages to publicans which would trigger the rudimentary informant network of the recently installed Rekef presence so that the word would get back to her contact that she had arrived. Even so it took a surprisingly long time before a Fly-kinden messenger tracked her down and handed over a folded and sealed paper.

There had been little care in the encoding, the overt contents gibberish, an obvious fake. She tutted over such sloppy fieldwork. From long experience she solved the code automatically, drawing from it her directions and the meeting place. Still shaking her head, she took a sure path through the city, for all that she had only just arrived there.

Her contact met her on his own, although she knew that he had been accompanied moments before, dismissing his hired guards once he saw her arrive alone.

"You must be Captain Havel," she said, eyeing a Wasp-kinden of middle years, a thickset veteran of more than one knife skirmish. He took the sealed orders from her, breaking them open with a thumb and leafing through them.

⁂

His mouth suddenly dry, Havel studied the Spider-kinden woman for a long time. The seals and signatures on the orders were genuine, beyond dispute, but that only made him even less happy with this encounter. "Your papers seem to be in order," he said finally, in a voice soft and hoarse from the scar across his throat, a memento of a botched negotiation with the Scorpion-kinden. "Good of the general to care about us. We thought we'd been forgotten, out here." He had been all of two years in Solarno, almost since the Empire had first taken an interest in the Exalsee. Havel had remained without orders for most of that time, and what had started as a routine of lying low and collecting information had gradually been corrupted by the very nature of the place. For he and his men had since found no shortage of opportunities to turn a profit on the shifting scene of Solarno's politics.

But now the Empire was suddenly interested again and Havel rapidly decided to present himself as a model officer of the Rekef Outlander because, so long as he was left in charge here, any indiscretions, bribery, sedition and mercenary work might stay unnoticed.

"The Empire's relationships with my kinden have suffered a blow just recently," said Odyssa a little later. The Spider-kinden was now reclining elegantly on a couch and looking slyly attractive even in her dusty travel garb. He would have been bragging and flirting with her had she been anyone else, but this was a Rekef lieutenant who, from her papers, seemed to have just crossed the infamous Dryclaw on her own, and that put him off. Like many Wasp men, he found very capable women disconcerting.

"So what's the deal?" he pressed. "You want us to step up the operation here?"

"You may have to eventually," she told him. "For now, though, be aware that there are Lowlander agents in Solarno, or shortly to arrive. The Lowlanders have decided to bring their war all the way out to the Sea of Exiles, and it's up to you to deal with them."

"That's easy enough. Any idea who they've sent?"

"Every idea, Captain." She smiled sweetly. "A Beetle-kinden named Cheerwell Maker, and a Fly named Nero. She is like most of her kind, too short and too fat. He is bald and really quite ugly. General Reiner would like this situation taken care of personally."

"I'll send him their heads packed in salt if he wants," Havel offered. Already he was beginning to relax. What had seemed like an unwelcome intrusion on his authority was now a chance to reassure his superiors that everything was going according to plan. Two dead Lowlanders and his position would be secure again. With that settled in his mind he relaxed more comfortably opposite her, his smile becoming more genuine. "Are you staying long in the city, Lieutenant . . . ?" He glanced at the papers but she forestalled him.

"Odyssa," she said. "And only overnight. Then I must return for further orders. However, if you have a place for me to stay in a safe house . . . or perhaps even just a bed?"

Although well used to dealing with Spiders, Havel felt his heart skip as she gazed at him, and he called out for a slave to bring them more wine.

Wasp-kinden! Odyssa laughed inwardly. Their Empire was the greatest power in the world, and yet they were such children. A little touch of her Art on this one and she could have him strip naked and let her ride him all around the outskirts of Solarno.

Teornis of the Aldanrael would be delighted when he received her report.

SIX

There was a strange hush amongst his fellow Moth-kinden as Achaeos returned through the lightless halls to his fellows. His thoughts were so soured by the Skryre's words that he barely noticed, barely even registered, that here, in his birthplace, something was very badly wrong.

He had expected to find his comrades crouched shivering against the walls, but they were on their feet and ready waiting for him, practically dragging him into the room.

"Where have you been?" Allanbridge demanded.

"Never mind that. We should leave now. There's nothing for us here," Achaeos said heavily.

"Blasted right we should leave!" the Beetle said. "They're coming!"

Achaeos stared at him. "They?"

"Some of your people flew in just now," said Thalric. He was sitting in one corner of the room, the only one not standing, and as far away from both Tisamon and Gaved as space would allow. "The Empire is coming, Moth. As of a few hours' time, this will be imperial territory."

A hammer struck somewhere in Achaeos. He had known, surely he had known, and yet it was a different thing to be told of it as a certainty. *I have to help them fight* was the only thought that came to him. His hands already itched to string his bow.

He glanced at Tisamon, because he found that of all of them it was the Mantis whom he trusted most. Tisamon nodded once. His clawed gauntlet was on his hand, and he was spoiling for battle.

"Your people are just . . . standing about," Tynisa added. "They're not even armed. They're just standing there, crowds of them, just waiting."

They have a plan. The Skryre had said as much. He only hoped it was a good one. "I don't think they're going to fight," he announced.

"Well, your people are supposed to be wise," Thalric said. "I once saw an air armada during the Twelve-Year War. They pitched up against a castle on a hill and pounded it with leadshotters until it had become a castle in the next valley. Let's face it, there's a lot of fragile carving on this mountain of yours."

"I don't mean to sound tactless, but can we bloody go?" Allanbridge demanded. "Look, they'll have glasses scouring every inch of your fancy stonework out there. What do you think they'll do, if they see an airship leaving this place?"

"You're right," Achaeos decided. Allanbridge's *Buoyant Maiden* was tethered closely, only a precipitous scramble. "Come on." Achaeos skipped out into early morning air that was just lightening.

Allanbridge clambered next out through the wall opening, clinging to the sheer mountainside by Art alone, and Tynisa followed behind him, then came Gaved who flew straight to the gondola and began preparing to cast off. Tisamon stayed back, having seen the pensive look on Thalric's face.

"You'll get on that flying machine or I will kill you," the Mantis warned.

"You think I'd jump ship now?" Thalric snorted. "There's nothing for me here. They'd hold me until they worked out who I was, then I'd be just as dead as the rest of you." Still, there was clearly a tinge of regret in him as he climbed through the window and made his way along the narrow ledge, wings flicking occasionally to retain his balance. Tisamon watched him, wondering whether he was really too injured to risk taking flight, or whether this was just an act.

As soon as the Mantis had finally joined them, running lightly along the ledge and jumping for the gondola, Gaved cast them off. Allanbridge instantly released the clockwork driving the engine and the propellers flew into life amid a delicate whir of gears. He then put the tiller into the wind and adjusted the vanes, and the *Buoyant Maiden* slowly began to tack away from Tharn.

"Look," pointed Tynisa, who was at the rail, leaning out. Beneath a cloudy sky there could be seen distant flecks of darker matter. The Wasp air armada was on its way.

"Airships," Allanbridge observed. "Big ones too, a half dozen at least. Can't see any small stuff from here without my 'scope."

"I can," Tynisa told him. "I can't count them up, but I think three dozen fliers."

"Not to mention probably about two thousand of the light airborne," Thalric added. He had not even come over to look. "They'll have them clinging to the dirigibles, everywhere they can, all wrapped in their woollies. I would, too, if I were in charge."

"Do you know who will be leading them?" Achaeos asked him, "and what . . . what will they do to my people?"

Looking back, they could see crowds of Moths lining the balconies and entrances of Tharn, hundreds of robed figures standing, blinking in the unaccustomed daylight. There were others amongst them: Fly-kinden and Mantis warriors. Way below, even the farmers had not gone to bed with the moon but now stood silently in their tiered fields, waiting, waiting.

"That's no proper army," Thalric said, almost contemptuously. "An expeditionary force—that's all your city merits. They'll have picked some officer to appoint governor of this place, if your people roll over. Nobody important, though. It's not as though this backwater has anything anyone would want."

Achaeos rounded on him, fists clenched. Thalric raised an eyebrow.

"What?" he asked. "Remember, you brought me along as your imperial advisor. Don't ask questions if you don't want the answers."

"I hate to break up a pair of friends," Allanbridge told them, having come back above decks, "but we've got a problem." He had a telescope out now, and had been raking it across the distant airfleet. "They've spotted us sure enough." Seeing Achaeos' expression he continued, "You forget we've got a real big balloon above us, and the dawn catches it just lovely. I count a couple of fixed-wings now coming to pay us a visit."

"Then make this machine go faster," Achaeos demanded.

"It doesn't work like that, boy. They're just plain faster than we'll ever be."

"But what will they do?" Achaeos remembered flying machines duelling during the Battle of the Rails. "How can we fight them?"

"Ah, well, that's the real problem," Allanbridge replied. He opened up a locker and brought out a big repeating crossbow with a latched hook that he now rested on the gondola's rail.

To Achaeos it seemed impossible that they should ever be caught. The airship was sculling along with a brisk wind, passing perilously close to the mountainside yet always being gusted past it. He himself would be hard-pressed to fly this fast for very long. So how fast could the Wasp machines be?

It was an agony of waiting, but soon he could see the fliers as twin dots against the sky, keeping close together, imperceptibly growing in size as they neared. But still the *Buoyant Maiden* clipped ahead, making more and more distance from Tharn, and yet not widening the gap at all.

Tisamon had gone down into the hold and now he reappeared with a bow, a proper Mantis longbow as tall as he was, and strong enough that he was forced to lean heavily into it to bring it to the string. On seeing this, Achaeos strung his own bow, which seemed pitiful in comparison. Nearby Tynisa stood with her hand on her rapier, looking angrily impotent.

She spoke to Achaeos but her eyes were on the growing specks. "What happened with your people?" He sensed she merely wanted to blunt the edge of her frustration.

"Precious little. They will not help us. They would prefer to cast me out. They are . . . they're scared."

"Of the Wasps, you mean?"

"Of the box."

Her eyes widened. "I'd have thought that would be their very thing."

"I thought they would help—that they would appreciate what I'm trying to do. But no, they . . . they, who are wiser than I am, are afraid of it. They paint it as something that twists anything it touches. And . . ." He stopped, suddenly uncomfortable.

"And?" she prompted.

"And they may be right. I think it has begun to work on me already."

Something zipped overhead, and they ducked simultaneously. Looking over the stern rail, Achaeos discovered the two flying machines were now close enough for him to see two men riding in each, one that must be directing it, while the other, sitting above and behind, was aiming some kind of big crossbow. The nearest of the two had begun loosing a few ranging shots.

Tisamon joined the pair of them at the stern, pulling his bowstring back level with his ear and waiting, his arm unflinching.

A crossbow bolt ploughed into the balloon above them, and then two more as the enemy repeater found its range. Tisamon loosed, sending an arrow flashing through the open air, but the shaft shattered against the hull of the enemy machine, and he cursed and reached for another.

"Will the canopy hold?" Gaved shouted.

"I told you, it's Spider silk and those bolts are just hanging in it. That's not what I'm worried about," replied Allanbridge. He had repositioned his own repeating crossbow on the back rail, but then Gaved suggested, "You stay with the engine. I'll do the shooting."

"Against your own folk?"

"They won't make any allowances for me if they catch us."

The two fliers were diverging now to pass by the airship on either side. Tynisa saw that they had two sets of fixed wings and a rear-facing engine, not so different from a craft she had ridden in once, when escaping another airship. She ducked as a crossbow bolt clipped the rail beside her, and just then Tisamon let fly his second arrow. The distance was considerable, but the Wasps had pulled in close to be within crossbow range, and Tisamon's great bow proved equal to it. The shaft flew true and the man handling the crossbow reeled back with its thin spine jutting from his shoulder.

Achaeos now loosed too, watching his shaft fall short and vanish into the air. On the other side, the second craft was drawing closer, the crossbowman tilting his weapon upward, still engaged in pumping shots into the balloon, whilst the pilot stretched out a palm toward them. In the next moment the Wasp's sting flashed at them, but it was nothing more than light by the time it reached them. They saw the flier pull in closer still.

The machine to port was falling further away but overtaking them, with the crossbowman trying to pull the arrow from his body. On the other side the flier was getting recklessly close, and when the sting lashed out again it charred the railing. Then Gaved was shooting back, exchanging shots with the crossbowman on the fixed wing. A bolt ploughed into the imperial flier's hull up to the fletching, and the flier reeled with the impact, a fine spray of liquid misting from the hole. Then Gaved himself fell back with a cry as a bolt split the rail and peppered him with splinters.

Tisamon and Achaeos were both loosing arrows now but the Wasp pilot swung the flier in and out erratically, letting the curve and plate of the hull take their arrows.

Thalric stepped forward, his jaw set, and threw an open hand out toward it. summoning the Art of his people.

With this step, I sever one more tie. His own sting lashed out, not at the men but at the machine itself, where the crossbow bolt had pierced the fuel tank. Instantly the flier was trailing fire. He had time enough to see the horror on the face of the pilot, his own kinsman, before the man pulled the fixed-wing into a dive, trying to get to land before the whole fuel tank caught. Thalric followed them with his eyes as far as he could, but the flier was soon out of sight beneath the airship.

Then the second machine was coming back, the crossbowman trying to manage his weapon one-handed and shooting erratically. Tisamon ran to the prow and nocked another arrow.

The flying machine was speeding straight for them. Tisamon held his breath, string pulled back all the way, and then let fly.

The arrow almost clipped the lip of the pilot's seat before piercing the man's armour and burying itself in his chest. The flying machine suddenly went arcing upward, performing an absurdly graceful loop before plummeting earthward. The wounded crossbowman kicked out, letting his own wings carry him down. Soon they were both out of sight.

"Will they send more?" Tynisa asked Allanbridge. "If they're so much faster than we are?"

"Faster indeed," he said. "But they've got just the smallest tendency, those fancy fliers, to run out of fuel. My girl's got a good westerly blowing her the right way, you see, and even if her engine winds down, well, we won't drop from the sky. No, they've had their chance. They'll not catch us now."

⟨|⟩ ⟨|⟩ ⟨|⟩

I am so very far from home, was his thought now, so many days after their escape from the flying machines, as Achaeos felt the encroaching of the night that, for most of his life, had been a time for waking and doing, rather than trying to sleep. *I am so very far from her.*

Magic was a remedy for that—magic that shunned the waking, sunlit world, but whose chiefest currency was dreams and visions.

In his mind's eye he had found her, Che, sleeping on a broad bed draped with silken sheets, curled up like a child with a slight smile on her face. His heart leapt to see her there. He had thought he felt her absence, before he tried this scrying, but he had not known just how much so until he bid her face appear in his mind.

"Che," he said softly. "I know you are asleep. I have touched you before, like this, when the need was utmost. Now I have found you again so easily. It must be because I love you."

He knew he had no guarantee that she would ever hear his words, even in her dreams, or that those dreams would be recalled on her waking, but he needed to talk to her, to touch her. Just looking at her made his heart ache, yet it was a love abhorrent to his entire kinden, seemingly against all reason, and despite that one that could not be argued with.

Che, I need to show you what I see, here. We have reached the town of Jerez, you see, which is like no place I have ever been to. I want to show it to you.

Her surroundings—the blur of them that he could make out—seemed almost palatial, with white stone, tapestries and rugs, a window with ornately worked shutters. It was a far cry from the heap of sticks in which he himself was spending the night, and which passed for a house here in Jerez.

He rose from the filthy mat of crushed reeds and went over to the doorway, looking out at Lake Limnia in all its sordid splendour.

I know your city lies by a lake or a sea, Che. Well, this is my lake. It was bloodred with the sunset and, although a far smaller stretch of water than the Exalsee in the distant south, it encompassed his entire northern and eastern horizons. Lake Limnia's edge was cluttered and uncertain, with stands of reeds ten feet tall springing from the mud, their tangle of brown roots sometimes sturdy enough to walk on and blurring the boundary between land and water. Torn from the lakeside but held together by their roots, similar reeds formed floating islands that scudded slowly across the surface wherever the wind took them. Some of the islands were large and stable enough to build on, for all that there was nothing but murky water beneath them.

Jerez squatted like a festering boil on the side of the lake, a haphazard collection of little buildings made from stick, mud and reed, hundreds of them ranging from single-room shacks to sprawling two-storey excrescences that were rickety, ugly and lopsided, increasing in number toward what was nominally the centre of the town. The only stone building stood in the middle, a fort the Wasps had built for their local governor. To Achaeos' amusement it was already listing badly as the soggy ground set about the business of reclaiming it, year by year.

Many of the locals lived out on the water itself: some of them on boats, but more on houses built on rafts. Clearly the Skaters liked to be able to move about easily and the shores of Lake Limnia comprised a maze of channels, shifting islands and floating houses. Achaeos had already heard from Gaved that the black market—the Black Guild as it was known—was strong here, since the Skaters could transport almost anything around or across the lake in secrecy. North of the lake began the wild and hilly country of the Hornet-kinden, who were the Wasps' barbarous kindred, untamed territories that were the gateway to many fabulous places beyond.

The Skaters themselves were still very much in evidence, and Achaeos studied them anew, for Che's benefit. *Do you remember Skrill?* he asked her within his mind. *She was your uncle's agent to Tark? I'd guess she must have been part Skater.*

They were a small folk, but almost grotesquely long-limbed. Every step involved a stalking, surreptitious and shifty motion. Though there were plenty of outsiders lodging in Jerez, the Skaters looked on them all with narrow-eyed suspicion, yet looked on their own kind with even more. They were blue-white of skin with long pointed ears, complementing pointed faces and pointed noses. Most of them wore drab, slightly ragged tunics that left much of the limbs bare, but some sported armour of tarnished metal scales. Almost all the adults seemed to be armed, and so far Achaeos had seen bows, slings, blowpipes, daggers, Wasp-pattern swords and even a few crossbows.

Watch them, Che. Watch how they set out. He fixed his eyes on one skinny creature that might have been female, watching closely as the Skater stepped out onto the water, then simply ran, skipping over the shallow waves, leaving nothing but a series of ripples to tell of her passage. They could all do this from an early age, for it was the Skater Art, and it was the last nail in the coffin of any Wasp attempt to control their smuggling and banditry.

But notice, he told Che in his head, *how they stay close to the lakeshore, amongst the islands and the reeds. I have heard stories of great beasts, fish and insects, out toward the centre. Also they say that the lake is haunted, with strange lights appearing sometimes, deep below. . . . Perhaps it is just talk to keep the Empire at bay, though I cannot imagine the Wasps being frightened by talk of ghosts and lights.*

He stretched and yawned. He must have been living with daylight kinden for too long. The nighttime, when his own people were most active, was becoming the time he felt a need for sleep. *Be safe, Che*, he exhorted her, across the miles that now separated them. *Be safe and stay safe.*

❖ ❖ ❖

Morning brought little joy to Jerez, but a spark of it to Gaved. He looked out at the lake, now soiled by the dawn, at the stinking collection of hovels that formed the town, and he thought, *I'm home.*

Not true, of course. He was a drifter by nature, with no home to speak of, but business had brought him here so many times that he had almost acquired a fondness for the sorry place, second hand and with no questions asked, the way one acquired anything in Jerez. And there were even a few dwelling here that he might almost call friends, or as near to friends as his trade allowed. *What's a friend anyway? Someone to watch your back, and resist the temptation to put a knife in it.*

He halted his step, still staring out at the lake, considering it. He had now seen a little of how the other half lived: Stenwold Maker and his extended clan of agents composed of all kinden; Tisamon and his daughter and their invisible bond; the joy of Stenwold's niece when she had met again her Dragonfly comrade.

I'll settle for the unknifed back and the freedom, he told himself.

"You're sure you know your business?" The Moth's voice came from behind him.

"Better than anyone. My contacts here will let us in on whatever's going on. You can't throw this sort of thing onto the waters without causing a ripple."

The man's blank, suspicious eyes tried to read him but, even before receiving the burn scar, Gaved's face had never been particularly expressive. The Wasp gave him a nod and set off down the crooked alleys of Jerez, thinking, *Trust always was hard to come by in this town.*

Three streets further on he stopped a Skater child, murmuring to it as though he was merely asking directions. The skinny creature nodded, took his coin, and ran off. Gaved continued on his patient way, hands shoved into the pockets of his greatcoat. He looked as unassuming as a Wasp could get.

Two streets later and the same child returned, whispering to his ear, "A woman follows you: Spider-kinden, young, and very pretty." Gaved nodded sagely, handed over another coin, and made a change of direction as though acting on the child's advice.

Well, no surprises. The girl reckons she can out-skulk the Skaters, but they were born for that *game.* It almost felt like relief, this evidence of their lack of faith in him. It added a sense of certainty to his life.

Time now to test other certainties, to see if they had rusted in the constant misting rain, for he had arrived at his destination. Of all the little shacks of Jerez this was perhaps the least prepossessing, barely more than an outhouse tacked onto the Cut Glass Export House, a Skater merchant cartel that specialized in buying in gems from the north and selling them on furtively to Consortium factors or imperial officers. Its clandestine associations with the regime were such that, even when posing under such an obvious name, it continued to operate within sight of the governor's fort quite unchallenged.

The little outhouse was bigger on the inside than it looked, because it had bitten at least three rooms out of the neighbouring Cut Glass, with more space under negotiation the last time Gaved had been here. The Glass itself put up with them so long as prying eyes did not turn on the Export House itself.

There was a sign dangling haphazardly from the slanting roof, and Gaved saw approvingly that it had been repainted recently. The rains that came almost every other day to Jerez, that were slanting down even now, were ruthless on paint and ornament of any kind. Jerez signs eschewed words; even the advertising was underhand. The Cut Glass itself used a broken mirror, and the swaying, spinning piece of board that Gaved had sought out bore a simple eye, looking left. For those that had use for their services, it was enough.

Gaved pushed the door open and ducked inside, shaking the rain from his cloak. The first room was low-ceilinged enough to make him stoop, and empty save for the ubiquitous reed matting on the floor and a fitfully burning rush lamp hanging from the rafters.

"Nivit!" Gaved called out. "Customer!"

"Come on in." A thin voice emerged from a doorway covered by just a tatty drape. The room beyond was much bigger and cluttered with half a dozen crates and a seven-foot statue of a robed Moth-kinden that Gaved recalled hauling in there, with some help, over a year ago. A lone Skater was perched on one of the crates, scratching inventories onto a slate. Nivit was bald and pallid, gaunt and hollow cheeked even for his kind. His script was immaculate, the tiny characters crowding each other to make the most of the slate's surface, but his writing pose was bizarre, with elbows and knees jutting out at all angles as he bent his long limbs to the task. The Skaters had clearly never been intended for literary folk.

"Well look who it isn't," Nivit crowed. "Himself, himself. Didn't think I'd see you for another half year at least."

"I always come back, sooner or later," Gaved replied.

"Word said you pitched up in an airship. Going up in the world, is it? Or just up and down?"

"I told them they'd not keep it a secret," Gaved admitted. Allanbridge had brought them down silently at night, pumped the gas out of the balloon and stowed it out of sight, the gondola abruptly transformed into a serviceable boat that they hauled through the mud of the shoreline until it was nominally afloat on the lake. Gaved had known that there was no such thing as a secret in Jerez, though. The Skaters saw everything. That was what he was counting on.

"So tell me, chief, what's the busy?" Nivit put down the slate. With elaborate showiness he extracted a little bell from inside his tunic and rang it once. A moment later a young Skater, a girl as far as Gaved could tell, darted from somewhere still deeper inside the building and took the slate back with her.

"*She's* new," Gaved noted. "Business is good, I take it."

Nivit gave a shrug, which transported his bony shoulders over a remarkable distance. "So I get lonely." Gaved knew that in a further room there rose rack after rack of shelves carrying hundreds of slates, with every transaction neatly ordered and dated. Nivit's powers of organization were the secret of his success.

"I've got a commission for us both," Gaved informed him.

"So long as Nivit gets his cut, lay it on me," the Skater said. "Who's the mark?"

"Not who, this time, but what. Something that's come to Jerez just recently. Something specialist and valuable, imperial contraband—or at least the Empire will be looking for it. Whoever has it will be aiming to sell it, but the price will be steep as steep." It felt good to be back here, working with decent, honest crooks like Nivit rather than for the Empire. Not that there was any escaping the Empire here either, of course. Most of the work the two of them had previously tackled together had involved catching imperial runaways. As well as his hunting skills, that was what Gaved had brought to the partnership: an acceptable Wasp-kinden face for their imperial patrons to deal with.

Nivit nodded. "Well, now, luxury goods, is it?" He smiled slyly. "Already got rumours coming in of some sort of auction, see. Nothing definite as yet save that it's really, *really* by invitation only, but stay with me and I'll pry out some details for you."

⦶ ⦶ ⦶

This was, for Thalric, the acid test. Like a child who had been naughty, he was at last being let out on his own. Tisamon, he realized, would be sharpening the blade of his clawed gauntlet, not so much in anticipation of betrayal but in eager longing for it. There was a man for whom the last 500 years of history might as well never have happened.

The Mantis had wanted to go with him, of course, but Thalric had patiently talked and talked, and eventually convinced the man that he, Thalric, could go places alone in a way that a Wasp could not if he were tugging a belligerent Mantis bodyguard-jailer. Since he had been brought along as their imperial expert, they now had to let him get on with his job, or dispense with him.

He had phrased it just like that, waiting for that speculative look to come to Tisamon's face. It had been a tense moment for Thalric, knowing that his wound would slow him too much, if it was death the Mantis decided on.

Instead he had read the man, a spymaster reading an enemy agent, and seen just a touch of confusion. Stenwold was not here, to give the word and endorse Tisamon's bloodletting. Tynisa had gone tracking the wretched mercenary, and her father's world was a simple one of black-and-white decisions divided by a blade's sharp edge. Now they were actually here he did not know how Thalric could be put to best use.

"I need to go out and gather information," Thalric had insisted. "I'm no use locked up here on the *Maiden*."

"Where he'd only get in my bloody way," pitched in Allanbridge, who had repairs to make to the gasbag, and so became an unexpected ally.

Tisamon's spines had twitched along his forearms, and his lips had compressed thinly, but he had eventually nodded and let Thalric go.

And so here he was off the leash again, in Jerez, back in the *Empire*. A Wasp in civilian clothes it was true—but then that was nothing unusual here. Jerez had so far never resisted imperial rule. There had never been a Skater army lined up against the black-and-gold. There had barely even been a local leader when the Empire first arrived, since the Skaters had seemed to choose and dispose of their headmen virtually every tenday. They had welcomed the Wasps in as the only way to contain the constant infighting and feuding that were so ubiquitous amongst them. Or that was the story, at least. Since then, Jerez had become the eternal thorn in the Emperor's side: a conduit for fugitives and contraband that the Imperial Army could not stopper. Worse, it was a corruptor of officers, for many previously honest men had seen the opportunity in using their power and rank to dabble in the black market and make themselves handsome profits. Added to all that, this loose, mobile town shifting about on the shores of Lake Limnia produced a bare pittance of tax revenue, tax gatherers who asked too many questions tended to disappear overnight, and any proper census of the town was just impossible. More than one governor had considered trying to wipe the place off the map, but then the Skaters would just pack up their possessions and creep over the lake to somewhere else.

Scyla was obviously familiar with this place, so Thalric knew there was no point in trying to find her directly. She was not who he was looking for, anyway, since she had merely been hired to grab this box for some imperial magnate. That meant that they would be looking for her, sending hunters after her, and there were places that imperial staff tended to frequent when sent to Jerez on missions like this. It was, after all, a regular occurrence for imperial spies to end up looking for someone in this midden of a town. Thalric now wanted to see if whoever the Empire had sent was unimaginative enough to follow the usual path.

The answer was clear enough once he had found the two-storey shack that served as a boarding house and tavern, and was known informally as Ma Kritt's Place. It had a veranda out front with a view of the lake, as if that would appeal to anyone, and Thalric could see three Wasp soldiers seated there at a rickety table, nursing their drinks. They too were in their civvies, but he could tell just from the way they sat that these were not only soldiers but Rekef. Someone high up was still using the poor old service to do his dirty work.

Thalric had found his ideal vantage point, leaning against the wall of a ruinous hut, with his hood up and ostensibly gazing elsewhere. He was a master of surveillance through the corner of his eye, and he had a good enough view not only to interpret gestures, but even to recognize faces.

The man he took to be their leader was called Brodan, and had been a sergeant newly called into the Rekef when last encountered, but must surely be at least a lieutenant now. Brodan had been Reiner's man, too, if Thalric was able to judge, and a sudden surge of hope came to him.

General Maxin might certainly want him dead, but Reiner . . . perhaps General Reiner would decide that he was worth protecting after all. If, for example, Thalric was able to haul in some useful prisoners, fresh out of Collegium, who knew what this box was supposed to be and why it was so important.

In his time Thalric had run a few double agents, and he knew the strange balancing point that existed there: to keep a turned agent in place, the original employers had to be kept sweet, had to be convinced that the agent was still true. Hence, the traitor must still have useful information to pass on to his former masters, even as he was sending their secrets back. The situation bred a strange kind of uncertainty, for the double agent became unsure about who he was betraying to whom. Thalric had been amazed how many had still professed, despite the obvious contradiction, that they still remained loyal to their original masters.

Of course he had never said to himself, *I would never do that, in their place.* He had never thought that he would *be* in that position himself.

But here he was now, in exactly such a quandary. What did he owe Stenwold and his people? Nothing. What did he owe the Empire, though?

The same nothing, but this was not about what the Empire could do for him, but what he could do for the Empire. Seeing his countrymen over there he felt such a keening sense of loss, of exclusion, as though he was peering into a warm room through a frost-touched window, locked out in the winter cold.

A quick step over to Brodan. *Good day . . . lieutenant, is it now? Remember me?* His mouth went dry all of a sudden. He wondered if Tisamon, or his wretched daughter, was watching from somewhere. If he acted quickly enough it might not matter.

He wavered.

He fell.

He stepped out into the open, heading toward the three reclining Wasps, trying to decide whether he was some greater degree of traitor now—and, if so, to whom.

SEVEN

On the waters of the Exalsee, Che watched a sleek boat with blue sails tacking between the islands. She had been on boats enough to recognize a Spider-kinden design, not so very different from the vessel that had carried her and Nero to Seldis.

It was a strange world out here: Spiders ruling a city of the Apt, Flies piloting warlike flying machines, barbarous Dragonfly pirates. It was beautiful, though, for the early morning sun had turned the great inland sea to liquid gold that rippled out to the distant horizon, the islands in it cast now in black velvet. Below her were the stepped streets of Solarno, the bold red roofs, the blazing white walls. The city was just waking, and she could hear the very beginnings of the bustle that she had encountered as they docked. A city of a dozen kinden. A city of sudden violence and strange politics.

"Early riser, aren't we?"

Che turned to see Taki standing in the doorway. The Fly-kinden was now dressed in a simple, much-darned tunic and trousers, not white as the Solarnese preferred but a dark grey. There was a pair of folded leather gloves thrust through her belt.

"Going to work on your machine?" Che asked her, recognizing clothes that wouldn't show the dirt or the oil.

"Yes, as it happens." Taki was a little taken aback by the observation. "My poor *Esca Volenti* took a hit or two in the scrap and, even before, she didn't feel quite in balance. I can't leave her repairs to the Destiavel's mechanics. They'll never get it right."

"You have . . ." Che made an apologetic face. "I don't mean to sound patronizing or anything, but you employ more artifice here than I would have expected. I was expecting the Spiderlands, if you know what I mean."

Taki smiled. "You've not seen the Spiderlands then, not properly. The Spiders love their gimmicks and gadgets too, even if they can't use them personally. There are cities down south that are just factory states, I hear, and Diroveshni—that's southwest of here on the Spiderlands edge of the Exalsee—makes the best parts for fliers and automotives. We get all ours from there. What you mean is that the

Spider ladies and lords don't want to *see* any of that sweaty, greasy stuff, and so they keep it far away from their nice houses. Now, how about breakfast?"

"Please."

Taki motioned for her to follow, and they tapped their way downstairs to find a long, low table in the Fly-kinden style already set out with bread, grape jelly, ripe tomatoes and thinly sliced meat. There were about half a dozen people there, mostly the local Soldier Beetle types plus a pair of Flies and a single Dragonfly-kinden who sat cross-legged and stripped to the waist, his arms and chest showing an arabesque of brands and scars. A second glance revealed to Che that Nero was one of the Flies, but he seemed to have become native overnight. He was now wearing the white tunic and loose trousers of a Solarnese, and there was a little box-like hat with a small peak covering his bald head. He looked up at her and grinned, and only then was she absolutely sure it was him.

"Well look at you, Sieur Nero," Taki said. "You're now looking almost civilized—for an old man."

"And you, Madam Taki, are looking positively barbarous. Did I overlook some local custom about wearing the worst of one's wardrobe today?"

Letting that comment wash off her, Taki took her place at the table and signalled for Che to elbow herself a space. "If you wish to fit in here," she instructed, "you will have to learn a civilized city's methods of addresses. None of your masters or madams. A man is 'Sieur,' Sieur Nero, and a lady is 'Bella' if she's your equal, but 'Domina' if she's your better."

"What if a man's your better?" Nero asked.

"How would I know? I've not met one yet," Taki said smugly, to snorts of amusement from her fellow Destiavel employees.

"These words are very strange to me," Che said. Having made no attempt to look like a native she did not mind showing her ignorance. "And the place names, too. You talked yesterday about . . . Princep somewhere."

The Dragonfly looked at her sharply, while Taki nodded. "Princep Exilla, yes. Bane of our lives, most of the time."

"Only, I know it's just a name, but it sounds as though it should *mean* something too. I wondered . . . in Collegium there are some ancient tablets that are inscribed with letters nobody can read. These words you use sound almost like a different language, or . . ."

"It's all the Dragonflies' fault," Taki interrupted. "Isn't it, Dalre?"

The scarred and branded man gave her a terrifying scowl that, Che realized later, was meant in humour.

"Dalre's people have been here a lot longer than we have—they came here way back in the bad old days to found their colony. They brought their own talk too, like a different kind of gabble to their everyday speech, so the words are close enough that you can almost understand them, but not quite. They use it only as a secret language now, but I think that way back it was kind of formal lingo for their bigwigs and wise men. It's like one of those private clubs for the gentry, where if you don't speak right you don't get in. After the Spiders came to Solarno and heard it spoken, they tell me the titles and talk are all over the Spiderlands too. Poetic, you know, just how the great ladies like it."

"So Princep Exilla means . . . ?" Che asked.

"The Exiled Princedom, or something like that," Taki replied. "And there are place names like that all over. Even ordinary streets here in Solarno. Speaking of which, I need to go down to the machine shop to make sure the greasy-handed ones aren't going to ruin my poor *Esca.* How about I take you and Sieur Nero to the Venodor, so you can get to watch how Solarno really operates."

There was a slight edge to her glance as she said it, and Che, while nodding in agreement, thought, *She wants to get us out of here. To keep us out of the way of her Spider mistress perhaps, but why?*

❖ ❖ ❖

"Who are they?" Che asked, raising her voice to talk over the rain. Taki leant out into the street from the covered forecourt of the taverna to see the group she had indicated, and sighed theatrically.

"You foreigners certainly know how to pick the best of our lovely city. Those, Bella Cheerwell, are chaotics." She glared at the little knot of blue-hatted men and women, mostly Solarnese but with a couple of her own kinden, who were standing at a street corner within the Venodor and glaring right back at Taki and everyone else. "You have those too, where you come from?"

The Venodor was Solarno's chief market, Che now understood. It was not decently located in a single open space but in dozens of cluttered streets in which, it also seemed, ordinary people were attempting to reside. Nero explained that this followed a pattern found throughout much of the Spiderlands.

"Agitators, you mean?" Che probed and, when Taki nodded, she admitted, "We have a few ourselves, I suppose. Students in Collegium who want this or that changed within the city, or protesting about someone somewhere else doing something they don't like. And in Helleron the protests can become quite violent, they say, but there's usually an element of crime involved as well." She shrugged. "That's what I hear, anyway."

"Near enough the truth," Nero confirmed. He had not even bothered to peer out at the chaotics, or else had already seen them as they arrived at the taverna. He just lounged on the wood-slatted bench at one corner of the low-walled forecourt, while above them the rain drummed on a waxed awning before sluicing off it in sheets.

"Well this lot can become as violent as you like. They're supporters of the Crystal Standard Party," Taki explained. "You have no idea what I'm talking about, do you? I can't understand how you get on in your Lowlands, without politics."

"We do have politics," Che said, feeling obscurely proud. "In Collegium our citizens cast lots to elect the greatest of us to the Assembly, so the city is governed by its people."

"That sounds quite mad," Taki told her. "I may have to go there, just to see this prodigy for myself. Stories of faraway places are always strange, it's true, but usually when you meet a traveller from those parts you find out it's all nonsense and they're just like we are. Apparently you're not."

"So what's all this business with rival parties here?" Nero asked.

"Now concentrate, as this will get complicated, you poor innocent foreigners," Taki warned them with a grin. She sketched a broad circle on the ground with her foot. "Here is the Corta Lucidi, which includes representatives from all the major families of Solarno. Each family has, oh, four, six, up to a dozen representatives, depending on their wealth, their status, the trades they control. And also the number of their supporters," she added, flicking an idle glance in the direction of the chaotics, who were now shouting out something hostile at several hurried passersby. The group of agitators was only half out of the rain but did not seem to care.

"Now this," Taki continued, now delineating a smaller circle with the toe of her sandal, "is the Corta Obscuri, which actually controls the city. This is made up of the lucky ones from the Lucidi that the chief party chooses which, needless to say, are its own supporters. At the moment it's the Crystal Standard that runs the Corta Obscuri, and so all the current Obscuri members are from Standard families. With me so far?"

The two foreigners nodded dutifully.

"Right, let's see if I can lose you with this next bit," Taki went on. "Now the Lucidi can call for the Corta Obscuri to be reformed at any time. And, if they have enough voices in the Lucidi, another party can take over and appoint a new batch of Obscuri. I should mention now that, aside from their spokeswoman to the Lucidi, nobody knows who's been picked for the Obscuri at any given time. Only those chosen know who's really running the show, so all we lesser folks know is which party runs the city this tenday. It's supposed," she added, with an ironic smile, "to prevent corruption."

"Why don't your Lucidi call for a new hand on the tiller every day, then?" Nero asked her.

"Because, whoever does ask for that, if it doesn't happen, that person is thrown out of the Lucidi and the ruling party can choose who fills their shoes," Taki told him. "So the important people's supporters get out on the street to intimidate the to work out why he was not moving. Only as he toppled sideways did she notice the pommel of the short, hiltless throwing blade almost buried in his neck.

Che leapt to her feet, scanning the crowd. The size of the brawl had shrunk to something the militia were now happy to deal with, and they began to wade in and club the remaining contenders apart. Behind them, the more opportunistic of the Fly-kinden were busy making hurried assays of the pockets of the fallen.

She noticed there was one man staring at her. He was not a local, nor of any kinden she recognized, perhaps some manner of half-breed. He was lean, russet-haired, neither tall nor short, dressed in a cuirass of bronzed scales and a shabby tan cloak. She could read absolutely nothing into his stare, as impersonal and distant as the stars, but he wore a bandolier of throwing blades and one of them—just one, mind you—was absent.

The thought made her stomach turn, but she went over to the dead Dragonfly and awkwardly withdrew the blade, a slippery and unexpectedly difficult task that had her hands slick with his blood. The stranger was still there, watching, when she straightened up. In the background Nero was swearing and wrapping cloth about his injured arm, demanding to know what she was doing.

She had expected the man to be gone, or to avoid her when she approached, ut instead he stood his ground, and she saw that a couple of the militia had oticed him too, but were studiously pretending they had not. Someone who was nown, then, and regarded with that particular brand of respect that had nothing do with being liked.

Closer to, he was slighter of build than she had first thought: not much taller n Achaeos, though broader at the shoulder. His face was gaunt and weathered, ossible to put an age to, utterly unknowable.

She held the blood-washed blade out to him and asked merely, "Why?"

It was back in his hand in an instant, without her even seeing him reach for Vhen he then smiled it was a window onto something truly alien to her—thing ancient and sad and very dark. He reminded her, she found with a , of Tisamon. That same melancholy darkness was contained in both of them.

Why not, if it pleases me?" His voice was nondescript, as undramatic as could ave undone his air of mystery. Then he had turned, and was striding away t a backward glance.

⦶ ⦶ ⦶

he street, from one storey up, Captain Havel was watching the same chaos yssa at his shoulder. He had started with a tight little smile, because if this he would be able to report a happy success to his masters, and not have bout the Rekef enquiring into his accounts. The streets of Solarno were

lesser people, and perhaps a few houses change party, especially the smaller families, who basically have to whore themselves about the place to make ends meet. But a lot of it is down to the shouting, because a lot of people start to jump ship when it looks, out on the street, that someone is getting stronger than they used to be. So maybe our citizens *do* get to choose who runs them. Just like yours, in a way."

"In a way," Che agreed weakly. It still sounded a far cry from either Collegium's polite power jostling or the elegant, deadly games the Spiders played.

"Anyway," Taki told them. "You two go ahead and take a walk about the Venodor, because I need to check on my *Esca*. Make sure you come back here, to Ahabi's Three Pillars. If you get lost, everyone knows where this place is. Keep your purses tight and don't get into fights. I'll be back here before the next bell tolls."

"Taki," Che let the question out at last, "why are you so interested? Why are you helping us like this?"

"I'm just a naturally friendly person," Taki replied cheerfully, but Che shook her head and the Fly girl grimaced. "It's because of the Wasps. You obviously know a lot about the Wasps, and I want to know more because, some friends of mine and I, we're getting just a little worried. Enough said for now?"

"Quite enough," Che agreed, and the little Fly slipped away into the side streets.

"So, what do we know?" Nero asked, after she had gone.

"The Wasps are here and not everyone likes them," Che suggested.

"And not everyone doesn't like them," Nero finished for her. "That girl isn't too sure about her own mistress—her Domina. Notice how she got us out of there before the Spider could start asking us questions. Believe me, it's very hard not to come clean with them, when they're putting their Art on you."

"So what do you think the Wasps' agenda is?" Che asked. "I don't see any . . ." She looked about her, and then looked again. "Actually there are a couple over there, just standing there, keeping an eye on things. It's almost as though they're a kind of . . ." She looked at Nero worriedly.

"Militia?" he mused. "So maybe one of the parties has started hiring them. Maybe imperial soldiers are moving into this city as mercenaries. Good ploy, that—I wonder how many they've got in Solarno so far. But it would take a lot of soldiers to put the clamps on a place as mad as this one. Our next move then—what do you think?"

"Gather more information."

"Right," Nero confirmed. "And I hate to say it, but I'm better placed than you, for that game. I thought you'd be a good bet, but I've not seen another Beetle-kinden on the streets save for the pale skin local kind, and you're not going to pass for one of them."

It was true, Che reflected gloomily. Not only were the Solarnese women all sand coloured, with dark or red-dyed hair worn twisted up at the back of the neck, but they were also mostly taller than she was, and leaner. "So you're off to trawl the gutters, are you?" she asked.

"While you get to be polite with all the lords and ladies. Make sure you stay close to that Taki girl. She's obviously flying in from the same quarter as we are where the Stripeys are concerned, even though she's got a bit of a mouth on her. Are you even listening?"

Che had been staring past him, but now she nodded hurriedly. "Stay with Taki, yes. Sorry, it's just . . . I had strange dreams last night."

"Bad ones?"

"Anything but," she replied, and then found herself smiling.

The shouting from the street corner mob had increased over the last minute or so, though they had been paying it little heed. Now, Che leapt to her feet even before she had quite realized what she had heard: the unmistakable sound of metal striking metal. Without intending it, her own sword was clear of its scabbard.

The arguing nearby had turned into a brawl, though nothing like the formal deadliness of the duel witnessed the previous day. Even as Che and Nero had been talking, another group had appeared from nowhere, most of them wearing the little red hat of yesterday's successful duellist. Their jibes and accusations had suddenly sparked fire: there was one drawn blade and then they were all at it. Knives and daggers and the local curved swords appeared in every hand, and from then on an undisciplined and bloody skirmish was inevitable.

Che saw immediately that most of them, even those that had brought swords, were not fighters by habit, perhaps even less so than she herself was. Tradesmen and servants, she guessed, with maybe a few who had shed a little blood before. They were now packed close, jostling and shouting, and trading overextended blows wherever they could, so that the daggermen had the best of it, and the whole sorry mess was coming right in their direction.

Many of the other locals were trying to get out of the way, so that the narrow streets running down to the waterfront were abruptly packed with fleeing people crammed shoulder to shoulder. Others, however, were joining in with abandon and, only adding to the confusion, many of them wearing no hats at all. Across the street a band of the local militia had already arrived, but seemed content to stand back and watch rather than wade into the maelstrom.

"Che," said Nero from somewhere above her. He had flicked aloft with his wings and was now perched precariously atop the awning, a foot resting on one of the poles. "Che, get out of the way."

She looked around, and saw nowhere to go. She was too heavy, too clumsy, to follow Nero. She had insufficient stamina to fly more than a short hop, and that could just land her right in the middle of them. Instead she backed away toward

the door of the taverna. Then the fighting mob had swept into the little courtyard, constantly eddying and turning, but never quite getting to the taverna's doorway, leaving a blade's length of clear ground in front of her as Che put her back against the stone wall. Beside her, in the doorway, a man who must be the proprietor had emerged with an axe-headed pike levelled, and was glowering ferociously at the knot of fighting men and women.

There were at least four bodies now lying further down the street, which the militia were picking over unhurriedly. Che looked around for the Wasp soldiers but they were nowhere to be seen. She tried to make sense of the scrimmaging throng, amazed that more people were not already bleeding to death on the muddy cobbles of the Venodor. A lot of the "chaotics" wore leather cuirasses, and the style seemed to be for slashing strokes that left long, shallow cuts, rather than fa stabbing. It was a style designed to prevail without demanding a death, and ple of the combatants had already retreated to lick their wounds. It seemed pure r ness to Che, but both sides seemed to have the same general purpose.

She never saw the assailant coming but instead she suddenly heard the of ripping fabric close at hand, and then swift motion beside her as Nero d through the awning and was abruptly perched on a man's shoulders. The m had been within arm's reach of Che a moment ago, was now staggering Nero clawed for his eyes with one hand, drawing his dagger with the o Solarnese tried jabbing his own long knife up at Nero, but the Fly ke position, wings buzzing in and out of sight, and then Che herself lung and ran her potential assassin through the gut.

He convulsed and fell forward, leaving Nero abruptly hovering as the man jackknifed to the ground, taking Che's sword with him. of horror—how much blood had she seen shed, how little of it h then Nero cursed and spun out of the air, a spatter of red sudden white of his clothes. He had twisted aside, by sheer Art and instir came in, so it had gashed across his arm rather than into his ribs. A hit the ground, Che found herself facing a lean Dragonfly-kinde on both cheeks. In his hands he wielded a long-hafted sword, as r In her hands was nothing.

He took a moment to note her vulnerability, his expressi lunged for her. None of the local posturing for him, he was ir retreated hurriedly, her calves striking the low wall of the co world went toppling backward. He turned his lunge into a for speed, and she saw that slender, lethal blade plunge str then jerk to one side.

It drove itself into the ground right beside her face with one knee on her chest, his expression bewildered. S

deceptively dangerous places where brawls started all the time these days, what with control of the Corta Obscuri up for the taking. In such conditions a pair of witless foreigners might easily fall foul of all manner of local violence.

Seeing the fighting spill into the inn's courtyard, he had become ecstatic, and careful to share such pleasure with his visitor, congratulating her on laying a good rumour trail.

The Spider woman's hands had squeezed his shoulders, as she pressed in close behind him. "It's easy enough to get these Solarnese to fight each other. Your agents are all in position?"

"Agents?" Havel had snorted. "That's too grand a term, but in Solarno there's no shortage of hired killers, either local or visiting. Princep Exilla practically turns them out as a national industry. But they'll do their job," he had assured her, both as the man currently impressing the Spider maid and as the officer about to impress her distant Rekef superiors. He had been so cocky, just then.

They had watched the killers dart in, the death of the Solarnese man followed by the swift strike by the Dragonfly. Havel had even leapt to his feet with a hiss of triumph as the Beetle girl fell backward, the killer stooping on her.

Then the man himself had toppled, and a sudden spreading gap in the crowd had announced the newcomer.

From his window ledge vantage point, Captain Havel twitched back as though from something venomous. "That changes everything," he muttered, staring at the one unutterably still figure amid all the confusion, the one whose aim had just felled the Dragonfly assassin.

"You know that man?" Odyssa asked him.

"How good are your eyes? Did you see the throw he made?"

"There was too much going on," she claimed, although she had seen well enough. Let him salve his newly hurt pride by educating her.

"A target on the other side of a street, and across a scattered mob of chaotics," Havel said numbly. "Oh, I know of him, yes. Cesta, they call him. Cesta the assassin. Quite the local celebrity, he is, though he doesn't often put in a public appearance like that."

"Spider-kinden? I didn't think—"

"No particular kinden, some mix of blood. He's almost a folk hero in this mad city, not because he does anything for anyone except himself, but just because he's so very, very good at his profession. All the street children growing up wanting to be like him, you know the type I mean." Havel's tone betrayed contempt for a mere outlaw risen above his station. "And he's neutral, I'm told. All the factions have tried to woo him. Word was he's taken to killing their emissaries to make them stop trying. I wish I knew what put him in that spot with the idea of protecting some clueless foreigner. Damn the bloody Solarnese."

She read it all in his face, the game suddenly gone beyond the board, his little scams and takes overshadowed without warning by this Lowlander intrusion: an intrusion that was suddenly not just two clumsy agents but had roots somewhere in the heart of Solarno's dark side.

He turned abruptly, putting Odyssa at arm's length. "You're going to have to carry a message for me," he declared, obviously regretting the words. Imperial priorities overrode even Havel's own profiteering, though, and he had to act fast now to prevent an even bigger mess that he might be judged by. "Take a message for me back to Araketka Camp. They'd better know as soon as possible that the stakes have just gone up."

After she had saluted like a good Rekef officer, she slung her pack and left. She travelled north through sufficient streets to check that she was not being followed, then doubled back toward the water, after reversing her coat, raising the hood, even changing her walk. This was all done without really thinking about it, letting the natural deception in her training and her bloodline take the reins.

She reached the low waterfront dive where she would wait for her man. *Not my man*, she chided herself. *Thinking like that will only get me killed.*

She consequently made her approach very cautiously, because it was quite true what they said: Cesta had killed potential patrons before, if he believed that they were trying to buy his political allegiance, rather than simply commission him to kill an enemy. By the time Odyssa saw him arrive and sit down at his customary table there it was already dusk. After the earlier downpour, when the wind had driven curtains of rain sweeping across its surface, the Exalsee was now a veritable mirror, a looking glass for the moon and stars.

He sat alone at a table that gave him a good view of anyone coming in, and offered a swift leap into the water if he needed to escape. That same table had been conspicuously empty before, whether by the landlord's instructions or simply because other customers knew that the assassin favoured it. She made sure he would see her as she approached. His instincts were, she was sure, like a bow drawn back. No sense in loosing them.

"You," he began, as she approached, "are playing a very complicated game." Despite her careful measures to evade the spies of Captain Havel, Cesta had recognized her at once.

She sat down, looking out across that beautiful dark expanse of water, seeing a lone galley struggle out from the shore, oars labouring in the utter lack of wind. "I thought it was assassin etiquette not to question one's employers," she said.

"I never learnt many manners."

She studied him then. His features seemed young, then old, as he tilted his head, shifting readily as the light caught them. Cesta was over forty, from her sources, but whatever his kinden, they aged as gracefully as her own. "You were late," she pointed out.

"On the contrary, I was in the nick of time. I always am."

"They nearly got killed," she said.

"Yes. *Nearly*."

"Isn't such drama counterproductive in your profession?"

He stared at her for a moment and Odyssa wondered if she had overstepped the mark.

"Drama is all," he said softly. "Drama is the why of it. I would have thought a Spider-kinden would understand, you who live your lives just for show. I do not kill because I love killing. I do not kill because it makes me rich. I do not kill because I have some cause or ideology to propagate. I kill for the same reason an actor steps onto the stage, or a good athlete runs his race. Because, in the fleeting second of the execution, I am excellent. I am complete."

She took her life in her hands with, "So why not become an actor, assassin?"

"Because I am very bad at acting, and no other reason. I have only one talent in life. My heritage has left me just that, and no more."

She dipped into her belt pouch, seeing a minute buildup of tension in him that was instantly gone when all she came out with was a roll of coins.

"You're owed this, I believe, and I'm sure you're a man who has few living debtors."

"Because of the insult," he said. "Not because of the money."

"Of course not." She slid the coins across the table top and without warning he pounced on her hand, pinning her to the wood with a pincer-like grip.

"Do you think I live in a palace, Spider girl?" he asked her. His voice was so soft she could barely hear it over the hammering of her own heart. "Do you think I eat off jewelled plates, or have a host of slaves to tend to me? Do you think that I, with who and what I am, could simply retire one day, to live like a Spider lord amid all the luxuries of the world?"

His grip was hurting her but she refused to show it, looking him directly in the eye.

"I cannot risk sleeping in the same place two nights running," he said. "And, when I sleep, I keep one ear open for the footstep on the stair, the hand at the shutter. I eat when I can. I have no friends, nor any trust to spare for them. I have a thousand enemies who have good reason to want me dead, a thousand clients who would rather I was silenced. What I own, Spider girl, is what you see: the tools of my trade. I have no use for anything I cannot carry. I cannot be tied down, neither to people nor to property. I have these garments, these weapons, and my reputation. That, then, is the life of a great assassin."

"But you are a hero to the people," she got out.

"To the people in general, perhaps, but I am an enemy to each individual one of them. Not one of them has so much as bought me a drink, and even if they did, I could not trust them far enough to drink it."

"But all that money—the amounts you ask?"

He smiled, and let go her hand, his fingers leaving stark white marks where they had gripped. "Perhaps I bury it. Perhaps I give it to beggars. Perhaps I invest in the spice trade. Perhaps I throw it into the Exalsee. When I am gone, no one will ever know." He regarded her doubtfully. "So much for me," he said, "but if I were an informed Solarnese, I would be more concerned about a Spider woman who is working with the Wasps, and yet attempting to preserve their enemies. What can be going on?"

"Well that will have to be my secret," she told him, rising.

He made no move to stop her but, as she turned, he said, "I feel that Solarno may become a very crowded place in the near future. Why do I think that, I wonder?"

"Perhaps you should take up travelling and spread that reputation of yours wider," she said.

"Oh, I rather think that my skills will still be needed here," he said. His look at her, in that moment, was entirely predatory. "You are very elegant, Spider girl, very clever and complex. Do not slip in your web making. I would not like to hear some other give me your name some day soon."

EIGHT

Balkus leant back along the raked seats of the Prowess Forum, watching as the Dragonfly-woman danced through the air. The sunlight that broke from the chamber's four doorways glittered on her armour so that she seemed to be clad in rainbows. The long-handled, short-bladed sword was a blur, passed from hand to hand, or sometimes held in both, but never still.

Felise Mienn was at her daily practice.

"He set you on her, did he not?"

Balkus looked over at the Spider-kinden, Destrachis, seated a few rows further up. He was a mystery, and that was something Balkus had no time for.

"He being who?" the Ant asked.

"He being Master Maker," Destrachis said. He was old, or at least looked it, for his long hair was greying. Instead of the easy grace his kinden usually moved with, he had retreated to a delicate, measured patience. Of course, as he was a Spider, it could all be an act, to put those around him off their guard.

When Balkus made no reply, the Spider-kinden continued, "Because he's going away."

"It's no secret Maker's going north," Balkus said. "And someone's got to watch over your woman there."

"*I* watch her," Destrachis said reasonably. "But perhaps you mean someone you can trust."

"We don't know you," Balkus agreed readily. "Furthermore, Maker's Mantis friend has taken a shine to her, but I really don't think he's taken one to you."

Destrachis's long face grimaced at that. "In Seldis and Siennis they tend to laugh at the Mantis-kinden and their grudges," he said. "Of course, the Mantids don't come there much. And, as for the rest, I'm perhaps the only Spider-kinden who'll ever admit to you that I cannot be wholly relied on. I've failed before."

"Haven't we all." Balkus turned back to Felise Mienn, still engaged in her exercise, watching in silence for a moment as she spun and glittered. She was beautiful, there was no doubt, but it was a beauty that would be dangerous to approach. Her very presence set him reaching instinctively for his sword hilt, and he fought off this impulse because it could be so easily misconstrued by a madwoman like her.

"It's something of a mystery, really," continued the careful voice of Destrachis. "Before it happened, she was never reckoned so good. She was trained, of course. She was a Mercer, and they're not exactly slack with sword or bow, but this . . . this mastery just seems to have fallen on her like a mantle, after her family was lost to her."

Balkus nodded, still trying to follow the shimmering movements of the Dragonfly-kinden, and finding that his speed of eye was not quite up to the task.

"Well it's all very pretty," he said, as dismissively as he could muster, "but I prefer my own manner of fighting." He patted the heavy bulk of the nailbow resting on the stonework beside him.

"Nobody's keeping you here," Destrachis pointed out.

"Like you said," said Balkus. "Sten Maker left me here with an armful of jobs, and keeping an eye on that one there was one of them—in case she goes mad."

"A waste of your time," the Spider observed.

"Says you. I've seen her and I've seen mad, and she's it."

Destrachis smiled, but it was a tired smile. Felise had been in Collegium for more than a month now without any sudden explosion of her madness. She had not even shown any inclination to charge off after Thalric. Yes, she was making every show of being sane now, and yet he knew it was not so. He felt like a man living in a tottering house that one night will collapse and crush him. "Oh, I'll not argue with that, friend," he said. "Only that, when it happens, you'll not be able to stop it."

"My girl here can stop near enough anything," Balkus said proudly.

Destrachis sniggered. "You might get the chance to shoot at her, but you would never hit her. Then her sword would cut that piece of artifice of yours in half."

He expected a quick rejoinder, but instead Balkus craned back at him, frowning. "It's Sarnesh steel, this. She could cut my nailbow in half?"

"That weapon of hers is one of the Good Old Swords, as we say, made in the old fashion that almost nobody remembers now, save amongst the Dragonflies, and perhaps the Mantis-kinden. A proper Commonweal noble's duelling blade, no less. They don't make them like that any more, but they don't have to, because they last forever."

Balkus gave a rude snort. "If they're so wonderful, everyone would be making swords like that still."

"Not everyone can devote so many years to crafting a single blade," Destrachis explained, silencing the Ant once more. When it seemed that he had given Balkus enough to think about, he added, "She's changed, though. I travelled with her from Helleron to Vek, and I can't remember her ever practising like this when she was hunting down Thalric. It's as though it's some new challenge she's preparing for . . ." His professional instincts were worried—that much he knew. Perhaps it was just the idea that Felise might become even *better* at killing people. *In the Commonweal they believe that madness can gift someone with a skill and vision that sanity cannot touch, and here in her I see the proof of that, but now she is taking that madness and reforging it, and why?*

"And you're meant to be a doctor," Balkus scoffed. "You want to know what this is about? I'll tell you right off."

"And?"

"She wants to impress someone. You know who I mean."

Destrachis looked at Felise dancing, the utter precision of it, and at the same time the passion that drove it. *Such a thing to overlook.* "I cannot think so. She has been driven many miles by the death of her family. Surely . . ." *Or has this lump of an Ant-kinden struck the truth, after all?*

"She'll be disappointed," Balkus added, "and I wouldn't want to be around when that happens, either. I like my nailbow in one piece."

"Disappointed? In what way?"

"You get to know a bit about the Mantids, growing up in Sarn, and besides, that one's madder than most. Tisamon, he's got a history. I picked it up in pieces, but that Tynisa's his own daughter, which meant there was a mother. I never heard of a Mantis-kinden who paired off twice."

"I'll freely confess that I don't know too much about them," Destrachis said. There had been enough of them about in the Commonweal, but their Lowlander cousins' hostile reputation against his kind had led him to keep his distance.

"Shame, when you think about it. Both as mad as each other, both widowed," Balkus mused. "Do well together that pair."

Destrachis sent him a stern frown, to make known his disapproval of such thoughts directed at his patient. Inwardly, his mind was spinning. Of course, Felise could easily know far more than he about the Mantids: as a Dragonfly, as a Mercer especially. The Spider-kinden doctor's former uneasiness now had a focus at last. He remembered when Tisamon and Felise had fought, how perfectly matched they had been. How there had been a *connection*, in the dance of blades, that neither of them could ever have managed by speech or expression or anything *civilized*.

So, in her mind, they would fight again—and she would win him, or else she would kill him, or he would kill her.

Perhaps, he thought wryly, she was approaching it right. Perhaps that was what Mantis-kinden meant by "love."

⦶ ⦶ ⦶

College engineers had restored the rail line between Sarn and Collegium within a tenday of the Vekken defeat, and the floods of returning refugees, mostly frightened-looking children, served to remind the people of Collegium that, although their Sarnesh allies had been able to send precious little armed support, they had yet played their part.

It was to be a time of confirming old alliances and, as Stenwold hoped, making new ones. The crisis point was reached, for the Lowlands must stand united now, or within the year to come the Wasps would roll over them, city by city.

It had been some time since he had visited Sarn, several years even. He suspected that the changes he now saw in the city were only months in the making, because Ant-kinden changed nothing that did not need it. They were a people of traditions, of set ways of doing things. Now someone had kicked over their nest.

It was easy to see how the Wasps had upset that familiar way of life. It almost seemed that a third of the walls of the city was spun in scaffolding, as though some great metal spider was saving the city for a later meal. The buildings along the road running beside the rails had all gone, demolished and then levelled to strip any enemy of cover, despite the fact that the main assault would most likely come from the air. The walls themselves were changing shape, from the original smooth curve that encircled the city to something spiky, with sloping, pointed buttresses jutting out to give defending archers more inroads into any besieging force, also battlements that curved up and out and then in again, so that sheltered crossbows could fire through slots above them at any airborne enemy. The summit of the wall was studded with siege engines and, as the rail automotive drew closer, Stenwold watched an impossibly spindly crane winching one of these into position. Some were heavy-barrelled leadshotters, some repeating ballistae plated in steel. There were others still that were new to him—racks of tubes that must be the new serial scrapshotters he had heard about, which would fill a space of air with enough loose metal to bring down anything flying through it. He saw the machines tilt and turn experimentally with hisses of steam leaking from their joints. All the wall emplacements were armoured with shields before and above to protect the engineers. Too heavy to be winched by hand, the engines were kept grinding back and forth by steam or clockwork.

They don't really know what they're doing, Stenwold decided, but it was still a hopeful sight. At least they were doing *something*. The Sarnesh, backed by the ingenuity of the Collegiate artificers, were preparing for a conflict with the Wasps that would come all the way to the walls of their city.

And he saw further emplacements beyond the walls, too: bunkers and entrenched weapons, that might or might not be connected underground to the city's subterranean levels where the ant hive housed the working insects that the city used as beasts of burden. He hoped this activity would impress the others as much as it impressed him.

Across from him dozed a pale-skinned Ant. His name was Parops and he was from Tark, and normally a Tarkesh would be risking death merely by coming to Sarn. Tark was in the hands of the Wasps, however, and Parops had been almost eager to come along with Stenwold. The last chance for Tark would be the utter defeat of the Wasps, and he was willing to break centuries of xenophobia to achieve that. It was enough to give a man hope.

If we beat the Wasps, Stenwold reminded himself. "If" was a poisonous word. *Let's beat the Wasps first.* For, in fact, even welding together a unified front against the Wasps seemed to be almost impossible, for everyone was pulling in different directions. It was like trying to shoo flies out of a window: no sooner had you swept them into the open air than they were back again.

Aside from Parops, he had come with only two of his staff: Sperra, who was now sleeping curled along the length of one seat and quite oblivious to the roar of the engine and the rattle of the wheels, and Arianna. Looking a little queasy, she sat pressed up against him with her head resting on his rounded shoulder. Travel by rail was the fastest and most efficient way to get anywhere these days, but it was a rough experience for the Inapt.

He reached for her hand and squeezed it, and she managed a wan smile. Before them, just then, the walls of Sarn opened up to swallow the train of open-roofed carriages in which they travelled.

When the automotive pulled in, they were ready waiting for him: it was hard to fault the Ant-kinden for organization. A small delegation had obviously been passed his mental image by some Ant that had once met him, and so they singled him out easily even as his little company disembarked.

"War Master Stenwold Maker." He found himself addressed by a Sarnesh woman robed in the Collegium style, which counted as a token of high respect.

"I suppose I must be."

"You have requested an audience with our Queen," he was further informed. "It is granted. Even now rooms are being prepared at the Royal Court for you and your fellows. Kindly follow me."

* * *

Nothing would have singled the Queen out from her fellows, save for the ornament that she adopted out of pity for the foreigners' confusion. She had not been born royal. Unlike Spider Aristoi the Ant-kinden put no stock in hereditary dynasties. The Queen's childhood had displayed in her an aptitude for command, decision-making, leadership. Such traits were watched out for, among the Ant-kinden. They were discouraged, in most cases, but sometimes these gifts shone in exactly the right way, and in such children they were cultivated.

She had been young for the post when made an officer, and very young when given her commander's rank, stepping easily up through the simple hierarchy that was all the Ants needed. Her ability, and the soundness of her judgment, marked her as exceptional in a race where conformity was the rule, but it was that rare breed of "exceptional" that managed to complement the whole rather than challenge it.

At thirty they had made her a tactician. She had been chosen from a hundred candidates, her every thought and action having been carefully scrutinized without her ever knowing that the Court was watching her. Never let it be said that the Ants could not keep any secrets from their own.

When she was thirty-eight the old King had died, and she had joined his other tacticians as they put their minds together even as his body cooled. The decision had been unanimous. In putting herself forward she had showed no personal ambition. They had simply measured one another by the standards of each other, and she had stood taller than the rest.

The absolute trust of an Ant city-state was a burden she was proud to bear, for all it weighed on her heavily. For eleven years she had lived with such iron responsibility, but never to this degree. It was the time of crisis that any Ant regent dreaded.

The Queen of Sarn now sat at her war table, on which maps and charts were pinned in immaculate order, updated daily by the clerks of her army. Eleven years ago she had been chosen as the supreme voice of Sarn, the fount of all authority, the ultimate origin of all orders. She knew that outsiders considered the Ant city-states to be merely autocracies but the truth was richer than that, infinitely more complex. The mindlink that laced them all together did not exclude her, nor did it make them her unthinking slaves. She was constantly present in the minds of her subjects as they were also an influence in hers. The Beetles of Collegium thought they had achieved government by the people in choosing their quarrelsome leaders by the casting of lots, but in reality they had no idea, no idea at all.

And speaking of Beetles, here was one arrived to see her, she was informed, and it was a name she had heard before.

She did not even need to glance at them for their reactions. She felt the presence of her tacticians supporting her. They were eight Ant-kinden men and women, the keenest military minds in the city, with a pair of Beetle women, an artificer and a merchant, to advise on matters less warlike. There would, she guessed, be little need of those last two in the next months.

Stenwold Maker, she reflected, seeing the doors open to reveal a stocky, bald man dressed in the folded white robes of a College master but looking as though he missed a sword at his side, approaching with a walk that still compensated for the blade he had not been allowed to bring in.

Tell me about him, she directed.

—He has been quite a maverick, causing trouble for the Assembly, came the first voice from among her tacticians.

—Reports confirm that he has been spreading warnings of the Empire for at least fifteen years.

—He was in Sarn six years ago, starting an agent network. We have the details of some of his contacts here, but not all.

—Reports suggest that he was in the thick of the fighting during the Vekken siege.

—His position at the College was in the department of history, but prolonged absences have punctuated his teaching.

Known associates . . .

The Queen waved that information away in her mind, and all this time Stenwold had been approaching the war table, hearing none of it, not guessing how he was being weighed up. *His character, then?* she said.

—Resourceful. Charismatic. He has been able to control the Assembly.

—He inspires loyalty in others. A good officer—for a foreigner.

—Do not forget that Beetles endure. He has endured a great deal.

"War Master Stenwold Maker," she began, and he gave her a stiff, somewhat paunchy bow. "Your Majesty," he acknowledged, and then gave a brief nod left and right to her council.

"We are pleased to find our allies in Collegium still in possession of their freedom," she said to him.

"We are pleased to still be in possession of it. I see you anticipate a siege here, your Majesty."

"We do, but no siege such as these walls have ever known. We have sent Fly-kinden scouts to investigate the Wasp army. It seems they have made fortifications for the winter, and their defences are intended against both an air and ground assault. We have therefore borrowed from their designs."

Stenwold nodded. "Clever," he admitted.

"And it may be that we can borrow from them even further," the Queen remarked, almost casually, and then fixed him with a steel gaze. "We understand an agent of yours who fought beside us may have escaped the Wasp forces with something of immense value."

"The reports of agents . . ." began Stenwold, holding up a hand, but she forestalled him.

"We mean the new weapon, that the Wasps turned on us at the Battle of the Rails." Even as she spoke her advisors were in her mind.

—Reports suggest that Collegium has been constructing their own version. It was unclear whether this was purely from first principles or . . .

—There is a Spider-kinden now waiting in the antechamber with a wrapped bundle of the correct size and shape, according to battlefield recollection.

She saw the Beetle glance sideways at her expressionless Tacticians, obviously guessing at their constant exchange and yet deaf to it. "War Master Maker?" she prompted.

"They call it a snapbow," he told her at last, bowing to necessity and the accuracy of her own intelligence. "Your own soldiers have seen its efficiency. My agent was able to bring me the original plans."

—There is more to this, though. He is holding back information.

He is entitled to, the Queen responded. *He is an ally, not a citizen.*

—We cannot risk the future of Sarn on the squeamishness of our allies.

—If we merely requisition the sample weapon he has brought, it could be reverse-engineered by our artificers.

In offending Collegium we would lose more than we gained, the Queen decided. "You can recreate this marvel?" she asked.

"And we have done so," Stenwold said. He still felt a stab of pain when he recalled those plans, the so-familiar handwriting of his student, Totho, who was working with the Empire now somehow, driven there by the curse of his blood and the fall of Tark.

On the crest of a wave of mental voices, the Queen announced, "We will set our artificers to the task, Master Maker. We will require the plans, therefore, in order to work efficiently at rearming our soldiers."

This was the moment he had been waiting for, but she had dropped it on him sooner than he had wanted, though perhaps not sooner than he had expected.

"I . . . The Assembly, that is, is unsure . . . the weapon is of a remarkable design. We fear to see it in general usage, you understand. We are therefore training elite groups of—"

"The weapon is already in general usage, Master Maker," she reminded him. "The Empire, we understand, is very large and has many, many soldiers. If it is to be defeated we cannot now stint on any advantage your agents have procured for us."

Stenwold pursed his lips, thinking of the golden future he had envisaged, and how the Sarnesh having the snapbow would change it. Oh, they were the best of Ant-kinden, without doubt, and had come so far in just a few decades. They were Ant-kinden all the same, though, so how long before their armies were at the gates of Vek or of Tark?

"I have not brought the plans with me to Sarn," he said.

—He is lying.

—He should be persuaded to send back to Collegium to collect them.

—I concur that he is lying. The Beetles clearly do not trust us.

—We cannot therefore trust them.

—We need allies now if we are to stave off the Wasp-kinden when they come.

"Master Maker," the Queen said softly. "We understand that you have been the man to cut through philosophical procrastination at Collegium, and to impart a keener view of reality than your people might otherwise have achieved. Allow me to do the same for you. We must defeat the Wasps at all costs. If Sarn falls, the Lowlands has lost its heart. We cannot stand on niceties or other such considerations. I wish you to think very carefully about how much our need for victory outweighs any other needs of your own just now."

"I understand, your Majesty. I have another proposal, though. I would like to use Sarn as a rallying point for those cities willing to send troops and aid in order to resist the Wasps. You are correct that Sarn is the keystone of the Lowlands, as matters now stand, and I am also aware that there is an alliance of Moth and Mantis-kinden north of here. So, as well as Collegium, we can hopefully bring several others to the table. We can then plan a unified strategy regarding how best to fight and how best to hamper the imperial advance. Would you be willing to consider this?"

"You do not deflect us so easily, Master Maker," the Queen remarked acidly. "You must come to accept that this weapon you have discovered is wasted in the hands of Collegium. You are builders and inventors but not warriors. That is our profession here in Sarn. To pass weapons into our hands is simply an efficient division of labour. However, I am confident that you will, after due thought, come to make the correct decision on this point. As to your own request, we are agreed. Let those who are prepared to stand against the Wasps send their Tacticians and embassies here in safety. We shall receive them all."

⟨|⟩ ⟨|⟩ ⟨|⟩

Stenwold backed out of the war room, feeling off balance and ill at ease. He had expected that Sarnesh agents would have sniffed out Collegium's new acquisition, and he had come armed with the authority of the Collegium Assembly to deny the Queen's logical request, but she had ambushed him with it before he was ready, launching him into the pitched diplomatic battle he had been hoping to defer. Nor was that battle won yet.

He wondered uneasily how far news of the snapbow had spread.

Back in the antechamber he rejoined Arianna, hugged her briefly, and then turned to look at the next petitioner ready to enter the war room.

It was Salma.

Stenwold blinked at him, seeing the same lean, hard-edged man he had encountered when recovering his niece. Salma all grown up, calloused and lean, standing here still in his brigand's armour as though he were not about to speak to a queen.

"Hammer and tongs," Stenwold said softly. "What are *you* doing here?"

"Merely a prince calling on fellow royalty, what else?" Salma said. His smile was the same old smile gleaming through a filter of time and pain. "It's good to see you, Sten."

"It's good . . . very good to see you," Stenwold told him. "I wish I'd been able to bring along Che or Tynisa."

The smile lingered, now sadder. "Those were the days, weren't they?" said the

Dragonfly. "How little we knew. Except you, of course. I listened to everything you said, and I still wish I'd listened harder."

"At least you listened. It took my own people a lot longer." Stenwold looked him up and down, this most unlikely of royal petitioners. "You're here on the business of your . . . surrogate people?"

Salma nodded. "My followers, yes. I come to barter like any tradesman. To horse-trade, in fact." Seeing Stenwold's expression he waved a hand dismissively. "It's a Commonweal expression, although more fitting than you'd think. Your own business here is your grand alliance, of course."

"Let us hope it's more than just *my* business," Stenwold said, and at that moment an Ant functionary was at Salma's elbow. The two old friends clasped hands, and Stenwold said, "Good luck," before returning to Arianna.

She raised the wrapped bundle questioningly, but he shook his head at her, relieved to be out of here without having to unsheathe it. She kept her questions to herself until they were well clear of the royal palace and pacing back through the well-ordered streets of Sarn proper toward the Foreigners' Quarter.

"So I carried this along for nothing then?" she said eventually.

"Well," he said, "We knew they knew that we knew how to make it, so to speak, but the Queen is not going to be derailed from her intentions." He grimaced about him at the perfectly grid-patterned streets, at the silent Sarnesh going about their lives without fuss or haste, at soldiers trooping past them carrying material to the walls. "I suppose I can't blame them, given that they were on the receiving end, but they really, fiercely want Totho's invention. I'm starting to worry about precisely what they'll do if I don't willingly give them the plans."

"The Assembly opinion seemed to be fairly unified on that point," she noted.

"The Assembly of Collegium, lucky fellows, aren't here facing the Queen of Sarn." He sighed. "I know it's an artificial situation. Old Thadspar wanted to keep it out of the wrong hands, and yet the Wasps already have it. And, anyway, the Sarnesh will capture one eventually, build their own copy, and then they'll have it too, and they'll only remember that *we* didn't want them to get it. And they want it *now*. They want to be able to put it to use against the Wasps next spring, and for the short term, of course, that's the best idea."

"And for the long term . . ."

"They will turn it against the world, sooner or later. No doubt about that. The temptation to win a few battles over their old enemies will prove too much. This weapon is dangerous enough in Wasp hands, but in Ant hands the possibilities are even worse."

Now they were securely inside the Foreigners' Quarter, approaching the elegant Beetle-style two-storey that was the Collegiate embassy. Once inside, past the guards and the functionaries, Stenwold retired to the suite of rooms that had been made available to him.

And there's the joke because, a month before, Collegium's own diplomatic staff wouldn't have let me in the door.

"You were right," he told Sperra. "She's a tough one."

The Fly nodded. "Rather you than me, chief."

"I take it not so good, Sten?" This came from the last man there, a fleshy creature with pale, bluish skin—an Ant from some western city-state at the fringes of the Lowlands proper. His name was Plius and he was nominally Stenwold's man here in Sarn. Stenwold had been in the game a long time, cutting his teeth on agent-running in a half dozen cities, and way back when he had first recruited Plius, Stenwold had taken him for what the world usually saw: an outcast trying to make his difficult way in a hostile city. Now, his customary pipe in his hands, Plius managed a wan smile at Stenwold, who smiled back and nodded.

With his extra years of experience, Stenwold had known as soon as he reacquainted himself with the man. He knew the telltale signs now of a man with divided loyalties. Either he had been blind to it before, or Plius had been turned fairly recently. They were still both playing the game as though it was not so but, somewhere along the line, someone else had put their mark on Plius, and Stenwold knew he could not trust the man any more, only keep him close and wait.

❖ ❖ ❖

Who is this man? the Queen asked, and this time the silent answers came more hesitantly.

—A nobleman from the northlands. He has been a student at the College.

—Reports suggest he was at Tark during the siege.

—He may be a spy.

—We have heard unconfirmed reports of irregular resistance to the imperial advance being linked to his name.

—Our knowledge of the Commonweal is almost nonexistent.

—Save that they, too, have fought the Wasps.

With no clear vision from her Tacticians, she used her own eyes, seeing a young man, too young to be standing before her in this weighty role. He wore a long leather hauberk reinforced with metal plates that would ill become the worst of her own soldiers, and yet he carried himself with a casual authority. Apart from that he was golden skinned, handsome, clear eyed, and he stood before her war council as though he was the lord of a realm and not just the chief of a ragged pack of bandits and refugees.

"Prince Salme Dien," she said, pronouncing the foreign name carefully. She was aware that he was studying her in return, unsurprised at seeing nothing but a woman of Sarn of middling years, with the same close features, brown skin and short-cut dark hair as all her kin. No doubt the lords in his homeland wore gaudy flowers of gilt and gems, compared with the token regalia she bore to identify her. Her look told him flatly that in Sarn they valued other things.

"Your Majesty." He sketched a bow that was obviously a shadow of something more formal.

"Your name is known to us, to my council and myself," she told him. "It has therefore won you this time, when our time is precious to us. Who are you, Dragonfly, and why should we heed you?"

"In the Commonweal it is customary to bring gifts when currying the favour of great men and women," Salma declared. "I have something you should appreciate, and also may serve as your answer."

She sent out a query, but discovered no aide awaiting him with bundles in the antechamber. "Speak clearly," she advised.

"In the Foreigners' Quarter I have, under lock and key, three Wasp scouts my men have caught. I have questioned them all I need to. They are now yours."

There was a murmur in her head, a sound of cautious reevaluation. "You are in the habit of catching Wasps without being stung?" the Queen asked.

—This may yet be a trap. Misinformation is easy to plant.

—Wasps are hard to take alive. They are more mobile than our own scouts.

"There is," said Salma, "a knack to it."

The Queen frowned at him. "And who are your men, exactly? Do you hold yourself a tactician now?" She said it with a glance of mockery at his travel-stained dress, the stitched repairs to his armour.

"Yes," Salma replied, quite seriously.

That stilled the voices in her head for a moment, and he let his voice step into the breach.

"The Empire has wrought a great change east of here. They have displaced hundreds, thousands, from their homes: people from Tark, from Helleron, from all the little communities between there and here. The roads are full of refugees, escaped slaves, wilderness folk: a great tide of humanity that the Wasps have driven before them, to shiver and starve through the winter. Now the Wasps have halted their advance so that they can accumulate more reserves of men and weapons, and we have regrouped too. We are the dispossessed, your Majesty, and we fight."

"You fight the Empire."

"We turn upon our creator."

—This is preposterous.

—There is no precedent for this.

—He is no more than a brigand with ideas above his station.

Because she was Queen of Sarn, one mental word silenced them. "And what are your plans, this winter, Prince Dien?"

He smiled at her. It was a smile baked hard and sharpened to an edge. "We are attacking the Wasps, your Majesty. We are attacking them, even as I speak, in all the little ways we can. My soldiers have disrupted their supply lines. My artificers have broken up the rails between their camp and Helleron. My Fly-kinden pass over their camp and lure out their soldiers into ambush or capture. My foragers take everything from the land before the Wasps can harvest it. My spies become their slaves in order to discover their plans. Can you say as much of your own people, your Majesty?"

The outrage about the table was almost tangible to him, loudly audible to her, but she felt as though, despite the others present, there were now only the two of them truly there in that room: the Queen of Sarn and this young man with his disturbing smile.

"You are here with a proposal, young prince," she informed him.

"Certainly," he agreed. "For the moment, the city of Sarn presents a line across which the Wasps dare not go, not until they are fully ready for their great battle. I have with me thousands who cannot fight: the young, the old and the wounded. I know Ant city-states well enough, and you will have hoarded enough within your walls to withstand a siege lasting years. You have therefore enough to provide for those of my people that I cannot."

"And in exchange you will make yourselves soldiers of Sarn?"

"No," he said. "Under no circumstances. We know what that would mean: to be the least valued, the first sent into the fire. We are free, your Majesty, no subjects of yours, nor of any ruler's."

"So, in return, what?" Her Tacticians were now hanging on her words, trying to keep up with the way the world around them had suddenly shifted.

"In exchange we will do what you cannot. We will tell you all that we discover about the Wasps. When they advance, we will harry their vanguard and ambush their baggage train. We are woodsmen, trackers, thieves and brigands, your Majesty, and we will become the very land about them, which turns upon them. We are not many, but we are still an army. More, we are an army without shield wall or formations, an army that moves swiftly, that has no home, that cannot be pinned or broken against a solid line. They do not know how to fight us. This is what you shall have, in return."

"And where will this proud independence of all rulers take you at the last, young prince?" she asked him, and he knew from the question that he had won, that she would agree.

"A city, your Majesty. A city west of here, where my people can stop running.

We do not know where it is, yet, or what it shall be called, but when we see the land just so, we shall build there."

The flurry of conflicting voices in her head rose high, some saying that he should be instantly destroyed, others that he should be used, but still more that he was an ally worth having, now and for the future.

For the future, she agreed, *If there is to be one for any of us, a new community built by those who have cause to love us is no bad thing. And it would not be hard to commandeer, if that were to become necessary.*

NINE

"Who else is aware of this?" asked Alvdan, revealing just a hint of uncertainty that was unbecoming in an Emperor. The news had shaken him a little.

"The servants within the harem, and of course the other concubines," General Maxin said. "Two other servants from the palace proper. They are presently being held to my order."

"Let it be known they have incurred our displeasure," said Alvdan, which meant death, of course: he had taken a liking to the phrase recently. "General, this could have just as easily been *our* throat laid open." He splayed his hands anxiously, feeling the charge of his sting build in them. The news was so fresh that he was still in his nightshirt, alone with General Maxin in his bedchamber, even his personal body servants having been dismissed.

"The chief of the harem guards shall be disciplined, your Imperial Majesty," said Maxin smoothly.

"She shall be more than disciplined, General!"

"Your Imperial Majesty, we must not draw unnecessary attention to this."

Alvdan looked at him, narrow eyed. "You mean the situation in Szar?"

"I do." General Maxin's mind was spinning, laying the pieces of his plan into place. Another step intervening between the Emperor and his Empire. Another few bricks in the wall he was building around the man, until it was General Maxin who would have sole access to the throne—and thus become the power behind it. "The Bee-kinden of Szar are extremely important to the war effort. You must know how much we rely on their foundries and forges. The presence of their queen here has so far guaranteed their loyalty. As a result our Szaren garrison is currently one of the lightest in the Empire."

"Have it strengthened then, and damn their suspicions," Alvdan snapped. "Who would inherit now? How do the Bee-kinden manage their idiot succession?"

"By simple primogeniture in the female line. There are two princesses and a prince, my records tell me." Maxin said. He had known of Tserinet's death for less than an hour but he had the most efficient clerks in the world within the Rekef's administration. "Maczech, the eldest princess, is currently a houseguest of the garrison commander, Colonel Gan, treated with all honour but still a hostage to her mother's good behaviour. The prince, her junior and not eligible by their customs anyway, is an Auxillian captain garrisoning Luscoa near the Commonweal border. The younger girl is about twelve and lives in Szar with her family. She is not of the direct royal lineage but a niece to the late queen. We must move carefully, your Majesty, and meanwhile I will ensure that Maczech is kept secure."

"Do so," Alvdan agreed, "and think up some excuse for tripling the garrison at Szar. Tell them we are suspicious of another Mynan rebellion or something." He sighed. "It seems today shall no longer be mine to dispose of. The Sarcad was to examine my sister once more, was he not? Let him know he should proceed in my absence, because I shall not have time to indulge myself."

⦉⦊ ⦉⦊ ⦉⦊

As if suddenly struck by a thought, or hearing a voice otherwise unheard, Uctebri grinned to himself, needle teeth stark white against withered lips. He was such a repulsive little man when he was not concentrating on impressing her, she decided, with his head bald and veiny, and his scant, lank hair thin and grey. His features were hollow, his lips wrinkled and the few fangs they concealed were like needles of bone or the lancing teeth of fish. On his forehead, beneath his translucent skin, was a red patch that constantly shifted and squirmed, and his eyes . . . his eyes were evil. Seda had not believed in evil before she met him. His red and piercing eyes seemed to stare into her very being, flaying her layer by layer.

But he claimed to be on her side, so that must be all right.

Seda, youngest and sole surviving sibling of the Emperor, did not trust Uctebri the Sarcad one fraction, yet still he was more on her side than anyone else she knew. He had a use for her, clearly, while to the rest of the world she seemed simply to be filling space. Or at least until Alvdan had decided on the succession, whereupon she would finally incur his displease, as her brother was now phrasing it. She would be then seen no more in the world of men, which was Uctebri's phrase, and one she marginally preferred.

Uctebri called her *Princess* sometimes, too, a Commonwealer title she had no right to, but that was pretty enough. In truth she could not even claim to be a Chattelaine, the half derogatory term for an influential Wasp's wife. She had neither husband nor household. Her life, her bloodline, had left her nothing but fear as an inheritance.

Seda had never known her grandfather, and her father had spared no time for her, but here was a surrogate relative of an older generation for her: Uncle Uctebri of the fabled Mosquito-kinden that they frightened children with. When he made the effort, he showed her exactly how his grotesque kind had survived so long. When he put his mind and his Art to it, he could show himself so engaging and compelling that she found herself forgetting his grotesque appearance and provenance.

He claimed he was preparing her for the ritual that her brother so much desired, a ritual that would gift Alvdan with eternal life. She believed none of it. What she did believe, though, was that Uctebri did not trust her brother. It was a sentiment she easily concurred with.

And so, by delicate stages, they had become conspirators.

She was supposed to be strapped to a couch, laid out for him to hunch over and probe and touch. When her brother was watching they would play the charade out. In his absence, however, Uctebri would use his Art to muddy the mind of her guard, then she could be unstrapped and sit up for a more civilized encounter.

"Your brother needs more to think about," the Mosquito informed her. His voice was a soft rustle.

"If he is growing impatient, surely you can baffle him, O Sarcad," she challenged. She liked to play at games of strength with Uctebri, and he gained a distant enjoyment from them that he would never draw from any experiment upon her body. Despite her royal bloodline that all but touched the throne, she was in fact alone and had nothing. He enjoyed seeing her test herself against him. In fact he encouraged it.

He had plans for her.

"Yes, he will grow impatient if my anticipated services are all he can expend his thought on," the Mosquito admitted. "I will have the Shadow Box soon but, until that oaf Maxin has recovered it for me, I shall attempt no ritual, either for you or for him. Until my wages are paid I shall have to take his mind off things."

"What do you propose?" she enquired.

He gave her a smile, a quick flash of those needle teeth. "Would your brother be distressed to discover one of his concubines was dead, do you think, Princess?"

"No, why would he care?" she almost laughed at the thought. "I can't think of a single man, woman or child whose death would discomfort him. Not even that bastard Maxin's."

Uctebri steepled his delicate fingers. "You do him an injustice, for at this moment he is particularly distressed. The death of one of his harem has just upset many of his plans."

She stared at him. "Explain yourself, Sarcad."

He drew close, raising one cold hand to softly touch her face. "I have known both kings and queens in my time, and in my long experience they are quite unsightly. What a bloodline you have! Your brother, so regular of feature, handsome and well proportioned—quite the hero king of legend. And you, my dear princess, what a queen you might make."

She shivered because, although the thought was not new to her, it was still the worst treason to express it. "The Empire has no queens. No woman can inherit."

"So says a history all of merely three generations old." Uctebri's lips twitched. "I am older than your Empire, and I know how these things can change. Maybe, if a certain bold young woman should begin to unfurl her wings . . . especially with her brother so distracted."

"Distracted by what? Tell me plainly, will you?"

"The Queen of Szar killed herself last night." His protuberant red eyes glinted, bleakly pleased. "She had been oppressed by dark thoughts for night after night. It was inevitable, really."

"You are a monster," Seda chided him.

"You disapprove, O Queen-in-waiting?"

She realized that, beneath it all, she did not. It meant so little to her, the fate of some woman she had never met. *How like him I am, at heart*. "Speak on."

"Naturally, the news is confined to the harem, and it is your brother's intention that it should stay there."

"I understand the nature of the hold we have on Szar and the Bee-kinden." She forced herself to look into those bloody eyes, but his Art had started working on her now, so that they appeared almost benign—the malice in them dissolving before her gaze.

"I rather think the sad news may become known in Szar sooner than might otherwise be expected," Uctebri said, delicately.

"You can . . . but of course you can. But this will damage the Empire."

"Which is a merely a weapon in your brother's hands at present. Time enough later to whip your subjects back into line," he told her. "For now, I think it best that your brother finds himself ever more deeply involved in matters both within the Empire and without. It is only to your benefit, Princess, because you will need all the space for manoeuvre that you can muster. You have a great deal of work to do, I believe."

"And should I start by granting the boon I see you about to request of me?"

Her remark left him absolutely silent, his red eyes gleaming as he examined her.

"I read it in your face, monster," she said softly. "Have I not done well?"

He suddenly bared his teeth in a smile of true approbation. "Oh, well done, Princess. My kind are not so easily read, after all. Your skills are impressive, but then you have survived by them these last several years, have you not?"

"Oh, I have, at that."

"You are perfect," he observed, with such utter sincerity. He was grotesque and hideous of spirit, and she was just a tool to him, but she was an implement that he valued and even had care for. It was a bitter truth that the Princess of the Empire had no other who showed her any greater regard than that, but it was a truth nonetheless.

"We shall meet again tonight. I shall have them bring you to me. My invention is limitless when it comes to finding excuses to enjoy your company. So you shall come to me tonight, and we shall enact a little ritual all of our own. It is time you were tested."

⦶ ⦶ ⦶

She dressed for him carefully. She wore a gown of red, in respect for his overriding obsession, that was worked with black in complex patterns at the hems. It was some Dragonfly war loot that had eventually found its way into her wardrobe, never worn before.

She sat before her mirror, with her body servants, and had them tend to her makeup as though she was to be flaunted before generals.

A test, she thought, *and what if I fail?* If she failed then, at least, when the worst came, she would look a true princess. In the Commonweal, where her dress came from, the women wore swords. She would have girded on a blade too, if custom had permitted. She still had her sting, of course, although she had never had cause to turn it on another human being. *Knowing Uctebri's passions, perhaps I shall have cause to turn it on myself.*

I am so alone that I must find this repulsive monster my ally, putting my life in his thin hands.

She stood up, seeing in the mirror a reflected Seda of the might-have-been. For a moment she could not quite recognize herself in that image. There was pride there, and strength, and a cruelty that had graced the eyes of her father and now her brother. A moment later she was clutching at the shoulders of her servants, dizzy with it, for she thought she had seen, behind that silvered doppelgänger, the flames of battle, countless airborne war machines and a thousand soldiers marching against a reddened sky.

The guard had arrived to fetch her. She noticed him start slightly at the sight of her, trying to match this formidable image with the princess he had seen last.

The room she was brought to was lined with black stone as a result of the vanity of some courtier of her late father. She guessed that, over the last few days, the servants had been kept busy polishing, so that floor, walls and even ceiling all gleamed. In the centre stood Uctebri, surrounded by a ring of tall iron candelabra. Each candle flame that he had lit was doubled and redoubled by the polished walls, until it seemed she and the Mosquito stood in a gloom pierced by a hundred guttering stars.

"You are on edge, creature," Seda observed. "More than usual I think. What has caught you by the hair this time?"

Uctebri showed his teeth, either in grimace or grin. He had little enough hair, in truth, and his scalp gleamed in the candlelight.

"Or have you decided to support my brother after all? It wouldn't surprise me, given that he is Emperor already. What can I offer against that? Perhaps this has been his game to tempt me into treason."

"On his slightest word, you would die, Princess," Uctebri said. "Games, he might play, but he has no need to see any proof of your perfidy. It is not as though his fraternal love for you restrains him."

"That it does not," she agreed. "So what, magician? What has got into you?"

He said nothing for a moment, just went on lighting candles. Then: "You make a remarkable show tonight, Princess. I had not asked it of you."

"Should the spirits of fate not see me at my best? You have prodded and pried and measured me all this while, but now you say there are tests still to come."

"It is now time to make my real test," Uctebri said, as he lit the final flame. His expression, shifting and flickering with the light, looked doubting as he turned it on her. "All this time I have informed your brother of the tests I have conducted on you, some of it true, some false, but for me this is the real test—and you *must* pass."

She felt a sinking in her heart. That was what was now different about the man: he was, for once, entirely serious. Gone were the coy insinuations, the mockery, even the grotesque flirtation he seemed to indulge in. Now he had become Uctebri the Sarcad, a magus of the legendary Mosquito-kinden, and he was about to determine her future.

"And if I fail?" she asked. She was used, through long experience, to appear calm in these times of trial. Her brother had put her through enough practice already.

"Then you will be of no use to me. We will be of no use to each other. I shall instead make what I can out of your brother's inferior clay." She thought she heard genuine regret in his tone. *He would far rather it was me. Can I take comfort from that?* She could not because, in her prolongedly precarious state, there was no comfort to be had from any source.

"Make your test, then," she told him. "What must I do? Run? Jump? Do you wish me to sing to you, monster?"

"My test has already begun. I simply require you to watch me and listen. I will know, after I am done, whether you are my suitable material or not."

"But all you've done so far is light candles . . . " she observed.

"Yes, so many candles." He moved about the room, seemingly aimless. The myriad darts of light confused her eyes. It was impossible to even tell where the walls were now, such was the multiplication of reflections. Surely he had stepped beyond this room somehow, she kept thinking, but then he would turn, and she had to take it on faith that there was a wall there that had turned him.

He was reflected alongside the constellations of candle flames, of course, but as she watched she felt her stomach start to turn, because she could not quite match them to him, some were too far, others too near. "Sarcad . . ." she whispered, "what are you doing?"

"Magic," and he continued his pacing. "Do you hear me?"

"Of course I hear you," she said, and felt that, even as she spoke, her words were covering some other voice that had given answer to the same question.

"We are at the crux," Uctebri said, and she was surer than ever that he was not actually talking to her. "Come now. Make yourselves apparent." His tone was still low, almost conversational. Shrouded in his dark robe he seemed to appear and disappear as he turned toward and away from her, his face pale in the candlelight, until she had lost track of which was the real Uctebri, and which were merely the reflections.

The reflections . . .

She concentrated her gaze on the marble of the floor beneath her because it was the one keepsake left of the room she had walked into. She had only the hard sense of it beneath her feet, for her eyes now saw just a distant perspective of lights and darkness and the scrawny faces of the Mosquito-kinden, and her ears told her that the space about her was vast, with distant, forlorn winds channelling forever through twisted passages . . .

The reflections were all solely of *him*. There were none of her at all.

"Be not shy," Uctebri murmured. "We must risk much so as to gain more. Come to me. Come *now*."

The nearest reflection turned to regard her, and she realized that it was not Uctebri at all. The neck was thinner, and there was a wisp of beard on its wrinkled chin. An older man of the same race, with the same bloodred and protuberant eyes. Some others lacked Uctebri's blotchy birthmark, and some, she saw, were haggard old women, as vile and balding as their menfolk. One by one they had all turned, and now every face there was staring at her, and she could not have picked Uctebri out from among them. The massed malevolence of that gaze, a score of desiccated, red-eyed monsters, rocked her and chilled her to the bone, but still she faced up to them. She stood her ground. If she fled now, she would, she knew, find herself beyond the stone room's vanished walls, never to be seen again.

"She sees us," one of the Mosquitoes declared.

"Yes," said another, one that she recognized a moment later as Uctebri himself. "Yes, she does." His tone was one of relief, and she knew then that she had passed his test.

"What . . . ?" Her voice came out as a croak, so she swallowed and spoke again. "What does this mean?"

"That you have entered our world," said another voice. Between the flickering light and the sheer number of them she could not discern who had spoken. "That we can make use of you."

"I have no wish to be made *use*," she told them. "I am no tool of yours."

"Yes, she will do well," said one of the women. "Your judgment is sound as ever, Uctebri."

"What does she know? How much have you told her?" asked another, suspiciously.

"Enough. Only what she needs to know," Uctebri said. "I intend to show her more, though. She can do more of her own will than when forced, but for that we must allow her a freer rein."

"You have the ear of their *Emperor*," said one, using the word with outright derision.

"And I know what sound will best reach it," Uctebri said drily, from wherever he was. "I have an errand for some servant of ours, whoever is best placed to travel to Szar."

"The Bee-kinden city? Why should those primitives concern us?"

"Oh, no great matter," Uctebri said, and at last Seda saw him clearly amongst the ranks of his peers, "save that there is some small piece of news they had best know."

⟨|⟩ ⟨|⟩ ⟨|⟩

The messenger almost fell from his horse as he reached the Skiel barracks. Guards were already moving in on him, shouting out challenges. He tumbled to his knees, one closed hand out to forestall them. He had been riding for days and nights.

"Identify yourself!" the watch sergeant snapped again—but now he was close enough to add "Sir," on seeing a lieutenant's insignia.

The messenger fumbled inside his tunic, coming out with a folded paper, thrusting it at the sergeant. The man took it wordlessly, beckoning a lantern over to read it by. A moment later he swore to himself and hurriedly handed the paper back. The lieutenant nodded, swaying slightly with fatigue.

"Get the horse stabled," the sergeant called out. "Get this man somewhere to sit down, something to eat and drink. Send a message to the colonel—the new colonel, you know who I mean—and tell him there's word for him."

The messenger let himself be escorted to the barracks mess hall, empty at this hour. He took a bowl of the wine they offered, ignored the lukewarm stew. These had been the worst few days of his life: not the ride itself, since he was trained for that, but there had been those who had done their best to stop him in the surest way. He was bringing word that they had tried to keep secret, and here he was, at last, in the same building as the man they were trying to keep it secret from.

A soldier clattered in, saluting him. "The colonel will see you right away, sir."

The messenger nodded, drained his bowl and slapped it down on the table. He was about to be let into the presence of a great man, a man he had worked for most of his professional life, and never seen. Dire times made for great opportunities. He followed the soldier out of the room and upstairs into the officers' quarters, and deeper in still, up through the ranks, up the ladder of prestige.

He was finally led in. Before him, at the desk, sat the man he had never met before, and unmistakable for all of that: a thin man fit for a harsh season.

The guest quarters in the garrison barracks of Skiel were warm enough, a fire banked high and shutters closed against the cold. A meal was already spread out for the man, cooling slowly, the food barely sampled and the wine untasted. From the look of him, though, one would think him cold and starved. He sat in a high-armed chair, at a desk on which four pieces of paper were laid out neatly one beside the other. He could have been a clerk, perhaps, some mere servant or functionary.

Save that these were the quarters reserved only for the garrison commander's most honoured guests—honoured, in this case, meaning most powerful.

His face was lean as a hatchet blade. Men had dreaded that face, in their time. Some still did. In the past, dread was simply something that it inspired, but just now, there was a hint of the emotion on those same lean features.

He was a general, after all, and there was a war on—but there was always a war on. The Empire was forever expanding, or consolidating, but that was not the struggle that concerned him. The Empire was young, therefore its hierarchies and loci of power were not quite settled. By the end of the reign of Emperor Alvdan II, long might he last, they would be finally determined, and either this man would then stand beside the throne or his enemies would.

Currently his enemies seemed to have the upper hand, so he would have to do something about that. In fact he was journeying to Capitas for that very purpose. This was General Reiner of the Rekef, and his enemies were General Maxin and General Brugan, also of the Rekef. It had become increasingly clear, ever since Alvdan II had ascended to the throne, that the triumvirate system of the Rekef could not continue. Since then there had been a polite little war going on: a war of allegiance mostly, as each general did his best to put his own men into positions of power and dethrone the favourites of the others. There had been the odd man left dead as well, because recently General Maxin had gone a step further than his opponents had dared.

There was a respectful cough nearby. Reiner and the waiting messenger both glanced over at Reiner's second, Colonel Latvoc, a grey-haired Wasp who had served him more than fifteen years.

Reiner raised an eyebrow, gave a gesture of one narrow hand, inviting Latvoc to report.

"This is Lieutenant Valdred, sir," Latvoc began, "one of my men in Capitas. He has . . . news."

The pause left no doubt as to the news' character. Reiner took note of the young lieutenant's pale face, and the hollow eyes that suggested this man had not slept in his determination to bring him this word. He nodded.

"Sir . . ." Valdred said. His uneven voice suggested he had obviously never been in the presence of a Rekef general before. "Sir, in Capitas, at the palace. . . . They say the orders came from General Maxin, sir—"

Something impatient in Reiner's eyes brought him up short. He glanced at Latvoc, who was carefully expressionless, and then swallowed nervously.

"Colonel Lodric is gone, sir—replaced. And Major Tanik and Major Skan as well."

All men Reiner had put in place. The general's lips tightened fractionally.

"The orders had the Emperor's own seal, but the men that have replaced them, sir, are all Maxin's men. I know it."

Reiner looked at him bleakly. So that was eight years' work at Capitas undone, all the men personally loyal to him thrown out of office at a stroke.

"But there's worse, sir," Valdred continued. He plainly did not want to say it, but his sense of duty forced it out of him, and Reiner respected that. "General Maxin is waiting for you to come, sir. He knows that you are planning it. He will have a reception planned for you. That is what I have heard, sir."

"The lieutenant here is in the Messenger Corps, sir," Latvoc explained. "A great deal of news travels through there, both official and unofficial."

It was a gamble now: go to Capitas, and who knew what Maxin might have in store for him. Maxin had grown so cursedly powerful, ever since the bloody work he had made of the Emperor's relations in order to secure the succession, eight years ago. He had not rested since then, either, and now he knew Reiner was coming, and had let out the news that he was ready for his old adversary.

Reiner was not without power or supporters, and Maxin would have gathered a whole new crop of enemies since then. Would any of them stir themselves to help a Rekef general, though? The Rekef ruled by fear, and fear, unlike love, did not outlive the possession of power.

"General Brugan has not responded to our messages, sir," Latvoc reported. "I do not think he sees General Maxin as the threat that he is. He seems to want no common cause with us."

Reiner turned to his papers. If not home to Capitas, then where? The answer was obvious, if unsatisfactory: to the provinces. Maxin had all the power in the capital, but there were plenty of provincial governors who owed their position solely to Reiner's favour.

The war was not over yet.

❖ ❖ ❖

The man and woman standing at one end of the roof terrace were councillors of Helleron, Totho knew. He watched as the portly man, dressed in gold-embroidered robes of Spider silk, laughed and pointed something out to the woman—something in the city below them. The Consellar Chambers of Helleron made great use of this roof, running a railed walkway all the way round it. Fly messengers used it regularly to arrive and depart, and the great and the good of Helleron often came here to gloat over their civic holdings, surveying a roofscape of fine townhouses that gave way, after a few streets, to smog-hung chimneys and the bleak and featureless walls of factories.

Helleron was now a city under occupation, and what had surprised Totho was how very little it had changed. True, there was a garrison force in, now: Wasp soldiers on the streets and Ant-kinden Auxillians from some far corner of the Empire. True the council was merely advisory to the imperial governor, who was a man beyond the social pale as far as they were concerned. Still, Beetles always endured. Beetles flourished everywhere. Totho, half Beetle himself, had never appreciated that so clearly before.

He was able to sidle close to the two councillors, so long as he did not stare at them openly. They took him for a servant and therefore overlooked him graciously. The woman was now pointing at some district across the city that was mostly shrouded in smoke. They were fighting there now, she declared. Fighting on the streets of Helleron! She seemed to think it was simply marvellous.

Totho knew what the fighting was about. A war was being won and lost on a daily basis in Helleron because, whilst the Council of Thirteen had meekly bowed the knee as soon as the Wasp armies had appeared on the horizon, there had been others who had been left out of the deal, and were now holding onto their power as tightly as they could. This winter, the imperial garrison was busily engaged rooting out the fiefdoms.

They were criminal holdings, areas of the city run by gangs comprising as varied a mix as could be imagined: home-grown Beetle toughs, magnates fallen on hard times, Spider *manipuli*, close-knit Fly-kinden families or knots of exotic killers like Mantids or Dragonflies. The Empire was not accustomed to sharing power with other authorities either legal or illegal, nor did the Consortium of the Honest wish for its profits to be diluted in any way. Some of the criminal fiefs had since fallen into line, paying their dues and taking their orders, whilst others had dug in and mobilized their fighters. Each tenday now the Empire took on another little band or alliance and smashed it.

Totho listened to the two councillors tell each other how wonderful it was, that their city was finally being rid of such trash. He noted that neither mentioned the secret deals they had undoubtedly made with those same fiefs, the profits they had squeezed from them or the commissions they had paid. It all made him feel ill.

He himself had betrayed his friends, turned his back on his whole previous life, but these rich and powerful councillors were a whole world of hypocrisy ahead of him.

The first few spots of rain started to fall, and he watched the superbly dressed councillors hurry inside. Totho chose to stay outside, as if the downpour could wash him clean of all his recent actions. After a short while, Kaszaat came and joined him.

For him the last month had brought and taken away many things, but it still had not taken her, though he had assumed, without even analysing why, that she would surely be long gone by now.

"I just heard the news. Another two factories for you," she said. "I congratulate you now, yes?"

He shrugged. "You know his thinking better than I do. You tell me."

"I think yes—but not all the way." She leant on the rail beside him, tugging her peaked leather cap down a little to shield her face from the rain. He let himself study her, for him a new luxury. Here was a woman a little older than himself, shorter and with the stocky build and dark skin that reminded him of a Beetle-kinden, and yet subtly different in every way. Her face was flat and round, and he had at first thought it expressionless. Now he knew that impassive front was partly due to being one of a conquered race within the Empire, and the rest he could now read, from experience. He realized that his own habitual expression was not too dissimilar, for his mixed blood had taught him to keep his feelings inward.

"How is the new project?" he asked her. His current duties meant that he was committed to actual manufacture, and had lost touch with the research and design that artificers coveted so much.

"You don't miss much," she told him. "You keep with your snapbows. The new work? He doesn't even let me see it. Only him and a few others, all day and all night in that factory, three, four days at a time. Then they come out and they sleep, and he gets his back seen to. You know how it is with his back, when he works too long."

Totho did indeed. Not so long ago he had found out why their master, the Colonel-Auxillian Dariandrephos, suffered as much as he did. It was a revelation personally horrifying but professionally intriguing.

"So you're all just cooling your heels waiting?" he asked, quite relieved. He was not on the team for the new project. Instead, Drephos had given him oversight of the snapbow factories, and a strict quota to be met. When the Wasp army took the field against Sarn in the coming spring, it could be a new dawn for warfare, although Drephos alternated his enthusiasm with damning doubts about the imperial generals' capacity to actually make use of what they had been given.

"You want to go see?" Kaszaat asked, and he glanced at her in surprise. Hidden somewhere in her closed expression was something close to mischief.

"You're not one to go against orders," he said.

"No orders. Nobody has said, 'Stay out while we're gone.'"

"He's come out of there today, has he?"

She nodded. "You're not curious?"

He realized he was, as he followed her down through the Consellar Chambers and onto the street.

Drephos had been the first ever Colonel-Auxillian. In fact they had created that rank purely for the benefit of Dariandrephos, the maverick half-breed master artificer. Endowed with that authority he had taken the imperial armies on to win wars and conquer cities. Totho had been impressed enough within days of meeting the man, but now, after seeing the fall of Tark and the routing of the Sarnesh army, he was convinced that Drephos could be the greatest artificer there ever was.

It was because he cared for absolutely nothing but his craft, Totho was sure. Drephos did not care about rank, save that it helped get his work done quicker. Similarly, they had chosen him as the first ever Auxillian to be named an acting governor, but he had only pressed for that position because, as Governor of Helleron, he could turn the city's industrial might to his own ends.

He had then brought his hand-picked team of artificers to Helleron to assist him. Totho was one of that team and so was Kaszaat, but there was only a single Wasp-kinden amongst them, and that was a moody old outcast who had spent more than ten years as a debt-slave. Drephos collected minds that could think in different directions. He had no need for time servers and conventionalists.

"This is the one," Kaszaat said. "Three days solid, nobody seeing any of them all that time. Came out this morning only." By now the oily rain was sheeting down on them, so they ran from overhang to overhang, trying to dodge the worst of it. Ahead of them was the factory she had pointed out, although it did not seem particularly remarkable to Totho.

"Who has he taken in there with him?" he asked, as they came up against the factory's wall, taking what shelter they could.

"The twins," she said, meaning the two Beetle-kinden in their team, who kept no company save each other, "And Big Greyv."

"The Mole Cricket?"

She nodded. Totho had never spoken to the man. That pitch-skinned giant had a sour look to him that did not encourage conversation.

Kaszaat unlatched the factory door, which was not even locked, and they quickly stepped inside.

Most of the interior was bare, which was the first surprise. The workbenches, the machines, all the paraphernalia of manufacture had mostly been stripped out, save for a series of complex presses intended to test the durability of materials under stress. Aside from that, at the far end of the empty space, there stood two great machines. Totho and Kaszaat approached them cautiously. The sound of the city was faint in here, for all the high windows were propped wide open to let the oil-pungent air in.

"We must have the wrong factory," Totho decided, looking up beyond the machines toward an observation gantry. Had Drephos and the others been standing up there to watch . . . what exactly?

"Fans," said Kaszaat wonderingly. "Just fans."

That was all they were: huge-bladed fans positioned at one end of a great open space but, on looking at them, Totho suddenly experienced a shiver of unease. He did not believe in magic, he was no Moth seer to brag of visions, yet some part of his artificer's being shuddered momentarily on seeing those stilled fans, and the emptiness all around them.

TEN

Thalric approached them without ceremony, simply dropping into a seat beside Brodan and saying, "At ease, Lieutenant." The general scuffle that followed had Brodan and his men half out of their seats, hands raised or already going for their swords.

There was a long pause, in which Brodan stared at him, surely trying to place him. Thalric leant back, waiting, looking as natural, as unconcerned, as could be.

"Major Thalric?" Brodan said at last, not quite sure.

"The same. But do sit down, Lieutenant."

Brodan did, and about them his men slowly relaxed, though not without a few puzzled glances.

"Well, it's been a while, sir," Brodan said. "Fetch a drink for Major Thalric," he ordered one of his men, who jumped to his feet and ran off into the rear of the grimy little Skater drinking hole. "I didn't realize you were in these parts, sir. I thought your work took you out west more."

Thalric smiled. "You know how it is when you do the work we do," he said. "One day in the Commonweal and the next in Capitas." Brodan, he was guessing, had never been to the capital. It was a good name to drop to get the man thinking of him as a superior officer, and so not to be questioned.

"Of course, sir," Brodan acknowledged. "Can we help you in any way in Jerez, sir? Or are you here with your own people?"

Thalric studied the man's face: blunt and honest, under a mop of dark hair, the look of a simple soldier, with a soldier's powerful build. But Brodan was Rekef, and therefore more than he seemed. "A little of both, perhaps. Tell me, Lieutenant, what are your orders?"

He had expected the man to be cagey about them, but Brodan sighed. "Retrieval—some piece of contraband. You know how difficult it is to find anything in this place, though. I'm of a mind to just start executing the locals until someone feels ready to tip us off."

"No great loss to the Empire if you do," Thalric agreed. It was almost unbearable, this moment of cutting nostalgia. Here he was again, a Rekef major talking with his underlings. He felt his exile—his death sentence—like a weight about his neck. How could he not belong here still? "You have leads, of course, or you've lost what craft I remember of you."

"Precious few," Brodan grumbled. "Oh, there's something going on, and some odd faces turning up, but getting to the truth in Jerez, well. . . . Before I made the Rekef I did a stint on the smuggler run here. Night after night out on the lake in little boats, getting eaten alive by the midges and watching the lights. We were out here a month, and they reckoned the trade just got worse while we were. These little bastards, sir, they knew just where we were sitting and what we were there for."

Thalric nodded sympathetically, hearing the rain patter harder around them. They relocated, by unspoken consent, to beneath the roof of the taverna, huddled in an odd pattern to avoid the leaks through the perished thatch.

"Of course," Brodan said, "eventually they reckoned someone in our company was on the take."

Thalric let that hang there, still casual in his pose, every muscle taut as steel on the inside.

"Unless it's a secret, sir, may I know what you're here for?"

"Investigating a threat to the Empire, Lieutenant," Thalric replied. "As always."

"A threat to the Empire, sir, right." For a long time, Brodan and Thalric just stared at each other, and then Thalric smiled again, feeling a strange release of tension.

"Your soldier's not back with my drink, Lieutenant. That seems lax discipline. You shouldn't stand for it."

"No, sir. I'll have words with him."

"When he gets back from the garrison with the others, of course."

Brodan's smile was not entirely devoid of regret. "That's right, sir."

"Well, I shouldn't underestimate the speed with which bad news spreads, should I?" Thalric was still slouching in his chair, quite obviously not the man for any sudden moves. The careless pose made them uncertain, and most of the soldiers obviously did not share Brodan's up-to-date knowledge of recent Rekef reversals.

"They made sure to get hold of anyone who used to know you, sir. They told us."

"I'm sure they did." Inside, he felt sick. *So close!* For just a minute he had been the man he used to be, and now . . . betrayal again. He seemed to be a magnet for it, either giving or receiving. He wondered what Brodan had actually been told.

Not that it mattered so much. Brodan was a good soldier and he would obey his orders. "They'll probably make you captain for this, Lieutenant," Thalric remarked.

"That would be nice, sir." Brodan's face remained without expression. There was, Thalric understood, no second chance here for him. Brodan was not the kind of man to let old times get in the way of duty. Thalric could remember a certain Rekef major very close to him who had been just like that, too.

The whole front wall of the taverna was open, just a mess of straw propped up on poles. Without tensing, without any motion to warn them, Thalric kicked the table over, leaping back in his chair with his wings flashing about his shoulders to fling himself backward, out from under the roof and into the rain-lashed air.

The sting seared from his hand, and one of Brodan's men was knocked over flat even as he got to his feet. Then Thalric dived away, streaking through the rain a few feet above the muddy ground, and knowing for sure that they would come after him.

A sting bolt hissed through the rain just to his left, and he flung himself sideways, casting himself down one of Jerez's wretched, rotten alleys and putting the thin barrier of a few inches of mud and twigs between him and his pursuers. Immediately he turned right again, trusting to the rain to cover him. He heard another crackle as one of them loosed a shot at him, but he did not even see the flash.

His wound was starting to tell on him now, slowing him down. Even as he flagged, one of his pursuers came bowling into him, and the pair of them tumbled end over end before splashing down into the mud, Thalric on his back, and the soldier kneeling beside him, blinking in surprise for a moment, but already extending his hand.

Thalric found inner calm, even as he raised his own open palm, knowing that he did not have time. When he saw the flash, he assumed that he had been shot, almost imagined the burning pain he should feel.

It was the flash of wet steel, not of searing energy, and the soldier's head was cut cleanly from his shoulders, his body toppling aside in the clenched moment before the blood started.

Thalric clambered to his feet, looking into the eyes of his rescuer, his tormentor.

"Tisamon," he gasped.

The Mantis had no expression, merely cleaning his steel claw before walking off without waiting to see what Thalric would do. There was no telling what he might have seen or guessed.

⁂

"Now what you got to understand," said Nivit, "is that there ain't been no grand proclamation that anything big's goin' on around here. Right?"

Gaved nodded, recognizing where the Skater's circumlocution was going.

"And also there ain't been no invitations come my way, tellin' me that anything like an auction might be held any day soon. Most 'specially there ain't been any sign that some real expensive, real exclusive thing—of about yea big to each side—is being flogged off some time soon, somewhere near where we're standin'. If you thought I'd heard that, Gaved, you'd be dead wrong."

The Wasp grinned despite himself. "And yet you've heard something."

"People are our business, Gaved," Nivit explained. His girl had meanwhile brought him out a little stack of tablets, and his long hands were sorting through them, apparently without his conscious involvement. "Now we always have odd fellas droppin' in here lakeside, to buy, to sell, to hide, to seek, you know how it is."

"I do," Gaved agreed.

"Only you can't help noticing that in the last couple of tendays the calibre of them has gone up and up. All sorts of grandees from the Empire and elsewhere, all coming in quiet like and just waitin'. Now what happens is, a few days ago some factor comes knocking with a commission. You ever hear of a Founder Bellowern?"

"I know the name Bellowern," Gaved confirmed.

"Big Beetle dynasty, people all through the Consortium. Rich and powerful. Well, this Founder's one of the elder sons, maybe the one who gets the whole pot eventually. So what's he doing lakeside in Jerez? Keeping an eye open for the competition. His man gave me a list of names and faces to look out for and, what do you know—here they all are, if you look hard enough. A good twelve names, and each with a history. Some of them we'd seen here before but most of them, no. This has to be different. This is special. So, old friend, how about you do some talking now, and I can just shut up?"

"Gladly." Gaved sank back carefully in the hammock-sling seat that Nivit's girl had strung up for him. The very feeling made him curiously at home. Perhaps it was just that here, beside Lake Limnia, a Wasp could almost escape his birthright. "There is a box—some mumbo-jumbo thing from the olden days. My principal wants it."

"Him and the world, too. Rich fella, is he?"

"Not especially."

Nivit made a derisive noise. "Then don't even bother showing. These names I've worn my feet out in trailing, they're rich enough each one of them to buy Jerez outright and the lake as well, or else they've got stuff to trade that makes that just about true. Take a look." Without Gaved having to presume on their friendship by asking, he passed over a tablet containing a shortlist of names that mostly meant little—but brief noted descriptions that soon gave him pause for thought.

Here was the wife of a Wasp colonel, a man who Gaved had heard was now the Governor of Maynes; there were two Spider-kinden *manipuli*, as the Spiders called their archplotters and politicians; a Dragonfly noble who must surely be risking his life even to step inside the Empire; another Consortium baron, and yet another Wasp whose name had been mentioned in connection with the Imperial Court. There were others besides: Moth, Woodlouse, and a gang of factors acting for a buyer of unknown kinden.

Gaved shook his head. "Word gets around."

"It certainly does." Nivit shrugged his bony shoulders. "Your fella's out of luck then, it seems."

"Assuming he's interested in *buying* . . ."

"Dangerous words." But Nivit was grinning. "You're thinking about the old times now, ain't you?"

Gaved was busy copying the tablet's contents onto a scroll that was already looking damp at the edges. The marshes of Lake Limnia were unfortunately death to paper of all kinds. "Old times indeed, Nivit," he replied. "Back when we did more than just hunt down runaway slaves for the Empire."

"It ain't *all* imperial work these days," Nivit argued defensively. "Mind, I know what you mean, and I wouldn't have thought you'd be the man for it, any longer. Thought you'd put that kind of work behind you." Stealing property was in a decidedly inferior league to tracking fugitives, but it had been a long time since Gaved had been so desperate. It sent a strange thrill through him, though, the thought of one last heist. He had never considered himself as a thief, just a recoverer of goods, a returner of lost property. The rest of the world had not been so indulgent with the labels.

"You'll help?" he asked.

"I ain't doing the legwork," Nivit stated. "So long as there's a cut for me, I'll get you what you need to know, but you can go fish for the goods yourself."

"That's all I need." Gaved smiled.

* * *

It was raining again on Jerez, which seemed to be the rain capital of the Empire, and possibly even of the world. Tynisa, wrapped up in a cloak, had found an overhanging roof to shelter under but, the way the wretched Skaters seemed to build, it was like sheltering under a sieve.

Yet they didn't seem to mind the rain. She had quickly taken a distinct dislike to the people of Jerez. They skulked about all the time, or when they were not skulking they were stalking. Merely watching them now, seeing them pacing along with their long limbs, all cloaked and hooded as if off on some sinister errand, it gave her the shivers. Before he had gone off to meet his contact, and therefore before Tisamon had instructed her to follow the man, she had asked Gaved himself what in the world these sinister little people were good for.

"Banditry, smuggling and covering up murders," he had replied, in all sincerity.

Some of them glanced at her occasionally: she caught glimpses of their pale, narrow faces, all angles and edges, but at least they minded their own business. She gathered it was not healthy, in Jerez, to pry into another's affairs.

Which was precisely what she was doing, of course, because Tisamon did not trust Gaved in the least. Tisamon probably trusted only two people in the entire world, and the other one was Stenwold. Having to work with the Wasps sat badly with him, he who had been killing Wasps since before she was born.

For herself, she couldn't trust Thalric an inch, but she was not yet so sure about Gaved. The longer she had to stand out here dripping beneath the feeble shelter of a Jerez eave, the less she liked him, though. He had gone into a tiny little shed shored up against the side of a larger building and, given how long he had been inside, it was clear that the whole structure was like Scuto's workshop in Helleron, where the internal divisions had not followed the lead that the external contours suggested. She was also becoming irritatingly aware that Gaved could have simply left by an alternative exit, and she would never have been the wiser.

But what, though? She could hardly burst in on him, kicking the door down, just to ascertain that she was still in a position to spy on him without his knowledge. Tynisa had never realized that being a Weaponsmaster would entail this much cloak-and-dagger work. She recalled now what she had witnessed of the way the Mantis-kinden lived—her own father's people. Primarily hunters and forest dwellers, stealth and shadow were bred into them, so for Tisamon this stalking of Gaved was a natural extension to her training.

A fair time had passed and he was still inside, if indeed he was there at all. The rain showed the same staying power, falling thickly across Jerez with monotonous patience amd ruffling the surface of Lake Limnia into a maze of ripples that the water-walking Skater-kinden could skip over as if it were solid ground.

It was also growing dark and, though her eyes were good for that, the stinging rain was making her job more and more difficult.

She flinched suddenly, glancing to her left. She felt sure she had abruptly noticed a stranger standing there . . .

Nobody in sight, so she frowned, wondering if she had caught some instant Jerez fever and was seeing things. Yet the image had been so clear: a slight, robed figure, like Achaeos perhaps, save that she knew it could not be him. Too tall for a local, proportioned more like a proper human being, but . . .

And in that instant she saw the figure again, standing just beside her. In an instant she had her sword out, whipping the narrow blade from beneath her swirling cloak.

There was nothing but the rain and the shadows . . .

She had been standing here too long, because now she had three or four Skaters closely watching the foreign madwoman jumping at nothing. She hid the sword away and returned to her surveillance. At least there was still a lamp burning in the little round window, so someone was at home in the rundown shack Gaved had entered.

The rain, running over the roof sign made the painted eye weep. The sight seemed strangely mesmerizing. It seemed to look out over its people, those hateful spindly creatures, and know nothing but sorrow. She found her own eyes drawn back to it again and again . . . and all the time some part of her was screaming that there was *someone standing right next to her.*

Gradually her eyes lost focus. Even the Skaters passing by paid her no heed. Still less did they peer into the shadows beside her, their eyes as proficient in the darkness as Tynisa's own, to see the hunched figure lurking there with its pale hand reaching out for her. The men and women of Jerez knew not to enquire into certain things. They had made their town a place where even the iron law of the Empire rusted, and such a place attracted certain interests that they did their best to forget about.

❖ ❖ ❖

"Tynisa?"

She snapped into attention. The rain was easing, and the lamp in the little round window was now extinguished. The cloud-mottled moon lent little light to the scene, but Gaved carried a covered lantern.

Gaved was standing before her, looking at her with an expression of genuine concern.

"Tynisa?"

"What . . . ?" She leant back against the slick wall, feeling oddly dizzy.

"Are you . . . drunk?" he asked.

"No, not drunk, not . . . anything. I just . . . I must have dozed off . . ."

"What are you doing out here . . ." His voice tailed off as she raised a hand to brush her rain-plastered hair back out of her eyes.

In a moment he had made a grab for it, but she was faster still, even feeling as off balance as she now was, stepping back and having the tip of her sword at his throat in an instant. His hand, which had been reaching, was now splayed open, directed toward her. For a second they stared at one another.

"Your hand," he said, closing his own.

"What about . . . ?" She looked down at it, saw the shallow gash that the last of the rain was still washing blood from. "How did I do that?"

She sheathed her blade once more, further examining the wound. It extended from her forefinger knuckle to the base of her thumb. The cut was slightly ragged and shallow, and she did not feel it at all. She sucked at it experimentally, tasting the salt of her own blood, which was already congealing.

"Are you all right?" Gaved asked slowly. "You came here to check up on me, I see. I suppose I can live with that. A friend of a friend saw you out here, and warned me someone had been watching the place for a very long time . . . I thought you might be Empire."

"You thought *I* might be Empire?" she asked.

"Why not? I keep telling everyone I'm not imperial, and you've no idea how hard I've fought for that to become even a token truth. Not all of us Wasps have much love for the Emperor."

"Gaved, when you came out, did you . . . see anyone else?"

She saw instantly that she had guessed right. A muscle twitched in his face, tugging at one corner of his mouth.

"Just for a moment," he admitted. "Just a shadow." There was something more, something he did not want to say, but at this stage she was too cold and wet—and, she had to admit, frightened—to care.

"Since I've now been found out," she said, "can I come inside?"

He nodded, still looking troubled. "I'll have Nivit's girl fix you something hot to drink," he said.

ELEVEN

Her name was Xaraea and she had been the first to see this coming.

That was the joke, really, because she was such a poor seer. Like any Moth-kinden of standing she had learned the mouldy principles of magic, but she had never had any particular gift for it. She lacked that specific kind of concentration that made it possible to pluck apart the weave of the world and then reknit it as she wished. She would never be a true magician, and that meant, in the hierarchy of Tharn, that there was a ceiling above which she could never fly.

Yet here she was and the future of her city—of her world—rested on her shoulders. She had her own talents, she had found: her own sort of concentration. While her peers had studied the workings of the universe, her lessons had been in human nature: politics, commerce, all the strings that bound each individual to each other. Xaraea had played the games of the Spider-kinden, even served as ambassador to them for three years, learning the trade of deception from the mistresses of the art. In short, she was Arcanum: the secret cult of spies and agents through which the Moth-kinden gathered their secrets, and feuded amongst one another.

They had found uses for her talents other than magic. She had a good mind for logic. She had intuition. She had a deft hand, too, that could be turned to many tasks. She had undertaken her first murder on her twentieth birthday. The victim had been another Moth who had never known that he had been judged and condemned. Such were the games of the Arcanum.

The Arcanum: it was a word merely whispered throughout the remnants of the Moth culture. Many other races had their spies and agents acting as their sword against treason and their shield from enemy eyes. The Dragonflies had their Mercers and the Empire its brutal Rekef, but the Arcanum was the oldest secret service of them all, so encrusted with traditions and exceptions that it barely qualified as such. It was a blade in the hands of any Skryre that cared to take it up, and it had been turned inward more often than not in the silent, secret struggles that the Moth elders waged upon each other, murder and blackmail and espionage based on prophecy and ancient philosophy.

When the Wasp Empire had commenced its Twelve-Year War against the Commonweal, the Moths had finally begun to take notice. Not till then, nor even as recently as a month ago, had most of them considered that this extreme might come: Tharn at the Empire's mercy. Xaraea's patrons had shown more foresight, though. Out of curiosity and divination, they had set her the task of finding a shield against the Empire.

Xaraea had gone into the Empire twice, masquerading as a slave, trying to understand this vital, bloody-handed new power emerging into the world. Her exit, with a faked death enacted each time to stave off their hunters, had brought back to Tharn more information than it knew what to do with. In the Days of Lore, her race had been noted for its understanding of the minds of others, but that faculty had atrophied ever since the revolution.

She had gone into that Empire and studied its workings, and sought out contacts, and installed her agents amongst the slaves and subjects of the Wasps. She had put out her feelers delicately, seeking some solution to the grinding advance of the imperial armies that would come to Tharn sooner or later. Delicately, through intermediaries of intermediaries and by the most fallible means possible, Xaraea had constructed the faintest outline of a solution.

How it had all come home now: Xaraea the intelligencer and spy, whose fragile plan would either save or doom her city.

It was bright day outside but the city had not gone to bed. Instead she looked out of the window, shielding her eyes.

The sky was full of airships. There were other flying machines, too, landing out in the fields, digging great ruts across them. Wasp soldiers swarmed in a cloud about them, and one by one they were dropping to perch on the countless balconies and the statues, or cling to the carved reliefs. Their hands were extended in open-palmed threat, but the people of Tharn stood patiently and offered them no harm, made no suggestion of resistance. Not a blade nor a bow could be seen. After all, what good would they be against the artificers' weapons that bedecked the flying machines?

Because it was her plan, Xaraea had to go down there to see if this desperate, infinitely unlikely clutching at fate could be made to serve them. She spread her dark wings and pushed off through the window, descending in a slow spiral to meet the rulers of the Wasps.

The new Governor of Tharn was arriving.

⁂

The Wasp felt a steadying as the airship's painter-lines were lashed to whatever could be found to secure them. He supposed that meant statuary and embossed carvings. If there was a strong wind tonight then there would doubtless be a few headless effigies amid the friezes of Tharn in the morning.

He was merely thirty years of age, and only a major. For one of his age and that rank, this honour was unheard of. True, he had been helped on his way, like a man boosted up over a wall by his fellows, but he had worked hard for it, too. He might have his handicaps, but they had taught him guile and craft until he had become as nimble a manipulator of opinion as anyone within the Empire.

His name was Tegrec, and he had been given the governorship of Tharn.

Of course that did not mean the Empire regarded Tharn highly, since the Moth hold was viewed as some kind of rustic appendix to Helleron, without industry, without wealth, without even a dependable source of labour, the Moth-kinden being a slim and feeble race. He had fought for this post, but had not had to fight too hard once his name was on the right lips. In that, he had been helped along.

"All secured, Major," said Raeka, his body slave. Tegrec went nowhere without his slaves, most especially his constant attendant Raeka, a slight, dark-haired Wasp woman, not pretty but clever and loyal. Behind him stood his personal guards, a brace of Mantis-kinden he had bound to him by understanding and manipulating their system of honour. They were prepared to be his slaves simply because he had assured them that, whatever else the Empire believed, he would never treat them as such. With such a concession he had won their hearts and minds.

His reliance on his slaves and his refusal to travel without them had given him a reputation in the Empire for decadence and a willingness to impose his power on others. Of course, they did not know of his handicap, his burden and his joy, that made all this so necessary.

I have been waiting for this moment for a score of years at least. Dare I call it fate? Perhaps I do.

Major Tegrec made a gesture and Raeka opened the door for him, turning a wheel and swinging out the disc of metal-rimmed wood. He could hear the not-quite-silence of several hundred Wasp soldiers waiting for him and, beyond them, in silence absolute, the Moths . . .

One of his Mantis bodyguards stepped out first, casting a suspicious eye over invaders and locals alike. He wore his clawed gauntlet, the blade folded back along his arm. Then it was Tegrec's turn, and he paused in the gondola's hatchway, seeing his invasion force snap to attention and salute. *No need for any of you, it seems*, he thought. *Are you relieved not to have to go down into those tunnels and passageways to root them out? Or disappointed that there's to be no rape and plunder?* He made sure they had a good look at him, standing there with one foot on the rim of the hatchway, one hand on the circular door, his nonregulation blue cloak, secured by a golden brooch, billowing heroically in the wind. Tegrec the conqueror, the only major ever to be made a city governor. An unassuming figure, really, which was why he wore the cloak, the gold armlets and the torc, all to convey the image of a rather greater man. In truth his hair was starting to recede and he was thicker at the waist than a Wasp soldier should really be, and not quite as tall as most. No matter, his soldiers and the Tharen Moths would only remember this moment of his arrival.

As he stepped down, his most senior captain came to salute before him. "No resistance, sir. None at all. Aside from knives and a few hunting bows, not even any arms to speak of. Of course, there may be others concealed further in."

"And what statement have they made? Do they wish to negotiate? Is this a surrender or merely a truce, Captain?" Tegrec loved the sound of his own voice, a cherished vanity: it was smooth and supple, and made up for the lack of height and hair.

"A woman speaks for them, sir," the captain said derisively. "She says they know they cannot resist our superior strength, therefore they will accede to the Emperor's authority."

"And you don't believe that," Tegrec noted. It was clear that this veteran soldier wanted his quota of violence. "It has been known, captain, that, whether through pragmatism or genuine enthusiasm, some communities succumb to the Emperor's legions with never a blow struck. Fly-kinden and Beetle-kinden, for example, all sensible and peaceable types. The Empire has, as yet, no Moth-kinden within it, but they are reckoned wise, so why should they not take the sensible course?"

"Sir, they are also said to be *clever*," said the captain, as though this was the ultimate insult.

"You expect an ambush in the dark? Well, it is possible." Tegrec had to keep reminding himself that it *was* entirely possible. The ground he stood on, the plans he had made, were all quite open to change. "However, we can torch their fields and besiege them, starve them out, destroy their carvings, even haul Mole Crickets up here to tear away their stone. They know this, captain, because they are not fools. I will parley with their leaders, and explain to them what the Empire shall require in terms of garrison, taxes and the like. I am otherwise willing to spare the Empire's resources, and the lives of her soldiers."

The captain nodded, clearly still not convinced. "Their woman, she said that their leaders—she called them something but I can't recall quite what—would be waiting to offer their formal surrender to you."

Skryres, Tegrec recalled, and the word made his heart race a little. "Very good, Captain," he said calmly, as Raeka stepped up beside him, bearing his sword for him. "I see no reason to delay, so lead me to them."

They brought him to the Tharen spokeswoman first, a slight, grey-skinned woman of close on his own age. She was dressed in the elegant robes that all Moths of a certain station seemed to wear. So colourless, all of them: grey stone and grey skins, grey robes and white eyes and dark hair. This one was attractive, though, in an exotic kind of way, and he had a reputation for lechery to maintain, both amongst his own people and the slaves he kept. Not Raeka, though, never her. She was too precious to him to use up and cast aside.

Knowing the eyes of the army were on him, he gripped the Moth spokeswoman's chin in one hand and tilted her head back so that he could admire her face, then her profile. In a voice that would not carry past his guards he said, "And you are Xaraea, I believe."

"I am, Governor," she said.

"And the . . . the Skryres are waiting, are they not?"

"For the pleasure of your company, Governor."

He could see she was on edge. They had never met before, but he had received so many messages from her, or from her Arcanum, that he felt he knew her. He could see the uncertainty behind the proud defiance.

"Take me to them," he directed.

The Moths had lit lamps for him. It was a considerate touch. The lit path led to an amphitheatre, its rings of stone seats quite empty of spectators, but the bluish white lanterns cast shadows there instead. Three Moth-kinden, none of them young, were awaiting him at the far end. Looking from face to face, he found he could not read them. If they were trembling at the change he brought with him or if they were contemptuous, even if they were plotting to betray him already, he could not tell.

"You may leave us, Captain," Tegrec said.

"Sir?"

"A simple enough order, was it not?" Tegrec arched an eyebrow at the man. "I have my guards, Captain."

The captain eyed the Mantis-kinden guards as if to say they were all very well, but they were not imperial soldiers. "Sir, are you . . . ?"

"Do you genuinely fear they will use their Art on me, to rob me of my wits? I assure you, I am proof against it."

"It's not that, sir, but . . ."

Seeing the man's expression, containing fear and hatred and doubt all mixed, Tegrec laughed quietly. "Surely you do not think they will . . . what? Bewitch me? I had not put you down as some superstitious savage, Captain."

"Of course not, sir." The man looked rebellious but saluted, and led his soldiers out.

And let us see if this gamble pays a dividend, thought Tegrec. *For if it does not, then neither Tharn nor I will do well out of it.* He nodded to his guards, and they stepped back a pace, leaving only Raeka immediately beside him.

Seeing the soldiers leave, Xaraea took a place halfway between him and her masters.

"Elders of Tharn," he said, his voice, even when pitched low, resonating about the chamber. "Skryres of the Moth-kinden, I am Tegrec, Major of the Imperial Army. Do I need any further introduction?"

"You are the one the Wasp Emperor has sent to rule over our city," answered the middle of the three.

"I hope I'm more than that," he told them. Despite their stern countenances he sat himself down on the lowest tier of seats. "A great deal of work has gone into bringing me here: *me*, rather than some other candidate for the governorship. My work and hers have brought this about, to name but two." He nodded at Xaraea, but she had her head down, in respect for her leaders, and did not notice.

"What do you bring down upon us here, Wasp-kinden?" said another of the Skryres. "We know your kind only too well."

"I bring the Emperor's rule."

"And what does that imply?" said the woman Skryre. Her tone suggested she was one step ahead of the conversation, knowing his answer already.

"An interesting question," he allowed. "The Empire is only here for two reasons: one concerns the skirmish that happened months before Helleron was even taken, in which your people killed a few of our soldiers. The other is merely a happenstance of geography, since the Empire doesn't miss out towns along the way. There is no more to it than that, nor any great burden on me—so I can be whatever kind of governor I like."

She smiled thinly. "And what would you like, O Governor Tegrec? What is it you want from us?"

The words almost stuck in his throat, and glancing at Xaraea was no help to him. In the end he could not simply blurt it out. He had hidden his handicap for too long. "Do you see this woman here?" he asked, indicating Raeka.

"Your slave, we take her for," one of the other Skryres remarked. Tegrec had the sense of much conversation going on between them that he could not hear, as though they were Ant-kinden who could pass words silently and freely among themselves.

"My slave, indeed. She goes everywhere with me and even sleeps at the foot of my bed. She is very useful, since she can read technical plans and evaluate siege artillery. She can fly orthopters and other such machines. There is one other reason, though, why she is so very essential to me. Can you imagine why?"

Although they made no sign of it, he was sure they already knew.

"She opens doors for me. They all think that a great affectation of mine, but in fact it is to hide a certain handicap I must live with. She opens doors because, faced with locks and latches, I can make no sense of them. You understand me."

The woman Skryre came forward, staring at him intently. "Yes, we see," she said. "You are Inapt."

"I am a freak amongst my own people," he confessed, without any rancour. "What they all take for granted, I can never be a part of. But there are compensations nonetheless. I was always a reader, as a child, and from that, once grown, I passed on to stranger matters. In my library I had several tomes acquired at the start of the Twelve-Year War against the Commonweal: books my kin could never comprehend, but I could."

"You are a seer," the Skryre confirmed, so matter-of-factly, but it was an endorsement he had not been sure of ever receiving. "You have taught yourself, then, from books?"

"From books, from Dragonfly prisoners, by whatever other means were to hand. And then the conquest of Tharn was spoken of, even before we had taken Helleron, and soon I began to touch on agents of your factor Xaraea here. From there it was a matter of making sure my name was coupled with Tharn's at every turn, and so, between your woman and myself . . ." He smiled. "Here I am, a major at thirty, and the Governor of Tharn."

"We shall not remain within your Empire long," said one of the Skryres, "Or at least so the majority of our futures show us. Either we shall be free or we shall be destroyed. The future you propose is but a thin thread in the weaving."

"State your terms," the female Skryre demanded.

Tegrec spread his hands. "I see no reason to impose any more on you than I must. A small garrison, for what more would be needed amid such a peaceful folk; some pittance of taxation too, for the Emperor is greedy for such things. Beside that, nothing needs to change. Continue to rule yourselves and your lives as you always have."

"As we always have," echoed one of the Skryres, in a sick tone of voice. "You have no idea of *always*, Wasp-kinden."

"Then *teach* me," Tegrec said, standing up at last. "I have come with an open mind. I have come thirsty for knowledge. I know you have taken students from other kinden before, though never from mine, but there has never been a Wasp like me before. Teach me, then, and make me one of you, and in return I shall shield you from the Empire. If you doubt me, then look within me—as I know you can, as I myself have even done with others."

They exchanged glances, and then one asked Xaraea, "Your spies, your agents, what do they say?"

"There are no certainties," she said. "But what choice have we?"

TWELVE

"No sooner do I discover that I have in my house an individual of culture and fame," Domina Genissa exclaimed, "than he is maimed by the Crystal Standard's ghastly mob!" She had Nero settled down comfortably in a bedroom that was clearly intended for much grander folk, and her own personal Spider-kinden physician had cleaned and dressed his wound, and then bound a sweet-smelling poultice to it.

"An individual of culture and fame, Domina?" Taki enquired doubtfully.

"When I first saw his face, my dear, I had just an inkling that it was known to me," Genissa declared. "I curse my weakness of memory, that the answer was so slow in coming."

Taki and Che exchanged glances, each as blank as the next.

"Why look above you, dear ones. Look over the door."

They did and, after a moment Nero chuckled. "Oh, neatly done. Very neat."

There was a painting executed in a single long band above the doorway, a scene that Che took to represent the Days of Lore, the "Bad Old Days" as the Beetles sometimes termed them. Here were Spider ladies and their lords reclining, scantily clad or sometimes not clad at all, eating grapes and sipping wine from golden goblets, surrounded by coiling vines and leafy trees, as though all this luxury was simply to be had on the bough for the asking. Mantis-kinden in archaic carapace breastplates duelled with rapiers and claws, and to one side she saw a Moth-kinden, a young man that Achaeos might almost have posed for. The thought made her sad, wishing him here with her.

She peered closely, then, to see the Shadow Box he had spoken of, but of course there was nothing of it. This was no ancient painting but a modern artist's romanticized portrayal. Nero's own, apparently.

"Yours, Sieur Nero?" Taki guessed, a wary respect in her voice.

"Look toward the bottom left," he suggested.

There were other kinden depicted in the picture, although the eye was carefully led away from them. Huddled in the corners Che saw Ant-kinden hauling casks of wine, Beetle-kinden hammering steel at a forge, Fly-kinden bearing platters of meats. One of the Fly servants was facing outward, looking over his shoulder and straight out of the painting: a bald man with a knuckly face.

"Better than any signature," Nero explained with satisfaction.

"But you said you'd never been to Solarno before," Taki said, genuinely thrown. "That's painted right onto the wall."

"That's because it's just a copy," the artist replied, grinning. "The original's in Siennis, but someone from here must have gone travelling there, and liked it enough to commission this copy. And it's a good reproduction, don't get me wrong."

Genissa's face had fixed slightly at first when he spoke, but now she warmed again. "I hope you are not offended, Sieur Nero."

"Flattered only, Domina."

"Bella, please. Bella Genissa. It would please me."

Behind her back, Taki raised her eyebrows at Che. "I take it you and Sieur Nero have much to discuss, Domina. A commission perhaps?"

"A commission indeed," Genissa said happily. "When he is fit for it. Until then I would hear of his business in the Spiderlands, for I am sure we must have mutual acquaintances."

"If it pleases you, I'll take Bella Cheerwell out to see more of our city, Domina."

"Of course, of course." Genissa waved them away, and Taki tugged at Che's sleeve.

Nero gave her a quick nod, as if to confirm: *I know what I'm doing here.* Che sent him an encouraging smile back, and then followed where Taki was leading.

Once they were out of earshot of the bedroom, and Taki had taken a precautionary look around for eavesdroppers, the Fly woman said, "Don't be fooled by any of that performance."

"By Genissa?"

"She loves that act, all the flowers and fluff, but don't forget she's the head of the Destiavel, and you can't be that without all your knives good and sharp."

"She's your employer," Che noted.

"Don't think I'm not grateful for it. Her money keeps my *Esca* in the air. She's also much better than a lot of the family heads. Still, she's no fool and right now she assumes your friend is a spy from the Spiderlands. That's what she's really talking to him about, though he may not guess it."

"Nero's smarter than he looks, as well," Che pointed out loyally.

"That can't be too hard. So, I'm going to show you more of the city. Do you know the best way of seeing Solarno?"

When Che shook her head, she continued: "From the air."

"You mean . . . from an airship? Or an orthopter?"

"That's just exactly what I mean. I'm sure I can find some pilot with a two-man who owes me a favour."

"Actually . . . I can pilot a flier." Ever since seeing Taki duel with the pirates over the Exalsee, the thought had been with Che. "Not well enough for fighting or anything, but I can pilot a flying machine."

Taki looked doubtful. "Well, I could commandeer you something from the house hangers, but . . ."

"I'd be really, really careful with it."

"I'm more worried about you, yourself. If I got into real trouble, I could always bail out and fly, but—"

"I *can* fly," Che insisted and, when Taki still looked doubtful, she let her wings flare a little, a shimmer passing across her shoulders.

"Sink me," Taki swore. "You really *are* a foreigner, right enough. The locals certainly can't, I'll tell you that much. I don't know how they ever dare take to the air. Bella Cheerwell, you have yourself a flying machine. This may all work out better than I'd hoped."

❖ ❖ ❖

The *Stormcry* seemed very fat and ungainly next to Taki's *Esca Volenti*, which comparison Che supposed was fitting enough. It—or *she*, as Taki introduced the machine—was a block-bodied fixed-wing with broad pinions that each bore a propeller, with an extra prop mounted above the pilot for good measure, ahead of a box-kite tail. The rear of the pilot's seat touched up against a compact little steam engine that drove all three, and Che suspected it would get particularly hot in just a short space of time. The entirety of it was built of light wooden planks, brass bound. Che had to admit that out here beyond the edge of civilization they seemed to know their artificing, at least when it pertained to flying machines.

"She's a reliable old girl," Taki said. "Not local, mind: she's out of the Chasme foundries across the water. We captured her from some Princep Exilla pirates years ago."

Che had looked over the controls, which had been devised to be as simple as possible. "I can fly this," she declared, sounding far more confident than she felt.

"Well, let's go for a spin, then," Taki declared for the benefit of all the Solarnese engineers and servants within earshot. Hopping up on a crate of spare parts, she added, whispering in Che's ear, "Just follow where I lead. I'm taking you somewhere special."

"But I thought we were—"

"Never mind," Taki hissed. "You want to know about Solarno and the Wasps? Well, then you can come along with me. One and only chance for the truth. You with me on that?"

"Of course."

"Then climb on in, and they'll start her up for you."

Once she had been wheeled out of the hangar onto the airstrip the *Esca Volenta* practically leapt into the air in a sudden flurry of wings, dancing into a long curve of waiting as Che's new machine was pushed next out into the sun.

They flung the lower propellers and she pumped the fuel frantically with a foot pedal, feeling them catch and start spinning, with the third engine firing a moment later. After that the propellers were dragging the *Stormcry* forward, hustling the machine toward the edge of the airstrip. The strip was high up, on Solarno's top level, well above the bulk of the city, and Che belatedly realized that if something went wrong she would come crashing down through someone's roof on the next tier down.

She brought to mind her lessons in aeronautics. She had not revealed to Taki that her practical experience of flying had been a single, one-way trip on a stolen Wasp fixed-wing, and then a few civilian ambles once she had got back to Collegium. She had to admit that the *Stormcry* was the best machine anyone had ever entrusted to her.

And then the fixed-wing was out over the city, and inexplicably not falling anywhere. It just powered off, twenty feet above the roofs she had been so worried about, and she was flying.

Whether winging by her own Art or by machine, she was clumsy at flying. She flew just like a Beetle-kinden, never meant to be in the air. But, whether by Art or artifice, she loved it. Whilst Taki waited on above in the *Esca Volenta*, she took a circle over the airfield and the hangar, thrilling as the heavy machine responded to the movement of the sticks. The *Stormcry* was no piece of precision engineering but had been built for someone just like her to use, someone who was no great pilot. She loved it.

She then saw Taki, above and over to her left, suddenly turn and head out across the city's shore, skimming over the Exalsee, and Che coaxed the *Stormcry* after her, vastly wider in the turn, but with a straight speed that allowed her to catch up with the orthopter out over the gleaming water and high over the scattering of islands that punctuated the inland sea: half black crags and half sandbar beaches.

She heard her own voice whooping with sheer glee. Taki was staying deliberately close, keeping a watchful eye on her, as she let the *Stormcry* sling low over the water, low enough that she could clearly see the knots of trees peppering the nearest island, with stone ruins jutting out from them, the remnants of a long-abandoned tower or fort. Then there was a sailing ship making stately progress across her path, and she pulled up and over, clearing the top mast by she knew not how little, before skimming back down over the water, weaving past another island, where a lone flag flew atop a dark peak.

Taki flew close, gliding for a second and waggling her wings, obviously trying to tell Che something. When Che failed to understand she pulled the *Esca* closer and closer, until Che had to pull herself away when it seemed that the *Esca*'s beating wingtips would graze her own fixed ones.

She caught a glimpse of Taki herself, making violent gestures at her to indicate: *Pull up! Higher!*

Then there was a shadow ahead of her, a shadow visible beneath the water.

Che dragged the sticks back, and for a moment the *Stormcry* bucked in the air, shuddering, and then she was pitching upward and the water beneath her had exploded—a great spray of it, high enough to spatter her even as she pulled away. Glancing back, she saw the giant creature submerging again. A fish, she realized, but one that could have swallowed her whole and taken a fair chunk out of her flying machine at the same time. If that water spout had struck the *Stormcry*, she could have been brought straight down, into the water and those waiting jaws.

She shuddered and went higher still, following Taki as she skipped the *Esca* further over the Exalsee, pausing only once near the far shore to let a parachute out in order to rewind her engine.

The shore here was trimmed with jungle, and indeed the deep and knotted green extended as far inland as Che could see, punctured here and there with the glitter of inland lakes. Taki was already bringing her machine down, circling and circling as if looking for something. Che decided to fly in a wider circle above, waiting for Taki to settle.

They passed along the coast a little way, and then Che noticed a river mouth where the trees had been hacked away a little, producing a narrow strip of the work of human hands against that vast ocean of green. Just there, the *Esca* was already descending in steep circles, and Che swung the *Stormcry* out over the Exalsee again, only to bring her back, coasting low, toward the village.

It was hardly a village, though: a trading post, she supposed, would be the closest description. It consisted of three wooden buildings that seemed to have fought their way momentarily clear of the hungry green of the jungle, and then some rabble of canvas huddled around them. A good dozen long piers extended out from the shore and, while some had boats moored to them, there were at least seven flying machines hitched there also, including the *Esca*.

Like the rest, the *Stormcry* was equipped for a water landing, and Taki had explained earlier that as long as she did not come in nose downward Che should be fine. It was a rough experience all the same, as she bounced the fixed-wing from the waves a couple of times, then managed to bring the engines down to an idle as she virtually paddled the machine in. Taki was already waiting on the pier to help her tie up.

"Welcome to the worst-kept secret on the Exalsee," the Fly announced, as Che alighted from the fixed-wing. "Welcome to Aleth."

"This place has a name?"

"This is a city as far as the locals are concerned," Taki told her. "The Alethi are nomads, Ant-kinden, and they're off in the jungles for months at a time, camping for a tenday and then moving on, always hunting and gathering. Their tribes all come here at some stage, though, and so do the traders from Solarno and Princep and Porta Mavralis. When there are natives in town, this is the busiest trading spot on the Exalsee, believe me."

"How?" Che demanded. "How could you even accommodate any reasonable number of people here?"

Taki laughed. "The traders live on their boats, while the Alethi build their little tree houses off in the jungle. Over there's a joint called the Clipped Wing, where everyone goes to drink and deal, and that next to it there's the big storehouse, where the goods get stowed until they're picked up. You see, you don't really *need* buildings—not when everyone knows what they're doing."

"So what are *we* doing here?" Che asked her. Whatever Taki might say about this place at its height, there were a few people about now, mostly green-tinted Ant-kinden who she supposed must be Alethi.

"We're going to visit the Clipped Wing," Taki replied. "I want you to meet some friends of mine."

⁂

The taproom of the Clipped Wing was barely that: a big open space, shutters flung open along the riverside wall, and the window space screened off with cloth mesh to keep out the insects. At one end of the room a few planks had been nailed to the tops of some barrels to provide a makeshift bar. Behind the bar itself . . .

Che ran forward a few steps, feeling instantly absurd because it could not be him. Indeed, when she looked again, this man was older, darker of skin and longer of nose. Still, it had been quite a shock. She stopped in the middle of the taproom, feeling foolish and upset.

"Why are you lookin' at me like that?" the barman growled. "I owe you moneys or something?"

"No, it's just . . ." Che bit her lip. "I had a friend who was . . . one of your kinden."

"That right?" The barman did not seem much interested, but amongst all those spikes and hooked thorns it was hard to judge his real expression. He was only the second Thorn Bug-kinden she had ever seen.

"Two, please, Chudi," Taki told him, flipping a coin onto the counter. The barman gave her a leer.

"Thought we'd be seeing you, once that bunch o' reprobates made it. Was just thinkin' to mesself, who could turn up that'd be more trouble than all o' them put together?"

"I love you too, Chudi," said the Fly, accepting two wooden mugs from him, and then heading off for one of the low tables that were shoved up against the walls. The mismatched band already sitting on the floor around it were currently the Clipped Wing's only other clientele, and they had chosen the table with the best view of the water.

Taki simply dropped in amongst them, leaving Che hovering awkwardly until the Fly used her elbows to make some room for her larger companion. As Che sat down, she was aware that all eyes were on her, weighing her up, perhaps wondering what use she was.

"This is Bella Cheerwell Maker," Taki told them. "She's come a long way, from the other side of the Spiderlands, she says, and she's heard we've got a Wasp problem here. Che, these ladies and gentlemen are some of the best pilots anywhere about the Exalsee. A little siblinghood, you might say."

Che nodded blankly, looking from face to face as Taki named them in turn. Scobraan was a heavy-set Solarnese Soldier Beetle wearing a leather breastplate on which golden wings were painted. Niamedh was a woman of the same kinden, her hair shaved close to her skull and the edges of an old scar reaching from either side of an eye patch. Te Frenna was another Fly-kinden woman, flamboyantly dressed, with a red scarf trailing from her neck. And "The Creev," as Taki named him, was a half-breed—native Solarnese bulked out with solid Ant-kinden muscles. The final member of Taki's little coterie was the most surprising.

"And this is Drevane Sae," the Fly announced. Sae grinned at Che with a face fiercely tattooed across the cheeks and forehead. He had a helm on the table in front of him with a curled metal crest, and he wore armour comprised of wood and leather. He was a Dragonfly, clearly, and Che had never seen anyone less like a pilot.

"She does me wrong, this little woman," he said to Che, his smile widening to show teeth that had been filed sharp. "I am no metal pilot, though. Rider, that is the word for me. These machine-shaggers can't match me and my bride."

Che made an uncertain noise in response and looked to Taki for guidance.

"Sae is the best insect rider that Princep Exilla has got," Taki explained. "These days they mostly hire mercenary aviators from Chasme, but there are enough of them still who do things the old-fashioned way."

"Old-fashioned and best," Drevane Sae confirmed. When he scratched at his stubble Che clearly saw his wicked-looking thumb claws.

"So you don't like the Wasps?" Scobraan said. "Well join us in a drink to that." He raised his mug and the others did likewise, leaving Che no choice but to follow their example. The liquor was harsh, yet almost tasteless, and made her gag.

"You told her already why we're of the same mind?" Scobraan asked Taki.

"Our little social club has a varying membership," the Fly explained. "Not least because on some occasions we do our best to shoot each other down. If you'd been here three months ago, you'd have seen a few faces who can't be with us now. Good friends of ours."

"But you said . . . you fly against each other?" Che looked from face to face, not quite understanding. "Are you friends or aren't you?"

"We are siblings," Niamedh said. "What we share, none who has not done as we do can ever understand. The wind and the sky's vault above. The rush of air against your wings. The world lying like a bowl below you."

"Working for different cities, different parties," te Frenna added. "So we fight, who wouldn't? When we're told to, or when we want. We're allowed to—that's the point."

"If Scobraan is asked by the Path of Jade to fly against the Destiavel house," Taki explained, "then he and I will go head to head, and perhaps I'll shoot him down, or perhaps he'll shoot me."

"You're like Mantis-kinden," Che said. "Or . . . no, you're like a duelling society, but with flying machines."

"Just like," Scobraan agreed. "But this time is different. Like Taki said, we're missing friends at this table, because of the Wasps."

"They've been in Solarno almost half a year now," Niamedh said. "Just a few at first, then more and more. They've wooed all the parties, with gifts and celebrations and promises of aid. Then we found there were their soldiers out on the streets, and sometimes one party had hired them, and sometimes another, like mercenaries, until sometimes they were about and nobody had hired them at all. But they were still going about their usual business, breaking down doors, making people disappear."

"And then Amre," Taki said. "Well, te Marro Amre-Stelo to you, but Amre to me . . ." She hesitated. "He flew north, to visit their grand Empire, to find out where they were all coming from. When he came back he was scared. He called a few of us to meet with him, every one of us who was in Solarno then. That was me, Niamedh and a couple more. Only when we turned up, before he could even tell us, the Wasps were right there. They . . ." She pressed her lips together and looked down at the table. Che was surprised at this, since the Fly girl had been nothing but cheery sunshine since they had first met.

"They had their swords," Niamedh said softly. "And that Art thing they do with their hands. It was all we could to do get ourselves out of their alive."

Taki looked up again, forcing a smile. "He was right behind me, was Amre. But he never made it out of the door."

"No proper death, that—dying on the ground," Drevane Sae growled.

Scobraan drained his mug and waved it at Chudi, until the Thorn Bug came over from behind the bar with a jug for refills.

"So perhaps you should tell us just what the Wasps are all about, Bella Cheerwell," Taki said. "Because whatever he knew, they killed Amre just to stop us finding out."

Che nodded slowly. "I won't be able to tell you anything you haven't guessed at, I'm sure," she said, "but I'll tell you what I know. We'll start with what you may think, which will be mostly what they want you to think. They're a military kinden, certainly, but they talk a lot about only being interested in trade and peace. They just want a little certainty with how they stand regarding your city, so they can concentrate on their enemies elsewhere. They like your flying machines, and they have gold to spare, so they're everybody's best friend."

There were enough nods around the table for her to continue.

"That's certainly what your leaders will have thought at first. And then the Wasps will keep coming, more and more filtering in, and people will start realizing that they really are a very military kinden indeed, and there now seem to be great numbers of them. By that time you'll have heard from some of their Auxillians—slaves by any other name, of many kinden, from many different conquered places. Your leaders will start to understand that the Empire collects cities, and how the Imperial boundaries are closer than they realized, probably just north of your mountains. You're aware your maps are out of date? And speaking of maps, you'll begin to understand just how many times the Exalsee could fit within the Empire. And then the Wasps talk pleasantly to your leaders and start to explain how best Solarno and all the other places here can keep the Empire happy."

Taki smiled, without much humour. "I can vouch for that sort of talk. They had some Wasp bigwigs visiting in the Destiavel house, and I heard some of the servants talking about it. You could write their speeches for them, Bella Cheerwell."

"And . . . well, this is where I need local knowledge. Your politics here seem very complicated."

The Creev spat, which Che took to mean that his home politics back in Chasme were simpler, but Scobraan laughed briefly,

"Sure enough. They're trying on each of the parties in turn, to see which is the best fit. And when they've got their feet in, and wiggled their toes a bit, they'll want to make sure *their* party controls the Corta Obscuri. And *stays* there."

"And the Empire will thus control Solarno," Che agreed. "And then one day you'll wake up and they'll introduce you to the new governor and garrison the Empire has been so kind as to gift you with, and Solarno will join the Empire without even a fight. And then the rest of them, every city around the Exalsee, with Solarno as a base to fly from. All of you, with no exceptions."

After she had finished talking they glanced at one another unhappily. She could see them wrestling with the scale of the problem. Their world was solely the shores of the Exalsee, just a dozen communities and the wide sky above the waters. The world beyond the northern ranges had always been a joke, to them: foreign people doing silly things.

"An Empire," said Niamedh with distaste. "All that—so many cities—all under one man's command?"

"It is you Solarnese who are strange," said Drevane Sae. "Your factions and families, pah! A body has one head, and a people one ruler. These Wasps, though . . . we thought of them as perhaps a few cities or nests or whatever they have. Somewhere beyond the Dryclaw, we thought. But not this."

"If they came against Solarno . . ." Scobraan downed his drink and waved Chudi over to provide more.

"They will come," said Taki. "They are laying their ground even now. Be honest with yourself: you know it. More and more of them will come. Right now, they're fighting the Spiderlands somewhere to the north."

"Capture Solarno and you can have a fleet at Porta Mavralis before they even know what's going on," te Frenna agreed.

The half-breed known as The Creev cleared his throat. "How are they getting in?" It was the first thing he had yet said. Che now saw that what she had taken for an armlet was in fact the iron band of a slave, ostentatiously loose enough to be pulled off his wrist and over his hand at any time.

"In?" Scobraan asked, bewildered.

"How many in Solarno?" the Creev asked, and then answered the question himself with, "Two hundred soldiers? Four hundred, perhaps? But who has seen five hundred soldiers cross the peaks? Even one by one, there would be talk. I fly often to the Toek Station, trade with the Scorpion-kinden there. No word do I hear of Wasps coming through in great numbers—and the Scorpions are good door-keepers. So how do they get in? And how many more?"

He left them all in an uncomfortable silence.

"The Wasps in Solarno have already tried to kill Che once," Taki said, for she had not doubted the hand behind the attack at the Venodor for one moment. "Now we know what the Empire means, how great a threat they really are, the knowledge that they killed Amre for. We have to let people know. We all have ears who will readily listen to us—in Solarno, in Princep and Chasme. We can let people know the Wasps are coming."

"And what?" Scobraan asked her. "A thousand thousand Wasps? Whole armies of them! You heard her. What are we supposed to do?"

"I heard her," Taki said forcefully. "Better than you did, I think. Where are these Wasps fighting? Here? Yes, soon enough. And already in the Spiderlands. And also in these Lowlands where Che comes from. And she said north even of there as well—in the Crommonwheel . . ."

"Commonweal," Drevane Sae corrected her, in a tone that suggested his people had not forgotten.

"So how much can they now spare for *us*? And if we make it expensive for them, if we make them pay dearly, they will lose their taste for it and weaken. What Bella Cheerwell is proposing is an alliance."

They stared at Taki, even Che.

"Well," Che said. "I suppose it would be. In a way."

"So if Solarno stands firm, if all the Exalsee stands, then the Lowlands and all the others will surely stand," Taki said. "Are we totally without influence? No, we are the pilots of the Exalsee. We are the best of the best. My Domina will listen to me. So make yours listen to you." She stood up. "Or do you think the Wasps will still give us free rein to fly and to fight, after their armies are camped about Solarno?"

One by one they stood up in agreement, Niamedh first—and Scobraan, wearily, last.

Che and Taki were the last to leave the piers, because Che knew she would need as much clear water as possible to get the *Stormcry* into the air. It was worth it, though, to see the others taking off. Scobraan's twin-engined fixed-wing, as barrel-bodied and bulky as he himself was, and armour plated to boot, growled its way into the waters of the Exalsee, rising from them magnificently, impossibly, like a rock miraculously taking flight. Niamedh's *Executrix* was a sleek orthopter, its prow crooked forward and then hooked back under like the arms of a mantis, the wings seeming too narrow to take her into the sky until the machine leapt forward with a single clap, wingtips tearing the waves, and then away. As te Frenna's heliopter spiralled upward from the water, Drevane Sae sounded a mournful, far-carrying note on the horn strung about his neck, and his glittering mount, all of thirty feet from antennae to tail tip, roared out of the jungle to perch beside him. It had a jewelled saddle with a holstered longbow to one side and a sheath of lances to the other. Finally, the Creev climbed into his own orthopter, *Mordant Fire*, a blunt-faced, ugly-looking machine whose bows were lumpy with half-hidden weaponry. He paused for a second, looking back at the two women, and then his funnels began smoking and his engine choked into life, and he was sweeping his way across the water, before battling into the air.

Taki had already hopped into the *Esca Volenti*, and Che managed to get herself seated within the *Stormcry*, despite the rocking waves. She started the engines and let their pull take her away from the pier, building and building momentum until she could put the flaps down and let the thrumming power of them rip her from the water and cast her into the air.

The *Esca* soared overhead, leading the way, and Che corrected her course, keeping well clear of the water, and letting herself ride in the wake of Taki's machine.

THIRTEEN

Even after a cup of the bitter root tea that Nivit's girl had brewed up, Tynisa had seemed shaken, oddly cold and light-headed from her lost moment in the rain. Gaved had been concerned enough about her safety to escort Tynisa to where Achaeos was awaiting news, which had clearly surprised her.

"Why?" Tynisa had asked him.

"What?" he had said, "I was going this way anyway."

She had given him a wry smile, and he had thought, *Spider-kinden women.*

Gaved had handed his copy of Nivit's notes to the fretting Moth-kinden, to show that he was at least earning his keep, then he had trekked back through the rain to Nivit's place, to make further plans.

An hour later found him having planned what little he could, agreeing with Nivit about who should be looked into and who avoided, or who amongst the Skater's old contacts might have heard a rumour or two about where and when. Beyond that they had settled into talking over old times.

"I swear, I'm staying this time, once this job's done," Gaved declared.

"Depends whose back you get on to," the Skater replied. "This many big fellas about, even I might take a holiday away from Jerez."

"I never learn." Gaved shook his head. "Every time I strike off from here, it's only the Empire that hires me. I am so sick of doing imperial errands."

The shrug Nivit gave him was eloquent. It said: *Which of us can escape his heritage?*

There was a single knock at the door, soft and polite, but with a suggestion of more force available if necessary.

They exchanged glances. After the thought just voiced, it seemed entirely possible that there were Wasp soldiers outside.

"There in just a moment!" Nivit shouted, and crept to the door quite silently, putting an eye to a strategic peephole. In a moment he looked back at Gaved and mouthed *Customers*. He quickly opened the door, and stepped back hurriedly as a large man entered.

Gaved stood up as he did so, and wondered instantly if this was one of the rich buyers Nivit had mentioned or, more to the point, whether this was the rich buyer of unknown kinden.

No, he realized as recognition came, *Beetle-kinden*. Beetle-kinden of a breed he had never seen before, though. Not Lowlander, not imperial either. The newcomer was very tall, stooping even once he was past the lintel, and broad shouldered with it. Despite the rain outside, he wore no cloak, but was armoured head to foot—though it was armour that Gaved for one had never seen before. Much of it was iridescent, like Dragonfly plate, but instead of greens and golds and blues, it was pale and milky, sheened with oily rainbow hues that danced in the light of the candles Nivit's girl had set out. The edges of the plates were gilded, with gold of a red richness that was also beyond Gaved's experience. The man's skin tone, in the guttering light, was not the rich brown of a Beetle-kinden from anywhere Gaved knew but pale as an albino, though his hair was dark, cut short and plastered back around his rounded skull. His mouth was wide, his eyes small, and he bore a staff that ended in some device, some cunning piece of artificing. As he came in, Gaved caught a brief glimpse through the open door of men, large and small, waiting outside in the rain, in the darkness.

He realized that he had never seen anyone like this before, despite the fact that here was a Beetle-kinden, a ubiquitous breed. This then was something entirely outside Gaved's well-travelled experience.

He glanced at Nivit. The Skater was standing very still. "What's it we can do, chief?" he asked his visitor, and his voice seemed a little fragile.

"You find people? That is your job?" the large Beetle said, and Gaved's uneasiness increased, because the man had an accent that was also entirely foreign to him. "Escaped people. Troublesome people."

"That's us, chief," Nivit agreed. The broad smile that now lit the big man's face was entirely unpleasant.

"Find her," he said, thrusting a square of paper out in one gauntleted hand. Nivit nipped forward to take it, and froze even as his fingers touched it. He barely glanced at it further before handing it to Gaved.

It was not quite paper, but something waxy, something a bit like paper but slightly greasy to the touch. There was a portrait on it, a picture of a woman. Spider-kinden would be Gaved's guess, although it was not quite so easy to tell. The picture was very exact, though, very detailed. Moreover, it was inscribed beneath the waxy layer.

"Find her," the stranger said.

Even in the face of all this, Nivit had not forgotten his professional priorities. "There's the matter of a fee, chief," he started.

The man reached for his belt, and when his hand came out, it was to display three lozenges of metal. "You shall have one now. The rest when you have restored our property to us."

Nivit timidly plucked one piece from the man's hand. Something in his expression, in his very bearing, told Gaved that this metal was gold.

"Sold, chief," the Skater said hoarsely. "Where can we—?"

"We will contact you, later. Meanwhile hold her for us." The man gave Gaved a level stare, and then turned, forcing his armoured bulk out through the doorway, and then heading out through the rain to his fellows. Some of those fellows, Gaved saw, were bigger even than their visitor, others as small as Fly-kinden.

Nivit closed the door, and then simply sat down on the rain-puddled floor with his back to it. "Oh cursing wastes," he breathed. "This is bad."

"Who was he?" Gaved asked. "Who were *they*?"

"I don't know. I just don't," Nivit said, and at the same time he was dissembling so badly that Gaved could tell it straight off.

"Nivit . . . ?"

"Don't ask me. We don't talk about it." The Skater's frightened look was genuine enough not to provoke more questions. "I bet you, though," Nivit went on. "I bet there's lights out on the lake tonight. I bet you any money you like."

He would not be drawn further. His hands, holding the bar of gold and the waxed portrait, were shaking.

◆ ◆ ◆

When Scyla opened her eyes it was there again: just a shadow, nothing but a shadow. She could have passed her hand through it, if she had dared: if she had not thought that to touch it, to fall under that shadow, would mean death.

She had always been one for darkness, had Scyla, for dark rooms and night-work. Now she crept off the end of her bed and threw the shutters wide. That had worked, before. When the shadow had first stood there, the glare of daylight had banished it.

She turned round. It was still beside the bed but it too had turned, craning over its shoulder, to look at her. The sunlight cut through, wherever it fell, but the dance of the dust motes kept its place where the darkness could not.

She had thought that this shadow was just a figment of her imagination, and then that it was a mere representation of whatever was contained within the box. By now she was realizing that this was an individual, the leader of the box's inmates, and that it was becoming more real each day.

It was fading slowly now. She could not look on it for long but kept glancing back and back again to check that it was leaving.

Or at least that it was ceasing to be visible.

During the last two days she had begun to think that it went with her everywhere, even outside under the sun. She had begun to notice where the rain did not fall quite right, or where there were shadows reaching along the ground where nothing could cast them, ripples in the puddles to suggest a footless tread.

Scyla was no great magician. Her talents and her training were only for deception. She was horribly aware that she was now out of her depth. She should have passed the cursed Shadow Box on to the Empire and then forgotten about it. Even the profit she stood to make from the auction was paling in significance as each day went by.

The shape, the twisted, spine-ridged shape of it, was almost gone now. She felt that she wanted to weep, to scream at it. Whoever had made the box had been a poor craftsman, for it had been leaking steadily since her touch had reawoken it. It was infecting her waking hours. It had already poisoned her dreams.

There were just a few days now until the auction. She must hold on to her mind until then. Then the box would become some rich magnate's problem, and she would listen carefully for the rumours of a great man thrown down or made mad. Or perhaps whoever bought it would be some Apt collector aware only of value and not of meaning, like the man she had stolen the relic from in the first place. Perhaps, even awake as it was, it would not trouble such a man. It might not be able to penetrate his dull and mundane mind.

It is in my *mind, though*. And what if she let the box go, sold it on, washed her hands of it . . . and the shadow still did not leave her?

Do not think of it. She would have done things differently, had she known better. She was falling apart. The box was prying at her constantly and she was just enough of a magician to understand what was happening.

Busy. I must keep busy. She would check with her factor here in Jerez to ensure the arrangements were properly made. Better still she would go abroad to spy on her potential purchasers. She would spy on her enemies, too. There were new Wasps in Jerez and she knew them for Rekef. Nobody could keep their secrets close in the Skater town, nobody except herself.

The Empire wanted its prize back. The joke was that at least two of her bidders would be imperial subjects, not averse to sneaking something special from beneath the noses of their peers. Self-interest was the universal rule of human nature, and the only rule she, too, had ever cared to obey.

Now, in the guise of a middle-aged Beetle-kinden man, she slipped from the room she was renting, out onto the waterlogged streets of Jerez. Even as she did, she made sure not to look down at the puddles, in case she saw the ripples and splashes of another's unseen feet.

* * *

Lieutenant Brodan watched his informant pad out of the room: a lean, sinewy Skater-kinden with the same manner as the rest—all anxious-to-please on the surface, all hidden impudence. Brodan had long ago developed a pronounced dislike of the entire breed.

He checked his notes, cataloguing who had arrived, and who had left, notables seen abroad on the streets, those who were well protected and those who were not. He knew an auction of some kind was taking place but he had no details. Nobody seemed to know much. Except there was a whole assembly of unusual characters in Jerez these days, and so they must know *something*. He would have to expand his researches to include one of them.

Choosing a target was difficult, for some had connections he did not dare disturb, while some had proved impossible to reliably find or follow. Others, like the Spider-kinden, were simply unknown quantities, and he did not want to overplay his hand. If he scared off the vendor, if the transaction just decamped to start up again in some other haven of iniquity like the Dryclaw slave markets, or up north amongst the hill tribes . . . well, in that case Brodan's career would be dead and buried.

It was a time for Rekef men to show themselves loyal. He was well aware that there were changes going on back home, by which he meant Capitas, a place he had never seen. Still, the regular lists of the newly denounced traitors kept filtering down to him, with some names added, and others crossed through with grim finality. He had no wish to find his own name included there, one day. It was that thought that concerned him far more than any hopes of promotion. These days a good Rekef Inlander agent had to keep running at top speed just to stand still.

He shuffled his papers once again, at a loss for a conclusion. The two Spider-kinden nobles had both invited him to drink with them, and each cautioned him against the other in no uncertain terms. One of the Beetle factors was dead. The Dragonfly had fled Jerez, probably on hearing word that Brodan was asking after him—but he would undoubtedly be back. Brodan guessed he and his servants were hiding out somewhere around the lakeside, that they would then fly in at exactly the right time to take part in the bidding. Brodan had men, or at least Skaters, watching for such a return.

One of his men came in, just then, ducking beneath the low ceiling of the little guesthouse room.

"Sir, there's an officer to see you."

"From the garrison?"

"No, sir."

Brodan stared at him, but the soldier was obviously not inclined to be any more informative, simply saluting abruptly and backing out of the room. Brodan hastily rearranged his papers in a face-down stack over to one side of the rickety little desk he had commandeered.

When his visitor arrived he stood up immediately, saluting.

"Easy, Lieutenant." He was a greying, slightly corpulent man, wearing a long overcoat half concealing the imperial armour beneath it. No insignia of rank, but none were needed.

"Major Sarvad," Brodan said. "I hadn't expected—"

"Oh, sit down, Lieutenant," Sarvad said mildly. Brodan knew him for a long-term Rekef Inlander, a cunning politician who skipped from camp to camp without ever binding himself to anyone. Small wonder he always seemed to survive the culling.

A soldier brought a three-legged stool for him, all the landlord could spare, and Sarvad and Brodan sat down facing each other across the desk.

"I've come from Capitas, Lieutenant," Sarvad explained. "They're not encouraged by what they're hearing from you."

"But I haven't . . ." *sent a report yet.* Brodan cut the words off short, but Sarvad smiled drily.

"That's just what concerns them, Lieutenant. Now, I told them, a man like Lieutenant Brodan, he's a perfectionist. He takes his time but it's worth it. So they told me, why not go and let him know just how *important* this matter is. You do know just how *important* it is, don't you, Lieutenant."

"I—I do, sir. Yes."

"Progress, Lieutenant. Where are we, then, and why aren't you already on your way home with your mission complete?"

"This area has always been notorious for covert activities, sir."

"Excuses, Lieutenant?"

"Only that it is never easy to find *reliable* sources of information." Brodan swallowed awkwardly. "The locals are a pack of lying wastrels, sir. They're all engaged in something illegal. They're loath to talk, and even more loath to tell the truth."

"I heard you had a man detained at the garrison. One of our own kinden."

"He denies all involvement, sir. He has produced references sending him here. I am waiting for authorization to properly interrogate him." A ray of hope. "I don't suppose—"

"I'm not here to do your job for you," Sarvad growled, his patience obviously fraying. "What else then? You must have more than that."

Not so much more, Brodan considered. "I had contact with a Major Thalric, sir. He's—"

"I know Major Thalric," said Sarvad, his eyes narrowing. "What did he want?"

"I think he's involved, sir. I have men out hunting for him even now."

"Hunting him?" Sarvad leant over the desk toward him.

"Yes, sir. He was on the latest list I received, sir. As a traitor . . ."

Sarvad's expression gave him no encouragement, and for a moment Brodan wondered whether his lists were in fact accurate. Then Sarvad settled back, his expression becoming more reassuring.

"I only meant to say, Lieutenant, that if you already had contact with him, I should think that no further *hunting* was necessary. He escaped you, it would seem."

"We will recapture him, sir, and then I'll need no permission to interrogate *him*."

"I doubt that he knows much," Sarvad murmured, half to himself, and then continued, out loud, "If he happens to die resisting capture, Lieutenant, or indeed whilst being put to the question, there will be no tears shed. You understand?"

"Perfectly, sir."

Sarvad left the dingy little guesthouse and, just a street away, found an excuse to duck into a narrow and shadow-cloaked alley, out of sight of any eyes. Then, although a big, old Wasp major had gone in, it was now a Beetle-kinden merchant who walked out and behind both faces lurked a Spider-kinden spy.

Always good to keep a close eye on the competition. Scyla nodded to herself. She had worked with Sarvad a few times, just a few years back. He had then stuck in her mind as a useful face to wear, for his political acumen meant that he could plausibly turn up anywhere, and was also unlikely to wind up at the sharp end of imperial displeasure.

Mention of Thalric was unwelcome, however. He knew too much about her, and she might have to hunt him down and kill him herself. Still, perhaps Brodan's men could now save her the trouble.

⟨|⟩ ⟨|⟩ ⟨|⟩

"You want Spiders? Over here for Spiders," announced Nivit's girl, who was taking her turn as tour guide about Jerez. Her name was Skrit, apparently, and she was certainly very young, although Skaters were so odd looking she could have been equally ten or sixteen. With her long-legged gait she moved fast enough that even Tisamon and Tynisa had to almost run to keep up with her.

A Mantis and a Spider keeping company within the Empire, and the remarkable thing was that nobody stared. In Jerez nobody's secret was safe, and at the same time nobody really cared. The locals lived in such a welter of gossip and speculation that any peculiarity of their visitors was picked up, turned over and soon cast aside.

They had the names from Gaved's list and were now taking a look at the new notables of Jerez. It seemed the best way to track down the box, or at least the auction of it, though everybody was being very closemouthed about the details for that event. Even Nivit had been unable to find out where and when it would be happening. Whatever Scyla had arranged, she was making very sure that, of all the secrets in and around Lake Limnia, hers was the one that did not get out. Achaeos had guessed it was because she had not yet set the place: the potential buyers would be notified personally in due course.

"And can't you find it by magic?" Tynisa had asked him. "You got us all the way here by magic. Why not just sniff the thing out and let's all go home?"

Jons Allanbridge had snorted at the superstition of such thinking. He was a practical man, partway through repairs to the *Buoyant Maiden*, the gondola of which still remained their base of operations. It meant that he and Achaeos were sharing—though not enjoying—a lot of their time.

"I know the Shadow Box is somewhere here, within or very close to Jerez, but for more than that I am altogether too close, it is too great. . . . It is like looking at the sun," Achaeos had explained. "And, besides, this Scyla, she has a little magic, a very little maybe, but she is used to *hiding* things." He had frowned then. "Tell me, Tynisa, have you observed anything . . . magical, whilst you were out on the streets?"

She had kept her face carefully blank at that point, thinking about the odd gap in her memory, the trance she seemed to have fallen into, the bleeding of her hand. She did not want to talk about it, she had decided. She would work that one out herself. She did not want Achaeos thinking that she was weak in any way.

Only when she departed with Tisamon and Skrit had she begun to wonder just where that decision had come from, whether it had been hers at all.

Since then, she and Tisamon had investigated four names on the list, and thus built up an interesting picture of life amongst the highest echelons of the collectors.

One had been a high-ranking Wasp officer who had been staying within the garrison but a few days before, or so the garrison servants had told Nivit. But the man had been arrested and imprisoned, and was even now under threat of interrogation; nobody knew why. Meanwhile, the wife of the Governor of Maynes, who had also been staying there, had gone to reside on a boat out on the lake.

"What is going on within the Wasp camp?" Tisamon asked, not expecting an answer, but it was something Tynisa felt better equipped to understand. She had Spider blood in her, after all, and so the puzzling out of politics should be second nature to her.

"Whoever wanted the box originally and sent Scyla to steal it," she explained, "they're here now. They still want it, but I'm sure they're not going to want to pay for it. The other imperial buyers are getting out of the way fast, or getting caught."

They had gone to look for a rogue Moth Skryre that Nivit had sworn was in town, with no success. The Dragonfly noble was also lying low. The Beetle-kinden Consortium factor that Founder Bellowern had been particularly interested in had since been found dead in a backstreet near the water, his throat slit and his guards nowhere to be seen. Clearly someone had seen a chance to rid the world of a little competition.

Now Skrit was taking them to see the two Spider-kinden who had journeyed so far north for the auction.

"They must have started travelling within a tenday of Scyla getting here," Tynisa said. "How could they even have got word so soon? Unless Scyla herself sent out airship couriers or something."

"Magicians have always been able to talk at a distance," said Tisamon, in a tone suggesting that everyone would know this, and therefore she should have learnt it as a child, "and also know something of the future."

Perhaps, if I had been brought up a Mantis, I would indeed have known that.

Tisamon's attitude to magic confused her. He accepted it unconditionally, whilst she still found the whole idea strange and unlikely, despite any proofs that had been shown to her. Moreover, he was distinctly wary of it. Even Achaeos inspired his respect, and there seemed to be a fear in him beyond that, deeply incised in him by his heritage and his blood.

And now we're in a town crammed full of magicians—or so I'm supposed to believe.

The two Spider-kinden were not hard to find, or shy of attention. They had taken over a guesthouse in its entirety, and had their servants deck the place out in silks of bright colours, reds and golds and azure blues. The whole front of the building had been thrown open to the fickle sun that morning, and Tisamon and Tynisa were thus able to watch the two of them holding court, one reclining at either end.

"They are good at hating each other," Skrit remarked enthusiastically. "Always hating, so they keep eyes on each other at all times."

"Very wise," Tisamon granted. Earlier he had named the two as "Manipuli," using a word which to Tynisa meant an intelligencer or spymaster, but apparently also meant a magician of a particularly Spiderish kind.

"We should have a watch set on these two," Tynisa suggested. "Still, I'm sure they'll be able to vanish away when the time comes."

"You want to see big man who pay the boss? Living just over there now. Moved his house yesterday." Skrit was reaching for Tisamon's sleeve, but he held it out of her reach, irritated.

"That would be this Founder Bellowern," he noted.

"What was wrong with his old house?" Tynisa asked.

"House was fine, he just not liked it where it was, had it moved," Skrit explained, in a jumble of words. There was nothing for it but to follow her until she had led them to a two-storey wooden construction that was nothing like the rest of the local architecture: square based, but widening as it rose, so that the roof was the broadest part of it, dotted with round glass-paned windows, and edged in metal besides.

Tisamon stared at it blankly, and it took Tynisa a while to recognize it. "An airship gondola," she said. "Like ours, but a whole lot bigger."

"Had it out on the water," Skrit explained. "Now he wants it inland. Put up his big float and just move it over, then float comes down and pulled down into the roof. Lot of work, that, no one knows why."

They digested this curiously, but neither could make any sense of it.

"Who's next on the list?" Tynisa asked.

"Not found yet. All hiding. You have all there are," said Skrit, sounding oddly proud of it.

"Well, they'll all know whatever there is to be known about the auction," Tynisa said. "We need to speak to one of them: who's our best wager?"

Tisamon looked back over his shoulder toward the big guesthouse but she knew that matters would go very badly for all concerned if he tried cutting the information out of those Spiders, whether they were magicians or not.

"This one," she decided. "Bellowern."

"Why?"

"He was the man who hired Nivit, and that shows initiative and open-mindedness. He won't be a magician, because he's Beetle-kinden. He's imperial but not army, not actually a Wasp." She shrugged. "And also I want to know what made him move his house."

Tynisa had not seen a gondola quite so grand since the *Sky Without*. Founder Bellowern's temporary home was now virtually the most sumptuous building in Jerez, larger in all dimensions than the genuine houses around it. It was also apparently impregnable. There was a hatch, but it was ten feet off the ground and looked firmly closed. The windows were too small for even a Fly to get through. Conceivably there must be hatches on the deck above, but she would have to wait until dark before climbing up there.

She realized she did not even know whether Tisamon possessed the Art to climb a sheer surface like this. It was always a social awkwardness, asking questions about another's Art, but she already knew that he could not take to the air as some Mantids did. His Art seemed concentrated in the spines on his arms and in the honed skill gifted to the Mantis-kinden in the simple business of killing people.

After they had been scouting out Bellowern's place for about ten minutes, a Skater-kinden child approached them. Tynisa stared at the creature without affection, for the locals' children were even less appealing than they were. The starved-looking thing, who could equally have been a boy or a girl, began a brief conversation with Skrit and then handed over a scroll. It was only after a moment that Tynisa spotted the relevance: the locals never used paper.

"It's from the man in the house," Skrit announced, for all the world as though she had just performed some public service. She held the rolled document out to them and Tynisa took it, breaking the neat seal and reading.

"To Master Mantis and Madam Spider: I shall be taking my ease shortly at the taverna delightfully known as the Bag of Leeches and you are cordially invited to join me in the open where we can both be assured of a minimum of surprises." Her mouth twisted wryly. "This is getting to be a habit," she noted.

"Bellowern," Tisamon said, and she nodded.

"We're on Skater-kinden ground, Tisamon. He's wise enough to have some local eyes minding his business. If we do meet him, is this going to get messy?"

Tisamon's expression worried her. He did not understand what was going on, and that made him jumpy, therefore dangerous. "We'll meet him," he decided. "If the Beetle does want a fight then I've no objections. But eat nothing, drink nothing while in his company."

"He's not going to be impressed with that."

"Good."

Skrit guided them to the place mentioned: there was a large leather bag hanging over the low doorway, but Tynisa was not going to prod it to test the claim. Like most of the Skater buildings, the front was composed just of poles, shutter panels taken away each morning to let the dank air in, with all the rot and fish smells of Lake Limnia riding on it. They chose a large, uneven-legged table with a good view of the street and sat waiting, but not for long.

The affluent-looking Beetle-kinden that arrived after them, only a minute away from being on their heels, was identified by Skrit as Bellowern. He had a retinue with him, and Tynisa felt Tisamon tense at the sight: a dozen Wasp soldiers out of uniform, but surely army men seconded to the Consortium, plus at least half a dozen servants. Tisamon's hand gestured briefly upward, and she saw a Fly-kinden keeping watch up there, between the roofs and the cloud-hung sky.

"Trusting sort, isn't he?" the Mantis murmured, as Founder Bellowern passed beneath the suspect leather bag and spotted them at their table. He was lean for a Beetle, but his dark skin and the receding grey hair cropped close to his skull were oddly reminiscent of Stenwold. He wore clothes in drab colours—black breeches, grey tunic and a dun shirt—but the cloth was all of the finest. Tynisa guessed from the way the tunic hung that he had armour beneath it, at least a leather vest and possibly more. At his belt there was a dagger that was almost a short sword, mostly hidden by a plate-sized buckler shield. As a result he looked less the merchant lord and more the successful mercenary captain.

He looked them over, clearly weighing them up, and then sat down opposite them as easily as if he had known them for years. At a gesture, his guards positioned themselves around the taproom while his servants stood respectfully a few paces back.

"I give up," Founder Bellowern said. "Who in the wastes are you?"

"A curious question," Tynisa said.

"I'm a curious man. You breeze in on a little airship, along with a Moth-kinden nobody seems to know, but whose name, my people inform me, is Achaeos—a new name to me. You could just be some pack of mercenary adventurers, a type that Jerez seems to attract like a corpse pulls flies. But then you start asking all the right questions to make it sound as if you're genuine players. So what gives?"

"You seem to be working on the assumption that we somehow answer to you," Tisamon said, low voiced. His eyes were passing from one guard to the next, and Tynisa sensed a slight uncertainty in him. It was, she knew, because the guards were not watching Tisamon. Instead they were looking elsewhere, looking outward. Then Tisamon's gaze passed on to the servants, where it halted once again.

Bellowern smiled. "If I was that interested, I could easily find out," he told them. "But let me tell you what I think: you're here with some two-bit quack conjuror who's got just enough talent to be aware that something's happening. Maybe he wants in. If so he's going to be disappointed. I don't say that to be unpleasant but the stakes are very high for this game. He simply can't afford it, any of it."

"So you're warning us off," Tynisa said. "You'll forgive us if we don't thank you for your wisdom and scurry away, right now."

Bellowern grinned at her, unexpectedly boyish just for that brief moment. "Just what I expected to hear. Am I supposed to have my soldiers muscle over now and bend some iron bars to frighten you? Or perhaps I should just make veiled threats. Hmm, let me think . . ."

Tynisa had to fight an answering smile. It was very like her first meeting with Teornis, and she had not expected that here. The Beetle before her had been a man of influence in the Empire for decades, and a man whose influence was based on trade, not on the all-important military. She should have foreseen a certain deftness of manner.

"Who is she?" Tisamon said abruptly, and Founder's entire bearing changed. All of a sudden his guards were watching, hands poised to unleash their stings. Caught off guard, Tynisa followed Tisamon's gaze to one of Founder's servants, a Spider-kinden girl, quite young . . . Or perhaps not wholly Spider? There was something odd about her, for certain.

"Why do you ask?" Founder said tightly, and Tynisa sensed that, for reasons beyond her, Tisamon's next words could easily give them the fight he had been spoiling for.

"I don't know," the Mantis said slowly. "What's wrong with her?"

"Nothing," said Founder, and the tension ebbed away invisibly, but sensed by everyone there. "Just a new acquisition of mine."

"A slave?"

Founder's smile was harder this time. "I had forgotten how much your kinden dislikes that trade. Well, you are in the Empire now, so fight a man for owning slaves and you'll have more work than you have years to do it in."

Tisamon's returning look was cold, but he said nothing.

"I believe you were warning us off," Tynisa prompted.

"Actually, I wasn't." Founder looked between her and the Mantis, as though weighing them on his merchant's scales. "You see, it may surprise you to know that I recognize that badge there, that both of you are wearing. I'm a man of strange interests, which is of course why I'm here at all." The smile, the harder one, broadened. "I don't know how much your little scholar is paying the two of you, but how would you like to work for me and earn yourselves a wage more worthy of your skills?"

"We are not mercenaries for hire—" Tisamon started.

Tynisa cut him off. "Tell us what you mean, Master Bellowern."

He smiled at her. "As I said, I know what that badge of yours means. I'm a knowledgeable man. To be amongst the real collectors you have to be. I was a roving factor for the Consortium for twenty-five years before they finally let me into their higher ranks, and I went to places you've probably never even heard of. We Beetles can go places that the Wasps can't, or won't. I've learnt a great deal, and I've found that history fascinates me, especially when it survives into the present, as that badge has done."

"You cannot think we would simply betray our current . . . employer," Tynisa said.

"I rather hope you wouldn't, in fact," Bellowern confirmed. "I don't know the details of your contract, though. You might be fee'd by the day or even the hour. I'm proposing two contracts, though, and I want you to consider them. I'll even buy you out of your current obligations if your master agrees. The thing is, as I said, I know that mark you wear. I'll ask your Mantis word of honour on any deal we strike."

"Even knowing what it is we seek?" Tisamon said. "You would take us to it, guide us to it, even knowing that?"

"With your word on it, Mantis, and your sworn oath, I think I would." Founder Bellowern smiled like a man who has leverage on his opponent. "But let's deal with the first matter first, as is always best in business. For the next few days, until that other business comes to hand, I feel myself in need of a little additional protection. Nothing more than that. Your badges suggest a level of skill I'd be willing to pay handsomely for. After that, well . . . we'll see how satisfactorily we work together, shall we?"

"What are you worried about, Master Bellowern?" Tynisa asked him.

"Just the usual. My peers and competitors are not principled people, so a little insurance is called for."

You're lying, Tynisa knew and, although his face was admirably bland, his eyes had flicked, just the once, to the mysterious Spider girl. This only confirmed Tynisa's suspicions. *Has the collector come into possession of some dangerous goods?* It seemed certain.

Tisamon was looking put out, but he was waiting for her to make her next move, trusting that she knew what she was doing. In this arena, where motive and feelings were the main weapons at hand, she was better equipped than he was.

"Master Bellowern, what can you offer us?"

"Fifty Imperials per day," he said smoothly. "But, as I perceive you are a Lowlander from your speech, that would mean about half as much in Helleron Centrals."

"Forty Centrals in Helleron coin, each. Double if we fight," she said, straight back.

Founder Bellowern regarded her impassively, giving no clue as to whether she had just oversold or undersold herself. "Agreed," he said at last, letting her know that he would have agreed more. "But what of your current contract?"

"We will have to speak to our patron," she told him. "However, I think he will be agreeable. As you guess, his purse is not large. Where shall we rejoin you?"

"I am aware that you know where I have made my temporary residence," he said. "I shall expect you there." He stood, and she saw a thought come to him that got through his calm façade to twitch at his face. "Come before nightfall, if you come at all. That must be a term of the contract."

When he had gone, she looked toward Tisamon, who was frowning, not at her but after the Beetle and his retinue.

"He does not understand all he thinks," Tynisa said. "For I am not bound by any 'Mantis honour.' I hope that does not disappoint you."

He made no comment on it. Instead he said, "I confess I am intrigued. What is he scared of?"

"There's one obvious way to find out," she said. "Let's tell Achaeos, and then we'll present ourselves for Master Bellowern's amusement. And perhaps, once he has us, he'll find other uses for us, such as removing the competition. There are people out there who know what we want to know. Bellowern isn't the only one, but he can lead us to the others."

FOURTEEN

It was more than Stenwold had expected, and it gave him more hope than he had seen in a long time. In this hall within Sarn, all the Lowlands were gathered against the storm the coming year would bring. The Sarnesh had reworked a barracks, taking out its internal walls and installing seats and a grand table for the greatest war council the Lowlands had ever seen. The men and women standing about it now showed that this had not been a wasted effort.

Stenwold himself represented Collegium. He watched the other ambassadors watching him. It seemed incredible to him, but his name was on all their lips. He was known across the entire Lowlands, as though he were some great hero of history.

This is *history*, he reminded himself. *We make it in this very room.*

The Queen of Sarn was there in person, a gesture which displayed the great faith and trust she placed in this council and in what it meant for the future. She had half a dozen of her Tacticians ranged behind her, for immediate advice, and even protection, if need be, and of course she had the whole of her city to call on if she needed more of either. Still, she had made a statement, taken a vital step. In refusing to delegate her presence, she had shown the world how much importance the Sarnesh placed on this.

There were two Mantis warlords here too, one from Etheryon and one from Nethyon, standing pointedly separate without staff or assistants. From their stance it was clear to see that they did not like one another. They were both women, and so was the slender, aging Moth who stood between them. In a move unprecedented, Dorax had sent a Skryre to Sarn for this purpose.

There was also a Tactician from Kes, with half a dozen soldier-diplomats behind him, and that was far more than Stenwold had hoped for. There had never been a Kessen ambassador in Sarn ever before. About a dozen blandly dressed Flies had come from Egel and Merro. They looked the sort to act irreverently but they were serious now. Their warrens were directly on the coastal invasion path. Beside them, Parops stood for the currently occupied city of Tark.

No one from the Felyal. Nobody from Vek either, but then the Vekken were still licking their wounds. Nobody from Helleron, although the Moth Skryre claimed to speak for her kin in Tharn.

A white-haired and bearded man, belonging to a kinden Stenwold did not immediately recognize, caught his eye. He was taking his place at the table, to the baffled looks of the other delegates. Stenwold caught at a passing Sarnesh servant and asked who this stranger was.

"His name is Sfayot," the Ant reported, after a moment's silent conference. "He speaks for the renegade prince."

"The . . . ?" Then Stenwold suddenly realized. *Salma! Salma has sent an ambassador? What does he think he's doing?* But, then, the fact that the Sarnesh Queen had allowed it spoke volumes. Just what exactly had Salma discussed with her?

"Feeling proud?" a sly voice asked in his ear. He looked about and found an elegantly dressed Spider lounging beside him, eyeing up the two Mantis-kinden.

"Teornis."

"Of the Aldanrael, at your service, and apparently that of the whole Lowlands." The Spider Lord-Martial sketched a bow. "Well, Master Maker, this is an impressive piece of artifice, but will it run?"

Stenwold looked about him at the faces, both familiar and strange, and then back at his own staff, consisting only of Sperra and Arianna. "All these people have not come here for nothing," he declared, and knew that he was right.

⦿ ⦿ ⦿

Two hours later, and he just managed to leave the room on his own feet, although, if Arianna and Sperra could physically have carried him, he might have requested it.

They had not come there for nothing at least. So far so good. They had come there, it seemed, for the snapbow. How glad he was that he had been so honest with the Sarnesh on the subject, for it seemed that everyone, even the blasted Moth-kinden, knew that Collegium had engineered one. Instead of any serious debate on the Wasp Empire, everyone had come with their demands for it, regarding who should have it and who should not.

The Sarnesh wanted it, and perhaps, as its first victims, they even had a right to it. He had known that. Of course, the Sarnesh did not want anyone *else* to have it. The Kessens, on the other hand, demanded that the Sarnesh should not be given access to the weapon unless they could have it too, and Stenwold could see their point. How long would Kes stand if the Sarnesh gained such a military advantage? He was so used to seeing Sarn as Collegium's staunch ally that he must now learn to view them as an Ant-kinden city-state in their own right.

Teornis, having lounged through most of the proceedings with an amused look on his face, had then taken the opportunity to say that, if Kes got it, then shouldn't the Spiderlands have the thing as well, whatever it was and whatever it was supposed to do? On the other hand, if the Lowlands could not agree on how to deploy this wretched machine, and yet still needed it in order to defeat the Wasps, he had suggested, mockingly, that perhaps it would best be given into the sensible hands of his people alone.

The Moth-kinden had, with a sharp word, restrained her Mantis allies from attacking Teornis across the tabletop. The Ancient League's argument was that nobody should have the snapbow, that the Wasps, as its sole holders, should be immediately defeated, and then all plans and examples of the weapon must be destroyed. They were obviously considering what great effect the device might have, employed against their own forces afterward. The Fly-kinden seemed divided on the subject, but one of them did have the initiative to ask whether a smaller version might be constructed. Only Parops and the white-bearded Sfayot had shown no great interest in the device, for the disposition of their forces was such that it barely mattered to them.

Of actual diplomacy, of alliance, of the war itself, precious little had been discussed. Instead Stenwold had become the anvil for all the hammers of the Lowlands, and his head was still ringing.

"They will change their tune when spring draws close," Arianna assured him, "Then they will realize."

"I am not sure this council will last until spring," Stenwold told her. "If I cannot solve this, then the snapbow may turn out to be the weapon that destroys the Lowlands after all, and before the Wasps even get a chance."

⁂

Elsewhere in Sarn, a servant waited in the Foreigner's Quarter. He was waiting by the rail line leading to Collegium, but not for a train. Instead, he glanced at the sky. He seemed, though was not, Sarnesh Ant-kinden, dressed in a simple servant's tunic, therefore nobody paid him much heed.

The messenger came without a word: a fat black fly the size of his fist, meandering over the bustling crowd of locals and visitors until it caught the scent the man had dabbed on himself. It dived for him, and he caught it in his hands, to scattered admiration amongst those standing nearest. He took it away to one side.

He was no Sarnesh, or at least not quite. A half-breed, but one of the rare kind where the face was that of either one parent or the other. He could walk unsuspected amongst the Sarnesh. His given name, Lyrus, was an Ant name. He could even hear their mind-speech, but he was none of them. He was Rekef.

He held the insect long enough to pluck the tiny rolled message tied between its legs. An uncertain way of communicating, this, but his handler was only a mile outside the city walls, a short enough sprint for a well-trained animal. He let it go, and the fly blundered aimlessly about the nearest wall for a moment, before buzzing away, understanding, in some crude fashion, that its task was done.

Lyrus had been well schooled. It only took a moment to decode the message.

Lowlander alliance must be stopped soonest. Destabilize Sarn as alliance centre. Sarnesh Queen must die. Approach Avt depot for details and wherewithal.

He folded the note and went over to a Fly-kinden food vendor, feeding the paper to the charcoal flames even as he haggled over the price of a meal. He then set off for the city gates. The Avt depot was two miles south down the Collegium line, a brisk enough walk for any Ant-kinden, or even for one who just resembled them. There he would take a delivery from one of the station's traders, and in that delivery would be included his further orders. As a servant attached to the palace, he had many duties that took him to many places. The beauty of his pretence was that no suspicion would attach to him. He was, even in the minds of his foes, a dutiful son of Sarn.

❖ ❖ ❖

It was evening by the time Lyrus paused at the gates of Sarn, just another Sarnesh Ant coming in with a basket on his back, just another Ant doing the everyday business of the city. There were plenty of soldiers about, but they were all for keeping their eyes on the new influx of foreigners and nobody spared a second thought for Lyrus. After all, he was one of *them* within his mind. They addressed him as brother and he hailed them in turn, smiling derisively at them in the hidden recesses of his head. They had no idea they were deceived, and most of them could not even conceive of it.

Loyalty: it was ingrained into the Ant mind. There were always mavericks, rogues, those who could not live inside the tight lattice of orders and duty. They left or were cast out, but they never quite lost their loyalty totally. Even those who were hunted down across the Lowlands, to die in some seedy alley on the swords of their brothers, did not quite lose that tie. In the moment of their deaths, Lyrus had no doubt, they found themselves reunited with what they had given up.

But he was different: Lyrus the half-breed and son of a half-breed sire on a Sarnesh mother. That part of him that was not Sarnesh was so mongrel that he had never bothered to untangle his antecedents. The one thing he had known, growing up in the Empire, was that the half-breed side of him made him automatically a slave, but the Sarnesh side of him got him cursed and whipped.

It had been easy enough, after that, to associate Sarn with all that was worst in the world. Then he had been found by the Rekef, and they had explained that he could yet serve the Empire and thus blot out the stain of his heritage. The younger Lyrus had been desperate for the chance.

He had spent seven years in Sarn since then, just being one of the locals, becoming known. He had worked patiently and tirelessly, a true Ant indeed, but all for the Rekef cause. He loved the Rekef. It was not just that they had given him a purpose, but he also loved their ingenuity, their resourcefulness. He knew that, back in the Empire, it was the Rekef Inlander they feared more, but the Outlander branch had to be twice as clever and find its tools in the most unlikely places.

He had met with his masters as instructed, outside the city. A few words had been exchanged, and a gift. As soon as he had hidden himself away in a storeroom at the palace, he took a closer look at it. It was a beautiful example of the weaponsmith's art: dark wood bound with brass, possessing four arms of sprung steel. It was a double-strung repeating crossbow, and the finest example he had ever seen—a fit weapon for a regicide. It was Collegium-built, and that could hardly be accidental. He was to be dubbed a Collegiate assassin, then. He knew there were already tensions between Sarn and its old ally, and this was where a wedge was to be inserted.

He knew that the Queen would want to meet with the fat man from Collegium soon. That would be his moment. He would have everything ready for then.

For Lyrus, being as quick as they came, it had been easy enough to secure himself a position within the palace. Always so eager to put in extra hours, always diligent, always careful beyond even the exacting Ant-kinden standards. The overseers placed real value on him, until gradually he had the run of the place. He had even attended the Queen herself before. Really, for someone with a devious brain, and the Ant-kinden Art to link minds, it was easy to achieve *anything* in this city.

And, of course, he would not be alone. His masters were sending two men to assist him. Not Wasps, for no Wasp could walk the streets of Sarn undetected, but a pair of Fly-kinden killers. Lyrus knew not to rely on them. They would be merely a distraction for the guards. Here, in his own hands, was the machinery for the alliance's destruction.

He was aware that he was not expected to survive but perhaps he could surprise his masters in that. If the business was swift enough, he might be the only witness whose story would be believed.

⊕ ⊕ ⊕

"How many soldiers do you have, back in Collegium?" Stenwold asked.

"Twelve hundred and seventy-four." Parops did not need to waste a moment thinking about it. Following the Vekken siege of Collegium, word about a renegade Tarkesh army had passed across the Lowlands and, one by one and squad by squad,

Tarkesh citizens had started to come out of the woodwork. Some had managed to flee after the death of the King, as the Wasps were finalizing their hold on the city. Others had been garrisoning villages or dispatched on other assignments beyond the city walls, and therefore had not been back in time to help defend their home. A few had even been Collegium residents or students at the Great College. Parops had thus become, without ever intending it, a rallying point. Some of his men were already, in their idle mental talk, promoting him to the rank of tactician.

Twelve hundred and seventy-four disciplined and motivated Tarkesh infantry, Stenwold considered. Of course, it would probably be more than that by now. That figure was the one that had come to Parops by the latest train from Collegium, therefore already a few days cold. It was an expensive proposition for Collegium to retain so many, but the Tarkesh were second to none as soldiers and Stenwold's people were only now starting to levy a real army of their own. The Beetle-kinden's numbers and equipment would be there, by spring, but not the discipline or the skill.

"Tell me," he said, thoughtfully, "will they be prepared to fight for Sarn?"

"Well, there's a question," Parops admitted. "And if you'd asked me whether they would fight *against* Sarn I'd give a quicker answer. But defending a foreign city-state . . ."

"Against the Wasps? Against the people who conquered Tark?" Stenwold pointed out.

Parops threw him an annoyed look. "Don't patronize me, Master Maker. Don't try to lead me by the nose. I know that in Collegium it's all peace and harmony and living alongside your fellow men, but remember we are Ant-kinden. We have *us* and we have *them*, and the Sarnesh have been *them* longer than the Wasps have. Would your Mantis friend stand up to defend a Spider city?"

"Yes," said Stenwold, surprising himself with the thought. "Yes, I think he would if I asked him. I'd never hear the end of it, though, and he would do it only because he sets our friendship so ruinously high. You, however, are not so bound to me, and you have your own people as your first responsibility. So if your answer is no, I will understand."

"My answer is that I would have to ask. We are not so very rigid as you foreigners think: it is simply that all you see is the order and the obedience. The debate between us is invisible to you. I will ask my soldiers, if you wish. So, it will come to that, will it?"

"Sarn is the front line now," Stenwold confirmed. "Wherever else the war may come, it will come here first."

"And if Sarn falls . . . then Collegium, the Ancient League, Vek . . . all the way to the western coast," Parops agreed. "Hence why we're here, and hence what you're trying to accomplish. I understand, Master Maker, and I can promise only that I will put all this to my officers, and they will put it to their men."

Sperra and Arianna came back just then, looking weary. They had spent most of the morning out and about in the city, Sperra waiting on the Royal Court, and Arianna gathering rumours.

"They told me that the Queen will desire another audience," the Fly told Stenwold. "She says for you to bring the snapbow."

Stenwold sagged. He had been standing up to talk with Parops, because that was part of the Collegiate debating style. Now he slumped into a chair. "I think we're where the metal meets," he said.

"I think you're right," Sperra said. "They weren't very polite about it either. I think they're running out of patience with all this talk."

"They're not the only ones," said Stenwold, but it sounded hollow. He would rather have spun it all out even further, in the hope that something would happen to rescue him from this standoff. "She's going to want to go into the next council with a snapbow in her hands, and to tell everyone that Sarn now have it, as a deal done. At that point we'll instantly lose from half to all of our alliance."

Parops shrugged. "If I were in her position, I would do the same. It is a tool she needs to defend her city-state, to counter her enemies."

"And after the war it will become a tool with which to attack her enemies in the Lowlands—or that is what they're all thinking," Stenwold said. "Everyone thinks that you can just stop history . . ." He looked at his hands miserably. "The fact is that, win or lose, the cursed thing is *here*. He built it, and it's here, and the world is different for it. Worse for it, too, I'll freely admit, but once a few have gone astray, once the Wasps lose a battle or if a thief makes off with one, then it won't be long before everyone has engineered their own."

"Everyone Apt," Arianna pointed out. "Some of us wouldn't know where to start."

"I thought your kin employed . . . people to do that sort of thing for you?" Parops said.

"But the Moth-kinden? And the Mantids? They've been trying to hold back time for five hundred years," she said. "You can imagine what they think of this."

"Is that what they're saying out in the Foreigners' Quarter?" Stenwold asked her.

"They're saying all manner of things, Stenwold, but it's a pattern I recognize. They're saying that the Vekken are going to attack here simultaneously when the Wasps do, and that Sarn should finish Vek off for good. They're saying that the Assembly of Collegium will fold if the Empire comes against it, and will then make a deal to betray Sarn. They're saying that the Ancient League will try to bring back the bad old days, and then make everyone slaves of the Moths."

"Nothing unexpected then."

"It's exactly the sort of thing *we* were spreading, back when . . ."

She did not finish the sentence, but he understood. Perhaps Parops did not know that she had been Rekef originally, but he was the only one in the room that did not.

"So you think the Wasps are active here."

"It would be surprising if they weren't," she said. "They're no fools, after all. They'll want to use our age-old enmities to break up this alliance, and they've got a lot of raw material to use. Half of the ambassadors are only here to keep eyes on their old enemies."

"I won't believe that," Stenwold said, with more force than hope. "I can't believe that. This *must* work. We have no other option. Everyone is thinking about what might happen after the war is won, but without an alliance we won't win the war! How can they not see that?"

"Because they're Lowlanders," said Arianna. She went to stand behind Stenwold, putting her hands on his shoulders and kneading the tension there. "I hate to say it, Sten, but you Lowlanders all look out on the world with one eye closed. Even you, Sten. You look a little further, but it's still mostly inward. In the Spiderlands we look in all directions, see all possibilities. Our brand of politics teaches us that. Even the Empire looks outward: it's young, aggressive, pushing at the borders all the time. That's why it's here."

"So what are we going to do?" he asked quietly. "What do I say, when the Queen of Sarn demands this wretched invention? Who do I betray?"

"So long as it's not me, and it's not yourself," Arianna told him, "I trust you to make the right decision."

A Sarnesh servant arrived then, almost on cue.

"Master Maker," he announced, "the Queen is ready for your private audience."

Stenwold glanced at his fellows and took up the prototype snapbow. *Who do I betray?* There was no answer, and yet he was running out of time to avoid that question.

"Lead on, Master . . . ?" he said, because he had no idea which of the Sarnesh this servant was.

"My name is Lyrus, Master Maker," the servant said cordially. "If you would please come with me."

FIFTEEN

Taki had used her second chute to rewind her engines, and Che was beginning to wonder how much longer her own machine would keep running. They were currently out over the middle of the Exalsee, a broad and island-studded expanse of sun-dappled water. That was when Taki suddenly pulled back, and Che could see her gesturing wildly, shouting something that could not be heard over rush of wind and the *Stormcry*'s low growl.

What? I'm clear of the water, was Che's first thought. Taki was still gesturing, though, swinging closer and then further away to try and convey some urgent message. Che almost thought she could hear her Fly companion's high voice over the engine's throb.

Despite herself, she looked down, and felt a chill as she noticed a shape in the water, a great dark ellipse. It was not some fish or water monster, though, but simply a huge shadow.

She looked up to see an airship drifting high above them, shimmering blue and silver and reflecting all the colours of the sky. The words of the Creev came back to her: *How are they getting in?* But, of course, an airship the same colour as the sky might go many places and not be seen.

At first she thought its pontoons bore four engines, but then she saw them fall away from the main craft, accelerating toward her. Orthopters: four of them.

A moment later she saw a finger-sized hole punched through the fabric of the *Stormcry*'s wing and realized they were shooting at her.

⁂

Taki threw the *Esca Volenti* round in a tight turn, wings beating furiously. Without thinking, her hands were releasing the catches that engaged the cogs of the rotary piercer mounted in front of her. With a low whine the weapon began to spin.

The sky arced round before her as, in her mind, Taki began working out how long she had left before her engine began to run down.

She could see Che making swift headway in the *Stormcry*, but two of the Wasp orthopters were stooping on her fast. Even in that moment of crisis, Taki had to admire the steepness of their approach. It looked as though the Empire could muster a few decent aviators, and that would make this contest more interesting. If Che had not been caught in the middle of it she would be enjoying herself already, but Che was no fighting pilot, not one ready to perform the dance of the dragonflies over the waters of the Exalsee. Even now she was dropping lower and lower, casting the *Stormcry* toward the nearest island in the hope of some kind of cover, but Taki was well aware that she would not be able to win out that way. This was not like land fighting, and cover was good only for moments at a time during a dragon fight.

She saw a minute glitter as the lead Wasp orthopter loosed its weapons, and she prepared to dive in on him. Somewhere in the back of her mind, she put two and two together and came up with four. Four imperial orthopters had dropped from the airship's mountings, which meant that the other two were . . .

She flung the *Esca* sideways in the air, virtually spinning on a wingtip. One orthopter rushed past her and a bolt of energy flashed from its pilot's hand, scorching a smouldering line across the wood and canvas of the *Esca*'s wing. Then the long darts of ballista bolts were slanting past her, and she danced her craft back and forth, ducking the other orthopter's shots. In her mind a clock was running, calculating just how long Che could hope to last without Taki's intervention.

The orthopter stayed right behind her, its missiles going wide. The flier had twin repeating ballistae bulking out its bow, alternate strung so that the release of the one fed into the loading of the other. She got a good look at this arrangement as she backed the *Esca*'s wings without warning, hanging and then falling out of the air so that the Wasp flier surged above her, and then throwing her wings into a blur to catch up with him. Repeating ballistae: the idea of it amused her. It was heavier and less efficient than her own weapon, but it was getting there. These Wasps were obviously worth watching.

She opened up with the rotary piercer, the firepowder-charged bolts whipping through the air far faster than the torsion-powered shafts of the ballistae, so that, just when he thought he had room to dodge, she punched through his hull with half a dozen separate shots. She had no idea whether the damage she had done was to the pilot or to the craft, but the Wasp orthopter abruptly faltered in the air and then dived dizzyingly out of the sky toward the unforgiving waters below.

Taki looked about wildly, trying to pinpoint Che again.

There! Almost skimming the water, just what her instructor had always told Taki never to do. *When you're that low, where can you go next?* But they had forced her down and, though her fixed-wing should have been faster, the two of them kept shooting and shooting, forcing Che to bank and turn in a desperate attempt to throw them off, squandering her speed for the fickle privilege of staying alive.

There was still one more orthopter pursuing Taki, and she felt the *Esca* shake all about her as she saw a hole ripped through the fabric of one wing. She swung her own craft around but the Wasp pulled out of his dive quickly, still keeping above her. She threw her machine at him and the two of them spiralled higher and higher, neither of them getting a shot in, each of them urging their machine to get above its rival. All this time they were getting further and further away from Che.

⟨|⟩ ⟨|⟩ ⟨|⟩

Another bolt lashed close past Che, gouging a furrow in the *Stormcry*'s side and throwing her into an involuntary yaw that nearly put one wingtip into the water. The Exalsee was dashing past so fast beneath her that she could only hope that any waiting monster fish would be unable to take advantage of this swiftly fleeing meal.

Che craned backward, trying to see her pursuers, but the rear of her cockpit blotted them out of view. The *Stormcry* groaned again, and she knew another bolt had slammed into some part of it behind her. She hoped it was nothing too important.

There was a little chain of islands ahead, most of them just jagged rocks jutting bare and grey from the water. *Taki, where are you?* She hurled the *Stormcry* forward, because she presented an open target here, over the water, and one that the Wasps were gleefully making use of.

Past the first island, just a barren spur of stone, and she sent the *Stormcry* sideways, trying to take advantage of its shadow. The bolts slanted down to her left, though, and she realized that one of the Wasps had gone high to continue lancing down at her, while the other was grimly following whatever paces she flung her machine through.

She had never thought that it might end like this: high-speed death in a flying machine, while fighting for her life. Surely that was a death for heroes and warrior-artificers, not for poor untrained scholars. The thought entered her mind that this was a death Achaeos would not approve of, and she had to clamp down on the hysterical giggle that followed.

Left around another jag of rock, and then right behind a proper island worthy of the name, that had a single stand of trees to screen her. The *Stormcry* suddenly faltered, a great gash carved into one wing, and she felt the differential drag from left and right. Her machine was not going to last that much longer, even though they had yet to strike anything directly connected with the engine. Or with herself, for that matter.

Something flashed behind her and, craning backward, she saw smoke being whipped away by the rushing air, and a sputter of flame that extinguished almost immediately. For a second her mind went blank, and then she realized: *He shot at me with his sting! How close is he?* Frantically she cranked her engine into a new gear, forcing the ailing machine to go faster. There was now a much larger island ahead, an entire hill of green rising from the Exalsee, with some kind of building perched on top. She would make for that.

There was another flash from behind, while ahead—

Che screamed on spotting, almost too late, a vastly long shape in the approaching shallows that was even then surging forward and upward. She flung the *Stormcry* skyward and sideways, nearly losing control entirely, watching the waters break and foam to either side as the monster lunged upward.

No fish, this, however. She had assumed it was just a similar spitting monster to the last one, but what broke through the waters was the jawed head of an enormous insect, surely three times the size of the *Stormcry* itself. She had a brief glimpse of an ugly, jointed snout, vast glittering eyes, as the monster lunged further, and its jaws gaped and gaped and gaped, unfolding and unfolding, telescoping outward until they rose high enough to pincer the Wasp orthopter's retreating tail. The speed of the flying machine dragged another ten feet of monster out of the water, its delicate legs folding close to its body, and for a second they both hung there, impossibly suspended. Then the jaws snapped closed, recoiling with irresistible strength. In another moment there was only the roiling water, no sign of monster, machine or pilot.

Che's heart was hammering so hard in her chest that she thought she might die. Then the other orthopter sent a bolt straight through her engine, which promptly exploded.

⦶ ⦶ ⦶

Taki felt the heat as the Wasp pilot launched his sting at her, but the *Esca* was moving too fast, and in the brief moment where his concentration was divided, she had flung her machine virtually across his path.

How brave are you? she asked him, as he had jerked his flier out of her way. A moment later she had loosed a single bolt into his machine, which was all that she had the time for. Her turn swept him out of her sight in the next instant, so she had no idea what she had achieved, if anything.

Taki came plummeting back now, looking for Che, letting the Wasp follow her if he dared. The sound of the *Esca*'s engine was not encouraging, for she was running out of stored power in the springs and had already used both her chutes. At this rate she might not even make it back to Solarno.

Ahead of her now she saw the remaining Wasp orthopter stooping on Che with its ballistae launching. She caught it utterly unawares and just let the rotary shoot, sending bolt after bolt into the orthopter from behind. After the second bolt she knew she was too late, as the *Stormcry* became obscured by smoke, and then by the brightness of flames. Taki screamed in frustration, seeing the Wasp orthopter virtually disintegrate ahead of her. The plume of smoke that the *Stormcry* had become was now diving straight toward the large island that she guessed Che had been meaning to slingshot around.

The *Esca*'s motor was sounding increasingly desperate, pitched higher and higher. That place ahead was . . .

That was Stokes' Island, she recognised, and it had a bad reputation. Che could still be alive, though, as the *Stormcry* was heading for a dry landing. Taki anxiously looked around for other Wasp orthopters, seeing none of them.

I have no time. It was agony, but she could not even land the *Esca* to go looking for Che, because she would never take off again if she did. With Che's help she might have been able to wind the motor, but never on her own. Nor could the little *Esca* carry Che, if she was hurt.

With a sob, she slung the *Esca* straight over Stokes' Island, and cast herself toward the northern shore of the great lake, and Solarno.

⟡ ⟡ ⟡

In the end the *Esca* did not have quite enough stored tension left in her to keep her wings beating and, 200 yards from the airstrip over Solarno, they stopped.

This was not the first time and, with a great heave, she threw the lever that fixed the wings in place, before resorting to her back-up power source, which was her legs. She felt for the pedals and began working them furiously, gliding in on the *Esca*'s slightly tattered wings, with only a single small propeller at the back providing her with a touch of extra lift as she ran it as fast as she could. She was not strong, being Fly-kinden and unsuited to this kind of strenuous work, so it took every ounce of effort to keep the orthopter from undershooting the landing strip and just ploughing straight into the city streets below her. But finally she saw the smooth stone of the landing field beneath her, and she hauled back on the stick, putting the breadth of the *Esca*'s wings against the wind, while kicking the orthopter's landing legs out ready. Her landing was not graceful, and abused components of the machine made noises that worried her, but for now she had no time to think about maintenance.

Taki hopped out of the cockpit and shouted to the nearest artificer, "Get the chutes replaced and her engine wound and ready to go! Now, man! There's no time to lose!"

As the startled engineer jumped up and ran over to obey, Taki collapsed onto her knees, her legs no longer able to support her.

There was a new clock counting away inside her head. It said: *How long can Che survive out there?* She kept insisting to herself that Che was still alive. Taki was not even considering the possibility of her friend dying in the air, dying in the crash landing or overshooting the island to plough into the Exalsee. Che might be trapped in the wreckage, though, and would almost certainly be injured. *How long, how long?*

"Taki!"

She watched the Dragonfly-kinden Dalre approach, looking exasperated.

"Where the reaches you been? I been looking all over."

"Look right here and you'd have found my *Esca* was out," she snapped at him. "Draw your own conclusions."

"Domina wants to see you."

"It will have to wait."

Dalre sighed, and dropped down so that he could talk to her face to face. "Look, little one, I know you're her favourite, but that doesn't mean you don't have to come when she calls. She wants to see you now. In fact she wanted to see you three hours ago. She's going spare, little one."

Taki stared at him. "That bad? Really?"

"Oh yes. Stuff is going on."

"Very nice. Very specific." Taki cast an agonized look back at the *Esca*. It would take them a little while to rewind her, to replace the chutes. She would have to make it quick, very quick. She would tell Genissa just that.

Leaning on Dalre's shoulder, she got to her feet. Her legs were still very shaky from all the pedalling.

"I'll go to her now. You don't need to escort me," she told the Dragonfly sharply. His doubtful look suggested that he wasn't sure she could even walk.

"Hey!"

She looked up and saw the foreigner, Nero, appear at the hangar's mouth. Her heart sank.

"What's going on?" he asked, and then, inevitably, "Where's—?"

"Come with me," she urged him. "I may need your help."

And she did. In fact she had to lean on him while her legs recovered. Meanwhile she told him everything: about the Wasp attack, the possible fate of Che. "How strong a flier are you?"

Nero considered. "Not strong enough to get out that far," he admitted. "Not my strong suit, is flight."

"And you're wounded too."

"A scratch."

"You were lucky to get away with just that."

"You know the old Art—our kinden's trick with danger," he told her, and she did. Even as the assassin had drawn back his blade, Nero must have sensed it and known to flick himself out of the way. He was clearly only annoyed that the blade should have cut as deeply as it had. "I can look after myself. Che, on the other hand—"

"I know, and I did my best," she said, more heatedly than she had meant.

"No criticisms. If you want me with you whenever you go out, though—"

"Can you fly a machine, at least?," she interrupted. "I'll need another pilot. From what I saw, the *Stormcry*'s beyond fixing, and I don't want to head out there in something that can't fight off the Wasps off if they attack again."

"Yes . . . the Wasps," replied Nero flatly.

"What is it?"

"I'm sure Domina Genissa will tell you."

◊ ◊ ◊

Everything hurt, as Che woke up. She was aware of that before she opened her eyes or paid any heed to what was going on around her. *Everything* hurt: her head, her back, her legs, her arms. Her left hand hurt particularly, but it was just a louder voice at the back of a clamouring crowd.

Her mind searched for explanations and she was reminded of one fateful night when she and Totho and Salma, and some girl that Salma had been wooing, had set out on an all-night drinking session. The following morning had hurt about as much as this one.

She had been in the fixed-wing, she recalled . . . the Wasps had been attacking her. She remembered the steam engine exploding behind her, the wood of the flier catching alight, the poor *Stormcry* burning. A piece of the fragmenting engine casing had struck the back of her head, after it spent most of its force on the panel it had burst through.

The machine had been dying fast, falling toward the island below. In a mad access of energy, half dazed and working on automatic, she had torn off her harness and thrust herself out of the cockpit, flaring her wings into being to catch the air.

She had not considered the speed the flier was going, so she had been caught by the wind instantly, buffeted along the entire length of the *Stormcry*'s anguished hull, seared by the erupting flames and choking in smoke, and then she had been falling end over end toward the island, her wings still flickering in and out of sight, catching her for a moment each time and then vanishing, unable to bear the strain. She had fallen thus in fits and starts.

She now opened her eyes.

She was caught in a tree. That was what struck her most. She was wedged in the crook of a tree, which probably accounted for much of the pain. There was smoke in the air, and she was afraid that she knew what that meant. As a Beetle girl properly brought up, what she felt about *that* was guilt. She had gone and broken their fixed-wing and she hoped that Taki and the Destiavels would not be too angry with her, but there hadn't seemed much option at the time.

Around the tree that she was snagged in were several others similar, and beyond those, even more trees and the faint suggestion of a grey stone edifice uphill from her. She recalled her view of the island from the air as forested, quite densely. Ideally she should now get herself either to the wreck of the *Stormcry* or somewhere else where a rescuer might spot her from the air. The ruin that she had seen capping the island would be the most obvious place to head for.

Of course the Wasps might also be looking for her. They could already be searching the island, so she would have to be careful. First, though, she would have to get herself out of this tree.

As she shifted, the branch supporting her gave way almost immediately, which solved that particular problem. Her wings caught her this time, and she landed heavily on the forest floor, but without any further apparent damage.

She stood up, wincing, and began trudging toward the sight of stone through the trees. It was her only landmark, everything else being quite foreign to her. The trees were of a type she had never seen before and she had no idea what else might exist here. It was not an island large enough to support some huge monster, she decided—then she decided that the huge monster might like to go off and swim and eat fish, and therefore could be very big indeed.

She tried to creep forward silently but the forest betrayed her at every step. She was just not physically built for such furtiveness. In the end, between the shifting carpet of leaves and the increasing gradient, she had to barge forward as best she could, and who cared about the noise she made? Then she found herself facing grey stonework.

A building, indeed, but now most definitely a ruin. Catching her breath, one hand on the tumbled stone of a wall, the scholar rose within her. Old, very old, she realized, for there was probably as much of it hidden beneath moss and drifted leaves and soil as there was still exposed. It put her in mind of a fallen tower she had seen some ten miles north of Collegium, beside the Sarnesh rail line. The architectural style was subtly different, but the age-born devastation very similar. That other tower had been a ruin before the revolution, six centuries ago and more. This building could be just as old, long undisturbed and decaying on this island.

She moved on, trying to get an idea of the original scale. This had been a single building, not a community, and quite expansive, but with a curious outline that only made sense when she matched it with the contours of the hilltop. The stones were large and she thought she detected carving on some of them, but now blurred out of all meaning. Of course she knew nothing of the history of this part of the world, though this did not look like Spider-kinden work, either current or past. More like the style of the Moth architects who had first planned the city that later became Collegium, or built that ancient tower lying to the north of it. Not the work of Moth-kinden hands, exactly, but of a people who had once shared some skills and thoughts with them, before coming to this far-flung place to build, and then to die.

That thought rang a stangely familiar chord in her. Something Achaeos had once said . . .

She perched on a stone, looking around her. It was certainly a melancholy place. Without evidence, she was convinced that these stones had not succumbed to time alone. If she closed her eyes she could almost feel the ghost of the building as it had once been, invisible now but somehow tangible. One symbol had been repeated often enough on these scattered stones that even the legions of time had not quite defaced it, and it spoke to her from ancient pages and from dissenting histories of how the world had been.

She had been around Achaeos too long.

When she opened her eyes again, she was not alone.

A lean, russet-haired man in a tunic of metal scales, crossed with baldrics loaded with throwing knives, was now leaning against a man-high section of broken wall. His features were so kinless, without reference, that it was the knives she recognised first.

"I know who you are. You're Cesta," Che declared, because Taki had told her all about this man, or at least those scattered and damning facts that Taki really knew. There was a strange dread within Che now, because she had more sources to draw on than just Taki's hostile recollections. Knowledge was now coming to her, piece after piece falling neatly into place. "How did you get here?"

"I suppose it would be grand to say that I was waiting for you, all along," he replied in his colourless voice. "In fact I happened to be on Old Scol, three islands down the chain, when I saw the smoke. A meeting as fortuitous as our last, perhaps?"

"And it won't do me any good to ask who's so interested in me that they employed you that time, either?" Che said. If she had been feeling less battered, less lost, then she would have left her next words unsaid. "I'm told you're only good for one thing—killing."

"More than that. I am not a killer. I am an assassin," he said with bleak pride, and the final piece fell, click, into place, and she *knew*. Not a half-breed at all, this one, nothing so commonplace.

I must be wrong. But she was not wrong. The sudden knowledge was as certain as it was mysterious. It was as though the stones themselves had told her, whispering it in her ear. *Oh, Achaeos, you taught me too much.* Yet it was some instinct of her own that had made the connection, knitting the tangled snarls of Moth-kinden history to give a name to his unplaceable features in this fallen stronghold.

"More than that," she echoed, "what if I said that I know what you are, and whose hands originally raised these stones?"

She had expected some arrogant sneering, but his entire face fell as slack as if she had stabbed him. He seemed utterly confounded.

"And how," he asked, "do you know that?"

"I am a scholar, a historian," she said. "And what my own people do not teach me, the Moth-kinden do." It had been a fraught time for them, setting her own histories against Achaeos's, until they had hammered out some view of the world they could both live with. Learning had been part of her life for so long she could not have stood by and let him dismiss it all, whilst his kinden were *all* scholars, with their own secret lore and traditions that were not used to competition. It had not been the prejudice nor the physical differences, but the sheer clash of knowledges that had been the hardest thing to resolve. His rotes of ancient wars and grievances that her kinden had known nothing of, the lists of his people's enemies, and a certain symbol—that jagged, angry mark—recorded for bitter posterity in Achaeos's people's archives.

"Moth-kinden?" he said tiredly. "So what tale do they tell?"

"That long, long ago there existed a clever, bloody-handed people skilled in stealth and deception, disguise and death." She recounted the story as Achaeos had told it to her. "That this people pitted themselves against the Moth-kinden's rule of the Lowlands, and turned their knives on the Skryres, who were the Moths' leaders. But they failed, and they were smashed, their entire people driven away and scattered, hunted down and wiped out, save for some few who fled into the Spiderlands and were never seen again. Or is this not the true story?"

"It will do." His earlier manner, that of the calm and inscrutable killer, had not recovered. "I may be the last of them for, aside from my father, I have seen no others of my kin. They did a fine job of dispersing us."

"Then you are a half-breed?"

"If we tended toward half-breeds, we would have become diluted beyond all measure, gone beyond even history's ken, but we breed true, the children born into the kinden of one parent or the other. We dwindle from generation to generation, but we cling on. Or perhaps only I, now. The last dregs of the Assassin Bug-kinden standing in the ruins of their last hall."

"Here?"

"Our monastery once. But your story is incomplete, for the Spider-kinden could still not tolerate us—we who were violent and sly beyond even their ways—and so they came here to the last stronghold of my race, and slaughtered all they found with the help of their slave soldiers. But some few must have escaped, as I myself am proof of. We are a stubborn stain on the world, one that will not wash out just yet."

"And . . . are you going to . . . ?" She clenched her fists. "Are you going to kill me?"

His sardonic look returned. "Are you yet dead? Then you may take the answer as no, for now."

She put a hand out to him. "If I know you, you should know me. I'm Cheerwell Maker from Collegium."

"Yes, you are." He clasped her wrist in that same warrior's affectation she had seen Tisamon use. "And you're tougher than you look. And you're here to fight the Wasps."

"To warn people about the Wasps."

"That may no longer be necessary," Cesta said.

"Tell me, whose side are you on?"

"That is one thing I can never tell you, because I have no side save my own and that of whoever pays me."

"And if the Wasps conquer Solarno?"

He shrugged, as if blithely unconcerned. "And do the Wasps have no need for a killer? Or else those that oppose them? Or I shall go to Princep Exilla—and if that falls there are lands more southerly still. My kind has passed from this world, Bella Cheerwell Maker. With the exception of yourself, and of the Moth-kinden who forget nothing, the world has forgotten us. Besides, we were always good at passing unnoticed. Even within the Spiderlands, no finger shall point at me and cry out what I am."

"So you don't care," she said, disappointed. "You're just a killer after all."

"Perhaps not even that. I am a shadow that the sun has not, for some reason, dispelled yet. I have sired no children. If I am truly the last, let my kind die with me. I would not wish my cursed blood on any other."

"And with your gifts you will do nothing?"

"Do you mean to recruit me, Bella Cheerwell Maker?"

"And if I do?" She knew she was overbold and put a hand to her mouth, too late to stop the words.

"You have not the gold to buy me," he said softly. "Besides, why should I take up arms in your cause? I am no idealist to jump to another's drum."

"Then you must leave Solarno and the Exalsee," she warned him, without force, her tired conviction coming from bitter experience. "You must go south or east of here, and then keep running, Master Cesta. The Wasps have need of killers but they'll bring their own, Rekef branded. I had a word with a Wasp, not so long ago, who tried to make a living as a freelance within sight of the Empire's borders, and he was not a happy man. The Empire beats a loud drum. You will have to run a long way not to hear it."

His lips twitched, but he offered no comeback, standing there in the wreckage of his inheritance. A moment later they heard the distant sound of a flier's engine, far off over the Exalsee, and Che jumped up but then hesitated. *Wasps? Or Taki come back for me?*

"Do you want me to find out who?" Cesta asked her, reading her expression.

"Why would you help me even in that?"

"Nothing I have said means that I can't like you," he told her. "I would kill you if I was hired for it, but it would still not mean that I cannot like you."

With that he was gone into the trees, leaving her to work his last words out.

⟨|⟩ ⟨|⟩ ⟨|⟩

When it was clear that it was the *Esca Volenti* passing low over the island, Che expected Cesta to simply melt away into the forest, but he was content to stand out on the beach with her as she waved at the repassing orthopter. Taki threw the machine into a tight turn and brought it down for an impeccable water landing. Moments later Che heard the drone of another engine, and a much bulkier machine rumbled down to the water, still managing to touch its surface as gracefully as a falling leaf. She recognized it immediately as the big, armoured fixed-wing belonging to the Solarnese pilot called Scobraan.

Taki put her head up out of the cockpit and was about to call over, when she spotted the assassin. For a second she had nothing to say but then she had hopped out and flitted from the *Esca*'s wing onto the beach.

"What in the pits are you doing here?" she asked the killer, sounding none too friendly.

Cesta's smile was cold. "I'm sorry, Bella te Schola Taki-Amre," he said smoothly. "Is this your island? Am I not welcome on it?"

"As far as I'm concerned you're welcome nowhere near me," Taki told him. He might have been almost twice her height, and a feared assassin as well, but she muscled up to him as though she was going to lay him flat. "You leave Che alone, you hear me?"

"Have I done her harm?" Cesta pointed out.

"Nothing you do turns out any good. Perhaps you forget that," the Fly replied hotly.

Che glanced between them nervously. "He hasn't done anything to me," she said. "We were just talking—"

"This isn't about you," Taki said sharply. "Just you remember that there are no depths that this bastard won't stoop to. *None*. He has no morality, nothing in him to make him care about others."

In answer to Che's uncertain glance, Cesta said, "True. All of it entirely true. The curse of our blood." She was not sure whether he was being genuinely flippant or hiding a deeper hurt.

"Are you coming or what?" bellowed Scobraan, his cockpit now open. He was looking up at the skies nervously. "Don't want to get caught on the water if they come back!"

Taki nodded. "Are you expecting a lift?" she asked Cesta drily.

"I have my own boat," he said. "No doubt I shall see you in the city, one of these days."

"Don't try to frighten me," Taki told him.

"Oh, come on!" shouted Scobraan, and Taki nodded, turning away from Cesta and visibly dismissing him from her mind.

"You'll travel on the *Mayfly Prolonged*," she said to Che, who recalled this as the name of Scobraan's craft. "Sieur Nero's there as well, he's got some bad news."

"Why do you hate Cesta so much?" Che whispered.

"He's a murderer."

"That's not it."

"Then whatever it is, it isn't your business," Taki told her. "I'm just glad to find you safe, Che."

"Did he kill . . . what was it, Amre? Your lover?"

That stopped Taki short, halfway into her seat on the *Esca*. "He was my half brother, Amre, and the Wasps killed him with their own hands. No, Cesta killed his own lover, for money. She happened to be a friend of mine, too, but that's not really the point."

⟨|⟩ ⟨|⟩ ⟨|⟩

The *Mayfly Prolonged* had hold space that just fitted Nero and Che crouching, comfortably enough for him but exceedingly cramped for her.

"So what's the bad news?" she asked.

"You know that Empire airship you had all the problems with," he began.

"Yes?"

"Well we reckon it was dropping off," said Nero. "Because there's a whole load more Wasp soldiers in Solarno now, enough to get everyone worried. I think it's starting."

SIXTEEN

She had walked into the garrison at Jerez without a word, picking up a guard to escort her as she did so. She looked like any stooped old woman in a dark robe, some emaciated grandmother hobbling with her cane, save that her eyes were red and glistening.

The guard from the gates then passed her on to a watch sergeant, who passed her to a duty sergeant, and she made no introductions or explanations, just latched onto each man in turn like a leech. Eventually they brought her to the man she sought, the man she had already sniffed out through the sloping corridors of the fort.

"Lieutenant Brodan," the duty sergeant began.

"What is it?" Brodan was at his desk, sifting reports dictated by his Skater agents. The sheer volume of fabrication had been wearing on him.

"Lieutenant Brodan . . ." The sergeant's face went slack. "I . . ."

"A message? A visitor?"

"A . . . visitor, yes. A visitor." The sergeant blinked, made a vague gesture at the robed woman. "This is . . . is . . ."

"What's wrong with you, Sergeant?" Brodan snapped.

"Nothing sir, I . . ." The man reeled slightly. "Excuse me, sir, I feel . . ."

Brodan looked from him to the gaunt face of the old woman he escorted and a cold shiver went through him. "Excused, Sergeant," he said quietly, and let the man get out of earshot before he inquired, "And what was that all in aid of?"

"Why, in aid of you, Lieutenant Brodan," she said, sitting down. Her voice was little more than a whisper.

"And who decided that sending me a hag was the best way to help me?"

Her lipless mouth curved mirthlessly. "There are those in the capital very interested in your success. They feel sooner is better than later, Lieutenant. So they have sent me to you. If it will help you, my name is Sykore."

Rekef? he thought momentarily, but she was surely not Rekef. This was no Rekef approach or technique. She was something else entirely.

"What help can you be?" he asked reluctantly.

"I can lead you to your enemies," she told him. "Do not think that I have been idle here in Jerez."

"I see no reason to trust you," Lieutenant Brodan said. Indeed, it was hard to see anything positive about his new acquaintance. She sent a distinct shudder through him, even though he was a Rekef officer, which was not a profession for the squeamish.

"Then you must make your choice. I am only offering you, after all, what you are here for, and no more. How easy to turn that down?" The creature's hissing voice was getting on his nerves. Pallid and hollow cheeked she was, and with red, staring eyes like something from a children's story. "I shall take you to your enemies," she repeated. "I know exactly where they are."

"You mean where they *were*," Brodan scoffed. "And how long ago was that?"

"Where they *are*. Where they will be," the creature insisted. Her bony hands twitched in her lap. "What can you comprehend? Nothing. So understand only that I know."

"And since when did I have enemies?" Brodan asked. "Everyone likes me."

"They are here to take what you seek, and that makes them enemies," his visitor said patiently.

"Collectors?"

"Not collectors but thieves. Thieves from the Lowlands," she hissed. "Enemies of your Empire."

"I thought you said you were working for the Empire," Brodan said suspiciously.

She curled her thin lips. "I am older than your Empire, so what should I care? Only that I am instructed to lead you by the nose until you have acquired this thing you seek, so here I am. If you turn aside my help, and then fail, it shall soon be known."

Brodan grimaced. It was true that the Rekef used some strange folk as agents, although this unidentifiable thing must be the strangest yet.

"I shall be watching you," he warned.

"Watch all you want. I shall even dance for you, if you wish."

He shivered again. *Is this Maxin's work then? Where did the general dredge this freak up from?*

"So take us," he said. "Show us these enemies that we're supposed to have. Let's sort them out."

She rose. "They must be stalked," she said, folding her hands primly before her. "Blood will be shed here tonight."

"This is Jerez, and blood is shed here every night," Brodan responded, wishing he felt as contemptuous as he sounded. Only ten minutes in a room with this monster, with the evening now drawing on, and he had begun to feel decidedly uneasy.

"Gather up your soldiers," she told him, and then her hand went up, her head tilting back as though she had scented something. "Gather them quickly. The blood has begun to flow. We must go. We must go now!"

◆ ◆ ◆

Achaeos had been suspicious, which Tynisa attributed mostly to his distrust of Beetle-kinden merchant lords. His own magic had failed to trace the box, though, and so he had at last given in with bad grace.

"If things go badly," he had advised, "find your way to Nivit's home. Gaved is there, watching over Thalric, and I understand that Nivit has people he can call upon to fight for him, insofar as these wretched little creatures ever fight."

"What about you?" she had asked, seeing they had found him alone. Jons Allanbridge, it seemed, was airborne somewhere, testing out the newly repaired *Buoyant Maiden*.

"I can hide as well as any Skater," said Achaeos. "They will not find me." He frowned, studying her closely. "There is something more to this?"

"Oh, no doubt," she said. "But there's only one way to find out what exactly, and that's to take up Master Bellowern's invitation."

Now she was hurrying along behind Tisamon, heading for the grounded gondola that Founder lurked in, as evening slowly grew over the sky.

"That Beetle is more frightened than he will admit even to himself. I wonder why," Tisamon remarked.

"His rivals, no doubt," said Tynisa. "Perhaps they have joined forces against him."

The Mantis shook his head. "More than that. No man becomes that great unless he can deal with the envy of rivals. It must be the box itself."

"Then what about that Spider girl?"

"Perhaps she knows where it is?" Tisamon said. "Perhaps he means for us to guard her." He stopped abruptly. "Perhaps that girl was Scyla the spy."

Tynisa also paused, unsettled by this new thought. "We can't rule it out," she admitted. "But, then, we can't rule out that Founder himself is the spy. From what Achaeos said, she can look like anyone."

"So this is a trap?"

"It could be a trap. Do you want to go back?"

Tisamon raised an eyebrow at her. "Why?"

She saw that he would rather that it was indeed a trap, something straightforward to turn his blade on. He was all anticipation.

"The rooms inside that thing are going to be low and small," she warned him.

"Let that worry them more than us. It negates their numbers," was all he thought of her concern. He set off again, faster, but Tynisa had felt a tickling sensation on her wrist. Inspecting it idly, she saw blood oozing there. Her mysterious scratch had opened up again, although she could have sworn that it was only shallow, a mere nothing.

"What is it?" Tisamon asked her. She shook her head, wiping her hand with a cloth, while keeping it from view. The scar seemed to have resealed itself rapidly. She had an uneasy moment, just a second of it, as though she was surrounded by a great chasm, yawning all about her, and she was about to topple into it.

"Nothing," she replied hurriedly. "Nothing at all."

They were admitted without delay into the gondola, heading up along a gangplank that two of Founder's men lowered for them. The interior had fewer rooms than Tynisa had guessed, with higher ceilings and more light and space. If not for a faint slant in the outside walls, she would have taken this place for a real house, even a regular house in Collegium. With the windows shuttered and gas lamps flickering on the walls, it could have been the sitting room of any College Master: rugs on the floor, bookshelves and paintings, even a little gilded automaton standing on Founder's broad desk, wound down and caught motionless in midstep.

The Beetle magnate sat waiting for them behind the desk, and there were two guards already present in the room. Tynisa looked further, and sure enough found the Spider girl standing in the shadows of one corner, staring wide-eyed at the newcomers. There was no indication as to anyone here being Scyla.

"You've taken your time," Founder complained. There was a broad-based decanter on the desk, but it was already mostly empty. "May I take it that your patron has released you?"

"We're all yours," Tynisa informed him. "Make what you will of us."

He nodded. There was an edginess about his glance that she needed no great skill to notice. "You expect your enemies tonight," she observed.

Founder stood up reflexively, one hand reaching for something below the desktop. "Don't presume to know my business."

"You will at least tell us who we are to fight," suggested Tisamon. Around them the guards were shuffling uncertainly, and Tynisa realized that they did not know either. Whatever hornet's nest Founder had kicked over, it was something he had not shared with *anybody* else. Anybody except the Spider, that was. Founder's new slave knew, Tynisa could tell. She knew, and she was terrified. Still, there was a raw, fragile look to her that suggested that *everything* frightened her. It was not a normal Spider-kinden look, but perhaps it could be used.

If he won't say, perhaps she will.

"I will tell you nothing," Founder said to Tisamon. "If they . . . If we're attacked, just fight. That's all you need to know."

"Perhaps we could carry the fight to your competitors," the Mantis suggested.

Founder's laughter in response was fierce and desperate. "Oh, don't promise what you can't deliver, Weaponsmaster, so just stay close and keep your blades ready. You want anything, ask Bradawl there, but no forays outside, no time off.

We now have our agreement." In a smooth motion he threw two pouches on to the desktop, heavy with coin.

With a smile, Tynisa scooped them up. It was, she reflected, a very large sum of money, the kind of money she had never dreamt of in her days back at the College. Perhaps there was something to be said for this trade after all.

She now hoped nothing would happen overnight to change that thought.

"Which is Bradawl?" Tisamon enquired.

"Here." It was a broad-shouldered Beetle with a breastplate over leather armour. "Lieutenant-Auxillian Pater Bradawl," he announced and clasped Tisamon's hand, wrist to wrist. "Hear you're s'posed to be good." His accent was not Empire but the homely, familiar tones of Helleron.

"Good enough," Tisamon agreed. He gazed at Tynisa, who threw another glance toward the mysterious Spider girl. "Perhaps we can talk, Bradawl," he added.

Bradawl certainly concurred, drawing Tisamon out of earshot of his master.

Founder was writing in a ledger now, turning up a gas lamp for better light to read by. A single menial came to refill his decanter, and Tynisa belatedly noticed that, of the big retinue the man had travelled with earlier, only the guards now remained. Most of his servants must be either elsewhere or dismissed for the night.

So as not to get in the way. It was an unwelcome thought. The two guards in the room were conferring with a third now, who just had come in from . . . Tynisa tried to work out the geography of the place, but it was impossible from the little she had seen so far: perhaps from the roof deck? She caught a few whispered words of the man's conversation: something concerning lights, and the lake. Founder's pen scratched audibly, abruptly, to a halt in a scar of ink. He cursed to himself and began writing anew.

She stepped a little closer to the Spider girl, doing her best to keep an eye on her and at the same time on the others in the study. The thought of the face-changing Scyla was close to her mind.

"So what's going on?" she whispered, hoping that another Spider face would be reassuring at least. The girl just stared at her.

"It's all right." Tynisa tried her best smile. "I'm not involved in any of this. You want to talk to anyone, you can talk to me. Are you from the Spiderlands? The Empire?"

"I am from nowhere you know," said the girl, but the words were unnecessary, and Tynisa felt a chill go through her on hearing that soft, strange voice. Just as she had known Bradawl was raised in Helleron, or that Bellowern himself was an imperial Beetle rather than a Lowlander, she realized that this girl's lilting and strange accent was utterly alien to her, more so than any she had ever heard in cosmopolitan Collegium or occupied Myna.

"Tell me, quickly," Tynisa said.

"They will kill me tonight," was all the girl said, and Tynisa could see that she did not want to be here within these walls, but that whatever was outside was worse.

"You, Weaponsmistress!" Founder snapped. "Over here!"

Tynisa cursed inwardly, but went over to the man's desk.

"You don't talk to her," Founder warned. "Nobody does." Tynisa expected him to add "Except me," but those words never came. Apparently, nobody at all talked to the mystery girl. "Now you stay close by me," Bellowern added, and there was nothing flirtatious in his voice. He took another swallow of wine, but it seemed only to leave him more tense.

"If we could—" she started, but he cut her off immediately.

"Just kill them," he said. "When they arrive, kill them."

She nodded, looking over to where Tisamon was sharing quiet words with Pater Bradawl.

The Mantis had expected Bellowern's guard captain to be hostile and resentful at these overpaid newcomers, but the man was a Beetle, as pragmatic as they came.

"I'm just glad we've got some replacement hands," Bradawl was saying. The darkness under his eyes spoke of missing sleep. "We lost three today."

"Lost to whom? How were they killed?" Tisamon asked.

"Just lost. Vanished off the streets," the Beetle explained. "Nobody saw a thing, so they claim, but then these Skater-kinden know when to keep their mouths shut. I told the chief that we should just get out of here, but he's set on waiting for this auction. The girl was just an extra, an impulse, and now we're paying for it." He stopped, realising he had said too much, and then deciding it did not matter anyway. "You and your woman had better be good."

"You don't know who the enemy is? Or who the girl is?"

Bradawl shook his head. "Just that we ran into her one night, and the chief must have seen something in her. She's really strange . . . and she's on the run, I know, nothing surer than that."

Tisamon glanced about. Despite himself, he found that the gondola's confines were beginning to oppress him. It was all too artificial in here, with the flickering lamps and the bolted-down furniture. "The locals . . . ?"

"Know what's going on, or something of it, right enough," Bradawl said. "They won't talk, though. Whatever it is, they live with it and they're scared of it, and they're in no hurry to get in the way. We're alone against it, whatever it is. We should just push that girl out of the hatch and be done with it, but the chief is fixed on her, wants to add her to his collection."

"A slave," declared Tisamon flatly.

Bradawl shrugged. "Mantis-kinden, what are you going to do about it? You're in the Empire, and everyone's a slave or a slave master."

"What was that?" Founder asked suddenly, loud enough to carry to them. They stepped back into his study to see him staring at his decanter.

"Sir?" Bradawl asked him.

"Someone go up to the roof and make sure our men are still there," Founder ordered. "And make sure they're armed and ready to fight."

Bradawl looked briefly exasperated. "There are two repeating ballistae mounted on the deck, sir, and four soldiers as well. Anyone who sends men against us will get knocked back hard, whether from ground or sky."

"You!" Founder pointed to one of the guards. "Go up there, now!"

The guard rushed out immediately, and they heard the sound of his boots clumping up wooden stairs. In the ensuing pause Tynisa sensed something occur, just a quiver in the floor and the walls. She looked across at Tisamon, who nodded. Founder was staring at the glass decanter still, as though it held some great secret.

The guard returned, reporting that the men up on deck were all present and alert, though Founder barely seemed to hear him.

"This is it," he said. "Look."

Tynisa saw it, then. There were ripples in the surface of the wine in the decanter, constantly quivering out inward from the glass sides. She could feel it now for certain, a thrumming in the wooden floor. Tisamon had his claw blade already on his hand, and she drew her rapier thoughtfully.

"The men above have seen nothing," Bradawl murmured. "So what is going on?"

There was a colossal snapping, twisting sound from below them, and the entire gondola lurched.

"From below!" Founder cried. He had snatched up a crossbow from beneath his desk. Bradawl signalled to his guards, and the three of them set off for "below," wherever that was. There was no need, though, for below was coming to meet them.

One guard had preceded Bradawl through the door, and headed halfway down some stairs before he came flying up again, knocking his two fellows flat. A monster emerged after him. At least that was what Tynisa saw.

In retrospect she realized it was just a man, but a man such as she had never seen before, seven feet tall, with a head and waist both too small and narrow for those huge shoulders and the massive arc of bared chest. His hands were huge too, each boasting a great hooked claw, while together they held a short, brutal-headed pike.

The man-beast bellowed something and Founder's crossbow bolt struck it in the shoulder, barely causing it to flinch. Bradawl took this chance to get to his feet again and lunged forward with his sword, the buckler shield in his other hand pressing in to ward off the pike head. The huge creature smashed him with the weapon's shaft, knocking him back down, and then Tisamon had stepped in and slashed a long line of red across its chest, sufficient to gain its attention.

It lunged with the pike, and he hacked another line across its chest, while Tynisa hovered behind him, just waiting for an opening. She could hear the guards coming down from the deck above, shouting questions and drawing blades. Tisamon was buying them a little time.

The creature abruptly shouldered forward, as if stung from behind, and Tisamon dodged round it, driving his blade in between its ribs in what was meant to be a killing blow. It shouted something at him again, with real words lost in a guttural accent, and then backhanded the Mantis with one hooked fist, sending him flying across the room.

It was already falling by then, but Tynisa lashed her blade across its throat just to be sure. Then she saw the next contenders appearing, and threw herself aside as their crossbow bolts punched up the stairway. She saw one of Bradawl's men take a quarrel in the chest, which passed straight through him, armour and all, to embed itself right up to the fletching in the wood of the wall.

Two small men had darted out from below, hunchbacked and long legged, frantically rewinding their massive double-strung bows, and even more frantically getting out of the way of whatever was following them. It turned out to be another of the hook-fisted creatures, its round head encased in a metal helm, and with no weapons other than its vicious hands. It thundered straight into the middle of the room. Bradawl put himself between it and his master, sword lashing out to cut it across the bicep, but it had already seen the Spider girl, and she was the one it was interested in.

Before it could take a step toward the girl, Tynisa had jabbed it in the back with her blade, sinking only inches into its leathery hide, and a pair of crackling blasts of stingshot had struck it across the chest from the Wasp soldiers now entering the fray. It charged them furiously, and Tynisa saw them raise their swords as they stood in the doorway that led to the deck. Founder meanwhile had loosed his crossbow again at some new target, and Tynisa whirled around to see.

The newcomer was a broad man, clad head to foot in pearl-sheened armour and brandishing some kind of slender lance. From his build alone, Tynisa would have thought him a Beetle. Bradawl lunged at him, his blade scraping off the unknown intruder's mail. In the next moment, the narrow point of the lance had swept forward to touch Bradawl's waiting shield. There was a sharp crack and a bitter smell, and Bradawl was thrown back across the room as though he had been struck with a hammer.

Tisamon was on his feet again, approaching the newcomer cautiously. Founder was still crouching behind his desk, hastily reloading his bow. He looked up at the armoured man and shouted something that included the words, "She's mine!"

The room was now getting very crowded, however spacious it had at first appeared. Tynisa cut across behind Tisamon to get closer to the girl, who was pressed as far into the corner as she could manage.

"We're leaving," she decided aloud. She saw that the Wasps had finished off the second huge man and were now taking cover behind furniture, trading shots with the little crossbowmen. "Tisamon!" she shouted. The Mantis was still standing between Founder and the armoured man, and Tynisa realized that she did not know how far his honour would stretch when it came to fulfilling this supposed contract to protect the Beetle.

The doorway to the deck above was blocked with Wasps, although the monstrous crossbows of the small intruders were taking a toll on them. There was only one other exit from the room and it involved going out the way all their enemies were coming in.

Tynisa darted forward, forcing the issue. The armoured man turned clumsily as she approached, lunging out for her with the lance. Tisamon took the chance he had thus given her, driving his blade home at the shoulder joint of the man's armour. It bit, but not deeply enough.

She ducked under the sweeping lance, saw its tip charring a line across the wooden wall. There was a leather pipe connecting it to the man's back, she noticed, and with a flick of her blade she cut it in half.

She was never sure, thinking back, whether that was the right thing to have done, for she felt instantly as though she had been punched hard, and there came a flash of blue-white light that seared all other details of the room from her mind for a second. Then she was lying on the ground, her head spinning, and the palm of her sword hand was raw and burnt, even the grip of her sword blackened. The armoured man lay on his back across the room from her, already struggling to get up with the help of his small servants.

"Come on!" she shouted to the Spider girl, and she saw fear and desperation fighting in the girl's expression, then desperation finally winning out. She dashed on past the armoured man in a sudden access of courage, but then a gauntleted hand closed on her ankle as she ran.

It was Founder who caught her, before she struck the floor, and Tisamon drove the point of his claw down into the gauntlet to break its grip, and then lashed a backhanded blow into the face of the man's helm.

The helm cracked, not like metal but like a shell, and the face beneath it was pure Beetle-kinden, though pale as a drowned man's and twisted in utter fury. The hollow voice emerging from behind the helm became recognizable words: "She is ours! You savages cannot take her!"

"Go!" Tynisa urged the girl, leading, the way to the front hatch. She had to pass the point where the intruders had come up through, and what she saw down there thoroughly frightened her.

A hole had been chewed in the bottom of the gondola, some machine or creature tunnelling up through the earth below to penetrate the wooden hull, but the tunnel was now entirely awash with water.

Even as she watched, there was a man down there, another of the huge, hook-handed creatures. As it half swam and half clambered to the surface, it was surrounded by a silvery nimbus that vanished as soon as it broke the water.

Tisamon was past her now, at the hatch, but he stared at it helplessly. It had been meant for Apt hands, and he could not manage the catches.

Founder literally pushed him out of the way. Behind them they could hear the last of his soldiers and guards being finished off.

He then had the hatch open, flinging it wide with a shout, as a bolt of energy struck him full in the chest, knocking him backward to the ground, his face fixed in a rictus of shock.

There were Wasp soldiers gathered outside, not those in the pay of the Consortium but the sort Tynisa was more used to.

There was no time to check whether Founder was still alive. Tisamon simply leapt out through the opening, dropping the ten feet of space to land in the midst of them, lashing out at them even as he fell. Two of the Wasp soldiers spun away from him, wounded, while the others scattered, seeking for cover from which to shoot.

Tynisa grabbed the Spider girl, who looked utterly horrified, and slid down the sloping hull, trusting to her Art to slow her fall. Her burden was no help at all, just clinging to her as though she had never climbed a wall in her life.

When it was obvious the girl would not do anything as sensible as run for her life, Tynisa had to drag her three streets away to relative safety before turning back for Tisamon. He was already coming, though, running after them at top speed.

"Where are the Wasps?" Tynisa asked him.

"They encountered our friends from inside," was all he said. He glanced away from her to the Spider girl, and Tynisa could see that he wanted to say that she would have been better left behind, but even so he was curious about her. Before he could speak, they heard shouting nearby, and the crackle of a Wasp sting.

"Away," he decided, and they ran off into the muddy streets of Jerez, the Wasps taking to the air behind them.

⁂

Nivit was out consulting with his sources but Gaved was supposed to be busy hiding people. He was nominally hiding Thalric, who was both an ungracious guest and an unwilling fugitive. The former Rekef man stalked about Nivit's premises, prying into the information broker's records and frightening Skrit. It was obvious that he would decide to leave soon, and then Gaved would get to find out whether he himself would decide to restrain the man, or even be able to.

When the knock on the door came, it was a relief to all of them. Gaved looked through the crack and then opened up hurriedly, bundling Tynisa and Tisamon into the room, and one more fugitive as well.

"No time to stop," Tynisa declared. "We have some Wasps to mislead. They're out searching for us and I don't want them looking here. Take care of the girl until we get back." She looked from Thalric to Gaved, getting little response, and then she and the Mantis were gone, the door swinging shut behind her.

""Take care of the girl"?" Thalric snorted. "Are we running a Helleron whorehouse now?" The new arrival looked at him in alarm, and then turned to Gaved and instantly flinched away from him as well. He saw her face.

He took a deep breath, feeling his heart lurch, and wondered at the vagaries of fate. It was the same girl, of course, unmistakable from the portrait, the one that the strangers had offered such a high reward for. Here she was in the flesh.

His first thought was of the bounty and how happy Nivit would be with this catch. It was the automatic reflex in his trade. His second reaction was to actually look closely at this wretched creature that parties unknown were so desperate to recover.

She was definitely something like Spider-kinden, but Gaved had travelled widely enough to note subtle differences: her skin was remarkably pale, her hair an odd compromise between gold and silver, and her eyes almost the same gleaming colour. Just as with the picture that was so uncannily lifelike, he was forced to conclude that she was not quite like any Spider-kinden he had ever seen, any more than she suited the Beetle-kinden clothing she had been dressed in, that now hung sopping wet about her due to the rain.

And she was clearly terrified, wide-eyed and trembling, which in a Spider would have indicated a remarkable lack of control, and of course she was not painted or made up as Spider-kinden, both men or women, almost always would be. She was a mystery indeed, but he could not rid himself of the thought that she was a potentially profitable one.

Thalric had approached her with a slightly disdainful look. "And who are you?" he asked her. She flinched back from him, and resisted his attempt to relieve her of her soaking cloak, wrapping it about herself even more tightly.

"My name is Cap . . . is Thalric," announced the ex-Rekef officer, neither harshly nor kindly. "Tell me who you are, and why they brought you here."

Gaved leant close, intrigued, seeing something in Thalric's tone catch with her.

"Sef," she said, and then repeated herself at Thalric's frown. "My name. Sef."

Not a Spider-kinden name, that, but I wasn't really expecting one, Gaved decided.

"So what significance are you in this, Sef?" Thalric pressed. "Speak, now."

"I don't know," the girl mumbled. "They took me and brought me."

"She's a slave," said Gaved, and Thalric raised an eyebrow at him.

"Oh yes?"

"You're talking like a master, she's answering like a slave," the hunter explained. "She's got the strangest accent I ever heard, but some things just don't change wherever you go." *Her accent is the same as her Beetle master's, and I'd never heard the like of that from anywhere either.*

"The Empire's a big place," Thalric said, studying Sef again. Her lips were pressed tightly together and she was trembling still.

"You'd have to go a long way," Gaved told him, "to find an accent I didn't recognize. Spotting the differences is part of my stock in trade. She's certainly from nowhere near here. So whose slave are you, girl? Where did you run from?" He could not quite match Thalric's authority, and eventually the other man repeated his question for him.

The word she said, unfamiliar and spoken in her unusual accent, that stretched some vowels and clipped others, meant nothing to them, but Gaved translated it as something like "Scolaris," which could conceivably be the name of some Spider city-state.

"Where's that, somewhere in the Spiderlands?" Thalric asked her, and she shook her head mutely. Thalric hissed in annoyance and moved forward—just a brief abortive movement—and Sef fell back, shielding her head as if waiting for a blow.

There was a long pause, Thalric considering her with contempt, then he shrugged. "We'll wait for the Mantis and his get to come back. Then they can explain why they've foisted this simpleton on us."

He stalked off to peruse some more of Nivit's records and Gaved tentatively approached the girl, crouching down and then sitting himself close to her, his back resting against the rough-cast wall.

"All right, then, Sef," he said softly, not looking at her. "So you're a runaway slave. And your masters are after you."

He had intended no more than to state the obvious, but he caught her look and it shook him. He knew the plight of the fugitive. He had lived the chase vicariously from following the trail of the hunted slave, the deserter, the thief. He knew the fear of capture, but the panic, the sheer terror on Sef's face, cut into him like a blade. She gazed at him with horror, and she looked around Nivit's hut with horror, and on the very ground and air as though it was a nightmare that she could not break free from. He had never before witnessed such cringing fear, until the moment her masters were mentioned, when it doubled and redoubled in her expression. She would be screaming now, he thought, if she dared, and so instead she was screaming inside.

He felt a sudden pang inside him—a brief moment of pain and regret. "They turned up here, you see, with your picture and a comfortable reward," he said, as gently as possible.

Something twisted within her, hunching her over so that her hair concealed her features. He could hear the violent shuddering of her breath.

"You might as well know that I'm a hunter. I track people down for money. I don't often get them delivered to me like this, but that's what I do. So tell me what I should be doing next."

He thought she merely shrugged, but then saw her shoulders quiver again, and caught a glimpse of tears on her half-hidden face. She was definitely not Spider-kinden, at least not of any breed he knew, for she would not have lasted a day in the Spiderlands.

"But if you tell me just exactly what you are and where you come from, maybe I'll come up with a reason to change my mind." He thought of what Nivit might say to that, and felt wretched for it. It seemed his curiosity had overmastered his habitual greed but, beyond that, the strangeness of her had got to him.

He gave her time, let her think, whilst Thalric cast occasional sharp glances at him, as though he was making her some kind of improper proposal. *Probably thinks I'm letting the race down by talking to lesser kinden.*

"I come from Scolaris," Sef whispered.

"That doesn't help me, girl. I've never heard of it. How far? In which direction?"

"It is down there." She gestured. "In the water. In the lake."

Gaved felt his stomach suddenly twist with something like vertigo. In the tense and unpleasant silence that followed he remembered Nivit's dark words about the lights beneath Lake Limnia. *Impossible.* He saw that Thalric had now stopped reading and was looking over at them, his expression frozen. *Impossible.* But he had already spent too much time here in Jerez and around the lake. Go to any of the Skaters' wretched drinking holes, find a bandy-legged creature too drunk to stand upright. They would soon tell you about the lights in the lake, about the boats that went missing, the strange wreckage sometimes found, all the other stories that the Empire had long dismissed as yet more lies such as the Skater-kinden delighted in telling, for no other reason than that falsehood was in their blood.

Do I really want to know this? "There's . . . a city in the lake?" Gaved enquired carefully.

"Three," Sef said tonelessly. "Genavais, Peregranis and Scolaris."

"Spider cities," Gaved said.

"Once," Sef confirmed in a whisper. "But not since the masters came."

"This isn't making any sense," Thalric snarled, disgusted. "She's mad. She must be."

She could be mad. Gaved looked into Sef's frightened face and decided he could believe that. It would be the easiest way to explain her, too . . . save for those others who were so desperate to regain her. Three cities that he had never heard of? Three cities in the lake . . .

He began to stand up, and she suddenly caught at the sleeve of his long coat, so that he froze halfway.

"I *want* to tell you," Sef hissed urgently, "because they don't want you to know. They will kill me just because they don't want you to know."

Gaved looked toward Thalric, but the ex-Rekef man simply shrugged and went back to his reading. Gaved slowly sat down again.

"So tell me then," he said.

"Ours. They were our cities," said Sef, keeping her voice very low, as though she was afraid that her pursuers would hear her from somewhere else in Jerez, or across the silent surface of Lake Limnia. "We tell ourselves, mother to daughter. They were our cities, and the masters were once our slaves, long ago."

"What masters?" Thalric demanded. "What slaves?"

Gaved sent him an angry look, but behind it he was still pondering. "Beetle-kinden," he then said. "The man who came to us was Beetle-kinden, coming out of a wet night, all armour and no cloak . . . Well, if he's from the lake he wouldn't need to worry about getting rained on."

"Beetle-kinden . . ." Thalric started off derisively, but then clearly thought about it, and Gaved guessed the path his mind was taking.

"In the bad old days, the Apt races were nothing but slaves in many places, before the revolution."

"Revolution, yes." Sef was looking from Gaved's face to Thalric's. "Our cities, that we made, that we wove and filled with air, but then they cast us down. We tell each other all of this, mother to daughter. They chained us with their machines and their weapons. They sat where we had sat, and cast us down to where they had once been."

"Only justice," said Thalric dryly. "Anyway, the Spiders of the Spiderlands seem to be doing well enough for themselves, so this lot must have been an inferior breed."

"Or just lacking enough space to manoeuvre," Gaved said softly. "Cities beneath the lake, and not great cities, surely—where could they go, when their slaves rose up against them?"

"You're speculating."

Gaved nodded. "And all we have is her word, and all that's probably made of is whatever folk tales she's cobbled together. Still . . ." He sensed the lake outside, that great expanse of water stretching past the horizon, unplumbed, marsh-edged, a haunt of Skater bandits and monstrous creatures.

"It's nonsense and she's mad," Thalric declared, though a little uneasily.

"Please," Sef said, tugging again at Gaved's sleeve. "they will come for me. They will take me back."

"You escaped all this," Thalric pointed out. "So it can't be that difficult. But why haven't we heard of this before."

"I was supposed to die," Sef said simply. "Master Saltwheel had us taken to his testing grounds, to his laboratory. We were supposed to die, to be killed by his weapon. But it ruptured the wall of the city. The others died, but I grasped the air and held it to me, and then I swam. The others died or were caught, but I swam and swam toward the light. We have escaped before. Into the lake itself, the caves or the deep water. They sniff us out, though. They always bring back the bodies, for everyone to see. There is nowhere safe between the walls of our world that we may hide from them. So I . . . I came up to gather air. I knew that Master Saltwheel would hunt me down, so I left that world."

The Wasps were now staring at her, quite blankly. She bared her white teeth at them, shaking constantly with fear and desperation and sheer frustration.

"To this horrible place!" she suddenly cried out, words long held trapped below now forcing their way to the surface. "To this horrible empty place! This open place where there is no end to it, and no walls, and where everything weighs me down! And the surface is too far away overhead and too great, so great, and the light of it burns my skin by day! And my throat and eyes hurt all the time, and . . . and . . . and . . . They will catch me eventually and kill me with the long, slow death, and it would have been better if Master Saltwheel had killed me with his machines than I ever came out here." Her hands balled into fists that were pressed close to her face, a face contorted with an uncontrollable horror of everything within her sight and knowledge.

"Saltwheel," Gaved repeated. Amidst this madness it was such an ordinary-sounding Beetle name that it chilled him all on its own.

"Weapons testing?" Thalric pointed out. "If any of this is true, how could they be Apt, operating underwater? You can't have any artifice without something so basic as fire, surely?" His eyes narrowed at Sef, who had fallen into a crouch, hands still raised to her face. "Answer me, slave!"

"We have fire," Sef replied, sounding almost proud. "We have fire. We fill our cities with air. But the masters, they have engines that need no fire, no air." She inhaled a long breath. "I have told you all now. They will hunt me down and they will kill me, but I have told you."

Gaved glanced at Thalric again, seeing that the other man's scepticism was almost entirely shattered. No doubt he was thinking like a Rekef again, thinking about a possible future threat to the Empire he had supposedly turned his back on.

Lake Limnia is out there. Gaved could feel it, its watery chasms, its unplumbed mystery. *If only I could see!* He would never see it, of course—even if it was anything more than Sef's imagination.

Best to hide her, though, just in case. He and Nivit could do that, if only he could convince Nivit to help. Best to hide her, whether this Saltwheel she mentioned was a Beetle of land or water.

The door rattled then and they all jumped, even Thalric. It was just Tisamon and Tynisa returning, though, pausing in the doorway at the sight of the pale and worried faces of the two Wasp-kinden within.

SEVENTEEN

The key to this venture was calm, and Lyrus embraced calmness as a constant companion. Here he was in the Queen's chosen audience chamber, which he and two other servants had set up and prepared not long before. Before fetching Maker he had held back to give the room one more look over. That was all the time he needed to ensure that the crossbow was properly hidden within the sombre drapes hanging to one side of the room's two lofty windows. He had unbarred the shutters on the windows themselves, and he knew that nobody would check them. Even with the Empire now looming so large in their mind, his kin here still did not think in three dimensions. Within the Lowlands the military threat to an Ant city-state was from other states of their own kind.

It was now all in readiness, with Maker and his entourage waiting in the antechamber. Lyrus took his place at the back of the room, knowing that he would be easily overlooked, seen as part of it. To the visitors he would be merely a servant, possessing a servant's customary invisibility, and to the Queen and her staff just one of their own people doing his job.

The Queen came in first, with only two guards. She would thus be making a show of her trust, as leverage for whatever she wanted from the Collegium ambassador. Lyrus caught the edge of the thoughts she conveyed to her warders, counselling patience but urging them to be ready if she decided to make her move.

For Lyrus it was a good sign. The more tension there was between Sarn and Collegium, the better this scenario would look.

The Queen stood waiting now: no round-the-table conference this. She had decided to try a new tactic. There was a fire burning in the grate as she stood there in her gleaming armour and long dark cloak, waiting for the Beetle to be summoned. This would be a heartfelt appeal, then, Lyrus judged.

The two guards had taken up position on either side of the door, and it occurred to him that he could kill her right now. The thought made his heart race and he fought to keep it out of his mind, so that not even a hint of his intentions might be picked up. This would be the culmination of his career. True, it could also be the end of him, but at least they would remember him. He would split Sarn asunder, one way or another. *To kill the Queen!* His masters would then admit that there was better blood in him than just tainted Sarnesh. The annals of the Rekef, the secret history of the Empire, would record him as a faithful son.

He was tired of living amongst these alien people who shared his face and skin, but the only way he could leave their house was through its rubble.

He found his fingers itching for the crossbow, but he stilled them. It must happen only with the Collegium man present. When he eventually made his move, anything might happen but, with only two guards to deal with, it seemed more than possible that Lyrus could be the only Sarnesh witness to the deed left alive, and who would the city more readily believe? If it was swift enough then even the last thoughts of the Queen and her escort could be extinguished before they betrayed him.

The Queen must have already sent the call, for the door opened and the fat Beetle came in, with a Fly-kinden and a Spider woman in tow. Lyrus scowled inwardly. This retinue complicated matters but Maker took his servants everywhere. They were all, of course, unarmed, for even her most honoured guests did not come into the Queen's presence with their weapons still at their belts. The burly Beetle clutched a cloth-covered bundle, though, and Lyrus guessed this to be the new device recently stolen from the Empire.

Responding to an unspoken thought, Lyrus came forward with a tray of wine decanted into Spider-made glass goblets. The Beetle and the Queen both took one and, before Lyrus could snatch the tray back, the Spider servant had helped herself as well. Acting every bit the contemptuous Sarnesh faced with foreign impudence, he returned to the window drape and set down the tray.

"Master Maker, this is no good," the Queen said. The Beetle made a show of eyeing the wine in surprise, but this touch of humour vanished into the ether. The Queen's face remained stern.

"It is a complex situation, your Majesty," Maker admitted. "I am sure, with time—"

"What time do you think we have?" the Queen cut him off. "How long now, before the war is upon us? This matter of these weapons, these snapbows, dominates us. You can afford to procrastinate no longer."

The Beetle grimaced, glancing sideways at his servants. The Spider stood there looking enviably relaxed, the Fly-kinden shuffling nervously.

"I will not send my soldiers to their deaths simply because you and your scholars do not believe we can be trusted with . . . this thing." The Queen gestured at the slender weapon in the Beetle's hands. "Make your choice, Master Maker, and make it now, for your time is up."

Quite, thought Lyrus and, though he would have liked to see the Collegium man squirm a little more, it was clear that his own cue was fast approaching. He reached into the drapery, grasping the stock of the crossbow. It was already loaded with a full magazine containing a dozen bolts. He had earlier tested the action, and it was as smooth and powerful as he could wish.

"Which would your Majesty rather have?" Maker was saying. "The snapbow or the Ancient League? The snapbow or the cooperation of the Kessen? That is the choice you are making."

Lyrus's Fly-kinden associates were waiting outside the unbarred windows, ready to burst in at the first sound of affray. Lyrus brought up the crossbow in a smooth and practised motion, and loosed.

⦶ ⦶ ⦶

The Queen of Sarn's lips moved to speak, and Sperra shrieked like a madwoman and dived at her. Stenwold, with reflexes he had not known he possessed, threw himself after her, seeing only that his single chance for a grand alliance was about to be inexplicably sabotaged.

The crossbow bolt lanced his thigh, right up to the fletching, the tip of it piercing Sperra's foot. They both cried out and then were both falling on top of the Queen, who had a sword half drawn, her eyes wide with shock. Her two guards drew simultaneously, running forward, and the shutters above them slammed open. All in that same moment.

The two Fly-kinden who hurtled in from above were wrapped up in dark cloth. One held a long dagger, dropping down on to the Queen and her assailants; the other simply flung out his hand and one of the Ant guards reeled backward with a blade in his throat.

Lyrus recocked and loosed the crossbow again and again. As the second guard moved in, he let the man reach down to haul Stenwold off the Queen, let the man jab at the Beetle with his sword, running a shallow line across his ribs, and then he shot the guard in the face. Lyrus himself would be the only remaining Sarnesh witness now, and he knew the guards had called for aid but had relayed crucially false facts about who was attacking. The Queen herself had not realized the source of the betrayal. *The foreigners are attacking the Queen!* Lyrus cried out into the ether. *Protect the Queen from these foreign assassins!*

⦶ ⦶ ⦶

Stenwold fell to the floor beside the dead guard, still unable to work out what was going on. Sperra was shouting something, crouching by the Queen, and then a Fly-kinden dropped on her, dagger raised. Even as Sperra saw him, and fell helplessly to the floor with her hands raised in feeble defence, Arianna had lunged forward, catching the Fly in the side with a blade Stenwold had not known she was carrying. The Fly assassin fell back, and she went with him, tumbling on to the floor as a crossbow bolt sped past them.

The crossbowman! Stenwold looked around wildly, before seeing a Sarnesh Ant armed with the weapon standing at the far end of the room. It was only the bolt in his thigh that convinced him the man was an enemy.

The main door was flung open, and more soldiers were pushing their way in, their swords drawn. The first man took a bolt in the chest, punching its way through his armour, and he fell back into the rest.

Stenwold found his hands tightening about the snapbow he had brought with him. Fighting the pain in his leg, he reached into his belt pouch, where he had some nailbow bolts intended for demonstrating the weapon. With trembling hands he now slotted one into the snapbow's breach.

Sperra was covered in blood, he noticed, and a crossbow bolt had pierced the Queen's body, just below her breast, and was quivering with the rhythm of her breathing. Sperra was trying desperately to get the woman's armour off to reach the wound, then flinched back as a narrow blade flicked past her to dig itself into the floor.

Stenwold raised the snapbow and loosed. It was clear the Fly killer did not possess the same Art that Sperra did, because he did not see the bolt until it had plucked him from the air, spinning him end over end to crash off one wall and drop to the floor.

Arianna had meanwhile killed the other assassin, but now she was backing off frantically, with Sarnesh soldiers running toward her. Stenwold, hands already fumbling a second bolt into place, shouted for them to stop. The Spider had dropped her knife, had her empty hands raised, when the first soldier simply clubbed her down with the pommel of his sword. Another, tight-faced, ripped Sperra away from the Queen and himself knelt down beside the wounded woman.

Stenwold turned to see the crossbowman level his weapon at the Queen again. He wore the faint smile of a man who might not survive the moment, but who would still win the game.

Stenwold loosed just before the other did, seeing the bolt strike him not in the chest as he had aimed for, but in the shoulder, upsetting the man's aim so that the crossbow quarrel went wide.

Someone grabbed Stenwold by the collar and hauled him roughly to his feet, racking him with pain. He looked up into the face of a Sarnesh soldier, and started to say that the crossbowman must be stopped.

He saw only a blur of movement as the man's mailed fist struck him square on the nose, knocking him cold with professional ease.

Stenwold came to slowly and reluctantly. Each further part of his body he became aware of made him regret his recovery. His head hurt abominably, his nose especially, though the pain in his back he attributed to the bare wooden boards they had laid him on. The crossbow wound in his leg was just a dull ache by comparison, though his ribs burnt from that seemingly trifling flesh wound.

On further discovery he found that the surface beneath him was a bed. It might simply have been the Ant-kinden idea of especial luxury, but this was more likely the kind of hospitality they extended to all of their prisoners. This room he was confined in was definitely a cell.

There was a wan light filtering in through a very high-up window, or a window that seemed high relative to himself. The cell was shaped like a circular shaft, and he had the uneasy feeling that the window was actually at ground level, and that his prison was sunk deep in the earth.

He sat up and groaned both at the pain and the sudden rush of memories. Following the assassination attempt, in the confusion, the soldiers had just struck out at all of them. His current residence suggested that confusion was ongoing.

Surely they can't think that we had anything to do with it?

But what would the Ant soldiers have witnessed, after all? Their Queen badly injured, two of her guards slain, a rabble of foreigners running amok. The Sarnesh with the crossbow—the Sarnesh traitor!—could have subsequently told them anything.

And the Queen had been no great friend to him, over the snapbow business. Well, now they even possessed the prototype he had brought. Perhaps they had decided it best to lock him away somewhere safe where he could raise no fuss. The alliance could now be falling apart just above his head, and he would have no idea.

Noticing that they had dressed the wound in his leg, he lurched over to the low door of his cell and began hammering on it, shouting for attention as loud as he could. Only silence followed, no running feet. He looked down at his hands, trying to think past the pain that held court about his broken nose, that was the loudest voice in his mind. What did he have left to bargain with?

The Sarnesh *needed* Collegium, surely. A generation of history must have taught them that. So they could not simply discard him. Things could be a great deal worse.

He tried to relax, but then realized he had not thought matters through. It *was* worse. For him, it was worse.

He had no idea about Arianna and Sperra. He had no idea if either of them was even alive. He was the big College Master from Collegium, so maybe he was worth keeping, but they—a Spider agent with a chequered past and a grubby Fly woman?

He hammered on the door some more. "Hoi, I have to talk to someone! I need to talk to someone, please!"

Arianna . . . The thought made him weak. He had only recently gained her for himself, woven a relationship between them that almost anything could have broken apart: an old, fat Beetle spymaster and a Spider temptress, late of the Rekef. It could have ended in so many ways, but not like this, *please.*

"Come on!" he shouted at the featureless door, even as the light from the window dwindled. "You must want to question me, at least? Talk to me, please!"

He heard the bolt shoot back, and he stepped away hurriedly. The door swung open, revealing a gas-lit corridor, low-ceilinged enough that the man standing there had to stoop. The visitor was Sarnesh, and for a moment Stenwold thought he was the crossbowman, but then realized it was just the same features, revealing the family-close kinship all the Ant-kinden possessed. If Stenwold looked further, he could see big Balkus there in the man's face—and even long-dead Marius, a friend from his student days.

The man regarded him doubtfully. He was dressed in the same chain mail as any other Ant-kinden soldier, purposefully just another anonymous guard.

"Well?" Stenwold demanded.

"I'm sorry, but I thought you had something to say to us," said the guard, and began to shut the door.

"Wait!" Stenwold said. "Wait, you have to tell me—what is going on with the Alliance? How long are you going to keep me in here? What about my companions? What's going to happen to us?"

The guard looked at him, expressionless, and Stenwold pressed on: "I am Stenwold Maker of Collegium. Look, there has been a mistake. A very terrible mistake. I was with the Queen, and—"

"Yes, you are one of those who assaulted our Queen," interrupted the guard, now much more coldly.

"I didn't! I was there, but I was trying to save her! Please, my companions can—"

"Questions are already being asked," the guard told him. "Your turn will come."

His tone made Stenwold falter. "Questions . . ." *Oh, we ally ourselves with them and we think that they are above all that, our friends the Sarnesh . . .* There would be special rooms, he knew, for questions. Rooms and *machines*. "Please, if I could just talk to someone—"

"Your turn will come," the guard said implacably, and then a new thought came to him, a message from elsewhere. "In fact it is here. How convenient." He regarded Stenwold thoughtfully, and then drew his sword. "You cannot escape, and if you attempt to attack me I will make you suffer for it, and my kin shall know of it."

"Yes, I understand, and I have no intention of making this mess any worse than it is already," Stenwold said tiredly.

"That is good." The guard's smile was thin and perfunctory. "Now exit your cell."

With a limping effort, Stenwold did so, moving slowly and carefully, keeping his hands always in plain sight. Beetle-kinden were physically tough, but a crossbow bolt through his leg would take more healing than simply a night in the cells.

He was guided through a series of turns of these low-ceilinged passageways, noticing constant side tunnels that he guessed might lead to the insect nest beneath the city. Certainly there were scuttlings down there from creatures that needed no light, and a bitterly acrid scent was evident. They were meanwhile progressing upward on a noticeable gradient and soon enough he saw windows again, small and barred and near the ceiling, and some of them able to be reached by steps, where a crossbowman could crouch to defend this subterranean undercity.

"Where are we?" he asked eventually.

"The palace," his guard replied. "A part of it you foreigners do not often see. You should feel honoured."

And then they were pushing through another door, and beyond it there was a room containing a desk. No sinister machines, though—not yet.

Sitting behind the desk there was a Sarnesh woman writing a report. She did not even glance up at Stenwold, but left him waiting for minute after minute.

He slumped to his knees, one hand pressed to his wounded leg. More time passed, then he cleared his throat loudly. She did not so much as pause in her writing. He began to wonder if in fact she were taking mental dictation from someone elsewhere in the building.

There was a second door to the room, and it opened without warning. Another Sarnesh woman marched in, like a close sister to the writer, with two guards immediately behind her. Stenwold flinched back instantly. They had the grim air of a death squad about them.

"Master Stenwold Maker of Collegium," the woman said.

"Yes, that is me."

The woman approached, staring at him, and Stenwold realized she was looking at his nose. The guard behind suddenly grabbed him, pinning his arms with a disproportionate strength and yanking him to his feet, while the woman reached up and took hold of his nose and twisted it.

Stenwold blacked out for at least a second. He came back to find himself kneeling on the ground, still pinioned by his guard, with blood running down his face, and weeping with pain. He looked up at his tormentress, eyes streaming, and demanded, "Why?"

"So that it will set correctly," she told him without sympathy. "For soldiers it is different, but I do not imagine that the dignity of a College Master is enhanced by a broken nose."

Stenwold tried to answer but the blood and the pain were too much for him. He had to be hauled back to his feet, and even then it was the guard who, seemingly effortlessly, supported most of his weight.

The woman and her escort then passed out of the room, and the guard had obviously been instructed to follow, as he manhandled Stenwold's bleeding bulk after them.

This time they were definitely moving through the palace at ground-floor level, but not in any part of it Stenwold had seen before. The room they paused in still had the barred windows, and benches about the walls which brought to mind a waiting room or antechamber. The Ants' customary lack of ostentation made it difficult to guess the purpose of much of their city from the furnishings alone.

"Sit," the woman said, and Stenwold was released without ceremony onto a creaking bench. He touched his nose gingerly but it was still too painful. At least the blood had now stopped, so he tenderly wiped at his face, trying to rid it of the worst of the gore.

He sensed another door was about to open, because the woman who had rebroken his nose now looked that way. When it did he forced himself to his feet, ignoring the reaction of the guard beside him, because it was Arianna who entered first.

They had not been kind to her, but neither had they been as cruel as they might. Her face was badly bruised down one side, and her left eye was swollen shut. Stenwold did not care, though, for she was alive! He shambled forward toward her, till the guard jumped on him, bearing him to the floor.

Something snapped inside him, and Stenwold twisted round and smashed the man across the face with his elbow, and with all of his might, spinning the Ant off him. He scrambled to his feet with a roar, but the Ant woman's soldier escorts had descended on him, and they held him firmly between them, and though he threw his weight on them, struggling with all his might, he could not shift their grip. The guard he had just struck put one hand on his shoulder, and immediately a searing pain burnt into him, accompanied by the smell of burning cloth and flesh. Stenwold screamed, dropping to his knees, and then suddenly, at the woman's unheard order, he was let go. The Beetle collapsed forward, feeling the raw, acid-burnt handprint where the Ant's Art had blistered his skin.

Then Arianna was kneeling by him, clasping him in her own bruised arms, hugging him close, and if everything was not suddenly all right again, it was better, so much better.

He forced himself to look up at the Ant woman. "What now?" he rasped.

"Now? Now nothing," she said. "We have ascertained the truth. You and your confederate will not need to be questioned after all."

"The truth? Then—?"

But he was interrupted by the door opening again. Another Ant soldier came in, bearing a small figure in his arms. Stenwold gaped at them, feeling Arianna's grip about him tighten.

The newcomer laid the figure down beside him, and Stenwold felt his stomach lurch.

She was twisted. There was no better term. It was an old, reliable mechanical torture, that had done this to her. They had racked her joints to make her talk and, as Fly-kinden had delicate joints and little tolerance for pain, he guessed they had gone on doing it until they were certain that what she said—what she must have screamed out over and over—was the truth. Stenwold felt his gorge rise, felt weak from sick horror at the thought. Arianna clung to him, even closer.

"Sperra . . ."

The Fly opened one eye and slowly turned her face toward him. She was alive, at least, but there were bandages about her head and limbs, and she trembled uncontrollably, reaching out a hand for Stenwold to hold. As her lips moved, and he saw tears leak from her eyes.

"Get me out of here, Sten," Sperra whispered. "Please."

"What have you done to her?" Stenwold demanded, feeling anger, futile and self-destructive, rising within him.

"We have questioned her. Thoroughly," said the Sarnesh woman. "We have also questioned Lyrus, who was attending on the Queen. We are satisfied that we know the full truth of the matter now. Lyrus had been suborned by the Wasp Empire. You and your associates were not involved in the attack."

Stenwold exploded, "You tortured her! You . . ." He wanted to say, *animals, savages*, but, no, this was the handiwork of the civilized, the darkness of a mechanistic people. "All she was trying to do was save your Queen! And what about your Queen? Could she herself not have told you what happened? Why this, curse you all!"

"Sten," Arianna said warningly, and he saw all of the Sarnesh grow tense.

"The Queen of Sarn is dead, Master Maker," the Ant woman said.

Stenwold found Sperra's hand at last and closed his own, so much larger, gently around it. The world had caught up with him again, as it always did. If the Ants had revealed any sorrow, any raging grief, at the loss of their leader, then perhaps he could have better understood. Their faces were as bland as those of statues, their loss shared only in the space between their minds—and just then he hated them for it.

* * *

I want to go home.

Stenwold leant on his staff because, although his punctured leg did not hurt as much as earlier, it was stiff. He stared about the table.

I want to go home.

But he had this one last piece of duty left to accomplish. Then he would go. If Sarn did not finally agree then it could fight its own cursed war. In the foreign quarter, waiting for him, was Arianna. She had wanted to be here too, but he had been firm. If there was trouble now, it must fall on his head alone. He would not risk another's safety.

Not after what had happened to Sperra—poor Sperra whose Fly-kinden Art had sprung her to the aid of the Ant Queen, and who had then paid for it at the hand of that Queen's subjects, and all for nothing.

Stenwold Maker watched the other ambassadors arrive. The sickness he felt in his stomach, which had started when he saw Sperra, had not left him yet.

Undercut at every side. If the Wasps had corrupted a Sarnesh, then who else here could be in their pay? One obvious answer was Stenwold's own agent. Plius was Ant-kinden from distant Tsen, and thus had no love for the Sarnesh. Plius also had secrets: Stenwold was spymaster enough to have seen that in his face. Plius evidently served two masters, two at least. The Empire had been in existence for only three generations but he had to admit it had learnt the trade very thoroughly.

Face to face, ranged about the table, these were not happy men and women. When the Queen had been killed they had all been hauled from their quarters and placed behind bars while the Sarnesh pieced together what had happened, extracted from the broken flesh of Sperra and the traitor Lyrus. Only the Spider Teornis had, by dint of Art and great persuasion, suffered merely a polite house arrest.

Stenwold glanced up to the head of the table, seeing there a middle-aged Ant-kinden woman, in full armour. The Sarnesh tacticians had since elected a King, but he had sent one of his council in his place. It seemed that trust was running thin in Sarn just now.

"Masters, hope of the free world," he began, trusting that his voice sounded less sarcastic to them than it did to himself. They stared at him suspiciously, as though he was cheating them in some petty mercantile business. The naked hostility evident amongst so many of them made him want to scream.

"You have known me, I think, as a patient man and the emissary from a city of patient and learned men. I hope therefore you have formed a good picture of my character. Our hosts, at least, have taken some pains to investigate it." Again that harsh edge to his tone. He forced himself back into a tenuous calm, and did not look at the Sarnesh tactician, although he was sure that she knew just what he meant, and that she did not care.

"Master Maker," Teornis spoke up. Stenwold glanced at him in surprise. The Spider wore a crooked smile, and looked briefly at his fellows to his left and right before continuing. "During this recent period of emergency, Master Maker, we have had some cause to talk to one another. Your name has been on many lips, and news of your arrest caused alarm, to say the least. Allow me to cast off my inheritance and be candid for a moment. I promise such a lapse shall not happen again."

There was a slight murmur of amusement from some of the others, and Stenwold marvelled at the man's ability to influence their mood.

"We are all enemies within this room," Teornis said. "We were never made to stand in one place and all look the same way. The commander from Kes hates our hosts. The lady from Etheryon hates me. Our hosts themselves, right now, are not enamoured of any of us." His smile broadened. "Not the most optimistic of situations, you will agree. But we are prepared to listen to Collegium, Master Maker. We will listen to you."

Thank you. "Then listen carefully," said Stenwold. "We are at war, all of us. The Empire is currently a threat to every city in the Lowlands, and yet here we stand bickering about a mere weapon. Not a weapon that cracks open mountains or destroys cities, but a weapon that a man may hold to kill another man. A successor to the crossbow, in fact, that in itself is barely more than a thrown stick with a little cleverness attached. I have heard fellow artificers speak of the march of progress. This thing, this snapbow, is not progress. It is just another way of killing someone and, even if it is an inch more efficient, then that does not make it progress. Progress is made by the improvement of people, not the improvement of machines." He was surprised at the sympathetic response to his words from the Inapt—the Moth-kinden and the Mantids—until he realized that they must have embraced such a view forever. He wondered whether, at this tapering end of the wedge, he had rediscovered some truth his own people had lost long ago.

No time for such philosophy now, old man.

"So the enemy have a way to kill people faster than they could manage before. You will say that we should have it, too, and I cannot say no to that. My own people, all our people, will soon become the targets of this weapon. Therefore we cannot cripple ourselves by casting it aside."

They watched him narrowly.

"So what, you say? What is the answer, then? I have only one, and I cannot force it on you. Collegium possesses the plans for this weapon, but there will be other chances soon for all of you who are capable of the artifice to copy and design your own. My current monopoly is almost fictional: it exists only in a saving of time. But we have so little of that left, and therefore I have something to bargain with.

"I will give these plans to the Sarnesh," he told them, seeing already the beginnings of their anger. "I will give them to the Kessen," he added. "I will give them to Teornis of the Spiderlands. I would give them to the Ancient League, if they would accept them. I would give them even to the Vekken, if they were here. I will give them to anyone and everyone who will sign a written oath."

That caught them unawares, even Teornis. They waited, and he happily let them wait a little longer before he enlightened them.

"An oath, I mean, that these weapons will be used against the Empire only. I know all too well that knowledge cannot be destroyed. They are therefore here to stay, these monstrous devices. An oath, all the same, that they will not be used against any other cities in the Lowlands, or against the Spiderlands. And an oath that you will take up arms against any city that does."

They clearly did not understand. He put his staff flat on the table, leaning forward. "Whoever breaks this oath will have more enemies than they know what to do with, and in this way those of our allies—our *allies*, you understand, who have given of their own resources already to defend us—those of our allies who cannot use this weapon are thus still protected from it. An oath of cities. An oath of alliance." He looked from face to face and heard his voice shake as he continued, "Trust, you see. Without trust we cannot succeed. Without trust we cannot stand together."

"And will you sign this oath, for Collegium? We understand that Collegium is even now raising an army equipped with such devices," the Sarnesh woman said.

Stenwold gave her a flat look, then delved in his pocket and brought out the much-creased oath he had laboured over. Before their eyes he unfolded it and signed it with his reservoir pen.

"It is done," he told them. "Who will be the next?"

They watched each other now, not him, and he feared they would not. *At least I can go home, then*, was his only thought.

"I shall sign next." Teornis took the oath from him and signalled for a servant to bring him pen and ink. "I know there are those who will not trust me, but I shall bind the Aldanrael by my mark, nonetheless. If they believe themselves to be so much more trustworthy, I invite them to place their own marks beside it. After all, the new-woven Ancient League lies a long way from my lands. I do not believe this new weapon has sufficient range that my anticipated treachery might endanger them."

He pushed the document across the table toward the Skryre from Dorax, ignoring the hostile glares of the two Mantis women who flanked her. The Moth-kinden, looking old and very small, looked at the paper and those two fresh signatures.

"We have nothing to pledge. We shall never use this deadly toy," she said. "We are at the mercy of all of you. This weapon shall likely be the death of us."

"Will the League draw back even now?" Stenwold asked her. "I do this to protect you, for what protection it can offer. Nothing we do or say will prevent the snapbow coming into general use here, as it already is in the Empire."

"Do not presume to lecture us, Beetle," she said, but she was tired, defeated. "It means nothing. However, the Ancient League shall put its mark to this."

After that, the oath passed about the table until it landed before the Sarnesh

Tactician, who had no doubt been communicating with her king and her entire city all this time.

When she signed, there was no great upsurge of relief in Stenwold, just the thought that he could leave this wretched city at long last and see his beloved Collegium once more. He forced himself to wait, even as the dignitaries filed out with their various expressions of suspicion and dissatisfaction, forced himself to remain the impeccable diplomat to the last. When Teornis appeared at his elbow, as silently and familiarly as his own shadow, he was not surprised.

"Masterfully done," the Spider said. His smile, as always, looked as genuine a smile as Stenwold had ever seen, and more practised than any.

"I am not meant for this," Stenwold sighed.

Teornis shook his head, seeming amused. "I only hope that we always remain allies, Master Maker, for you would be a formidable foe."

"High praise from the Lord-Martial?"

"And well deserved." Teornis's smile twitched broader, and even that reaction, seeming so spontaneous, could just as easily have been deliberately contrived. *With these Spiders I truly cannot ever know.* The thought turned him to reflect on Arianna, and he dismissed the association quickly.

"You should listen for news from the east, War Master," Teornis advised him. "It is at least passably pleasing this season."

"There is some new winter fashion, is there?"

"A new fashion in warfare, indeed. One hears on the wind that a certain protégé of yours has been causing the Imperial Army some degree of embarrassment."

⁂

Where the Seventh Army had come to rest after the Battle of the Rails there had once stood a Beetle-kinden farmstead. That was gone now, and in its place was a series of wooden fortifications that the Winged Furies had put up during the winter, in anticipation of retaliation from Sarn. They were Wasp field fortifications, though, nothing the Ant-kinden would have recognized: slanting walls and overhanging ledges, bristling with sharpened stakes, to make the camp as difficult to attack, from ground or air, as the Wasp mind could devise.

But there were still losses the walls could not guard against. There always were. Scouts went missing; foraging parties sometimes failed to return. The land beyond the fort was the hunting ground of Sarnesh rangers, of bandits, brigands and desperate refugees. This, though . . . this latest news had brought General Malkan out to see for himself. He required the evidence of his own eyes to understand the true scale of the attack.

There had been a troop transport coming down the track from Helleron, packed with men and supplies, going at a speed that only well-maintained rails could allow. Three miles from the fort, there had been a series of explosions that ripped apart the engine automotive and suddenly the tracks had been gone, hurled aside into splayed and coiling shapes, and the entire convoy had come off the rails, carriages shunting into carriages, the straight line of the transport's passage thrashing suddenly like a whip.

The corpses had gone by the time he reached the site. Travelling with a guard of six hundred men was time consuming but Malkan was not a rash sort. He was the youngest general the Empire had and he fully intended to become the oldest, in good time.

"One hundred ninety-seven men died in the initial impact," one of his aides was recounting without emotion. The man was his intelligence officer, almost certainly Rekef, and probably did see this number as nothing more than that. "Over four hundred injured, best count."

"And then?" Malkan prompted, though he knew already. The word had run quickly through the entire Seventh.

"And then the convoy was attacked, sir," his aide said. "The soldiers trying to exit the train came under shot from both north and south of the tracks. We estimate that another three hundred and twenty men were killed outright before any defence could be mounted."

"And that defence consisted mostly of staying under cover and keeping their heads down," said Malkan, wondering what he himself would have done in the circumstances. "Engineers, I want news!"

"Sir." One of his artificers left the rails and ran up to him. "Judging from the wreckage it could have been either a steam-expansion bomb or triggered steam pistons making the tracks jump. Just simple mechanical force to unseat the automotive, nothing flammable until the automotive's fuel lines ruptured in the impact."

"So?"

"It's a simple and robust device, sir, but whoever set it would need to be a skilled artificer in order to gauge its precise disposition. It must have been initiated on a pressure trigger, sir. The trains aren't regular enough for a clockwork timer."

"Could you make such a device in the field?"

"You could assemble it, but the parts must have come in from Sarn."

"Or Helleron," Malkan mused, "or Collegium." He had already heard the reports of some soldiers who had survived the attack, reports that gave descriptions of the attackers. No disciplined Sarnesh Ant-infantry, these, but a rabble composed of different kinden. A rabble with a common mind, like bandits but more organized . . .

"What of our scouts?"

"Two have not returned, while the others report no sign of any large force nearby," his aide confirmed.

"They won't. After you achieve this kind of success, you scatter, then rendezvous later . . ." The attackers had taken their own dead with them, but their departure had been hurried. There had still been clues: crossbow bolts, discarded weapons . . . yet there was no pattern, nothing uniform. Malkan ground his teeth. He could send men after the missing scouts, but whoever had not wished to be seen would have moved on by now, or alternatively it could become an ambush.

"I want those rails repaired in double time," he told the engineer, who saluted and returned to his men. Malkan pondered the situation for a while, putting himself in the position of his enemies as best he could. "Keep at least two hundred men here to guard them, though. I'd come back, if I were him, and kill the artificers as they worked."

"There is a lot of rail line between here and Helleron, sir," the aide noted.

"Indeed, so get a messenger off to Helleron . . . better send three, separately. We need a new way of transporting supplies and men. Just march them overland if they have to."

"Yes, sir."

The Seventh had been relying on the rail line to Helleron over the winter. It would now be a difficult adjustment to make, going back to old-fashioned methods, but it might be for the best. Simplest done was simplest fixed, as the artificers always said.

The dead men were a waste of resources, the broken rails and automotive an annoyance. What was really concerning General Malkan was the loss of almost five hundred snapbows that the attackers, whoever they were, had made off with, having deliberately targeted the carriage they were in.

"Explosives . . . and these new weapons . . ." he murmured. "If it weren't for that . . ."

"What, sir?"

"In the Twelve-Year War . . ." he began. It had been the cause of his meteoric rise through the ranks, his conduct at that war's end. "Toward the end, they were always springing surprise attacks, ambushes. They had inferior discipline, inferior equipment. We had broken their field armies by then, so they had to make up for it in tactics, using the land itself . . . those Dragonfly-kinden . . . I want to know any news received about Dragonfly-kinden."

He stared out across the broken ground, hearing the hammering of the artificers as they straightened the rails, and knowing that his enemy was somewhere out there, staring back at him.

EIGHTEEN

There seemed to be a Wasp soldier on every street corner, as though they had already occupied Solarno without the courtesy of letting anyone know. In the open-fronted tavernas the conversation hovered about them like a fly over fruit, but never quite touched on the awkward questions.

Che, Taki and Nero had gone out into the market district to see the true scale of the problem, with the Dragonfly Dalre and a couple of others shadowing them in case of trouble. It was hard to judge accurately, though, as the Wasps were spread out in groups of no more than two or three, but it seemed impossible to go *anywhere* without at least a glimpse of their black-and-yellow presence.

Nero had left them a short while ago, to undertake some aerial surveillance, and they had taken a table at a taverna to hear what the Solarnese themselves were saying. The uneasy local consensus seemed to be that one or other of the political parties had invited them in, or was even hiring them as mercenaries. That was the only way the locals could account for such an influx of foreigners in their midst. The idea that the Wasps might have an agenda of their own was not spoken about.

"The problem is," Taki said, "it'll become true. One of the parties will decide to make a deal with them, and that's just the start of the downward slope. The Wasps will keep that party strong, and the same party will rely on the Wasps all the more."

"I don't think the Wasps are likely to wait that long," said Che. "They'll soon be making demands to whichever party looks most gullible. Will that be yours, do you think?"

"I don't have a party," Taki reminded her. "I'm not into politics. All I want to do is fly." She considered the thought further. "But it could be the Destiavel's party, the Satin Trail, that I'll grant you—or else the Crystal Standard lot. The Crystals are in the Corta Obscuri now, and they might risk a lot to stay on there. If they don't alter their fortunes, word is there'll be a new Corta soon enough, and then they'll be out."

"What about the other cities of the Exalsee?" Che asked. "Will they step in?"

Taki looked almost horrified. "That pack of pirates and lackeys *interfere* with Solarnese politics? If Princep and Chasme and the rest turned up here protesting against the Wasps, the only thing it would do is have every local inviting Wasps to marry their daughters and take over the family businesses. No, this is a Solarnese problem."

"Then we have to talk to Genissa."

"Domina Genissa is not happy with the Wasps," Taki agreed. "She just doesn't like the look of them, and with her that counts for a lot. Mind you, she's generally a good judge from first impressions, and like a lot of the Dominas she doesn't want something new coming in and changing the mix. Actually, the only people who would really welcome that happening would be the Path of Jade crowd, and that's because at the moment they're in danger of dying out altogether. Mind you, they're in for all sorts of odd ideas, like banning slavery and the like. Not the sort of thinking your Wasps will want to encourage."

Che was about to reply when she noticed a pair of Wasp soldiers approaching, their attention clearly fixed on either her or Taki. She felt for her sword hilt, loosening it in its scabbard. Taki moved away from the table a little, allowing herself room to fly.

The lead Wasp, obviously the one in charge, was both shorter and leaner than most of them, but he bore himself with an air of arrogant confidence that made up for his lack of stature. His barred cuirass was fashioned of leather, not the metal bands the imperial soldiers normally wore. His hair was still tawny but he was older than Che had first thought, with a little burn scarring evident about his chin and neck. As he arrived at their table he nodded to Taki, ignoring Dalre and the other Destiavel men, who had stood up warningly as he approached.

"Do I address the Bella te Schola Taki-Amre of the Destiavel?" he said, fumbling slightly over such unfamiliar names.

"What of it?" Taki asked him suspiciously.

"My name is Lieutenant Axrad of the Aviation Corps," he said. "I have sought you out to congratulate you on your flying."

Taki stood too, sizing him up. "And what would you know about my flying, Sieur Axrad?"

Axrad smiled bleakly. "I flew against you, Bella Taki-Amre, over the Exalsee only yesterday. You downed several of my comrades, and damaged my flier enough that I could not continue our duel."

Taki glanced at Che, and then turned back to him, obviously reevaluating the situation. "You're a pilot?" She remembered the one Wasp machine she had not been able to pursue, just taking a single shot at it before heading for home. "That's not a title to lay claim to lightly, in this woman's city."

"I am aware of that," Axrad said. "While I consider myself the best of the imperial fliers in this region, I admit to having nothing but admiration for your skills, Bella Taki-Amre. I know it is likely that we shall cross swords once more, but I wish you to know I bear you no ill will, and if it is your fortune to send me to the waters I shall consider it an honour."

Che had been waiting for the catch here, the threat that the man's words must surely be leading to, but she saw now there was none. It was just a normal exchange in a world she was not part of. She glanced at the other Wasp soldier, and saw him looking bored and shuffling, and no more included than she was.

"Well, Sieur Axrad," said Taki slowly, "I think you understand our customs better than most. You also flew well. Tell me, do many of your—what was it, Aviation Corps?—think as you do?"

"Not so many, but I am not the only one. For my people, to fight is to live and to excel is to succeed. We are a warrior kinden not without honour on the field or in the air, though I am aware that some of my kin do not show the nobility of spirit that befits them. I wished to speak with you in order to redress this."

He was standing so stiffly, so awkwardly, that Che finally realized that he was actually frightened. He was a newcomer petitioning for membership to a club, and with no guarantee of receiving it. He wanted *acknowledgement*.

A flick of Taki's wings took her up on to the tabletop, and matching his eye level. "You've surprised me, Sieur Axrad, and I think we have something we can talk about. Would you join me?" She indicated a table further across the Taverna's courtyard. Che opened her mouth to protest, but Taki's warning look told her that this was not a matter for her to interfere in or eavesdrop on.

"I must warn you right away, that my respect for you does not compromise my loyalty to the Empire," Axrad announced.

"I would not expect it to," Taki said, and with that, the two of them moved out of earshot, heading to the other table.

Che caught the look of the other Wasp soldier, now consigned to standing out in the street while his superior amused himself, and she almost felt a kindred spirit there. Then Nero returned, pausing to hover in midair as he spotted Taki's new companion.

"Apparently he's a pilot or something," Che explained dismissively. "So what did you see?"

"Enough to guess at a little secret the Wasps have here," Nero said grimly, keeping his voice low. "They're scattered all over the city, but they're working in cells, each group of them checking in with a single soldier over and over. Not an officer, mark you, or at least not always—mostly just an ordinary soldier. I think they've got a mindlink between about a dozen Wasp-kinden across Solarno, just close enough together to stay in contact. They can do that, a few of them, though as far as I know it's a rare Art among their kinden. It means they'll be able to act all together, however separated they are."

Che nodded, her eyes fixed on Axrad's back. The news was not getting any better.

⁂

Instead of the dingy confines of the Clipped Wing, it was an elegant drawing room, its high-arched ceiling supported by seemingly too-slender pillars with gilded capitals, and whose expanse was painted with a scene of aquatic creatures engaged in improbable play together: fish, water beetles, insect nymphs and the like. Che had exchanged her audience as well. Instead of half a dozen aviators intent on her words, there was nearly a score of Solarno's great and good here, Spider-kinden all, and some with red cravats for the Satin trail, others with green and gold sashes for the minority Path of Jade, and a single old Spider who wore purple satin about his brow and draped over his shoulders in a kind of scarf, representing Che knew not what.

The grander surroundings, the most prestigious company, none of it changed the speech she delivered, which mirrored the words she had given the pilots: *this is the Empire.*

They were a far-from-attentive audience, though. As she explained, as passionately as she could, about the scale, strength and danger of the Wasps, they talked in low voices amongst themselves or perused books taken from the shelves on the far wall or simply stared out of the windows. Even the servants that passed back and forth across the room seemed to pay more heed, as they offered food and drink in an unending supply. Some of those assembled here were doubtless in the pay of the Wasps, so it was a certainty that the imperial agents within the city would soon get to hear of this. As they had already tried to kill her twice, there seemed little point in hiding her opposition from them. Displaying it thus openly, however, seemed to be having little effect, for the nobles of Solarno, all members of the Corta Lucidi, and all gathered here for this one purpose, seemed barely to care. Even Genissa of the Destiavel, who had organized this entire venture after hearing Taki's representations, seemed engrossed in talking gossip with her neighbour.

Che drew to a close, her final point petering out, feeling like an actor whose audience has seen better.

"Any . . . questions?" she asked, falteringly.

"You've seen all this yourself, have you?" a well-dressed, elegant man near the back enquired. "These armies and soldiers and machines?"

"I've seen enough of them. I was involved in a field battle against them—a battle that they won."

"But why would they come here? It seems such a great deal of trouble," a woman observed. "Who says they aren't here just as mercenaries? I've heard no proof either way."

"The Wasp Empire does not hire out its soldiers as mercenaries," Che insisted. "Those men out there are openly wearing imperial colours. They are here as an advance force, ahead of an invasion. They have already divided your people, it seems."

"My dear girl, we were quite divided enough before they ever showed their faces," Genissa remarked, prompting a polite ripple of laughter. "I think these Wasp-kinden could be useful to us. After all, they have rather polarized the common folk of the city."

"Please believe me," Che said. "You can't *use* the Wasps, not like that. They're not going to fit into your . . ." she nearly said *petty provincial politics*, because that would have been true, but fortunately she held it back, ". . . into your parties and factions. They're bigger than you and, if they want, they can field an army with more soldiers than Solarno has citizens. They don't seek alliances and they don't make deals. Their foreign policy consists of one objective only: conquest."

"That's all very well, but I can hardly see an army bothering to come all the way through the Dryclaw and then over the mountains, just for Solarno," one of them said. "I really think you're making far too much of this."

"But there is an army approaching even now," Che insisted. "They're shipping soldiers over the mountains in airships."

"I think we're missing the important point here," said one of the dignitaries of the Path of Jade, waving her hand languidly for attention. "All this Empire business is all very well, but nobody's so much as mentioned a word about how we can turn this against the Crystal Standard!"

Che sagged in despair.

"After all," the same woman went on, "these Wasp creatures are unpopular allies, and yet the Standard have embraced them. I'll wager there have been more than a few seats shifted because of that. If the Trail will stand with us, we can call a Corta election and have the Standard thrown out of the Obscuri before you can say 'done.'"

"A Corta Obscuri run by the Path of Jade?" someone scoffed.

"Well, of course not," said the woman. "I'm simply suggesting that we will support you in return for a few concessions that should be easily sketched out . . ."

"But what if the Standard won't let go?" Che demanded. "What if they call on the Wasps to keep them in power?"

There was a round of patronizing laughter.

"My, how dramatic you foreigners are," said one of them. "We're not going to put them into permanent exile, just take over for a year or two. You just don't understand the way things are done here."

Che gave up. They were right, of course, but the barrier to mutual understanding fell both ways. If she was to find help here, it would not be amongst Solarno's rulers.

⦶ ⦶ ⦶

The news broke by evening that the Crystal Standard had apparently, possibly retrospectively, invited the Wasp-kinden in, ostensibly for the sake of Solarno's stability given the riots and mobs so often afflicting the city.

But stability was the last thing that such news brought. In all the taverns and chocolate houses the gossips were soon abuzz with it, and opinions were stridently voiced. The grassroots support for the Satin Trail and the Path of Jade were talking in hushed, angry voices, and for once they were not at each other's throats. As long as the Wasps had just seemed unwanted foreigners lurking on every street corner, the Solarnese had been content to ignore them. Now they had been legitimized, local people suddenly knew whether to hate them or not. The Crystal Standard's followers stood by uncertainly, finding their new allies coolly arrogant and disdainful of their company, whilst the two other main parties—and half a dozen lesser parties nobody normally bothered with—began to voice their opposition in stronger and stronger terms.

The Crystal Standard recognized this as just the everyday Solarnese citizens' participation in politics. The Wasps, however, did not.

One squad of a half dozen Wasp soldiers found itself taunted and threatened by a pack of locals, who waved their narrow swords and accused them of being filthy foreign mercenaries who should go back where they came from. The Wasps, of uncertain temper at the best of times, loosed their stings onto this mob, killing several men and women outright. When the crowd had recovered from its shock, it charged at the soldiers, who retreated to the rooftops still shooting in retaliation. All in all perhaps three Wasps and twelve locals were killed before the citizens turned and fled.

The Wasps counted it as a great victory, but there was a hurried meeting between the Crystal Standard leaders and Captain Havel, who now found himself responsible for it all.

"This must stop," he was told. "Your men must exercise control."

Captain Havel was not entirely sure that they were his men at all. He was still technically the Rekef officer in command of Solarno, but there was an army colonel, still currently north of Toek and the mountains, who had given these soldiers their orders and outlined their tactics, a man who had never been to Solarno nor ever wished to until he could claim governorship of the place. He had written to Havel and made that last wish very plain.

Havel had lived comfortably here in Solarno for many years, and enjoyed a prosperous and hedonistic lifestyle while doing so. He was determined to cling on to that privilege, which meant no outright invasion, no bludgeoning use of Wasp power to inflame the city. He passed on his strict recommendations to the imperial forces, but with the knowledge that his kinden were never inclined to take insults meekly, while to the hot-headed Solarnese an insult was as common as a greeting, and therefore shrugged off as easily. It was a clash of cultures that could now go badly wrong very quickly.

By nightfall there had been no buildings yet burnt, and only half a dozen more deaths, so he counted himself lucky. It would take many tendays for the Solarnese to adapt to this new power in their midst, and meanwhile that army colonel up north would not stop moving his troops in. The airships would already be on their way back to the city laden with full complements of fighting men.

Havel felt his grip on the situation rapidly loosening. He needed to talk to Odyssa, he realized, for she would instantly understand the situation. After all, these native Solarnese might be mad for fighting, but it was Spider-kinden who actually ruled Solarno. Surely Odyssa could soon think of some way to appease them.

He met her in a private room of an eatery called the Sawbouys, enjoying a view out over the water. He called up a bottle of the house's best wine and the flank of freshwater shrimp that the place was famous for. The feeling of luxury, of living well, was soon calming to him, for it told him that he was keeping ahead of the rising wave of disaster that threatened to crash down on him,

He ate with a fierce passion, while Odyssa merely picked at her food and eyed him with amusement.

"I'm at my wits' end," Havel confessed. "The situation is, as they say, deteriorating."

"But surely this was inevitable," Odyssa said. "Was this not the imperial plan all along?"

"Do you think they tell me anything?" Havel said bitterly. "But, no it wasn't, not to my knowledge. Not this soon, at least. It's that cursed colonel out north of Toek, who just can't wait to get his men moved in here. He's going to end up unifying all of Solarno against us. All of the Exalsee, even. I wouldn't have thought it could be done but, little by little, he's managing it."

She shrugged. "So things are happening a little faster than planned."

"It's not as simple as that," Havel replied. "I had everything already in hand here, so it's an insult to me and to the Rekef. I could have annexed Solarno virtually single-handedly, with no need for all this." *And I could have made a fortune doing it.* "Now the army will sack half the city because this colonel won't keep them in check. Hundreds of our soldiers will die. It's just . . . such a waste. You're a Spider-kinden, so you're used to doing things with a little intelligence. You must be able to see my point."

"I think I'm beginning to," she agreed. "I take it you want me to send a message to the colonel?"

"Conveyed with the Rekef's greatest displeasure. Just tell him whatever it takes to get him off my back," Havel almost pleaded with her. "He doesn't understand how delicate the situation is here. He's just a stone-headed soldier with no appreciation of politics. All he's interested in is the governorship, and what good will that do him when his new subjects are bringing the place down around his ears?"

"You might be best off resigning yourself to what is inevitable," Odyssa warned him. "I'd be surprised if you can stop it now."

"Oh, I'll stop it all right, don't you worry," Havel assured her. "I've been in this city a good while now. I know how things work. I know how to keep the pot simmering and yet never quite boiling over. You'll see. Without any more provocation from that fool out in the desert, I'll soon get Solarno settled again." He breathed a deep sigh. Now he had said it, it even sounded possible. "I can even use the men he's already sent, make them a proper police force to back the useless militia the Solarnese have. They'll come to see us as invaluable, you'll see. We shall creep into their hearts. This town has its nobles and its councils, but really it's ruled by the mob, as each fresh demonstration shakes up the Cortas and their magnates. We shall control the mob. We could even start our own party here."

"I see what you mean," said Odyssa at last, as Havel took a swallow of wine. "You're right, and it is almost a Spider-kinden way of doing things. Almost. Naturally we'd add a few layers of complexity to it, whether it needed it or not."

"I try to be as simple as I can, so that I won't forget anything," Havel said.

"And if the colonel wants his war anyway?"

"Then let him go invade somewhere else, because Solarno is mine," Havel told her. "Surely the Rekef should be able to whip one over-ambitious officer into line."

"It should."

There was a reflective pause, both of them sipping at their wine. Eventually Odyssa continued, "I think you're right."

"In what way?"

"I think you could draw it back from the brink after all."

Havel nodded emphatically. "You're cursed right I can. Just give me a tenday without this colonel breathing down my neck, and I'll be back in control."

Odyssa considered him speculatively, noticing the sweat spring up on his forehead. "Yes, I think you could. You're a clever man, for a Wasp-kinden."

"I'll take that . . . for a compliment," he said, blinking at her.

"There is one thing you've failed to consider, though, and I feel that I should warn you of it."

"What's . . . what's that?"

"What if someone else wants the war?"

He goggled at her, mouth half open but no words forming.

"Layers upon layers, you see, Captain, in interweaving strands. You really are quite good at this, for a Wasp, but I fear you're no Spider-kinden."

She saw his hand twitch reflexively, but no flash of energy came from it. A moment later he had toppled sideways onto the floor.

Odyssa stood up, brushing down her tunic, an old habit kept from after her first murder. She sometimes thought the Rekef had nothing to teach her that she had not been born with. She would now pay the Fly host of this eatery enough to forget who she was. She had two men close at hand of equally uncertain memory, ready to dump Havel's body somewhere easily discoverable. Then she would put her Rekef hat back on, and run to the Wasp encampment at the oasis beyond Toek, and there tell the colonel, whom she had been steadily inflaming, that the Rekef officer in charge of Solarno had been murdered by the locals, and therefore the hour of his conquest and governorship was at hand.

NINETEEN

It had been a tiring day. His new responsibilities were making demands on him he had not expected. Totho had never seen himself as a factory overseer.

But that was not quite true, if he was being honest with himself. Every artificer who rose to the top of his trade should be guiding lesser craftsmen, having them work to his designs, delegating the burdens of his trade. Of course he had wanted that, but seen no chance of ever achieving it.

He had not wanted this, though. Drephos, Colonel-Auxillian of the Wasp Empire, had taken him on eagerly as an apprentice, but the folk of Helleron were not so open-minded. It all seemed insane to him, but that was only because he had done his best to forget his childhood, even his studentship spent at the College. A half-breed was never popular. A half-breed was cursed by his mixed blood. Collegium was a cosmopolitan city and even there Totho had never been allowed to forget the stain of his birth that was so plain in his features.

Here in Helleron, blood mattered greatly, and the local Beetles were hard on half-breeds. People like Totho got given the worst jobs, or worked in the criminal fiefs, or else starved and begged. Then Drephos had come along and been made governor of all Helleron, and set Totho up as master of whole factories, giving orders to foremen and artificers who spat at him behind his back, and stared at him mutinously when he faced them.

It had affected their work. They had dragged it out and dawdled, and even turned out shoddy pieces in the belief he was not artificer enough to know the difference. For a tenday he had agonized over it, trying to understand how he could make them see he was not a bad man: how could he win them over to his side?

Today he had awoken with his answer: he could not. He could be the most generous and even-handed overseer the city had ever seen, and to them he would still be just a half-breed.

So today he had gone in with a squad of Wasp soldiers. The Wasps cared for half-breeds even less, if possible, but Totho was Sergeant-Auxillian now and he simply gave them orders in a calm, clear voice that was obeyed. They all knew he had Drephos's ear.

He had not waited for the first slight to emerge. He knew just how it would have worked back at the College: the workers here would have behaved, good as gold, until the soldiers left. He had singled out three people that he hoped were the ringleaders.

He had ordered the soldiers to drag them before him, and he had hoped even then that a few words of warning would be enough. Their expressions had remained mulish and sullen, however, promising further mutiny.

They *had* been mulish and stubborn, he assured himself, in retrospect. *It was not just my imagination.*

He had ordered them to be whipped. So the soldiers had whipped them, and gone on whipping them until he had spoken loud enough to stop them. From that he had gained a large degree of fearful obedience from the workers and a small amount of surprised respect from the soldiers.

For the actual flogging they had been tied to machines inside the factory, where everyone could see. Totho had stood on the overseer's gantry with the leader of the soldiers, gripping the rail and waiting for that wince-inducing moment when the lash came down.

It never came: the lash rose and then fell, but the wince never manifested, and there had been something changing inside him, something born in him when the first cry came up. Not remorse and not regret, but something like satisfaction.

You bastards have kept me down all my life, he had thought. *Now see how you like it.*

Once the whip had stopped cracking, he had told the silent factory floor—silent save for the whimpering of his victims—that any future failings would be punished by death, and at the time he had meant it.

Now he looked back on that, all of it, and tried to see it as Che would, tried to feel appalled by what he had done, but that was harder and harder the longer he worked for Drephos. He no longer asked himself what he was becoming, for he knew now that he had already become.

⦃|⦄ ⦃|⦄ ⦃|⦄

Kaszaat came to him that night, as she often did, moving her smooth brown body over his in rhythms that were a language older than talking. He did not know it but she could read his mood and his history from his lovemaking: the more gloomy and the more grim his day, the tighter he clutched at her and the fiercer his passion, seeking in her body what he could not find in the shadow-world he had come to inhabit.

This time, though, he found something different in her: a desperation and a need. She wept when the climax came, her nails biting into him, thighs locked about him in a furious grapple.

He thought she would turn away to sleep then, but still she lay upon him, trembling slightly, and he closed his eyes and let the sensation of his own skin explore the pressure of hers upon him.

"Totho," she murmured at last, almost too softly for him to hear.

He made a questioning noise.

"After the battle, what happened between Drephos and you?"

Immediately he tensed, feeling his stomach lurch. How he would like to forget what had happened then, his betrayal, and his later confusion in trying to work out just who exactly he had betrayed.

"It was the prisoner girl, no?" Kaszaat asked. "That Beetle girl they brought in. As soon as you heard of it, you were different."

He said nothing.

"Totho, I'm not stupid. You're no Spider-kinden. I read you. You knew her."

He sighed, heavily. When she received no more answer than that, Kaszaat jabbed him in the shoulder. "Curse you, you bastard! Just speak to me."

"Yes, I knew her," he said.

"More than that?"

"What?" He sat up, half displacing her. "What do you want?"

"The truth," she said. "Because I, too, have a truth. I want to tell you a truth, but I need to trust you. Can I trust you?"

"Can *you* trust *me?*"

Her eyes blazed. "Yes, Totho. You think you're the only one with secrets? Nobody else has anything to hide?"

Well, yes. "I . . . What do you want to hear? I knew her from the College. I . . . liked her. I liked her very much. Happy now?"

"No," she said. "More than like—you *loved.*"

Why is she doing this?

"I don't know." Honesty prompted him to add. "I thought I did. Perhaps I did, but I don't know."

"You let her go."

He said nothing.

"You made a deal with Drephos. You gave him something in return for this girl's freedom," she persisted. It was not true, of course, but not so very far off.

"He . . ." *Why not let her in on the madness?* "Drephos wanted the snapbow plans spread further, for his wretched march of progress. So he had Che . . . had the girl take them to the Sarnesh."

All quite back to front, but it almost made more sense that way. He saw it was something she had never even considered, and he could hardly blame her for that.

"So Drephos, he trusts you," Kaszaat remarked.

"Does he?"

"No," she told him. "I know, because he came to me. He told me to get what I could from you. To sleep with you, bind you to close me. He knows sex, knows how it is used. He does not understand, but he knows the purposes."

He may not have the equipment left, Totho thought, considering the terrible accident that had stripped Drephos of so much. The notion that the man might have found a mechanical replacement was so horrifyingly incongruous that Totho nearly choked on it.

"So, so why are you telling me this now?" he asked her.

"I don't know," she said. "Why am I? Perhaps because of what they brought out of Drephos's factory today—you have heard about that? The twins told me. They are cold, those two. They talk almost never, save to each other and Drephos. Yet they talked to me, then. They had to. It was too much to bear in silence."

"The corpses? I heard there were bodies."

"Forty-five dead, prisoners, all of them, from the fief battles," Kaszaat whispered. "I heard their faces were black, with eyes popped almost out. Poisoned, that means—but that makes no sense."

Totho felt something twist in his stomach, some artificer's inner instinct trying to speak to him.

"He has a new weapon," Kaszaat said softly. "Something even better than the snapbow, to use against the Sarnesh."

They lay together for a long while, Kaszaat sliding off him to nestle under his arm, with her head resting on his chest. *Would it feel like this with Che?* He realized that he would never know. So Drephos had found a new way of killing people. Did it matter, though? Could Totho criticize, having done his own work so well?

"What are we doing here?" he murmured. "Why don't we just leave?"

"Because there is a sword," she told him, "And here we are on the right side of the guard . . ." Her voice shook and she stopped.

"What is it?"

She would not say, but she clung to him closer, she who had always seemed the more experienced of them, in all walks of life, older and wiser in so many things.

"Kaszaat, please," he said. "I promise you I'm not spying on you for Drephos, or the . . . the Rekef, or whoever else you think."

"I don't think that. Not *you*." She made a single painful sound of amusement. "Who would trust you to do that? You have only recently turned your back on the Lowlands, turned your weapons on your friends. You're a spinning wheel and nobody knows where you'll stop. Why else would Drephos point me at you?"

The cruelty of it cut him. He pressed his lips together and said nothing.

"Oh Totho, I'm sorry," she said after a moment. "I'm sorry, but I am frightened—who can I trust? What do you think of me, you, who love this other?"

"I don't know. I . . . I like you a great deal . . ."

"Totho . . ."

"What? Tell me, please. I need to know—"

There was something cold now at his throat. A blade? It was the work knife he had left beside the bed, as sharp as any artificer could desire.

He felt no fear at all.

"Are you going to kill me, then?" he asked her. "For what reason?"

Her hand was shaking, which worried him more than the knife itself. "How could you turn yourself on your own people?" she asked.

"You mean the Battle of the Rails? They weren't my people. They were Sarnesh," he said, almost without thought, but the subsequent response he came up with was hardly better: *I have no people.* In the end he just continued, "You've worked with Drephos for how long, now? You can't say you didn't know what he was doing. You were up there with him—with me—watching them bombard Tark into ash. What did you imagine he wanted your skills for?"

He was getting angry, which was unwise considering the knife, but he could not see what the problem was, why she had suddenly broken out of her shell like this.

"I am safe with Drephos," she whispered. "So long as I serve him, I shall never see his weapons turned against me. I need never fear."

"So?" he prompted. Gently he reached up to take the knife but her grip on it was too tight.

"They say there is trouble come to Szar," she said heavily. "They say the Queen is dead. They say there are soldiers now coming to my own city. They say that . . . there will be an uprising, and that it will be put down."

"And you think we'll be sent there?"

"I know it. I can feel it. Totho," she said. "But I can't do it. Not my own. I'm not as strong as you."

Strength? Is that what it was?

At last she released the knife, and he cast it aside, hearing it clatter against the wall.

"Will you tell him about this?" she asked.

"No," he said, shocked. *What does she think I am, some kind of traitor . . . ?*

Quite.

"Never," he insisted. "Trust me, please."

"Totho, I cannot find a way out," she whispered. "I have worked for him for too long. Now I will pay. He will kill me."

He had nothing to say to that. He knew Drephos was a man devoid of most emotions, but that his march of progress was a mechanized inevitability whose wheels would grind up anyone who stood before it. Instead, he held Kaszaat close, wanting to reassure her that Drephos would not harm her, or that he, Totho, would protect her. Both statements stuck in his throat, and he could not get them out.

TWENTY

Colonel Gan was, by his own estimation, the luckiest man in the Empire. Not only had his family connections ensured him a colonel's rank at a very young age, but, for the last seven years, he had revelled in the governorship of the most profitable yet docile city in the Empire.

The palace at Szar was magnificent, larger even than the great eyesore that the old governor of Myna had installed. As the local Bee-kinden built either single-storey or underground, it easily overlooked the entire city of Szar, and if the Bee-crafted architecture was more elaborately carved, every wall finished with intricate frescos and designs, then still Gan believed that the sheer scale of his palace showed his kinden's superiority over them.

Colonel Gan made a point of taking his breakfast each morning on a different side of his great multi-tiered edifice, surveying his domain. Sometimes he entertained his officers there, or imperial dignitaries passing through, also Consortium factors or men of good family, but once a week he allowed himself a special treat. He had observed, when he last visited in the capital, that the Emperor Alvdan II—a man whom Gan admired above all others—ate breakfast with the rather pleasant-featured Princess Seda once a week. Such fraternal devotion was much noted and debated in the courtly circles Gan preferred to move in and, though Gan himself had no well-born sisters, the city of Szar had nevertheless provided him with a suitable alternative. He considered that he was bringing a very imperial touch of sophistication to this city when he dined each tenday with its native princess, Maczech.

Maczech herself was not exactly the most becoming of women. Compared with the Wasp women that Gan favoured, she was distinctly short and dark and round-faced. She was a genuine princess, though, adored by the local populace with that slavish devotion they awarded to all their royal family. In thus showing her to her own people, as a guest at the mercy of imperial hospitality, Gan was demonstrating his hold on their city. Not that they needed such a reminder, of course, the Bee-kinden being so wonderfully spiritless. Left on their own, they worked twice as hard as any Wasps would have done, hammering away at their forges, their furnaces and machine shops, churning out armour and blades and machine parts that they then dutifully shipped off across the Empire. The final capture of Szar had been a considerable leap forward for the Empire's industrial capability, and here was Colonel Gan looking out over the dawn-touched city and relishing the spoils of it. Who cared that he himself had neither lifted a blade nor shed one drop of blood in its capture?

And here now came the princess: these Bee-kinden had no idea of how to dress, not even their royalty: the dark-featured girl wore only a drab tunic with a black and gold gown open over the top. He insisted she dress in imperial colours on such visits. He knew it rankled with her, but it was important that there be no doubt about whose wishes were counted more important.

But after all, I am not a tyrant, he reminded himself, and smiled at her. She smiled back, a little stiffly. She had learnt that her smile could be valuable currency, sometimes. He did not believe, of course, that she held any affection for him, but she needed things from him and she knew that she had to play the game to get them. If she kept him in a good mood, then she could ask him to intervene on behalf of her people, to lessen any punishments, lighten workloads, or even have messages passed on to her brother, who was off on Auxillian duty elsewhere in the Empire. She met a lot with her people, he knew, even the lowliest of them. She seemed to visit at random across the city, though dogged always by her imperial guards. Gan knew that such movements were guided by the thoughts of her fellows, for many of the Bee-kinden could speak mind-to-mind, as the Ants did. It was an Art even some Wasps could boast of, although Gan himself had never bothered to master it.

She demurely sat across from him, whereupon a Wasp came forward to pour some watered wine. Gan glanced up at him curiously.

"Since when do those of my own kinden do such menial work?" he asked, wanting to add the man's name and then realizing he could not remember it. "When you're finished here, go and get a local to serve us. I'm sure you must have other matters to attend to."

The Wasp server hesitated, glancing at Maczech. She was watching him through half-closed eyes, but Gan had the odd feeling she was actually more alert than usual.

"Well, speak, man. Is there something concerning you?" he enquired.

"Yes, Colonel," said the servant reluctantly. "I understand there is currently some disruption amongst the household servants, so I volunteered to serve you rather than force you to wait until they are put in order."

"I approve," Gan said and, as the man turned away from the table. "Disruption, you say?"

"Yes, sir." The servant turned back and glanced at Maczech again but Gan waved him to continue. "Well, sir, they seemed . . . rather unruly this morning. Suddenly unwilling."

"Nonsense," Gan snapped, his good humour evaporating. "The Princess's people are the most sweet-natured in the whole Empire. Why, I'll wager that Colonel Thanred in Capitas does not have a city as well ordered as mine."

"Of course, sir," the man said, retreating.

"I will have to review the service arrangements," Gan remarked. "Perhaps I have an overzealous overseer or some such problem." He turned to his guest. "Or perhaps you should speak to the staff here at the palace, as you often do to your people throughout the city, Princess."

"Perhaps I should," she agreed almost casually.

An officer came stepping out onto the balcony, not even pausing to glance at the view but stomping over to the table and saluting sharply.

"Is this urgent?" Gan asked him. His morning was being thoroughly spoilt, he decided.

"Colonel," replied the officer, whose insignia proclaimed him a captain. "Orders directly from the Emperor."

Gan froze, goblet halfway to his lips. If there was anything that could ruin his day it was a communication direct from the capital. The Emperor could strip him of everything he now enjoyed with a single word. He took the proffered scroll carefully, as though it might be venomous, and broke the seal. A moment later he glanced up at the captain and asked, "What in the wastes is this?"

"A present from Capitas, sir," said the captain, with a hard smile. "Five hundred men for your garrison. I came ahead with my staff to prepare billets, because they'll be marching into Szar any time now, sir."

"What am I supposed to do with another five hundred soldiers?" demanded Gan. "Considering all the places in the Empire that surely need reinforcements—"

The captain actually had the gall to cut him off. "Not my business, sir. If you'll excuse me, but I need to prepare lodgings for five hundred men."

He saluted again, then turned and left without waiting for Gan's say-so.

"Someone at the capital has gone quite mad," Gan declared. "Perhaps they're having another shot at the Commonweal, and need us as a staging post. Still, since the war pushed the borders further out, we're a long way from anywhere troublesome."

Princess Maczech was still looking after the captain thoughtfully.

* * *

When the five hundred soldiers finally arrived at the gates of Szar they did not find it the cheerful, hard-working city they had been led to expect. As they marched down the Regian Way toward the palace, they saw Bee-kinden come out of their little six-sided huts, or stop the hammers of their forging, and just stand and watch. The further they went into the city, the more the numbers of the watchers grew, until there were scattered groups of fifty or sixty men and women all standing, silent and surly looking, to see them pass by.

There were no words uttered, no raised fists or shouts of defiance, just that eerie silence as though they had walked into an Ant city by mistake.

And the thought in the minds of all the citizens of Szar was, *So, it is true, then, what the strangers say.*

⁂

Sergeant Fragen and his handful of men moved idly through the great market at Szar, scowling at the locals. Something was up, Fragen knew. First that new captain had turned up with half a thousand troops, all now jostling for space within the governor's barracks. Now the order had come through that patrols were to be upped to five men each. Fragen had been used to walking the streets of Szar with just one other soldier for company. The locals were a docile enough breed. This was not like Myna or Maynes, where you could get a knife in the back if you ventured down the wrong alley alone.

A Bee-kinden youth crossed close before his path and he cuffed the boy angrily. Szar was a nice assignment for a middle-aged sergeant and now someone upstairs was trying to provoke things. That new captain, no doubt. Everything had started going wrong since he arrived. And the new soldiers, they didn't understand how things worked around here, how a man could more readily take his ease a little more. All fresh and shiny new out of the capital, they were too keen by far.

Fragen decided that there were probably a few Rekef boys amongst them, too. He knew the governor had always kept his nose clean, but perhaps those days were gone. Perhaps some other big noise from the imperial court wanted a bite of Szar. Whatever it was, it was bad news for the ordinary soldier on the street. Fragen preferred easy assignments.

He and his men meandered on between two rows of stalls, watching the Bee-kinden slip out of their way hurriedly. They were like slaves, these locals, only you didn't even have to chain them up. They had somehow enslaved themselves. Fragen grinned at the thought. When he was younger he had considered the Slave Corps as a career, but it had seemed to involve too much travel, too much dealing with dubious characters like the Scorpion-kinden. This kind of life was far better.

He stopped by a fruit stall, where a sullen-looking old man had baskets full of oranges and peaches set out in the wan sunlight. The peaches must come from the north, Fragen guessed, out of the new Dragonfly provinces. Absently, he drew a knife and dug an orange out of the pile with it, biting through the rind.

He had done so a hundred times before, but now the old man was actually glaring at him. As far as Fragen was concerned, any imperial soldier could help himself to what he wanted. It was an attitude backed up by the Empire itself.

"What?" he snarled at the old fruit seller, and the man looked down, now unwilling to meet his gaze. It helped that they were not exactly impressive physical specimens, these Bee-folk. They had broad enough shoulders, and they worked hard, but Fragen was a good five inches taller than the loftiest of them. They were an inferior breed, to be sure: a dirt-grubbing little people in their squat, many-cellared houses, and if their craftsmanship was skilled, then it was wasted on them. They should be grateful that the Empire was here to teach them about the benefits of a grander life.

"Sir," one of his men warned, in a slightly uncertain tone. Fragen looked round to see a pack of the locals standing further along the row of stalls, somewhere between a dozen and a score of them, young and middle-aged men, and even young women. They were clustered together for mutual support, but they held staves and sticks, and he saw a couple of axes in there too, and even a poleaxe near the rear.

For a second he hesitated but he was, after all, a sergeant of the Imperial Army. He could hardly back down from a mere rabble of Bee-kinden peasants. Instead he led his men straight toward them, seeing the wretches shuffle back a little, yet hold their ground.

"What's this, then?" he demanded, as he approached them. "This looks like a riotous assembly to me. Clear off, the lot of you. Get back to your work before I take it out of your hides."

He was forced to a halt. They were drawing closer together, but going nowhere. Their dark, flat faces remained inscrutable. He saw a few knuckles tighten, fists clenching on their stave hafts.

What is this? For a moment he was baffled. *Are these really locals, or have they come in from elsewhere?* The next nearest Bee-kinden were miles off in Tyrshaan and Vesserett, though, and yet the men and women of Szar had never behaved like this, never attempted to question imperial rule.

"I gave you an order!" he shouted at them. Behind him, his men had drawn their blades, and he saw that sudden show of steel send a ripple through the little band of locals. "You disperse right now or I'll make an example of you, you just watch."

He levelled his hand at them, and he saw them trying to muster courage, and failing. They would not go, yet nor could they act. He would obviously have to make their minds up for them.

With a curse, because it had been a reasonable day until then, he loosed his sting, punching one man off his feet into the arms of his fellows, with a blackened circle in the centre of his chest. The victim was dead before his friends could let him go, and by then Fragen and all his men had their hands levelled, making it plain that they would kill every man and woman of the mob unless they broke up.

One man, the man with the poleaxe, abruptly dropped his weapon and backed off, and then they were all going, suddenly running off and scattering amid the stalls.

"Right," Fragen said vaguely. He looked at the petrified stall holders about him, at the peasants with their bushels and baskets. "Someone clear that filth away," he ordered them, pointing at the corpse. "Give it to its family or throw it on the waste heap, I don't care."

"Sir!" called out one of his soldiers, more urgently this time. Fragen turned to see another band of Szaren citizens approaching, filtering between the stalls, in groups of three and four, men and women of all ages.

He saw steel there, a lot of it: enough arms and armour that at least two in three were equipped as soldiers. *Where could they . . . ?* But it was obvious enough. A few had the heavy russet-painted breastplates that the old Szaren army used to wear, but most of them were now wearing imperial armour and carrying army-issue cross-hilted short swords or crossbows or spears, all crafted in Szar by the Bee-kinden. Others had the traditional Szar axes, each broad, curved blade balanced by a wicked back-spike. Many had squat triangles of sharp bone jutting from their knuckles, the gifts of their own Art.

Fragen tried to estimate their number but stopped when he realized there must be over a hundred of them, and more still coming.

"Sir! Pull out, sir?" the soldier enquired nervously, already backing off.

"Stop where you are!" Fragen shouted at the mob. "This is an imperial city, and any attempt at resistance will be taken out of your hides and your families! You know that, surely, you stupid peasants! Now back to your jobs! Back to your factories! Who do you think you are?"

The crossbow bolt lanced through him just as he finished speaking, causing him to spit the last word out with a spray of blood. Fragen stared at the fletched end of it jutting low down in his chest, and then he toppled over.

His men, already thoroughly unsettled, launched themselves into the air, wings unfurling to dart them toward the governor's palace and the safety of the garrison.

It was the first such incident, but, by the time the soldiers had alighted on the palace balcony, it was no longer the only one.

When Colonel Gan returned to his favourite balcony again, it was under heavy guard.

Parts of Szar were already burning. He could not believe it: his beautiful, peaceful, affluent city tearing at itself like a mad animal.

"Look at this," he whispered in awe. "What has happened? Are we at war?" Were there foreign agents in the streets stirring up this dissent? Agents that could work so suddenly and efficiently as to upset two decades of absolute peace?

He felt like yelling at the city, shouting at it angrily as if it were an unreasonable child. He felt that a single slap should rightfully bring the place back in line.

"You, go fetch me the Princess," he pointed to one of his men. "And where is that new captain? None of this started until he got here!"

As the first soldier ran off, Gan saw the very same captain approaching. The man was still in his dusty armour, stepping into view while he gave some final orders to a Fly-kinden kitted in imperial uniform. The small man took flight and was heading away eastward even as the captain saluted his superior.

"What was that about?" Gan demanded suspiciously. "What game are you playing, Captain?"

"That was a message for the rest of my soldiers, Governor," the captain replied, as though it was the most natural explanation in the world.

"The rest of your . . ."

"One thousand of the imperial army, all fresh from the garrisons of Capitas," the captain confirmed.

"One thousand . . ." Gan stared at him aghast. "Captain, I demand that you tell me right now just what in the wastes you've stirred up here."

"Not I, Governor, but someone realized it was coming," the captain said. "I should introduce myself, Governor. I am Captain Berdic of the Imperial Army, also Major Berdic of the Rekef Inlander."

Gan drew in a sharp breath. *They really are everywhere.* He made sure that his posture and voice did not give any hint of his disquiet at what the man had said. "So, am I under investigation then?"

"That remains to be seen," Berdic said noncommitally. "What exactly is going on in your city, Governor?"

"You tell me!" Gan snapped at him. "Clearly you knew it was coming!"

Berdic shook his head. "Governor, there are riots everywhere on the streets of Szar. There are parts of the city now held entirely by the local insurgents, so that the north and west are closed to us until further notice. Elsewhere it is only by putting all my soldiers onto the streets that peace has been maintained. Beyond those safe limits the population of Szar is arming itself for war."

"War?" Gan was dumbfounded. "Against me?"

"Against the whole Empire." Berdic shook his head. "Even my thousand troops may not suffice if this entire city takes up arms. It has been a while, maybe, but I'd wager these people still remember how to fight. Were you yourself here for the siege of Szar, Governor?"

"No, and neither can you have been since you're far too young."

Berdic smiled without humour. "I have, however, read my histories. These Szaren Bee-kinden were fanatics in battle, true berserks. That is their Art, just as we have our stings and the Ant-kinden can speak mind to mind. That, Governor, is the barrel of firepowder we must now keep the spark from."

In spite of himself Gan felt his initial antagonism toward the man draining away, leaving a kind of cold fear behind it instead. "What do you advise?" he asked quietly.

"I heard you sending for Princess Maczech," Berdic said. "That's a good first step. Have her speak to her people. Convince her first that if Szar rises up, then the Empire will soon put it down hard. Tell her about all the men, women and children who will be strung up between pikes, the slaves sent off to other cities, the punishments meted out to her people already settled elsewhere. Tell her all of that, for it will be nothing but the truth. Now, excuse me, I must attend to the soldiers. I will leave enough men in the palace to defend it, but the rest must be a visible presence on the streets."

He marched straight off without a salute, leaving Gan biting his lip and trying to work out where it had all gone wrong.

They escorted Princess Maczech to him within minutes. He looked into her face for signs of the madness that had gripped his city, but saw none of it there. She even smiled at him.

"Princess," he said, gratefully. "The people of Szar are currently engaged on a course that can only lead to their destruction. Look down there, how they are tearing up their own lives! When the Emperor hears of this, he will have one man in twenty impaled outside the city. You must address them immediately. Will you now speak to them?"

"The Emperor already knows," said Maczech, so softly he barely heard her.

"I don't understand," was all he could reply.

"How is it that everyone knows but you, Governor?" she asked him.

He stared at her, feeling his innards twist.

"My mother is dead," she told him. "The Queen of Szar is dead, and her funeral wake will see you burn."

His mouth was open, lips moving, but at first no sounds came. Then finally he got out, "Then you are Queen! I declare you Queen now! You are still mine, so calm your people."

Her smile cut through him, flayed him. "I am nobody's," she announced, and the commotion started inside the palace itself.

"I am Szar's," she said, reaching out to touch his face. The acid of her Art seared him like a brand and he fell back, screaming. His guards started to lunge forward, but abruptly there were Bee-kinden everywhere—the palace servants, old men and old women, girls, even children: throwing themselves at the Wasp soldiers, literally hurling themselves on their swords, so that the Wasps were forced to cut them down, to burn them with their stings, or hack them to the ground with bloody blades. And meanwhile Maczech . . .

Maczech was at the balcony's edge, and wings flowered from her back. Gan reached out an arm, hand opening to scorch her, but an aged woman grabbed at it, forcing his palm against her stomach, so that when he loosed his sting it tore through her. And Maczech was gone, already in the air and dropping toward the contested streets of her city.

Gan stood at the edge of the balcony as his soldiers killed the last of his servants, with the crisp red imprint of her hand vivid on his face, staring after her and shaking with fear and pain.

TWENTY-ONE

The rain in Jerez had stopped, literally. The water was suspended in midair, a field of shimmering droplets impossibly held in place, each one with a twisted reflection of the moon glimmering in its heart. When Achaeos stepped forward, they ran against his skin or broke against his robe in a myriad dark patches.

There were people abroad this night, of course, for the locals did not mind either darkness or rain. Here they were, frozen in place with the raindrops while going about their innumerable shady errands. He paused to examine the strange Skater physiology, distinctive for those freakishly long limbs, the narrow faces with their long, pointed noses and ears.

Somewhere out there was a presence not frozen in place, a presence waiting for him to find it.

This is a dream. But there was no such thing as "just" a dream for the Moth-kinden. They had dozens of categories: dreams serendipitous and dreams intentional, dreams prophetic and dreams malign. This, however, was a dream he had been seeking for many nights, for this was a *seeing* dream. He was trying to find the Shadow Box, but had already realized that it was a hopeless search. In Jerez he was just too close to it. Its power was everywhere, leaking out into the darkness, and he could not pinpoint it.

And now this, a proper seeing dream—but to see what?

Achaeos paced through the streets of Jerez, feeling the ubiquitous rain break across his skin and dampen his hair. When he stood still he could sense movement, others abroad this same night. He was not the only one to have this dream. That meant gates had been opened, tonight, that could not be easily closed.

Should I call out? But how foolish would that be? He could not simply stand here, in this dream-Jerez, and start calling for help like a lost child.

But you called for help before.

He started in shock. That thought had not been his own.

He tried to work out whereabouts in the town he was. The lake lay to his right, its expanse of water suspended in frozen ripples, dotted near the shoreline with the further-flung natives, with great stands of reeds, with little boats that had set out on clandestine errands.

A movement again: he turned, and for a second he thought there was a woman there. He had a fleeting impression of bulging red eyes and a hunger-pinched face.

Nothing there. Only the night.

We heard you call us. We call you now.

"Who are you?" he whispered, but he already knew, and with that knowledge he did not want to meet the thing that called to him.

You waste your time. You have not come to us. You have not found us. It was the voice of the Darakyon, but fainter, hollower. The voice of the Shadow Box.

They seek us, all of them. They are grasping even now for the line we throw only to you. Little seer, little neophyte, come to us.

"Where are you?" he demanded, louder, beginning to run through the frozen rain. He had another quick glimpse of one of his pursuers, a man of his own kinden wearing a silver skullcap, his face deeply lined.

Here.

And it was there.

He tried to stop, because to touch *that* would be to die, and he skidded, feet slipping from under him, so that he fell at its . . . where it rose from the earth.

There was a shape there resembling a woman, the lean frame of a Mantis-kinden warrior, except the reaching, grasping thorns and briars had pierced her a dozen times over, arcing and leaping back and forth through her flesh, that had sprouted darts and barbs like a Thorn Bug, and prickly leaves as well. Spiny brambles ran up and down her, and through her, and they twisted her skin, which was pale and human in places but elsewhere hard and shiny like the carapace of an insect. Her arms were simultaneously a Mantis woman's with the Art-grown spines jutting from her forearms, and a mantis insect's with great folding, raptorial hooks. Her face glittered with the facets of compound eyes, and scissoring mandibles worked inside a human mouth.

I would die . . . There was no doubt of that. Achaeos scrambled back a few paces, staring. Even his eyes, which knew no darkness, could not quite take in that piecemeal, shifting figure, but he knew that it was ancient and mighty—and in pain.

"Do you . . . have a name?" he whispered.

The lips and the mandibles both worked together, but neither matched the voice that now reached him,

I was Laetrimae when I lived. You must find me, Achaeos.

"Show me," he said. "Quickly, before the others get here."

The creature nodded and strode off into the unnaturally arrested town, without another word. Achaeos choked to watch her, for it was the naked Mantis woman who took each step forward, but once her foot touched the earth the briars and vines thrust up through it to rake across her and impale her over and over, and her skin ripped open with the barbs and thorns, and healed over in the gleaming green-black exoskeleton of her kinden's beast.

He got to his feet and hurried after her, after it . . . the spirit of a Mantis woman trapped between life and death for five centuries, constantly degrading and corrupting and yet still remembering her own name.

He knew that others, many others, were presently seeking him out. The other collectors and perhaps worse, all those who had the magical skill to seize upon this open portal and follow the thread. Laetrimae was pacing ahead sedately, but each step carried her such a distance that he was forced to run even to keep her in sight, and there was perpetually a flock of shadows behind him, squabbling over his tracks.

Until the tortured Mantis-creature paused at a door, a lowly place near the lakeshore where a sprawling guesthouse sagged, its walls at conflicting angles. She grasped the doorframe with such force that the wood splintered, and thorns and creepers grew out from her into it, and split it further.

And then he knew. He looked wildly about him for landmarks. He had to remember this place, when he awoke . . .

And Laetrimae grasped him about the throat in a vice-like grip, killing spines razoring his skin, and he felt her thorny branches questing at his flesh, eager to drink his blood.

And she said only, *Remember*, and branded that place on his mind so that he would never ever forget it.

❖ ❖ ❖

Achaeos awoke with a cry, startling Tisamon, who had been keeping watch outside. The Mantis almost kicked the door off its hinges just to get in. Beyond him, Achaeos saw that it was night still, and thus the best time to go to work.

"I know where it is!" he yelled. "We need to move now."

"Who's we?" Jons Allanbridge demanded, not a ready waker at this hour.

"Myself," the Moth replied. "Tisamon, and Tynisa, and—"

"And me?" Thalric asked sardonically. "You brought me here, yet you've had precious little use of me yet."

"What about Gaved?" Tynisa started.

"No time!" Achaeos insisted. The Wasp hunter was still at Nivit's place, with the strange girl they had rescued. "Now—we go *now*. Allanbridge, you stay here. Can you get your machine ready to leave?"

"It takes hours just to fill the canopy!" the artificer informed him.

"Well, just . . . do something," Achaeos said, almost hopping from foot to foot. "But we must go, please!"

"So let's go." Tisamon pushed past him out into the night. He stopped right there, as if scenting the air. Tynisa came out after him, sensing nothing. Her hand was bleeding a little, she noticed. That wound was unusually stubborn.

Achaeos had his bow ready strung, and he pushed past her, rushing off into the street and then looking left and right as if getting his bearings. For once the rain in Jerez was petering out, although the night sky was blotted with heavy-laden clouds.

Then Achaeos was off, and at a fair pace, too. Tynisa instinctively moved when Tisamon did, and it was only after she heard the running footsteps behind them that she realized that Thalric had come with them after all.

Useless, she decided. *He can't even see in the dark.* But Thalric was keeping pace nonetheless, using what little light bled out from under the doors of drinking dens and brothels. *Another one to watch for now.* He was dangerous, and she could not trust him. *He'd sell us all in an instant.*

Achaeos kept stopping for bearings, but most of the time he did not even look around him. Whatever guide he was consulting seemed to be entirely within his head.

"Did you hear that?" he asked, but even Tisamon had heard nothing.

"We aren't alone." Achaeos stared back the way they had come, and Tynisa fought down a small sound of horror because there was a pale mark across his throat, like a jagged and irregular scar. His blank white eyes met hers for a second, and she merely shivered and shook her head. Then he was running again.

As they took off after him, Tynisa was sure that something passed overhead, but when she glanced upward, she saw nothing.

⁂

Across the city there were others suddenly awake, but with nothing in their minds but disappointment. The young seer who had somehow merited such a guide had managed to lose then.

Sykore the Mosquito-kinden was one. She had hoped to catch even a glimpse of the place, a street even, so that she could have Captain Brodan searching each house there, but the boy had been too fast for her.

It did not matter, of course, so long as it was Achaeos who actually took possession of the thing. Sykore had her agent in the seer's camp, unknown to all. The Blooded Ones of the Mosquito-kinden knew their trade, and they guarded secrets that even the Moth-kinden did not speak of.

What concerned her most was that it might not be Achaeos's hands that eventually closed about the Shadow Box. She had not been swift enough to follow, but she had a feeling that there had been one other who had. She had a sense of age and power, the musty taste in her mouth that spoke of her kind's ancient enemies, the Moth-kinden that had driven them to near extinction.

⦶ ⦶ ⦶

His name was Palearchos, and he was old now, too old for this. He who had first flown at five years old—considered unthinkably early to develop the Art—he was finding it a labour now, and even more so when he screened himself in darkness so that even a Moth-kinden's eyes could not see him.

He had come from Tharn originally, but there were now five decades between him and the Tharen halls, and it hurt. Five decades of exile, and he had laughed at them when they cast him out.

I am a Skryre, he had told them. *The world is mine to shape. I do not need you.* And he had departed for his adventures, his schemes and plots, and he had revelled in his freedom from their interference. He had travelled the world, and seen things that they had only read of.

But now he was old, and he had been sick for a long time, sick for the company of his own kind and for the carved stone halls of home.

This would be his lodestone, to bring him home. This would be his invitation, so that his bones could at least be laid in the deep sepulchres, and his name remembered. But only if he *possessed* it. The young seer, that appallingly untrained boy, could not be allowed to take it from him.

And yet somehow *it* favoured him. Palearchos felt it keenly, this loss of faith. It was not just his own people had turned against him, but their whole world, too. He would therefore have to take it in both hands and force it to recognize him. How dare the box call out to this weak young stripling, and not to him!

He was an old magician and, as such, he had spent years of his life in other people's dreams. When the Shadow Box had at last opened, and thus compromised its hiding place, he had been deft enough to pick up that trail. When the dream had snapped shut, he had leapt from the window of his meagre lodgings and begun labouring flight. It would be a race, but he was in the air whilst the fool boy remained on the ground.

But they ran fast and he was not the flier he once was. It would be close.

I am too old to start this hunt again! He felt even older now, his wings stuttering on his back. Once he would have had disciples to seize the box for him, but they had all gradually fallen away, disillusioned with his outcast status. Now only his magician's arts could furnish him with help. He tried to compose the tattered spells, born of an ancient discipline almost fallen into utter disuse these days. He reached out, seeking those wretched spirits he had bound to himself long ago, expending his dwindling strength in an effort to give them momentary form.

If you want something done . . . The strain of the flight thundered in his heart and lungs, but he kept going, with no time to lose. He was too old, too old . . .

⦶ ⦶ ⦶

Scyla's eyes snapped open in the certain knowledge that something significant had happened. She looked about the little low-ceilinged room and tried to work out what had changed.

Nothing . . . nothing . . . but yes. She was no great magician but she had developed a little of that sense, and realized there was magic afoot. *The damned box.*

It rested on the rickety little nightstand beside her. She could easily reach out and touch it, but she held back. She had the uneasy sense that it was not *precisely* where she had left it.

The shadow figure was absent, at least, although the other shadows of the room seemed to bristle with briars and sharp-edged leaves.

Damn you, Mantis-creature. She was a Spider, she reminded herself, and Spiders would always get the better of the warrior-kinden that so much hated them. She would take this tatty fistful of superstitions and sell it to the highest bidder, and thus make her fortune.

She stood up, reaching automatically for her belt with its twin knives. These days she slept fully clothed because she could not bear to be naked in the same room as the box. *It watches me.*

She allowed her senses to drift, listening out beyond the roof, the walls. For once there was no shroud of rain to drum on them.

But there had nevertheless been a sound from above . . .

Instantly she grabbed up her pack from the floor, and reached quickly for the box. Then there was a shape at the window, which came darting in. Her hand found her knife hilt and she had the weapon from its scabbard and flung across the room into the intruder in one smooth motion.

◊ ◊ ◊

Even as they came within sight of the low-built guesthouse, they saw the figure fall back from the window. It was a Moth-kinden in a grey hooded tunic just like the one Achaeos wore, now clutching at a knife buried hilt-deep in his throat. The body became lost in the shadows even as it fell, seeming to vanish there entirely. Then Thalric shouted out a warning and smashed his shoulder into Tynisa, knocking her sprawling on to the muddy ground. Achaeos and Tisamon were both running back toward them, and Tynisa had her rapier out, turning on the Wasp furiously, but the flash from his hands almost blinded her. She felt the heat of it, but it swept above and past her, and she heard a cry of pain. Then there was a second Moth-kinden spiralling down to land on hands and knees. Tynisa made to go for the injured man, but Thalric's second sting hurled him ten feet away and, as he landed, the darkness consumed him and he was gone.

She glared at Thalric and only then noticed the arrow that hung loosely at his shoulder, stopped from penetrating deeper by his armour. There was a clatter of blades at the doorway, and she saw that Tisamon was duelling.

The figure that had come down to fight him was dressed in Moth-kinden greys, an open robe fluttering over a leather cuirass. She was no Moth but a Mantis like Tisamon, her features oddly shadowy and blurred, and she had a claw on her hand to match his. Tynisa made to intervene as they circled, but Tisamon made a hissing sound to warn her that it was his fight alone. Then they were in motion again, their claws a shadowy blur in the darkness, and the Mantis woman had driven Tisamon all the way across the façade of the house before he could take the initiative from her and drive her back. Despite her keen eyes Tynisa could not even follow the dance of metal and, after two abortive dashes forward, she realized that she would not get in through either the front door or the narrow window until Tisamon was done. Achaeos, meanwhile, took to the air, vaulting over the combatants and hurtling in through another window.

The shack stood in a row along with its neighbours, wall adjoined to sloping wall, but there would be a back way in. She glanced at Thalric, who had obviously decided it was safer to stay with her, and then they were both running.

⁂

Achaeos was inside, but he had not arrived first. As soon as he pushed into the guesthouse's common room a surge of power confronted him, halting him as effectively as if he had walked into a wall.

There was a robed figure standing in the middle of the floor: an old Moth-kinden man. Achaeos could just see the edge of the silver skullcap beneath his cowl.

"Who are you?" he demanded.

"I?" The old man smiled thinly. "I am Palearchos the Skryre, but who are you, boy, that this thing calls out to you? You are nothing. A pitiful magician, a lost cause, and yet it chooses *you*. Who are you, boy?"

"I am Achaeos of Tharn."

"And who is that?" Palearchos remarked dismissively. "A nothing. A nobody."

Achaeos tried to reach for his knife but could not, his muscles now locked rigid. He had not even felt the spell fall on him.

"Now," Palearchos said, and at that moment a Spider-kinden woman burst into the room, with a pack slung over her shoulder. Achaeos stared at her, seeing a middle-aged woman without either the cosmetics or the Art he expected from her kind, a woman worn by life, with deep lines on her face, caught in surprise by this unexpected scene.

That is Scyla, Achaeos realized. He had seen her face before in what he had thought to be a death rictus, after he had put an arrow in her outside Helleron.

"And you must be the thief," Palearchos told her. "You have hidden this thing well, but not well enough. Now you will bring it to me, and, shortly after that, you will both be rid of me."

Achaeos saw the woman freeze and then her eyes and mouth tighten as she fought against the coercion of the old man's magic. He thought that she would break away from it, at first, but then she took a heavy step toward Palearchos, and he realized that she had lost. He himself tried to shatter the old Skryre's hold on him, but he could not. Palearchos held them both firm.

From outside there was a woman's cry of pain, and a moment later Tisamon burst into the room with blood smeared on his metal claw and on the spines of his arms. Palearchos rounded on him furiously, teeth bared, and Achaeos saw the Mantis flinch away from the magician's power, stumbling back out of the doorway.

We taught his kind well, to be afraid of our power, Achaeos reflected, but whilst he and the Skryre had both been distracted, someone else had taken advantage of the moment.

Scyla hunched forward, as if moving against a gale, and plunged her knife into Palearchos's ribs with all her strength. Before the old man had even begun to fall she had kicked the rear door open and was running out into the night, leaving the blade still embedded in her victim. Achaeos felt the old man's hold leach from him, and then he was running after her, wings blossoming darkly from his back.

But she was gone. When he got into the night air, she was already gone. Scyla had evaded them yet again, and she was one whose trade was made for hiding. She was gone, and the box with her. He ran down street after street, searching frantically, but she was gone.

Thalric and Tynisa had arrived when he returned. They and Tisamon were gathered about the old Moth, and Achaeos saw that Palearchos was just clinging to life.

He knelt by the old man respectfully because, in spite of everything, they were kin, and furthermore Palearchos had been a Skryre. A renegade now, Achaeos guessed, but a Skryre once.

He took the old man's hand, and the white eyes, narrowing into slits of pain, sought him out.

"You, boy . . ." came Palearchos's faint voice. "You are of Tharn, you said . . ."

"I was," said Achaeos softly. "I do not know whether I am still. That will depend on the circumstance of my return."

"I had hoped to see Tharn again," said the old Skryre. "Here on the edge of the world . . . I had thought that, if I could bring this thing to them, this prize, then perhaps they would forget what I had done, the path I had travelled. So it ends, boy. Understand this, if you travel the same road as I."

Here was a magician of power, the strongest Achaeos had ever matched skills with, dying like a beggar on the floor of some filthy Jerez guesthouse. *Is that my fate?* The thought made something inside him squirm, as though it was a future he had already seen and hidden from himself.

"They would not have taken you back," he whispered, whether to himself or Palearchos he did not know. "Not with the box, because it scared them. They want nothing to do with it. If you had come to them with it, they would have driven you away."

Palearchos let out a long, slow sigh. "So," he said. His blank eyes found Achaeos's. "And *you* will have the box, will you?"

"If I can," the young Moth confirmed. "And if it will have me."

The old man's face twisted in what Achaeos took for pain, only recognizing it as rage when too late.

"Unworthy!" spat Palearchos, and his power seared its way into Achaeos's mind, into all their minds, like red-hot metal.

Thalric dropped instantly. Without defences against the Moth's assault, the blast knocked him instantly cold, and he fell to the floor in a clatter of armour. Tisamon had begun keening, hands clasped to his face, battering himself against the walls. Achaeos heard Tynisa scream in outrage and agony.

Palearchos was now dying, on the very threshold of that final all-consuming dawn, and he was doing his best to drag them all into the fire with him. Eyes bulging, teeth bared, his face was locked in a grimace of effort. Achaeos felt the man's mental grip clawing at him frantically.

So much stronger than him, this man, but dying, his reserves drained. Achaeos mustered his will, fighting back in order to free himself. A moment's liberty was all it would take. He caught a glimpse of Tynisa clutching at her arm, racked with agony. Tisamon was roaring, slashing the air around blindly with his spines, getting uncomfortably close.

I was never good at this.

In that moment Achaeos looked straight into the old man's madly vindictive eyes and tried, not to oppose, but to twist. It was as simple as letting a stronger enemy's sword fall askew by taking a side step, where to simply block the stroke would be to have his own sword shattered. For a split second that crushing grasp slipped off him, and Achaeos lunged forward.

It was not his mind that he lunged with because, even dying, the old man's defences would have swatted him down. He jabbed one hand forward and struck the hilt of Scyla's knife as hard as he could—driving it yet deeper into Palearchos's body.

And the old man was no longer dying, but dead. A spasm of shock coursed through his body and then he was gone. Tisamon collapsed to his knees, one hand still to his head. Achaeos heard Tynisa's ragged breathing behind him, saw Thalric begin groggily to stir.

We still live, but we have gained nothing but pain this night. He had wasted the chance the ghost had given him.

Outside, the bodies of Palearchos's ghost warriors had been reclaimed by the shadows. Even the arrow that had decorated Thalric's armour was gone. Nothing was now left of the old Moth exile but his corpse.

⦶ ⦶ ⦶

They limped over to Nivit's place, to find Gaved keeping watch for them still. He was sitting with the pale Spider girl, who flinched automatically as they entered, her eyes constantly fearful. Achaeos had assumed it was Tisamon who inspired that fear, but she stared at all of them with the same blanket horror. She had never seen their kinden before, not Moth nor Wasp nor Mantis. Or so it was if her story was to be believed.

"Nothing," Thalric spat in answer to Gaved's look. He was in a foul mood and Achaeos knew it was because he did not understand, could not understand, what had been done to him. He had been talking already about suffering a sudden stab of pain from his old wound, inventing excuses for himself.

"You didn't get the box?"

"No, we did not," replied Achaeos shortly. He was feeling tired, but worse he was feeling wretched. It seemed the task was beyond him, even when he was helped all the way.

"We'll just have to take it at the auction," Gaved suggested.

"Oh, of course," Tynisa snapped at him. "Well, let us know when you actually finish your job, hunter, and track it down."

"A man could take offence at that," he replied, maddeningly calm.

"So, take offence."

"Especially when he'd searched it out already."

Achaeos could see that Gaved enjoyed the utter silence that his revelation brought. The Wasp hunter reached out and took Sef's hand. As the girl looked at him, her face lost a fraction of its fear.

He is a professional, Achaeos reminded himself. *His livelihood is information, tracking, and to do that he must be able to ask questions and gain confidence.*

"She knew all along?" he said.

"Founder Bellowern kept her close," Gaved explained. "So very close that she was right there when Scyla's factor revealed to him the meeting place. Daft girl's known it all this time."

TWENTY-TWO

Odyssa was not going to miss this place.

For a city ruled by her own people, Solarno was too much like any city of the Lowlands for her taste: mimicking the grace and delicacy of the true Spider-kinden way of life and yet never achieving it: a raft of petty politics floating precariously on a sea of squabbling, uncontrolled natives. Oh, she knew that, for many in the Spiderlands, Solarno possessed great sentimental value, but Odyssa did not see the charm, and nor did the Aldanrael, the family she served. Solarno had become merely a gamepiece, and in any game some pieces were inevitably sacrificed.

The sky was dark with clouds scudding south and east across a scarred moon. She would not see it when it arrived, but she would hear it. It was only that sound she was waiting for, that last confirmation that she had served her part in the war. Nobody would know, of course, outside the secret councils of the Aldanrael, but that was how the game was played. She was not in it for the personal glory.

She would not even be here when the fighting started, and had no wish to present herself to the colonel for a full accounting of her activities. He was no fool, that man, for all that she had played him so effortlessly. Given a chance to make his own investigation, he might even begin to suspect how his hand had been forced. No, she would not be there to suffer his recriminations. Her stay in the Rekef was now over and, as soon as she had her confirmation, she would go home to Siennis.

She wondered briefly how the Solarnese would now cope: would the rival parties coalesce or merely fragment? What would the assassin Cesta do, or the pilots? How would the other cities around the Exalsee react?

She was not cruel, in terms of how Spider-kinden were measured, which meant that she had no qualms about consigning this city and its thousands of inhabitants into the hands of an angry Empire, but at the same time she had no great wish to see it. She would wait with interest for the news to filter west.

They, none of them, understand my kind, Odyssa thought, *for they are all amateurs, playing in the shallows. Our webs are invisible to the best of them, Lowlands intelligencers and Rekef spymasters alike. The Ants think we do it for power, and the Beetles think we do it for money, and the Mantids think we do it from spite, but they none of them understand that we do what we do simply because it amuses us to live this way, and because we are jaded . . .*

There was the sound she had been waiting for: a low, slumberous droning noise up high and distant in the sky, coming with the wind from the north, as though some insect of unheard-of size was making its patient way toward the coast of the Exalsee. It was not, despite imperial claims, the largest thing ever to fly. The Beetles of the Lowlands had larger that they used for transport and freight. It was the largest thing to fly solely for war, though. The Wasps were an unimaginative people, but their artificers sometimes had a spark of poetry in their souls, and thus they had named the thing *Starnest*.

To the north, the army would have already taken the mountain-pass trading post of Toek, scattering or cowing the Scorpion-kinden who used the place as bandit's lair and tollhouse. That was a mere diversion, an afterthought, however. She was hearing the vanguard of the true assault even now.

To think that one can brew war out of only a pair of Lowlander agents and a dead Rekef officer. But the Wasps were so predictable: prod their nest enough and they would sally out of it, raging for battle. She wondered how far the colonel would search for evidence of the great enemy plot to suborn Solarno for Lowlander purposes. Once he had secured his governorship, perhaps he would not even care.

The droning was louder now, and she wondered how many in Solarno had woken to it, or paused in their nocturnal vices to listen. The sound of an airship was not so rare, hereabouts.

She only hoped that Teornis had played his part as well. He had a more complex net to cast by far, and he was only a man, after all, for all his noble blood.

It was close to dawn and she must leave now, or risk herself being caught in the web she had so carefully spun. Odyssa turned on her heel and headed for the city docks, where a small fishing boat was already waiting for her. Its captain had no idea how fortunate he was to be leaving Solarno right now for Porta Mavralis.

Odyssa smiled at that. It was her gift, she supposed, to spread good fortune wherever she went.

* * *

In Che's dream she was by a very different lake, the details of which seemed to fade in and out of focus. From somewhere there was a terrible voice calling, and she felt a tug inside her every time it cried out. That tug was what bound her to Achaeos, and she knew that the great voice was calling for him, drawing him to it.

In her dream, she was hunting desperately through hovel-lined streets, trying to find him before the voice did. The air was full of glittery little knives that she realized were raindrops, all held fixed in place. She had the sense of frantic movement all around her, as though parties unknown had broken into her dream, and were ransacking it for something they had lost.

The terrible voice called out again, closer this time, and she caught sight of a grey-robed figure flitting ahead of her, drawn helplessly closer to the monstrous summons. She cried out his name, but the beckoning voice drowned her out with its wordless yearning.

She saw, ahead, something that belonged only in dreams, and only in the worst of them, something that shifted and writhed with thorns, an abomination still recognizable as human. Achaeos was approaching it almost eagerly, and she screamed at him in warning and tried to run, but pain began to flower all about her. The raindrops had turned into wasps and they were stinging her, forcing her away. The combined hum of their wings had turned into a thunderous buzz . . .

"Che! Che! Get up, now!"

She jolted awake, staring into the darkness, forgetting for a moment that she could banish it with a thought.

She banished it instantly. There was Taki standing in the doorway, her hair wild and uncombed, her canvas flight clothes still unbuttoned after being so hastily donned.

"What?"

"Che!" the Fly-kinden shouted at her. "Get up. Get your stuff! Just do it, please!"

Then she was gone, and Che could hear behind the Fly woman's pattering footsteps the sounds of fighting: sword striking sword, the cry of someone in pain.

Inside the building.

Che was abruptly out of bed, wearing nothing more than a tunic, hearing the house of the Destiavel come under attack.

More than fighting, though . . . what am I hearing? But the fighting itself was coming closer, and it blotted out whatever telltale sound she had caught. Hastily she grabbed her artificer's leathers from the low table where the house servants had folded them, struggling into them as best she could, finding them suddenly too small, too starched, snagging her fingers in the arms. She thrust her head back into the open and began buckling the leathers at one side, the latches clumsily slipping in her grasp.

She looked up as someone appeared at her door, and froze on realizing it was not Taki. This was a Solarnese man wearing a white tunic and trousers, with a slim curved sword in his hand. The dim light from the corridor showed that his sash and flat-topped hat were dyed blue: the Crystal Standard, Genissa's political enemies.

Bare-legged still, and with her leathers flapping loose, Che dived for her sword, snagging it off the table and wrenching at it desperately, hoping that it would simply slide smoothly from its scabbard for once. It did not oblige, and the whole baldric came with it. As she lashed it sideways to free the blade, she whipped the startled man across the face with the weighted buckle of the belt.

She would never know what he might have done otherwise, but after that affront he came for her, rushing forward with his curved sword dancing in a flicker. With another great heave, she swept her own blade, sheath, baldric and all, in its way, and the strap tangled about his sword so that they were drawn in close, face to snarling face. As his hand went to his belt for his dagger, she finally drew her own sword from the tangled scabbard and ran it straight into his stomach.

She remembered to keep good hold of the hilt this time, so that his own weight pulled him off the blade. She looked toward the half open door and saw Nero standing there, still bandaged from his wound, and looking a little surprised.

"What's going on?" she panted.

"The politics hereabouts seem to have gone to the wastes overnight," he said, looking every bit as baffled as she was. "Taki wants us out of here," he added, and to Che that seemed to be as good an idea as any.

She finished dressing hurriedly and the two of them got to the main atrium of the Destiavel house without meeting any other enemies, although they had seen plenty of bodies by then. That was when Taki found them, rushing up with Dalre and a handful of the house guards at her back. "We have to leave," the Fly girl urged. "Have to get out of the house, now."

"No argument here," Nero assured her.

"What's happened? Why is the Standard attacking you?"

"The *Standard?*" Taki was gaping at her in disbelief. "You think that's what this is? That pack of clowns?"

"Then what . . . ?" Che began, but Taki was already running ahead, shouting for them to follow her.

There was still fighting at the main door, but Taki had found a side door that was clear, and they got out into the street unmolested. Instantly three of their guards were dashing off around the side of the house, to catch the attackers at the front unawares. Dalre and a solid-looking Solarnese man stayed with them.

"Taki, will you please tell me what is going on?" Che demanded. "Is this . . . is this just some other mad thing you people do every month, or something?"

"Cheerwell, do you Beetles never look *up?*" Taki asked of her sharply.

Che did look up, and a moment later she fell to her knees, hearing Nero swear at the very same sight.

There was an airship hanging over Solarno, a massive tapering thing with a rigid-framed airbag, supporting a gondola that ran almost its entire length. There was a whole constellation of lights along its sides, lamps hanging from cords that cast a surreal moon-like glow across the city, and up onto the bulging sides of the balloon itself.

The gondola was riddled with holes, a not-quite-regular pattern of openings, and for a moment Che thought that Solarno would suffer the same incendiary fate as Tark. But this was no sophisticated bomber, and the *Starnest* had only one function in war.

Things were dropping continually from the holes, and those things were fighting men, who opened their wings halfway down to glide earthward into the city in squads of twenty and fifty. The airship was full of Wasp soldiers, who were now descending on Solarno in their hundreds.

"And look there, our old friends," Taki said, pointing. Che recognized their outlines against the clouds: two other airships, which would have been huge if it had not been for the monster they were escorting, and each equipped with four pontoons for docking orthopters. Some of the flying machines had detached already, and begun gliding over the half-sleeping city.

"But what are they doing?" Che asked numbly.

"They're invading," Nero informed her. "They're seizing the city."

"And they've scared the Crystal Standard into helping them," Taki added. "But if they keep dropping that many men from that ship for much longer, they won't need any help from anyone. Come on."

"Come on where?" Che asked.

"What do you think they'll do to you when they catch you, Lowlander?" Taki demanded. "We need to get both of you out of here—to the Lowlands, to Princep, to anywhere."

"The docks?" Che suggested. "A boat?"

"No, the airfield, before it's too late," Taki insisted. "Now follow me. Nobody knows a quicker way from here to the airfield than me."

⦶ ⦶ ⦶

Solarno was a city turned mad and thrashing. A hundred yards from the Destiavel house, another noble's mansion was in flames, with fighting at its doorways so fierce that Che could not tell whether those inside were trying to escape or those outside only wanted to throw themselves into the fire. She saw no distinctive sashes on any of them, suggesting some private grudge meeting a settlement of opportunity. Everywhere the Solarnese were busy killing each other, and occasionally Wasps stood looking on, heedless of whether their supposed allies were winning or not.

All those factions, all that talk about their ruling councils, and in the end it was just a barrel of firepowder waiting for the spark. The parties of Solarno had finally been galvanized, after the initiative forced on the Crystal Standard by the Wasps had broken the fragile balance. Left to themselves, Che guessed, it would have been a simple night of violence, and then stability would follow the sunrise. But this time the Wasps would fan the flames and, in the morning, Solarno would have become an imperial city. The people at each other's throats would blink in the dawn light and realise that they were no longer free.

Taki had been leading them swift and straight, sometimes running and sometimes flying, but without warning she stopped, staring ahead of her. In front of them was some taverna or other, which did not seem to Che in any way special, except that it was being looted. The front door was broken in, with young men and women tearing up the interior in search of valuables. Che noticed the sashes of at least two parties involved, and guessed that this was again a private venture and not the work of political partisans.

"Taki?" she asked. "What is it."

"Just . . . you can't understand," the Fly said. "It's not ever going to be the same, is it?"

"You can fight the Wasps—" Che started.

"It isn't the Wasps. You really don't know. You've only been here a few days. I'm Solarnese, and this is my home. That . . . that was where we all used to meet: me and Niamedh and Amre and the rest. That was where he died."

Her half brother, Che recalled, killed by the Wasps. Now the very planks of her memories were being torn up.

"Hey now, if we're going to move we should move," said Nero edgily. He had a knife in his hand. "This is getting worse than at Tark."

"Look!" Che gasped. A flight of Wasp soldiers was feathering down two hundred yards ahead of them, blocking their path. They fell from the sky in eerie silence, glimmering wings outspread, and as the first few touched down, a handful of others ran from a side street to join them. One seemed to be giving hurried orders, pointing down alleys and indicating precise sections of the street. Che recalled Nero's suspicion about there being Wasps in Solarno with a mindlink. How else could such a tidy operation be controlled?

The Wasps were now advancing directly down the street, and as soon as they reached the looters they simply started blasting away with their stings, killing half a dozen and instantly scattering the rest. They were shouting something, and Che picked out the words, "Curfew!" and then, "Everyone inside!"

"We have to leave!" she urged Taki, and saw with a shock the tears glinting on the Fly woman's face. The expression itself remained resolute, though, and Taki glanced quickly about them and then chose a side street that would lead them around and beyond the advancing Wasp squad.

Che glanced up, as the rattle of an approaching orthopter grew loud, seeing the flying machine skim the rooftops as if keeping a watch on progress below.

"Taki, if we take off, they'll see."

"That they will!" the Fly called back.

"But they'll come to try and stop us," Che told her. "They'll fight us."

"They'll fight *me*," said Taki grimly. "And so let them!"

Further away, across the rooftops, a Solarnese fixed-wing, none that Che recognized, was making a tight circle, duelling with a Wasp orthopter in a complex tangle of loops that eventually took them both out over the Exalsee. The flying machine that had just passed overhead made a ponderous turn and set out to give its colleague aid, passing so low that it rattled the tiles of the roofs.

"What about your mistress?" Che suddenly realized. "What about Genissa? Shouldn't you be looking after her?"

"She's off already," Taki replied. "She's gone to rally the Satin Trail, and she's got guards enough. You two are *my* responsibility."

There was a slight hitch in her voice, though, which told Che that this responsibility was self-imposed.

Over them the bloated length of the *Starnest* hung like a great deformed moon, and still there were soldiers descending from it, like seeds drifting in the wind. In their squads they fell on the city, and wherever they landed they took control, killing any citizens who were under arms out on the streets, loudly proclaiming their curfew and then setting off to bring ever-greater sections of the city of Solarno under imperial rule. Despite their orders, and the mindlinked men who tried to coordinate them, they were Wasp-kinden soldiers still. With the city of Solarno now helpless against them, they broke down doors, they looted and raped. They put the brand of the Empire on yet another lesser people, and believed only that their ability to do so was all the right they needed.

⟨|⟩ ⟨|⟩ ⟨|⟩

At the airfield Taki and her charges arrived at the hangar just before the Wasps did. Even as the aviatrix went rushing for the safety of the *Esca Volenti*, they were dropping onto the airfield beyond, their ready-drawn swords glittering in the hangar lamps.

The three fugitives were not the only ones to seek sanctuary here. There were at least a dozen mechanics caught out by the airborne invasion, several others who were most likely pilots on the same mission as Taki, and some who were simply ordinary people of Solarno who had hoped that the elevated field might prove safer than the city below.

There was at least a score of Wasps spiralling down outside. Taki paused, with the cockpit of the *Esca* half open, biting her lip.

Che called out to her. "Where do we go now?"

The Fly glanced back at them, and Che realized that, in the rush of relief at seeing her machine undamaged, Taki had almost forgotten about the people she was escorting to safety. The Fly boosted herself up onto the *Esca*'s hull and turned to look at the dozen other flying machines sheltering under the hangar's roof.

"That one!" she pointed, and Che saw a squat, barrel-bodied machine, a four-vaned orthopter that could only be a cargo hauler. It looked sturdier than the *Stormcry* had been, but also slower and surely destined for the same sorry fate.

"Isn't there something fleeter?" Che demanded.

"Just get *in* it!" Taki ordered her. The first crackle of a Wasp sting sounded outside. The engineers and pilots, and whoever else was armed, had formed up on either side of the hangar door. Several of them had crossbows, and Che saw Taki reach into the *Esca*'s cockpit and come out with a little double-strung bow of her own. Nero had already unslung and tensioned his bow, and now hopped up onto the hood of a half-dismantled fixed-wing, so as to get a clear shot at the enemy. Che noticed him wince with the effort.

She hurried over to the heavy orthopter, on which the inspiring name *Cleaver* was painted in square, solid letters. It was fashioned of wood bound with iron hoops, just like a barrel, and it was bigger than she had first thought. The craft looked altogether too heavy to get off the ground. Doggedly she hauled herself up the metal rungs bolted into the side, and began to fumble at the catches.

The Wasps were trying to force their way into the hangar but they had not expected the resistance and the first volley of bolts had cut four of them down. An enterprising pilot had even brought his craft's rotary piercer about and got a volley of bolts off into the Wasps as they began to muster. In response the soldiers tried a sudden charge, hands blazing. Che saw at least two of the defenders fall back, seared with smoking wounds. There followed a brief moment of close-combat fighting, short swords against knives and the curved Solarnese blades, and then the Wasps had taken to the air again, repelled. A ragged cheer went up from the hangar's defenders but, even as their cries still echoed, there were more Wasps gathering outside, the survivors of the first assault and now a dozen more. Che was grimly certain that an alert had already gone down into the city itself, as the Wasps would want to subdue the airfields most of all.

She had the round hatch open at last, and squeezed herself through, dropping abruptly into more space than she had expected. The *Cleaver* looked so heavy from outside, but it was almost entirely hollow, a dedicated freighter. A single wooden chair, looking like it had come from someone's house, had been nailed into place behind the navigation stick, and Che saw that her only visibility would be the strips of sky viewed through two slots cut into the orthopter's nose. She was no seasoned pilot but she had surely flown more elegant machines than this in her time.

And unarmed again. Taki doesn't trust me to survive an air fight. Not that the *Cleaver* could have managed that anyway. *It must move through the air like . . . like a Beetle, I suppose.*

She put her head out of the hatch to see where Nero was, and found him crouching atop the half-finished machine. At that moment he was loosing an arrow with great concentration, sending it winging out past the defenders, only to skip across the empty ground between two Wasps. An artist he might be, she realized, but an archer he was not.

If only Achaeos was here, she thought, and then, *I hope he's coping better than this.*

Taki shot off her crossbow, and then crouched behind the *Esca* to crank the arms back. The Wasps were making progress into the building now. Too many of the Solarnese were dead or lying injured on the ground, and the remaining defenders had fallen back to take cover behind the flying machines, allowing the Wasps the shelter of the doorway. To Che's horror she saw another Wasp orthopter fly past by the hangar mouth, turning slowly in a course that would bring it in to land.

"Nero, come on!" she yelled. "Taki!"

"No use," said the Fly girl, slotting a new bolt into place. "We can't get out past them. They'd destroy the *Esca*, destroy any machine that tried to escape." She sounded fiercely bitter, thus denied the sky.

"Hold your shot!" shouted someone from immediately behind the Wasp lines. "The next man to loose will be put on a charge!"

Slowly the Wasps stopped shooting, still holding to the cover of the doorway. The defenders then cautiously followed suit.

"Is Bella Taki-Amre within?" yelled a voice, and Che recognized it as belonging to Axrad, the Wasp officer pilot.

"What do you want?" Taki called out.

"I thought I might find you here. Here or in the air." Axrad appeared at the door, silhouetted against the lamps glowing outside. It was as if he was daring the defenders to shoot him. "We have unfinished business, you and I."

Taki slowly released the tension on her crossbow. "Are you asking me to take this outside?" she asked.

"My thoughts exactly," Axrad replied.

"And what about everyone else?" she enquired.

"What about them?" His tone showed that he had not even considered this.

"I have two noncombatants here who are not part of this fight," Taki said desperately. "I wish to get them safely out of the city."

"Then they will provide the stakes," Axrad suggested. "We two shall duel, and if you happen to defeat me, our soldiers here will let everyone depart where they will, either go to fight again or go to flee. Is that clear, Sergeant?"

Che did not hear the other man's response but assumed it must have been positive.

Taki slipped the crossbow back into the *Esca*'s canopy. She headed around her machine's wing as though to see Axrad better, but when she was passing nearest to Che she said, "They won't keep their side. He means it, but I bet they don't. Once I'm in the air, get going. They'll be busy watching us, and not you."

In a louder voice, intended to carry to Axrad, she announced, "I'm all yours. Let me wheel my *Esca* onto the field, and then we'll finish our business."

TWENTY-THREE

"This must be Lowlander work," the Emperor Alvdan hissed. He stood in his nightshirt, a dozen guards gathered about him. One fist was pressed nervously into his chin. "This can be no coincidence."

"It seems likely, your Imperial Majesty," Maxin allowed. He was not going to tell the Emperor that his own agents had sensed no warning of this, nor caught any Lowlander spies. *Let us hope the Emperor asks no questions about this*, he thought. Today was not the greatest day for the Rekef and, whoever had failed in this, Maxin was the man standing here with the Emperor in the predawn darkness.

The word received had been that urgent: Major Berdic had been emphatic and his messenger insistent. The sight of the Fly-kinden man marching into the palace, in order to rouse the Emperor and the master of the Rekef, would stay with Maxin for some time. The man's face had exhibited blank fear, but he had witnessed the plight of Szar and he knew his duty. Maxin had been forced to commend him for it.

"If Szar . . . goes, how does it affect our campaign?" Alvdan asked.

"Hardly at all, your Majesty," Maxin assured him. "More in logistics than any serious threat to your power. And rest assured that Szar will not leave our hands. Somehow the news has got to these backward people that their Queen is dead." He felt a moment's qualm in saying it before the guards, by force of long habit, but the secret had somehow leaked out despite all his precautions. Another failure attributable to his Rekef, if the Emperor should enquire further. Best to keep the man's mind on the problem and not the causes of it. "Our manufacturing in the West Empire will be disrupted until these rebels are put down, of course, but we have the Beetle city of Helleron to take up the slack as far as production goes. There is really only one matter worth troubling you with, your Imperial Majesty, and that is how far to go in punishing the Bee-kinden for their audacity."

"Punishment?" Alvdan queried, the word bringing him back to himself. "Do not think that we are a fool, General. Revolution is like a disease, and just one infected city can make it spread. We read the reports, and not just yours either. We know Myna was close to an explosion last year, and simmers still. It was not so long since Maynes was also in open revolt. The whole West Empire has been turbulent since the Twelve-Year War. We do not underestimate this development, General. We cannot shrug it off. Something therefore must be done." He lowered his fist at last, glaring about him at his guards. "Something *final*, General, because we have relied on Szar for too long. The Bee people are stubborn: they submit their backs to the lash and care not."

"Your Majesty?"

Alvdan's eyes were now quite clear, and his voice quite calm. "We have preempted you, General—even before this latest news. When we first heard that Szar was stirring, we realized that they had heard. We knew that they would rise up, because she . . . she was the only thing holding them in check. When her leash finally snapped, we knew they would make their pathetic attempt at freedom. Now Colonel Gan has lost the Princess, who will become Queen, and they will all be up in arms. Your reinforcements will not hold them. No, we need a greater rod to chastise them with than just the army."

Maxin glanced sidelong at the surrounding guards but they remained carefully expressionless. The Emperor thus taking the initiative in this matter was an unwelcome development. Alvdan was no fool, but Maxin was not wholly sure of his judgment. After all, he was supposed to live on a diet of whatever Maxin fed him, and that did not always include the entire truth.

"If I may ask . . ." he began slowly.

"Oh, General, look at you!" Alvdan said, with a bright smile. "Do you think we don't need you any more? Nonsense! You are still our closest advisor. Our . . . no, we shall not quite call you brother."

I remember well what I did to your brothers, on your command, Maxin thought.

Alvdan was plainly thinking the same thing. "We would call you a friend, save that Emperors have none. You are chief amongst our servants, and you must be satisfied with that."

"An honour, your Majesty," Maxin confirmed.

"Of course. General, we now intend to make an example of Szar," Alvdan explained. "We have sent for a very special man, an executioner. He shall teach the provinces that the Empire is to be obeyed in all things, meekly and instantly. There shall be no spreading of revolution. Every city in the Empire shall know the name of Szar. It shall be the key to unlock all future revolutions, the cure for the infections of rebellion for all time to come."

"But who have you summoned, Majesty?" said Maxin, almost impatiently.

Alvdan uttered a name, and it was a moment before Maxin had rifled through his capacious memory, but then he understood.

Maxin was a killer, who had taken the life of others for his own advancement so many times, and had countless more killed on his orders, but when he now put the idea together, the latest reports, the results of the tests, he shivered a little.

Szar is about to enter the histories, he considered. *In fact the histories may be the only place left for it, when this is done.*

⟨|⟩ ⟨|⟩ ⟨|⟩

He said I would notice no change.

The mirror was a fine piece of work in the shape of an hourglass, with a frame wrought from gold and silver filigree within which the shapes of dragonflies and butterflies hung suspended on fine wires. This was some trophy from the Twelve-Year War which had ended up, when nobody else had wanted it, here in her chambers.

It showed Seda only what she had always seen: a pale-skinned and slender Wasp-kinden woman, hair coiled neatly atop her head, with a vulnerability in her gaze that had been bred by long exposure to death and the cruel whims of her brother. Seda brushed back a lock of hair, and tried to see in the glass any sign of the magic that Uctebri claimed to have imbued her with.

Magic is subtlety, he had explained. *It is better to work with the properties that exist, than seek to create something that is not there. You are already an admirable specimen of your kinden, therefore I shall merely hone your beauty.*

It struck her that nobody had ever used that word to describe her, and that it should be left to the decrepit, blood-marked Mosquito to speak it made her sad.

If Father had lived, where would I be now? Married, no doubt, though to no one of her choosing. Alvdan, her brother, had never considered matching her with anyone, not even with his closest lackey, Maxin. He feared the ambitions of any children she might produce, let alone the ambitions of any husband she took, which would grow just as inevitably.

The one blessing of the revolution, Uctebri had told her, *is that it meant magic's day had passed. Why a blessing, you may ask? You did not believe in magic before you and I met and, among your fellow Wasp-kinden, all the way through the whole Empire, there is no belief in it. Superstition, you say dismissively to yourselves: ancient myth and foolishness. Thus it is that the simplest tricks of any magician can blind all eyes, because you Apt all accept whatever happens to you as if it made some kind of mechanical sense. A man goes suddenly mad and slays his close friend and, where once he might have said, "I was enchanted," now he says, "He had it coming to him." He invents his motives after the event, and never thinks of the subtle influence that inspired him.*

Seda shivered. Perhaps the look in her eyes had changed since she met Uctebri, whatever he said about her being unchanged. They now contained a knowledge and a worry more even than she remembered. He had opened doors that were better closed.

And yet he offered her escape, from her brother and from the death sentence that was ever stayed but always present. So she had made her compact with him, and now she could not turn back.

She had applied her makeup with a care and understatement that any Spider maid might be proud of. The gown she wore was pure white, and it cinched tight at her waist to emphasize the curve of her hips and her breasts.

I am beautiful, she realized. Perhaps it was just Uctebri's spell weaving breaking through, but she saw her reflection and knew it to be true.

Her first suitor arrived shortly after: the lean and aged Gjegevey. The Woodlouse-kinden counsellor stopped in the doorway, seeing her reclining on a couch as if waiting for him. She saw that banded grey forehead of his lift in surprise.

"Your, mmn, Highness," he murmured. His eyes had narrowed and she knew he must be sensing the enchantments that Uctebri had put on her. That was why she had summoned him first.

"We have spoken before, Gjegevey," she began, "and I know you are no fool. I am sure, therefore, that you have heard rumours."

"Certain appointments have been, mmn, mentioned," the Woodlouse-kinden replied. "You know that I am, ah, fond of you. As a daughter, perhaps—or a great-granddaughter, might be, hmm, more appropriate. Yet I fear for you."

"The company I keep?" she asked him.

"Indeed. You have made, hrm, close association with a creature of more power and evil than you realize."

"You fear for my virtue?" She gestured for him to sit beside her.

"In a very real sense, your Highness." He poled himself across the room on his long legs, stilt-like with age, and lowered himself onto the couch.

"Gjegevey," she continued. "I have been as good as dead for eight years. They might as well have buried me in my father's coffin. But now I have a chance, and this man is my patron in that. If he possesses power, as you suggest, then at least he bends it to my advantage."

"And if he is evil?" the Woodlouse enquired.

"I am a princess of the Wasp Empire," she declared with pride. "My father made war on thousands and subjugated a dozen cities, and I am his daughter. What my brother has done, so would I, if I had seized the throne and not he. Let mystics plot and scheme, old man. Let it be the sacrificial knife or the sting of a common soldier, the victim makes no distinction."

He remained silent for a long time, not looking at her, and any hint of his thoughts was lost in the eternal melancholy of his face.

"Do you abandon me now?" she asked gently. "Do you find yourself poised on the brink of a descent you had not meant to undertake? You have served the Empire since before I was born, and you cannot have been naïve for so long."

"No, no," he admitted, his voice just a whisper. "Only that I had, mmn, thought perhaps that you . . . But you could not have lived in such innocence." He studied her closely then, watery eyes peering from a long, deeply lined face. "I came here to the Empire as a slave, but also as an agent for my, mmn, people, yes?

I would thus act for my own people in guiding the Empire away from us. . . . Not in these last twenty years have I so much as thought of that purpose. Whatever I might wish, I am as imperial now as any Wasp-kinden. No, I do not, hhm, abandon you. I shall serve you, if I can."

"Good. I am glad of that." And it was true. She liked Gjegevey, in a strange way. She did not think of him as a slave, barely even as a foreigner, for he had always been there. "I am to meet General Brugan shortly."

Gjegevey nodded sagely. "A wise choice, if you can, hrm, win him over. He has never been one for allies, though. You will have to work carefully on him."

With Uctebri's help, I shall win him, even so, she thought, and shivered.

General Brugan had remarkable eyes. They were pale grey, so pale as to be almost colourless, like a clear sky reflected in steel. They were the only remarkable feature about an otherwise mundane-seeming man: his fair hair was cut short like a soldier's above a heavy-jawed, brutal face, and his solid physique now running to fat about the waist. He strode in, clad in an edged tunic and leather arming jacket, and paused just inside the doorway, staring at her.

He did not look like a spymaster, but then she had met all three of the generals of the Rekef, and only Reiner did. She would soon need the Rekef, or at least some support within it. If the Rekef opposed her undividedly, then no amount of support from any other quarter would count. She could not woo General Maxin, and she had heard that General Reiner had gone to ground in the provinces, having lost out in the recent jostling for power. Her father had been careful to spread the weight of the Rekef across three separate pairs of shoulders but it was common enough knowledge that General Maxin, currently the Emperor's favourite, was not the sharing sort.

And here was General Brugan. He had been a long time off in the East Empire, long enough for people to forget about him as he went about his duties. Now he had come back, perhaps in response to Maxin's powermongering, and here he was.

He is not so bad, maybe. She could not genuinely guess at his character but he was younger than Maxin, more athletic looking than gaunt General Reiner.

"My servant said you were asking for me," he said. His voice was wary and his eyes were suspicious, but they lingered on her. She felt her heartbeat pick up slightly, not at the close attention but the thrill of being able to wield influence at last, of whatever sort.

"Your servant was correct," she replied. "It has been a long time since you were in Capitas, General, but I remember you. Will you not sit?"

"You were but . . . a child then," he said, and she revelled in that slight catch in his voice. He approached cautiously, like a man suspecting a trap. "I have been away too long, it seems."

"Or perhaps you have returned just at the right time, General," she said. The words sounded awkward to her, but they stopped him, made him blink. He looked about the room swiftly.

"We are not overheard, General, nor are we watched." A thin and whispery voice in her head made her start briefly, and then she repeated what it had told her: "save by your own followers."

"You are well informed," he noted.

"You know where I grew into a woman, General, and under what restrictions. I am as well trained as any soldier in my own particular arts of survival."

"I'll wager so," he agreed, and sat down on the couch across from her, watching her carefully.

"You are worried I am merely bait for General Maxin?" she said. She expected a harsh reaction to that name, but instead he smiled slightly, eyes still fixed on her.

"I am not," he said. "I have always had my eyes here inside the palace, whatever he may have thought. I know you are no friend of his."

"Does that mean that you trust me, General?"

"I would not be such a fool." But his voice was strangely hoarse.

"General, my brother is always in Maxin's company these days. Your eyes have witnessed that much, have they not?"

"They have indeed."

She leant toward him, wondering if Uctebri was working in his mind also. To think that she might be flirting at the same time with the cadaverous Mosquito-kinden was worse than unsettling, but she kept her mask up, moistening her lips, looking into those remarkable eyes of his and hoping not to discern a tint of red within them.

"It is your duty to detect treason, is it not?" she asked.

"As a general of the Rekef Inlander, it is."

"But treason against what, General?"

"Against the Empire, Princess Seda."

Her heart was in her mouth, but for joy, only joy, at such a grand concession. It was not only the title he gave her, a Dragonfly honour she had no true right to, but that he had named the state, and not the man: the Empire not the Emperor. She knew that Uctebri must be within his mind even now, with his unsuspected magic, but the thoughts he was teasing out from General Brugan were only those already grown there, buried deep beneath the man's sense of duty and honour. Uctebri was just bringing the hidden part of Brugan into the light, perhaps a Brugan hidden even from himself.

"Treason against the Empire is a deadly foe for all of us," she said, leaning even closer, finding him leaning in too, until mere inches separated their faces. His heavy features did not seem so coarse now, not with those shimmering metallic eyes to illuminate them. "I imagine it can occur even at the highest levels."

"At the *very* highest," he confirmed, so entranced now that he seemed a decade younger, years of harsh duties, betrayals and caution falling away from him, and she knew, just as he said it, that he was now hers.

◆ ◆ ◆

The acting governor of Helleron was beyond the social pale. He held no dinners or dances, for nobody would have attended save under duress. He went to no entertainments, lest he darken the mood by his very presence. He was like the Empire's bastard son, the Emperor's favourite half-caste artificer-king and, save for his few apprentices, he had no intimates. Except for the demands he made of Helleron's manufacturing power, he had no involvement with the city's running.

It was a storm through which blue skies could be detected, the magnates of the Council said cautiously. In the Consellar Chambers they met, as they always had before the conquest, and ordered the daily life of the city. Within those walls it was as if General Malkan had never come to visit them and, so long as they adjusted their plans to fuel Drephos's constant needs for manpower and raw materials, they were left to run the city however they chose.

It could be worse, was their hesitant thought, once their initial revulsion at the governor's heritage had worked itself out. The Wasps might easily have installed a more interfering governor, a military dictator, some greedy grafter who taxed and robbed them: a man, in short, closer to their own nature. Drephos's haughty isolation was aggravating, but it was not bad for business, and in their hearts the magnates could almost find forgiveness. *At least he leaves us alone.*

And behind even their love of money and profitable trade were the other thoughts, left unvoiced. *He is a monster, but not the worst kind of monster.* Certainly the Wasp soldiers on the streets were a touchy bunch, so there were deaths, though of nobody important. A few buildings burnt, a few small traders were executed, but this was just the result of the Wasp-kinden's natural exuberance. With a tyrannical governor constantly goading them, things could be much worse, especially for those who had more to lose.

Still, the very standoffishness of the Colonel-Auxillian inevitably bred curiosity, so the city fought over any scrap of gossip he generated. The simple news that a messenger had come to him from the capital was seized on hungrily. Drephos was a self-contained man: he staved off paperwork and managed with no constant string of orders coming in or reports going out. It was as if the Empire had thrown up its hands in despair over him, leaving him to do what he did best. Nobody else understood his work enough to dictate to him.

Until now.

For now a panting Wasp-kinden had arrived at the Consellar chambers, waving a sealed scroll at a garrison sergeant whilst blurting out the half-breed's name. Orders for the Colonel-Auxillian, straight from Capitas, absolute priority, no excuses.

He is in one of the snapbow factories, the messenger was told, and the man set off there straight away. Enough of the seals on the message were recognizable for the garrison sergeant to know the messenger had not been exaggerating his missive's importance.

⦶ ⦶ ⦶

"I am informed," said Drephos, "that the balance of the Sixth Army will be with us in a matter of tendays, bound next for Sarn. How many snapbows can you give them?" His clear tones cut through the constant clatter of the factory floor that rose up to them.

"Perhaps another two thousand," said Totho, without even needing to think about it. "We did dispatch a rail shipment not long ago, although you know what happened to that. General Malkan has sent a messenger for more to be sent by automotive convoy."

Drephos made a dismissive noise. "I am unimpressed so far by the Seventh's ability to hold on to whatever we give them. First the troop train and now, I hear, the last supply convoy was ambushed as well. Give whatever you have to the Sixth and let the generals squabble over it themselves."

Totho nodded, gazing down on his busy workers, the banks of engines that were cutting out his machine parts, rifling the barrels, casting the ammunition. He sensed, more than saw, as Drephos moved closer to him, one metal hand and one living one closing on the guardrail.

"I hear you have solved your discipline problems," the master artificer said.

"I have, sir."

There was a pause, and Totho glanced sideways at the Colonel-Auxillian, to see him staring out across the factory floor in an oddly distracted way. This was the first time that Totho had seen him in several tendays, for the man's own projects had kept Drephos entirely secluded. Behind them both, the massive form of Big Greyv the Mole Cricket-kinden made the gantry groan in protest. The man was huge, a ten-foot-tall obsidian block with fingernails like chisels, but he was Drephos's artificer of choice to work with, possessing a patience and care as impressive as his bulk. He hardly ever spoke, and Totho guessed this was another reason Drephos had chosen him for the new project.

Kaszaat, standing in the Mole Cricket's shadow, seemed infinitely fragile.

"And you have continued experimenting, of course?" Drephos prompted.

Totho had not realized that he knew. "I've been tinkering with the snapbows, sir. I've being trying to add a built-in magazine to improve the shot rate." As always, he warmed to his topic once he had started. "The problem is that use of a nailbow's spring and lever mechanism shakes the aim and therefore halves the useful range, while gravity feeding jams too often, and clockwork—"

"Is too expensive and takes too long to make," Drephos agreed, clearly pleased with his persistence.

"How . . . ?" He had not been actually ordered not to speak of it, but the shroud of secrecy about Drephos's recent researches had been so plain. "How does your own work go, sir?" Totho asked.

"How indeed," said Drephos vaguely, not being evasive but genuinely considering. "The coming war with Sarn shall be remembered, Totho. There shall be names immortalized in the histories."

If anyone survives to write them. Drephos's current strange detachment worried Totho, for normally the man was inclined to be expansive, even boastful, about his work. Now, though, he had clearly chanced on something that seemed to have shaken even his customary composure.

"Tell me, what do we work toward?" the Colonel-Auxillian asked unexpectedly.

"Sir?" Totho glanced over his shoulder at Kaszaat and Big Greyv, but neither provided any answers.

"Archetypes," Drephos said, almost too quietly to be heard. "Just as they say there is a Wasp archetype, a knowledge of which gives the Wasps their Art, and likewise with all the other kinden, so too there is a weapon archetype, Totho. Can you grasp that? A weapon of weapons where to simply grasp the hilt, to simply *possess* it, is to slay your enemies? No contest of skill needed, no inclement weather or defensive wall, but death, delivered pristine and precise."

"This . . . this is what you are working on?" Totho asked.

"We approach it, Totho. We do approach it," Drephos replied, then shook his head as though to clear it. What he might have said next was lost because just then a soldier pushed past Big Greyv and onto the gantry, with a scroll thrust out toward him. Drephos took it disdainfully and moved a little way off to read it. The reading took him a matter of seconds before he turned on the messenger with the word, "Impossible!"

"Those are your orders, sir," insisted the messenger implacably.

"I have work here," Drephos snapped at him, "and I am not finished. Go find someone else to do your dirty work."

"Not *my* work, sir. You see where this message comes from?"

Drephos looked back down at the scroll. The messenger would have noticed nothing, but Totho had known the half-breed artificer long enough to spot a slight widening of his pale eyes.

"So . . ." Some of the fight had now gone out of him. "This is absurd. What do I know of such a business? There is no option, then?"

"You have been commanded *personally*, sir," the sergeant replied smugly, and Totho knew that he was enjoying being able to snub this half-blood of superior rank. "And, if you note, you are requested to take your work along with you."

The idea, however, did not seem to appeal. For a long time, whole minutes, Drephos stared down at the summons. His mind was elsewhere, charting webs of logistics, of numbers and calculations. Totho saw his lips twitch over and over, baring his teeth at whatever task was being forced on him. Kaszaat and Big Greyv looked as blank as he. Whatever had arrived from Capitas had come without a hint of warning.

Drephos bared his teeth to emit a long hiss. "Totho, find me a deputy from the engineering corps to take over here."

"Sir?" Totho stammered out. *Is it about me? Am I named in that note?*

"You're coming with me. I'm taking the whole team, the projects, the lot. We shall also take the big freight automotives. I shall continue to work even on the way there. My work is much too valuable to disrupt."

"But where are we going, sir?" Totho asked him.

"Inform the others, too," Drephos said. "We are sent to Szar."

Kaszaat's face remained a mask. Totho could only guess at the turmoil beneath.

TWENTY-FOUR

Lake Limnia at night, and the great expanse of moonlit water was chopped into a million pieces by the drizzle, blotched by swathes of reed, pockmarked by the shadows of Skater rafts and boats. It should have been nobody's idea of a pleasant sight.

Tisamon stood by the shores of Lake Limnia and stared across the rain-dappled waters. Every so often the clouds grew ragged enough that a despairing slice of moon could claw itself free of them, and then its clean, pure light appeared in the lake itself as only a pockmarked, ruined reflection, a face given over to disease and ruin.

If I was a seer, what omens would I make from this?

Around him the Skater-kinden padded on their stilting errands and left him be. Of course there might be other travellers about tonight. Any moment a patrol of Wasps could troop down between the leaning shacks, with arrest or execution on their minds. In truth, he had hoped for that, but for once the Empire was maddeningly absent and his claw remained unbloodied.

He was alone with his thoughts, and he was finding that uncomfortable, because it meant they strayed from the business at hand: the mysterious box and the forthcoming auction. When his mind was let free, to coast like a kite in the gusting wind, it asked the same question, *What is* she *doing now?* It had been a long time since Tisamon had been plagued with such imaginings: seeing pearlescent armour, a long, straight sword held perfectly poised, the curving talons of her thumbs, the elemental grace of her fighting stance. *Is even this place, even the great distance I have placed between us, not enough?* He had hoped that she would recede in his mind, along with the miles that separated them, but he might as well have brought Felise Mienn with him.

She is so swift, so deadly! How close she came to killing me, when first we met. There had been no other, not for a long time, to challenge him so. There had only ever been *one* other who had set his blood racing in the clash of blades.

Atryssa, forgive me.

The spectre of Tynisa's dead mother walked before him then, with accusing eyes. Mantids paired for life, it was well known, and many were those who then lived out long years as widow or widower. *For life* always, and he had bound himself to Atryssa, given her a child even, and now . . . *this*, *her*.

He tried to banish the Dragonfly duellist from his mind, but he could no more do so than he could defeat her, blade to blade. She danced and dodged, and was before him still. He felt like weeping, and then he felt like killing.

"Hoi, Mantis," came a voice, and he whirled about, his claw raised to strike. Nivit had hailed him from a safe distance, though, the bald, angular little man regarding him cautiously.

"Is it time?" Tisamon demanded.

"They sent me to fetch you," the Skater told him, his expression carefully neutral. "Anyone else looking out over the lake like that, I'd say there's a girl in it, but you, I reckon you're just thinking about cutting throats, am I right?"

"Nothing other," Tisamon agreed shortly, and stalked past the other man toward the looming hulk of the grounded *Buoyant Maiden.*

⦶ ⦶ ⦶

Scyla had hidden her auction house the best way possible, by having it come into being only when she was ready to sell. Founder Bellowern and the other buyers had discovered only days before, through a succession of bewildered Skater messengers, where their prize could be won.

Bellowern was not the only one to have fallen by the wayside. It seemed that collecting the exotic was a hazardous business within the Empire. Nivit guessed that almost half the wealthy and the powerful who had come to Jerez in response to Scyla's invitation were no longer there. Some, like Palearchos and Founder Bellowern, were dead. Others had been arrested by the Wasps in the Empire's own futile attempts to find the box. More had simply decided that the stakes were not worth the gain.

Out on the lake, in the gathering dusk, Scyla's gold now paid for a diligent team of Skater-kinden to piece together a great raft. They towed mats of reeds behind their rowboats or sailing dinghies, thus to haul the pieces of Scyla's theatre into place. There were walls, too, a building as grand as any native home in Jerez taking shape entirely out on the water. Soon the buyers would congregate there, narrow-eyed in suspicion of each other. Soon Scyla would have to appear there too, from behind whatever mask she was wearing, and present them with the Shadow Box.

Achaeos and the others sat in Nivit's office and planned. Jons Allanbridge had already gone to stoke up the *Buoyant Maiden*, now repaired in readiness for the anticipated getaway.

"Out on the lake," said Thalric.

"Of course out on the lake," Nivit told him. "Business on the lake's standard practice hereabouts. I'd have thought you'd known that."

Thalric sought out Sef, who was sitting close to Gaved. Despite rumours in town of strange hunters abroad at night, there had been no further attempt to take her. "The lake," Thalric said, "has become different to me now. What is the plan, then?"

"Scyla will have guards," Tisamon said, "or lookouts, anyway. If nothing else, she has no guarantee that one of her genuine buyers will not try force. Water is not our element, not the best for employing stealth."

Nivit's expression said *Speak for yourself*, but he glanced about at the others, waiting.

"Also, we cannot rely on magic," Achaeos remarked. Thalric snorted at that, and even Tynisa looked doubtful, but the Moth shrugged. "It matters not. There are other magicians, even Scyla herself. Believe in it or not, we cannot hide ourselves with magic."

"Nivit, can you get a boat?" Thalric asked.

"No problem there. We've all kinds of boats here. What're you doing with it? My people can see better in the dark than you think. You'll never get a boat there without them spotting you."

"I don't need to." The Wasp smiled drily. "This is old spycraft for you: when you can't go round the back, just walk in the front door as though you were meant to be there. Why is everyone punting out to this place, anyway?"

"Because they want the box," Tynisa said, seeing where he was leading.

"Well then, why not us? Only Scyla herself will know who's genuine. There will be other buyers coming out of the woodwork that nobody else has guessed at. So let's just walk in."

"And then?" Gaved asked dubiously.

"And then we take it," Thalric said. "You people want this thing, whatever it is? Then we take it. We kill Scyla, and we kill anyone else who gets in the way." His smile broadened in the pause that followed. "Squeamish, after all? Then be thankful you have someone of my profession here. This is nothing new to me. I'll wager your Stenwold Maker would agree, and I see Master Mantis there is nodding. This is just an operation like any other. We have arrived, made our plans, gathered our information, and now the operation must be wrapped up, the objective recovered, and then we're gone into the night. The Rekef Outlander do it every day."

"You're a cold one," Tynisa said. Thalric's smile only acknowledged her statement.

"He's right," said Tisamon. "This is how it must be."

"And if they won't let us in armed?" Tynisa asked. "I wouldn't, if I were Scyla."

Thalric displayed his open hands to her. "When am I unarmed?"

"You're assuming that we'll trust you with this business," she told him. "You're not one of us, Thalric. You're only here because your own people want you dead."

His smile withered. "And be glad they do, because you need me. I'm hard where the rest of you are soft, with your Collegium-bred philosophy and humanity! Not to mention the mystic, and the renegade who won't face up to his own birthright."

At that, Gaved had a slight smile, a fighting smile. His fingers flexed, but Thalric sneered at him.

"Tisamon's got steel, perhaps, but he won't stab a man in the back like I will, and right now you need a bastard like me."

He looked from face to face, challenging them to gainsay him. "I know, you don't trust me. Do you think that wounds me? I'm Rekef, so I'm used to being distrusted."

"How happy you must be," Tynisa told him.

"I'm not seeing many smiles in this room tonight, and if you have another way of doing this, just tell me. Will you have your Beetle pilot coast his airship in, and hope they mistake it for the moon? Will you swim beneath the raft and bore a tunnel up through it with your knife? Mine is the only way that gets us in safely, and it must be by my own choice of men or none at all."

"*Your* choice?" Tynisa demanded.

"This is a high-risk enterprise," Thalric said. "If there is an assault from without, Scyla will instantly flee, and you will neither catch her nor even recognize her. But if we are present there amongst the buyers, what can she do? To achieve her aim she must stand before them, she must present the box. At my signal we will strike. Speed and surprise will win the day for us. I shall take the box and fly to shore, while the rest will cover my retreat, and then make the best escape they can."

"One change to your plan," Tynisa interupted, holding his gaze.

"Name it."

"Gaved takes the box. You fight your way out with us, Thalric."

"Agreed." He did not hesitate a moment. "You and the Mantis and Gaved are to be my cadre."

"I'm flattered," said Gaved acidly, and then Sef tugged at his collar.

"Not on to the lake," she whispered. "You must not."

"It's you they're looking for, not us, these aquatics of yours," Thalric reminded her. She glared at him and, to Thalric's obvious amusement, the other Wasp put a protective arm about her shoulders.

"We won't be away long," Gaved reassured her, "and he's right. Just sit tight here."

"They are still searching for me," she said, biting her lip.

"If you are so fearful of being caught, why have you not left already?" Tisamon demanded harshly. He had never shown either interest or sympathy for the Spider girl.

"Left?" Sef breathed, as if there was a world of horror in that world.

"Left for where?" Gaved challenged. "She's already on the brink—the very shore—of her world. Where does she know to go to?"

"And the great hunter will look after her, will he? Bit of a career reversal, isn't it?" Thalric asked him.

Gaved's look was humourless. "I will do this job because I promised Master Maker I would. After that, Rekef, I'm gone, and if I take her with me, is it any business of yours?"

⦶ ⦶ ⦶

Gaved had worked in and around Jerez long enough to learn how to row, and now he powered the little boat forward with heavy strokes, staring fixedly at the receding shore beyond Tisamon and Tynisa, his passengers.

Sef he had entrusted to Nivit's care. He did not want to even think of that but, of course, rowing freed the mind wonderfully for random thought. *Nivit and I, we go back years.* Nivit was primarily a businessman, though, and Gaved was being sentimental. *We should sell her back to the lake creatures and be done with it.*

He liked to think that, in his line of work, the people he hunted down were criminals, the wicked and the reckless, on the run from justice. Even when he knew that they were merely escaped slaves or fugitives from the torturing hands of the Rekef, he still liked to think that. He liked to feel he was in the right.

Thalric, an uncomfortable presence in the boat's bows at Gaved's back, would see "right" as identical to being in the Empire's interest, or at least would have done so before his fall from grace. Gaved, however, had never quite been able to coax himself into that point of view, and that was why he had spent his life working twice as hard as any imperial soldier just to put a distance between himself and the Emperor.

But I always came back, he reflected. It was hard for a Wasp to make a living alone. Somehow he had always found that the contracts he undertook bore the imperial seal somewhere upon them.

At least Sef was no concern of the Empire. *And I will not sell her to the lake Beetles, and I must hope that Nivit is not tempted to do it. I must hope that our long friendship buys me that indulgence.* He had even ceded Nivit all of the gold Stenwold had paid. *I am a fool in so many ways.*

Thalric stared out across the misty lake, seeing the occasional flurry as one of the locals skimmed across its surface on some private business. The dark seemed to bring them out in numbers, but then they were creatures best suited to shady business—and so was Scyla. She had always preferred to deal under cover of darkness, preferring to hide even her changeable features.

He wondered if she could even recall what she truly looked like. Did she have to reassemble her own true face in the mirror first thing every morning, and did it then drift, from day to day?

We shall have a reckoning, you and I, he decided. He had nothing personal against Scyla but such a reckoning looked very likely, and it should be himself, Thalric, who dealt with her. He, who had once run her as an agent of the Wasp Empire, should be the one to bring her down.

The great raft was looming up and he saw several boats there already, with Skater-kinden men standing ready to take the painter line. He put a hand on Gaved's shoulder to halt his rowing, and the little craft coasted the remaining feet until two Skaters captured its prow with their long arms and tied it up. He put a few coins into their hands, good Helleron Centrals that the Skaters preferred to imperial currency. With that evidence of his prosperity from Stenwold's diminishing bounty, no further questions would be asked of him. It was exactly as he had hoped. Scyla had chosen this place for its advantages, but she must live with its drawbacks too.

He stepped onto the raft, with only a flick of his wings to keep his balance, feeling the twinge of pain in his side still from where Daklan had stabbed him outside Collegium. He normally prided himself on healing quickly, but just now he was glad to have been able to heal at all.

Scyla had miscalculated, of course, in her lust for secrecy. She thought she had her buyers where she wanted them. She believed herself safe from intrusion out here on the lake, far from any shore.

Thalric smiled a little at that thought. He did not know how well Spider-kinden could swim but he knew that they could not fly. Let her squirm how she liked, there would be no swift escape for Scyla this time.

The others were joining him cautiously on the raft, looking not like a rich buyer's retinue but more like nervous thieves. Tynisa was pressing at her hand, and he saw that the narrow wound there had opened up yet again.

* * *

To Lieutenant Brodan, it seemed clear that the murky waters of the lake were a metaphor for where his career was going. *I must be mad, to be out here with this wretched woman. Certainly my men all think I'm mad.* He could see it in their faces. They had followed him out here, in the rain and cold, but they were heartily regretting it. They had been kicking their heels amongst the reeds for two hours now, waiting in the dark. Occasionally a Skater would spot them as it padded across the choppy waters, and Brodan was sure they would all be laughing at the skulking Wasp-kinden.

It's just like the last time. He remembered many fruitless nights spent on or by this lake, trying to intercept contraband that seemed to be able to turn invisible at will. Pillaged loot from the Commonweal had been flooding through Jerez: whole libraries of books, armouries of mail and weapons, treasure beyond counting, yet Brodan's investigators had found such a tiny fragment of it that he suspected the Skaters had given it up out of pity.

And there she was, the source of all his problems. The wretched old creature was perched on a hummock and staring out at the water. She seemed to be whispering to herself and he wondered if *she* was actually mad, this whole business her private lunacy. That would explain a great deal.

"I am losing patience," Brodan said through gritted teeth. "There is nothing for us in this."

"*Losing* patience? Were you ever gifted with that?" Sykore said sharply, and Brodan unsheathed his sword in automatic response. She turned her head to stare at him, baring her pointed teeth in a hideous grin. "Oh, perhaps one day, Captain, but not on this night. You need me this night." Her red eyes fixed him to the spot. "They are out there now, as is the box—that and your renegade Thalric, and his Lowlander friends, all together."

Brodan looked back at his carefully picked handful of men, all of them crouching alongside him in the reeds by the lakeside. They were his strongest fliers, able to make the distance between here and the raft while keeping their strength for the fight. "Then what are we waiting for?" he demanded. "If there is any chance you know what you're talking about, then we should go right now. We take the box, we leave. And meanwhile we kill anyone who looks at us funny."

"And which is the holder of the box? You cannot tell and, while you decide, she will shift and change and lose you," Sykore told him flatly. "No, you have no chance until the box is revealed. I shall know immediately, and then you shall go and take it. Not until then, or it shall be lost in the mist. I am afraid, Captain, that you must swallow your impatience and wait."

"You go too far," he murmured, but he knew he would not follow up the implied threat.

Sykore glanced back to the lake, baring her teeth in a derisive smile. She had seen into his mind, seen how desperate he was to bring back the box, not for any great purpose but for fear of failure. Like so many of these Wasp-kinden, Brodan lived a life entirely dictated by fear—fear of his superiors' wrath, his peers' plots and his inferiors' ambitions. *If only the conquered could see their conquerors as I have, they would rise up in revolt tomorrow*, she thought. *And they would die for it. Fear is the greatest motivator, fear can make a man fearless, so long as you make him fear you more than he fears any other.*

Sykore settled back, heedless of the cold and damp, waiting for that magical moment when the Spider-kinden magician would produce the box out into the chill air, whereupon she would send Brodan and his people across the waters.

⦃⦄ ⦃⦄ ⦃⦄

"They're coming."

Nivit froze midway through checking an account, watching Sef's head come up and scent the air like an animal. Something guilty twitched inside him. He had just been thinking about the lake people and their promised bounty.

"They ain't coming," he said dismissively.

"They are," she whispered. "I can smell them."

Nivit snorted. "Oh, right, what do these water Beetles smell like, then? Other than rotting reeds and lake water?"

"They smell of the poisons they use in order to work their machines."

Nivit stared at her. "Girl, that almost made some sense," he said, and put the tablet down to approach the door.

"I can smell them," her hollow voice continued, like dead leaves, "as they can scent me and, though I have done all my kinden know to hide myself, yet they have found me at last . . ."

Now that she had mentioned it there was indeed the faintest whiff of something bitter and oily on the air, and Nivit tried to remember whether he had smelled the same when those lake people actually had come to his door.

"You . . . you stay away from the door, why don't you," he ordered, and Sef obediently retreated away into the darkest recesses of his hut. *Obediently*, that was the key, and what made her story ring even a little true. She did exactly what she was told, like no Spider ever did, even a Spider that had been enslaved. *This could be easier than I might hope for.*

He went sideways from the door over to one of his spy holes, peering out into the darkened street outside. *Girl's probably imagining the whole thing.*

Even as the thought came to him, he spotted a little pacing shadow, a long-legged, hunch-backed figure a little like a Skater, yet not to be confused with them. He jumped to another spy hole and found himself looking at a broad-shouldered form whose outline showed the armour plainly. Two other large figures were waiting in the shadows nearby.

What had she called the man—Saltwheel? A good Beetle name, but these lake dwellers were not good Beetles. Now Saltwheel, or whoever, was coming over.

Coming about the bounty. Got the money on him, like as not.

Nivit glanced back at the Spider girl, grimacing. Gaved was always too soft, and he'd taken a shine to Sef, but in time he would get over it.

The Skater smiled bitterly. *I am going to curse myself for this in the morning . . .*

But it was very clear to him how the land lay just now. The lake dwellers wanted her back, but not because she was their slave—a class uncared for and unmourned from what Sef had said. They wanted her back simply because she could tell people about them.

And so can I.

Once they had Sef, they would have no need of Nivit either, not to pay for his services, nor to suffer to talk.

He rushed to the rear of the shack, grabbing Sef's wrist and dragging her into Skrit's room. Here was one of his secrets, and he saw Skrit staring up blearily at him from her bed, wondering what was going on. However Nivit was not interested in her but in the crank at the back.

Most Skaters were not Apt: they were not a technical race, not given to artifice or machines. There was a minority that were, though, and this was growing, generation to generation, as Nivit's kinden slowly underwent a transformation.

Nivit himself was Apt, and he wound the crank as hard as his skinny arms could manage, till a hatch opened smoothly and silently onto a back alley, even as a mailed fist rapped sharply at his door.

He cocked his head at the new-gaping entrance, and Sef stared at him wide-eyed.

"Go," he hissed, but it took Skrit pushing her forward before she realized what he meant. She looked almost more frightened to be forced to escape alone than on first scenting the lake dwellers coming.

Then Nivit was padding for the door to confront them, one hand close to his knife hilt.

⁂

Sef shivered in the sudden cold outside, finding herself on an unfamiliar street in this horrible abscess of a community, alone out under the great dark sky. She was glad for the darkness, both because it would hide her from the servants of Master Saltwheel (although not the master himself, for he was proof against the dark) and because she had not yet adjusted to being exposed beneath the sun and her skin burnt red after only a touch of it.

But here she was lost on the streets of this place called Jerez, and somewhere, somewhere close, there would be Master Saltwheel and his servants and slaves patiently groping through the dark for her, and she had nowhere to go. The Skater

Nivit had just cast her out. The land Beetle Bellowern was now dead, his floating palace sacked and his men slain. She was utterly alone.

She had fled the lake because she had known that there was a world out there beyond its skin. She had never guessed how different it would be, though. So many times she had gone from the jewelled envelope of Scolaris up to the lake top, to gather air and to spy on the busy, spindly-limbed surface dwellers. She had never guessed how difficult it would be to actually *live* out here, with the heat and the cold, the wind and the appalling void of the sky above. She wanted now to go home to the great arched chambers of Scolaris, but that was one place she could never return to. In the final analysis there was only one star in the sky for her to aim at.

She must find Gaved. He could protect her from the great world and from Master Saltwheel. He had gone across the waters, though, with those others: the stern killer and his Spider-kinden student, and the angry one who hated everyone and himself as well. They had gone to get something that they needed.

She looked down and found that her feet had taken her, without pause or thought, straight to the edge of the lake.

Down there, in the fathoms of darkness, hung the bright cities of her people, stolen from them by the Beetle-kinden, but she was just one missing slave. With the precautions she had taken to mask her scent they would not realize at once that she had returned to the water. If she was swift, she could find Gaved before they detected her, and Saltwheel would still be searching the streets of Jerez, never guessing that she had returned to the waters.

She sloughed off the clothes they had given her, as she would need to swim swiftly tonight. She called on her Art, surrounding herself with a coat of air to sustain her.

A moment later she had sliced into the water in a smooth dive, carrying a silvery sheen with her, next to her skin. With a speed that no land dweller could have matched she darted off into the water, heading further out into the lake.

⟨|⟩ ⟨|⟩ ⟨|⟩

"My next lot, then," the Fly-kinden called, in a high voice cutting across the crowd. "A folio of plans and designs with alchemical notation dated to within fifty years either side of the Pathic revolution. Their condition is poor, but more than six in ten of the papers can be read. This item is believed to originate in what is now Collegium and represents the much-debated 'Illuminate' school of semi-scientific thought."

He strutted back and forth on his raised platform while a Skater-kinden servant carefully displayed a crumbling leather folder that rested on a silver tray under the cover of a parasol. To Thalric it looked like much of nothing, but there was a quickening of interest amid the small crowd of buyers and their servants. He had not considered that this would be an auction of more than one treasure, but he realised now that Scyla had been stockpiling a few choice acquisitions for just such an opportunity as this, and therefore perhaps many of the buyers now here would have no interest in the box whatsoever.

Scyla herself had made no appearance, or at least not that he could tell. Her proxy here was doing a fair enough job of managing the bidding, encouraging, jibing, pushing up the price, whilst she presumably waited around in the shadows somewhere, hiding behind someone else's face.

Bidding on the mouldering documents was brisk, and Thalric wondered what truths they might contain, what secrets of the days when the artificer's craft was just dragging itself out of the morass of mysticism. No doubt it would moulder afresh in the private collection of one of these plutarchs here. He saw a pair of Beetle-kinden bidding against each other stolidly, with single fingers lifted to advise the auctioneer, and a Wasp-kinden woman as well, elegant and grey, her eyes sharp. He wondered whether she was somehow wealthy in her own right, or whether she was merely acting as factor for another.

Probably the documents, however old they looked, were faked. That seemed more than likely, for few here had any idea just how easily Scyla could make herself disappear, so that there would be no direct repercussions for her.

The rain was starting up: the venue had a waxed canvas extended over the auctioneer's podium to keep his wares dry, but the buyers themselves sat on benches out on the open deck. Thalric guessed that this temporary raft might not have supported the weight of a roof and, anyway, the Skaters were not known for the solidity of their architecture.

He had not noticed which, but one of the Beetles had become the lucky owner of the documents, so the Fly-kinden, dressed as elaborately as any servant to Spider-kinden princesses, now trotted out the next lot: an enamelled silver statue in the Commonweal style, beautiful in execution and pornographic in subject matter, with the acrobatic couple's wings delicately picked out in gold lace.

Thalric passed his eyes over the audience for the hundredth time. There was no possibility of finding Scyla in it. He had thought that their association would have allowed him to spot . . . just something, some gesture, some stance, but she was as anonymous as a corpse on a battlefield, lost amongst the flesh of others. There were plenty of others, too, for nobody had been so trusting as to come here alone. Thalric's little band had therefore attracted no comment.

The Fly continued his banter, up on his stage, the treasures of the world passing through his hands. Some of the bidders left, their one goal attained or thwarted. Most were staying on. There was a feeling—Thalric caught the scent of it—of anticipation, as if they had only been marking time for something greater.

"My final lot, then," announced the Fly-kinden, and Thalric went cold within himself. It was not the proprietary tone, which the Fly had been using throughout, or the fact that the small wooden box had not been presented by a servant but plucked straight from a pocket. Rather it was something in the tilt of the head, that way of standing, that was familiar to Thalric. He was trained to recognize such things, to see through disguises.

But this? It was impossible, and yet he knew it for sure. His instincts were certain, absolute. He had seen her before in the shape of a Beetle, in the shape of a Wasp-kinden officer, in the shape of a Mynan woman. She had even infiltrated Stenwold's people in the form of one of his own students, and yet Maker had not known.

He leant back so that he could speak to the others without being overheard. They were all on edge from the moment the Shadow Box had been displayed.

"This curiously carved casket," the Fly-kinden was saying, "of Mantis-kinden workmanship, very delicately done, and dating to around the time of the Pathic revolution, or very shortly thereafter, this item is believed to be of great ritual significance to the Inapt people of that period."

"It's *her*," hissed Thalric. "The Fly is her, I swear."

"Her or not," Tisamon said, "it is time." His claw was already on his arm, without his having had any chance to buckle it on. It was a night of wild ideas and Thalric's veins sang *magic* to him. Tonight he could believe in anything.

He turned back to the Fly—to Scyla—who was concluding her patter. They were all unarmed here aside from the Mantis, but he was a Wasp. He sensed Tisamon behind him, about to make his lunge.

Let the Mantis take the brunt, he decided, waiting for the man's move.

It came, but not from Tisamon.

The Wasp-kinden woman, whose identity Thalric never discovered, suddenly shouted out a command and half a dozen men from various points across the room suddenly lurched forward. They had appeared to be there as independent buyers or their retinues, but abruptly they were as one and drawing knives, rushing for the stage.

Someone else wants to receive the prize without the price.

Thalric did not need to make a signal. Tisamon was already past him, knocking over a Beetle-kinden collector in his rush forward. His claw swept in and he caught the nearest knifeman in the back, without even slowing, vaulting the stricken man's body. Another knife wielder was wrestling with some other guard in the crowd, who had misinterpreted the move as an attack on his master. Three had gained the edge of the podium but one had already fallen, stabbed by one of Scyla's hired locals.

The Fly-kinden, Scyla in poise but utterly otherwise in looks, surged forward as the first man, a Beetle-kinden, tried to jump on to the platform. Thalric only saw her hand go in, but there was a knife in it when it withdrew, and the man fell backward. Then the Fly spotted Tisamon.

Thalric saw, actually *saw*, the shape of her face flicker, and he wondered whether she recognized who Tisamon was, or whether Spiders, for all their disdain, still had nightmares about the avenging Mantis warrior who might come for them one day.

Two of her Skaters tried to get in Tisamon's way, with short swords in hand and wearing cuirasses of metal scales, but he had killed the both of them swifter than Thalric could follow him. A third was struck down by Gaved's sting as it lanced over the heads of the crowd, which was becoming more chaotic by the moment. The wiser collectors were making their exits, and others were trying to send their men against the stage itself, or against those who were trying to attack it. With hands and elbows, Tynisa was fighting her way through the crowd to take the box as soon as Scyla was brought down. Thalric used his wings to wrench him up from the throng, feeling a stab of pain for his efforts, but he needed a clear shot.

Abruptly the air itself was busy. He saw a dozen Wasp soldiers appear from over the lake, their crackling sting bolts already lancing the crowd. Some of these newcomers landed close to Tisamon on the stage, but he killed them even as they touched down and before they realized their error. Tynisa dispatched another one, lancing a borrowed knife between the armour plates covering the man's back. Thalric felt his sting burning the palm of his hand in anticipation, but he held it back.

They are still my people, he thought, and besides he had other prey tonight.

Scyla had backed away, her outline shimmering slightly, until the wall that backed the auction house platform was at her shoulder blades. *Trapped*, thought Thalric, *trapped by her own devices*. A true Fly-kinden would not have left herself so helpless.

He watched Tisamon lunge for her. And she flew. Thalric almost fell out of the air himself, because she was most definitely Scyla, her Spider face shifting in and out amongst those Fly-kinden features, but she had stolen the Fly wings along with the face, darted over the startled Tisamon's head and out into the night.

Thalric let out a shout of anger, at his own assumptions as much as at her escape, and Scyla turned to look round, despite herself. Their eyes met briefly with a shock of recognition.

He felt the blast of his sting searing his palm as it departed, saw it strike the Fly-kinden body, that became abruptly a Spider-kinden body, and send it spinning, unfit for the air, doubled over about the charred hole he had torn in her. The box dropped out of her fingers, and he was instantly rushing for it, aware that Gaved was on the wing too, the pair of them converging and yet too slow, both of them already too late.

The impact of his shot had knocked her past the rear wall of the auction place, beyond the edge of the raft. Thalric saw Gaved pass in front of him, watched Scyla's body tumble from the borrowed air into the water, to vanish into the darkness.

And the box went too and, although it was wood, it was gone in seconds, as though whatever it contained was as heavy as stones.

For a second, Thalric was tempted to dive after it, into the chill of Lake Limnia, but he and Gaved both pulled themselves up before breaking the surface.

Thalric swore to himself. He did not care about the box itself, but failure cut deeply. He circled back over the auction raft, which was rapidly emptying, and saw Tisamon and Tynisa finish off a handful of patrons who had decided that the pair were to blame for whatever had happened.

He was just returning back over the wall when he heard Gaved cry out in astonishment. Looking back, he saw something emerging from the water—something that was slender and pale.

It was an arm. Out of context, it took him far too long to realize that. It was an arm and hand, and the hand was clutching the Shadow Box. It was Sef, reaching out from the water as one born to it, her hand, her arm, then her head sliding out into the air till she was exposed up to her waist in a shock of spray. She cried something wordless—or a word the Wasps did not know—and Gaved dipped in the air toward her.

* * *

There was something beneath her, Gaved saw. Although it was dark, he saw a great pale bulk rising beneath her. He had no way of knowing how huge, how far away, but it seemed to have scythe-like jaws, and it loomed larger and larger as it rushed upward to pluck her from the water's surface.

Gaved dived down without a second thought, and she held out the box to him, her eyes wide with terror.

"Yours!" she cried to him, and he pitched lower, almost skimming the surface, and caught at her arm near the elbow. She was slippery with lake water, but he locked his fingers into her flesh and wrenched her upward, his wings powering as hard as they could. He was a good flier, Gaved, since his profession demanded it, chasing fugitives for miles at a time, but he was not so good as to be able to drag her entirely from the water. Still, he fought to do so, hauling her up and up, fighting against her weight, as she cried out from the ferocity of his grip. The Shadow Box teetered in her hand.

She was now out past her hips, then her knees, and he felt his lungs straining, the constant beating of his wings sapping his strength. Then she was clear, toes leaving the water's meniscus, and he strove for height—enough height to escape the monstrous thing that was coming behind.

Abruptly she felt lighter and he was climbing rapidly. For a mad second Gaved feared that the thing in the water had scissored her in half, but then he saw that someone else had caught at her other arm. To his lasting surprise he saw Thalric, face white with the effort but flying upward and upward, staring fixedly ahead as if at some goal.

Gaved followed his line of sight and saw the most beautiful thing he could have wished for: Jons Allanbridge's *Buoyant Maiden* bobbing over the lake like a second moon, with a rope ladder already unreeling toward them. He saw Achaeos at the rail, a drawn bow in his hands, the arrow leaping past him to dart down at the surface of the lake—only to be intercepted by one of the Wasp soldiers who had been swooping in behind. The man howled, not badly hurt but knocked aside by the impact, dropping in a moment of shock toward the broken water.

Looking back, Gaved saw the giant thing from the lake break the surface briefly, beside the auction raft, and he would never know whether it was some colossal insect or perhaps—just perhaps—some device of the lake dwellers below. The question would remain to haunt his nightmares.

Then they were at the ladder, and Sef grasped for it with her free hand and scrambled up it as swiftly as she could. Gaved cast himself up, too, and over the rail, falling to his knee, utterly drained. Thalric dropped down beside him, clutching at his side and grimacing in agony.

"Thank you," Gaved said to him.

"She had the box," Thalric replied flatly, through pain-gritted teeth.

Down at the auction raft, Tisamon and Tynisa had made bloody work of Brodan's soldiers, and anyone else who tried to challenge them. Most of the buyers had now fled, by boat or by air, so when the *Buoyant Maiden* steered herself ponderously over the raft, with ladder unfurled, there was none to contest their exit.

TWENTY-FIVE

Coming home was the sweetest thing he had ever done: Stenwold, sitting in the train carriage with Arianna huddled against him, her head resting on his rounded shoulder; and poor bandaged Sperra sleeping fitfully, sprawled across a whole seat. On the other side of the carriage, Parops sat with his head tilted back, his eyes closed: whether asleep or awake, Stenwold could not tell.

But it was Collegium the rail automotive was pulling into, with the white spires of the College visible over the rooftops, with the dome of the Amphiophos right before them. Collegium, that jewel of civilization, which planned no invasions nor tortures.

He had given the new weapon of the age into every hand that wished it. He would now be responsible for the world that such an act created. It was easy for the great and mighty to sign their scraps of parchment, easier still at the time to convince themselves that they intended to keep their word. Expedience was the great eroder of moral stances.

Arianna made a vague sound and pressed closer in against him, so he put a protective arm about her as he stared bleakly out of the unshuttered carriage window.

Collegium had not changed so much, but it had definitely changed. There were companies of militia drilling in what had been the Stockhowell Market: awkward-looking Beetle men and women, and various other kinden as well, some in heavy chain mail and others in breastplates worn over heavy buff jackets. He saw halberd heads weave and dip, and crossbows shouldered in mock threat.

He kept looking until he saw a company equipped with the slender, silvery snapbows, industriously going through the motions of loading them. He had operated one himself, of course, and he knew how effortless it was. The weapon seemed to have severed all connection between the hand that pulled the trigger and the man that fell dead twenty or fifty yards away.

But it is a Beetle weapon, he realized. Totho had wrought it well. The Wasps were still half savage, without the iron discipline of the Ants or the broader understanding of his own people. The Wasp-kinden were well suited to skirmish and raid, to vicious assaults and angry reprisals. His own people were civilized and coolheaded and, because of that, they would take to this new weapon as nobody else. *In time*, he thought, *we could conquer the world with our reason and our good intentions. Let us hope that our future shall not suffer from the Wasps teaching us how to make war.*

The train shuddered to a slow stop, at which Parops reopened his eyes.

"Returning to your men, Commander?" Stenwold asked him.

"I have spoken to them. They will march," Parops agreed. "We will go because, if Sarn falls, the entire Lowlands will tumble with it. It will be the first time, I think, that the Ants of our two cities have fought side by side."

"Long may it last," said Stenwold, though he knew that it would not.

He took Sperra straight to the College infirmary, where the most skilled of Collegium's doctors would do what they could for her. She clutched at his sleeve briefly and he felt ill at having failed her.

⦶ ⦶ ⦶

The next morning he received visitors almost as soon as he was dressed. His drawing room was busy with a dozen functionaries, including two faces he knew: Lineo Thadspar, still Speaker for the Assembly of Collegium, and Teornis of the Aldanrael, who had returned to Collegium on the same train.

He studied their faces, the lined old Beetle and the smooth, agelessly handsome Spider-kinden, and he noted their expressions.

"I take it the news is not good."

"No worse than expected," said Thadspar wryly. "We knew it would come to this."

"The Wasps are marching," Stenwold predicted.

"They are, indeed. You have a source in Helleron, you will be surprised to discover, who has been sending missives by Fly-kinden messengers. He signs himself Woodbuilder."

Stenwold nodded. That would be the Helleron councillor Greenwise Artector, of course, who would be in a position to see a great deal of what went on in that occupied city. He did not speak the name, though, for his old habits as an intelligencer suggested it might be unwise. "What does this Woodbuilder have to say now?"

"That a new army is marching from Helleron—the Sixth, known as the Hive. It marches to reinforce General Malkan's Seventh, and from there on to Sarn."

"As you say, nothing unexpected."

"And he says also that he has given information to the Lord of the Wastes, so that that gentleman may impede the Wasps as best he may. I must confess I can make nothing of that message."

"I think we can, Master Thadspar," said Teornis. "Stenwold, you have a protégé, do you not, who is making a name for himself in Sarn and out in the wilderness."

Stenwold nodded slowly. "Salma, yes."

"Apparently this Lord of the Wastes has been attacking Wasp supply convoys," Thadspar explained. "Presumably aided by your Woodbuilder's intelligence. All very complex."

"It boils down to the same thing, though," said Stenwold. "Sarn must be defended, and the attack will come sooner rather than later. Do we have men we can send to Sarn's aid, just as Sarn has aided us?"

"I'm sure we do, although I have not had much involvement with the merchant companies . . ." Thadspar started.

"Perhaps you should not commit your soldiers so hastily," interrupted Teornis. "I fear you are not the only man with news, Master Thadspar."

The two Beetles stared at him, waiting.

"I am afraid there is another Wasp army, numbering I know not what, presently marching south from Asta to Tark. Word has come from the Dryclaw to my people, and was waiting here for me when I arrived. From Tark, I imagine that force will move on westward down the coast, through Merro and Egel, through Kes and the Felyal, and then to here. The Wasps want Collegium, as you already know."

"And your people, what will they do?" Stenwold asked him.

Teornis smiled. "Why, Master Maker, I have no idea. We are an independent, free-spirited lot. We might do anything." The smile hardened. "There are webs, though, of my own spinning, and we shall see what has been caught in them, by and by."

⦶ ⦶ ⦶

The *Esca Volenti*'s clockwork motor started with a whir of cogs, and a handful of the mechanics began nervously to wheel the orthopter out past the Wasps, onto the field. Beyond it, Lieutenant Axrad's own vessel was lazily powering up its wings with a deep grumble of its mineral-oil engine. The Wasp pilot threw Taki a salute before dropping into his cockpit and closing the hatch.

Back in the hangar, Che had already returned to the *Cleaver*, familiarizing herself with the controls. She heard Nero climb in behind her.

"We're going as soon as Taki's taken off," she told him.

"Right you are." He stood behind her, holding on to the back of her seat. "Roomy, this, but you can't see a thing," he decided, and she heard the hatch rattle again as he opened it for a better view.

Out on the field, the *Esca*'s two wings began working their way up to a blur, and then the flying machine's legs left the ground and slowly folded in, taking off on the vertical. Axrad's heavier machine prowled stubbornly along the airstrip before slowly lifting into the air with great beats of its own four-wing arrangement. Then they were both aloft, spiralling about one another, gaining height: for a moment the sole point of concentration for everyone watching below.

Even when the *Cleaver*'s engines started up, there was a moment before anyone could distinguish the new sound from the two fliers receding above. Then the barrel-bodied fixed-wing was already moving, dragged forward by its propellers and advancing slowly on the open hangar mouth. It was an unlovely thing in motion but it was solidly built, shouldering aside a smaller vessel that obstructed it in its hunt for the sky. Che felt it lurch and kick as she wrestled with the controls. It was taking all her strength just to keep the craft on a straight line.

I hope it's livelier than this when it gets into the air.

"Che!" Nero called down to her. "Trouble!"

The Wasps had noticed them, at last, or perhaps they had simply begun loosing their stings on the bystanding mechanics. Che saw several of the Solarnese go down. A moment later the *Cleaver*'s hull thrummed under scorching impacts.

This is a wooden flier, Che reflected, *with an engine that burns combustible fuel.* She needed to get into the air immediately, where the swift passage of the *Cleaver* would hopefully put out any burning on the exterior.

A moment later she was sprawling on the floor beside the pilot's chair, rubbing at her eyes and coughing at the smoke, whilst the narrow view-slit had acquired a charred new edge. She smelt burning wood behind her, and heard Nero clattering down from the hatch to stamp out whatever smouldering had started. The *Cleaver* was listing noticeably to the left, as she flung herself back into the seat, hauling at the sticks. By now the Wasps were concentrating their attacks, and the whole front of the *Cleaver* shook alarmingly. She heard wood splinter with the force of the combined assault and knew that, however solid her vessel looked, it was just like a wooden eggshell if they could apply enough pressure.

She threw the engine into a faster gear, and felt the cumbersome fixed-wing surge forward. At the same time the attacks fell off, becoming fewer and fewer, and she assumed that the Wasps must be throwing themselves out of the way. She peered cautiously through the damaged slot, hoping that she was still on course.

To her astonishment the Wasps were all dead. She caught a glimpse of their scattered bodies, a good dozen of them at least, before they vanished beneath her view. There was only one man standing there, a gaunt silhouette against the lights of the landing field. As the *Cleaver* advanced on him, he boldly waited until the last moment before ducking under its wing, and it was then that their eyes met for just a brief moment.

Cesta, the assassin.

Could Tisamon have done that? Che wondered. *Killed so many, so swiftly?* She imagined those little throwing blades flicking out in twos and threes, the Wasps falling before they even realized they were being attacked.

Thank you, Cesta, she thought, and then she was fully out in the open air, and she sent the much-abused fixed-wing over the airfield, putting everything she could crank into the engine, feeling the wheels lift from the earth just a moment before the *Cleaver* overran the edge of the field, teetering over the city of Solarno below, and then it flew.

⁂

Axrad broke away from the spiral, casting his flier over the city in a long, broad arc that gave Taki plenty of time to see that he had begun the fight.

Honour amongst Wasps, whatever next? She threw the nimbler *Esca* away from him, flitting back above the airfield, noticing the ponderous bulk of the *Cleaver* at last get airborne.

Good, she thought. *Now I fight.* She thumbed the lever that uncovered the rotating piercer and then danced across the sky, looking for Axrad.

He was above her already, swinging in from the sun, just as a good pilot should. She knew that he would do so and the *Esca* danced aside from the glittering lance of his repeating ballistae, and then ascended straight up without warning, as poised in flight as any insect, so that Axrad swept right past her, pulling furiously out of his dive even as he did. She put the *Esca* through three turns, spinning in the air, and shot at him, the piercer clunking over and over, sending its long bolts past his cockpit. But he was better than that, for he dropped his orthopter almost to street level, so that she had to stop shooting for fear of killing some innocent citizen. He then fell out of sight altogether, hidden momentarily by the roofs of Solarno, and no doubt terrifying anyone who happened to be passing beneath.

Taki soared overhead, searching for him, and without warning his flier flurried up out of the city, repeater firing as fast as it could reload itself. A bolt tore a narrow hole in her wing before she rolled the *Esca* out of the way, and then they were chasing over the rooftops, him directly behind her, and Taki always keeping out of the line of his ballistae.

She then saw that they did not have the sky to themselves. There were at least a dozen other vessels, of differing loyalties, flying above Solarno in this dawning light. Dragon fighting! The phrase had reached Solarno from the people of Princep Exilla, who enacted the same kind of duels astride their insect mounts, but it was among the pilots of Solarno that the practice had found its true home.

And amongst the Wasps, too, because Axrad was proving very, very good.

In a moment the city was gone from beneath them, and Taki was skittering across the dawn-reddened expanse of the Exalsee. *Can't get too far from Che*, she realized, and threw in one of her special tricks. It would normally be impossible in anything other than a heliopter, except that of course the *Esca Volenti* was special, endowed as it was with its little beating halteres that gave it more control and balance than any other man-made thing around that inland sea. With a single flip of her wings the *Esca* was simply facing the other way, for a moment speeding impossibly backward, away from the city, until the wings wrestled the orthopter to a momentarily stuttering halt and then plunged, back toward Axrad.

She held down the trigger, watching the piercer bolts flash toward him, striking sparks wherever they struck. His orthopter faltered in the air and seemed to drop, and then she had passed over it, and a craning look backward showed her that he was gaining height again, holed but not damaged, swinging in behind her doggedly.

She was enjoying herself now. Her city was being invaded, and her friends were fleeing it and needed her help and guidance, but it had been a long time since anyone had given her a run as good as this.

Then Axrad was soaring away, deliberately breaking off his pursuit, and she was instantly looking about her, toward all quarters of the sky.

There they were: two more Wasp orthopters angling in, lining up on her. Axrad had given her the only warning that he could, and she now turned to aim at them, flying right in their faces with her rotary piercer blazing, firepowder spitting the bolts at them far faster than any ballista's tensioned string.

These were not Axrad, however, just Wasp pilots with basic training and no great skill. One of them dropped almost instantly, so swiftly that she must have struck straight through the cockpit and killed the pilot. The other swung wide of her, but she turned within his turn and her rotary raked the underside of his craft, scoring several hits but nothing that hampered him.

The Wasp orthopter rocked again, as another craft flashed past before them, causing both Taki and the Wasp pilot to haul their fliers out of the way. It was a big, armoured fixed-wing, and Taki knew it at once for Scobraan's resilient ship, the *Mayfly Prolonged*. She dropped aside and saw the Wasp pilot take the bait, pointing on the apparently ponderous ship and shooting. A few of the bolts stuck, but most simply rattled from the *Mayfly*'s armour, and the Wasp was getting so close, so very close. Taki herself would never have fallen for it, but then she was already wise to the tricks Scobraan kept concealed within the *Mayfly*'s plated hull.

It was over before she knew it, the Wasp orthopter ripping into fragments without warning, as Scobraan's incendiary struck it and exploded, and for a hundred yards the blazing wreck continued on its course before losing its integrity and dropping from the sky.

Then the *Mayfly Prolonged* shook and shuddered, and Taki saw a line of holes being punched in its wing as Axrad dived on it from above. Scobraan threw the fixed-wing in a straight dash across the rooftops, trying to use his engine's greater power to offset the nimbler orthopter, and Taki put the *Esca* pointedly behind

Axrad, not shooting, but inviting attention. He broke off his chase of the *Mayfly* and made a surprisingly tight turn, so that they were for a moment heading straight at one another.

Perhaps he thought that she would be the first to flinch, but they shot at the same time, repeating ballista against rotary piercer, bolts flashing swiftly between them.

There were very few Fly-kinden amongst the fighting pilots, as the martial mindset did not sit well with their race. Those there were, though, were very good indeed. They were lighter than other pilots, so they could fly defter machines. Their reflexes were second to none.

A bolt ripped into the *Esca*'s hull, ripping apart the canvas and narrowly missing the motor beyond. Another gashed the right wing, and a third shuddered to a halt somewhere amid the folded landing legs. She saw the impact of her piercer bolt even before the ensuing flash of flames, and knew that she had landed a auccessful strike in Axrad's engine. Only then did she dart aside, pulling the *Esca* round in a steep turn to come back and check what she had done.

She spotted Axrad's machine by the smoke, as she came back to it, saw it falter in the air, and held off her attack. Before she had flown past, she spotted the man as he climbed out of his cockpit and jumped, wings flaring to catch him, and she found that she was glad he had survived.

Another time, she told herself, and went to look for Che and Nero in the *Cleaver*.

⟐ ⟐ ⟐

They found land at Porta Mavralis, the sole outpost of the Spiderlands situated on the shores of the Exalsee. Here Taki called on favours and raised credit in the name of the Destiavel, and obtained barrels of mineral oil for the *Cleaver* and a winding engine that the *Cleaver* could carry to retension the *Esca Volenti*'s clockwork engine.

"We must fly to your home, you and I," Taki explained to them. "We have a common cause now."

"Ain't you worried about what's going on back home?" Nero asked her.

"I shall return to Solarno, but first I want to see your war. I want to understand what the Wasps are fighting. And perhaps I want to find help for us."

While she was waiting for her fuel, the battered bulk of Scobraan's *Mayfly Prolonged* dragged itself into port, listing dangerously. The burly Solarnese had only bad news: names of the pilots killed or fled, the well-known buildings burnt, the imperial flag of black and gold unfurled over the houses of the great and the good.

Taki asked him to come with them, but he declined. "I'm for Chasme," he told her. "That's where we're mustering and gathering allies. We will strike back when time gives us our chance. I hear Niamedh made it out, was heading to Princep Exilla even. The sea . . ." He stopped for a moment, shuddering with fatigue and emotion. "The whole cursed Exalsee will run red with blood before those Wasp bastards get away with what they've just done."

Taki nodded vigorously. "Hold out, then," she said. "Che and me, we're going for help. Her people, who are fighting the Wasps already, they'll see us right, I'm sure. It's a long haul, but for a couple of fliers it's not so very long. I'll be back, Scobraan. So you just wait for me."

Che's return to Collegium was so much faster than the sea voyage of her departure. The *Cleaver* might have been slow for a fixed-wing but it danced effortlessly down the coast, and Nero had found a hatch in the underside to peer from, and call out landmarks for navigation.

"There's Kes," he said at one point. "Looks like a navy gathering there. Wonder how far away the Empire is right now."

At last, and after many stops to refuel and rewind, they had sight of Collegium. Che was leading the way with the *Esca* following docilely behind, and Che wondered how Taki was taking it. She was so far from her home now, seeing more of the world in this frantic flight than she had witnessed in her whole life. The Exalsee and its independent cities lay far behind them now.

⦁ ⦁ ⦁

There were more lines on Stenwold's face than she remembered, and his greeting was full of simple joy at seeing her so well when others were not.

"Uncle Sten, this is . . ." Che paused to get the complicated name right, "te Schola Taki-Amre, an aviatrix of Solarno. Taki, this is my uncle, Stenwold Maker."

Taki squinted up at the bulky Beetle. "You're the one who set her onto our city, are you?"

"I am sorry for your loss, but you know we all fight the same enemy now," Stenwold told her. "The Wasps will acknowledge no borders or limits to their ambition."

"Yeah, well, I saw that all right," Taki said. She kept blinking about her at the buildings of the College, so very different from the red-roofed houses of Solarno. "Sieur Maker, I mean to return to my city soon, and I'd be glad of whatever you could spare me. Consider: the more trouble the Wasps get from Solarno, the more their attention is taken off you, right?"

In reply to that, Stenwold took her to see Teornis, and Che explained haltingly that their mission had failed. Instead of allies they had found only another Wasp conquest.

Teornis had merely nodded sympathetically.

"It may not be so hopeless as you think," he said gently. "After all, Solarno is a Spider city—not Spiderlands, perhaps, but it has a sentimental place in the hearts of many of my people. If things get so very bad, they say to one another at home, there is always Solarno to retreat to. Solarno is a place where my people can play their games in miniature, for smaller stakes, so I rather think that there are some who might take its invasion poorly. Perhaps this will finally motivate some of the Aristoi families to take a stance on the issue of the Empire."

Stenwold had been watching him closely as he spoke and, with those last words, something seemed to break through on Teornis's face, some little window onto the mind that lay within. Stenwold was not sure whether he had been shown it deliberately, or caught that rarest of things, an unguarded thought from a Spider mind, but it seemed to him that Teornis was privately delighted with the news that Che had brought.

⟨|⟩ ⟨|⟩ ⟨|⟩

And then, five days later, while the Assembly was still collating news of Wasp military movements, the *Buoyant Maiden* was sighted drifting toward Collegium.

They were all there to greet it, even Sperra, who had found herself able to fly a little the day before, just a dozen yards before exhausting herself. Jons Allanbridge's airship touched down with unusual solemnity aboard, though, and the faces of its passengers were dour.

Tynisa was first out, and it was to Che she went.

"I'm sorry," she said, trembling, almost falling into her foster sister's arms. "Che, I'm so very sorry."

TWENTY-SIX

Night brought no peace to the shores of Lake Limnia. The slap and ripple of the water was underscored by the chirr and buzz of a thousand insects that raised a racket enough to drown out anything that had happened further out on the water.

Every so often the water would take one of their chorus, either by the flier's own clumsiness or through the predatory skills of some lake dweller. There would be a deep plunk punctuating the nocturnal serenade, a few errant ripples not caused by wind or weather, then no more.

Then something more substantial struck the water near its edge, raising a great sheet of spray that battered against the reeds. For a second there was nothing but the waves washing back and forth, and then something was crawling out of the shallows, dragging itself through the mud, tearing at the lakeside vegetation for purchase. The insect choir was joined by the gasping and choking sound of a man fighting for life.

And then stillness, save for his ragged breath. His wings had failed him at the end, but close enough to shore that the water had not claimed him. He had stretched himself out there with his feet still in the lake, every muscle strained, his wounds burning with a slow fire.

Lieutenant Brodan lay on the lakeshore and felt out the extent of his injuries. The Mantis had scored a long gash across his right arm and side, raking him with pain, but it had only sliced shallowly over his ribs and not cut into anything vital. He lay still and tried to breathe, wondering if life was even worth it now that he had failed the Rekef. Better to die, surely, than face whatever repercussions his superiors would dredge up for him.

His men were dead, every one of them. Only a superior prudence garnered from experience had kept him alive, and that would prove a double-edged sword when the accounts came to be tallied.

There was a rustle nearby and he craned his neck to see the shabby, shrouded form of Sykore picking his way toward him. He tried to stretch an arm out toward her, to burn her for her betrayal, but she hissed at him disdainfully, planting the end of her walking stick on his chest, causing an agony so severe that he nearly passed out.

"Foolish," she said. "Foolish Wasp. Fool of a Rekef. Can you accomplish nothing by yourself?"

He glared at her, furious but impotent. The haggard creature sighed and removed her stick from him, baring her pointed teeth in annoyance. "We must have the box. You only want it for your silly games, but my master *needs* it. He shall have it. I shall save you and your reputation, Lieutenant Brodan, since it falls to me." Sykore hissed. "I shall risk more this night than I would like to but, just as you, I must account to my superiors, and their punishments for failure throw the devices of your Rekef into shadow."

"What are you going to do?" Brodan got out.

"You would not understand," Sykore told him. "Nor would you believe." Inwardly, she steeled herself. Spying on the Spider-kinden girl was easy enough, thus seeing the world through the link of blood that she had forged. How much could she borrow, though? How far could she take it? Could she hold the Spider long enough to have her bring the box?

She thought not. The link had become fragile and, besides, the Moth seer would surely detect it if she borrowed so heavily.

She must expose herself, her own body, to danger. None of her kind relished that, for by nature they were lurkers in the shadows. She was loathe to risk so many decades of precious life in such an attempt, but the tools available to her were now few. She had only her own hands with which to take the box.

"Await me near here," she told Brodan. "I shall come to you with the box, if I can."

He stared at her sullenly, mistrustfully. She scowled at his ingratitude.

"I shall save you, Lieutenant," she told him flatly, "both from your own stupidity and the wrath of your lords. Think simply of that." And with that she was hobbling off into the night.

◆ ◆ ◆

The *Buoyant Maiden* had received a few new scars from Wasp sting shot, most notably a smashed steering vane that had made even their return to Jerez problematic, and so Allanbridge had taken her away for emergency repairs. The next morning would see them sailing for Collegium, leaving this sodden town behind them at last.

They would not be sorry to leave it.

"For me," Gaved informed them, "this is as far as I go. I won't be on the airship with you tomorrow." Sef was cradled in one arm, wrapped in an ill-fitting robe that Nivit had somehow been able to procure.

Nivit regarded his old partner doubtfully. "No way you can keep her here," he pointed out.

"Not here," Gaved agreed. "We'll find somewhere, though. Somewhere . . . somewhere beside some lake that has no cities in it."

Nivit chuckled scratchily. "Never thought I'd see you become smitten."

Gaved shrugged. "I'm just sick of the life, Nivit. I need a break from it."

"You'll be back at it, wherever you go. You're a hunter born."

Sadly, Gaved agreed that it was probably true.

Nivit's offices were getting crowded now. Thalric was asleep, or feigning it, recovering from the stress he had put on his wound, having commandeered Nivit's own bed. Tisamon sat in one corner, perhaps meditating, perhaps just keeping an eye on the two Wasps. A frown on her face, Tynisa was bandaging her hand, which was bleeding yet again. Achaeos watched her until she met his gaze, then he gave up on looking at anything else within the shack but the object he held in his hand.

Shadow Box. Box of Shadows. Soul of the Darakyon.

He had not expected it to be so beautiful, so very elegant, its surface intricate and twisted, wrought of unknown wood, layer on layer of carvings, so that within the outermost cage of briars there were deeper and deeper details to be discerned, creatures and trees and mere suggestions of form. Form and *movement*.

He blinked, he whose eyes knew no darkness. Yet here it was, this mythical concept he had heard so much about but never seen, for there was no box within the carvings, no core to it at all but merely a darkness at the box's heart. His seer's senses were blinded by it, a caged piece of night that was likewise to magic as staring directly at the sun was to the eye, so great and potent that it could not be properly viewed.

What am I to do with this, now I have it? What would the Wasps have done with it, ignorant as they were of the magical arts?

What indeed? Was there merely some demented collector in the Wasp Empire, some man of great political power and no true knowledge, who had somehow set his heart on this thing that held the death of an age within it? Or perhaps . . .

Perhaps someone in the Empire truly understood what it was. A Wasp magician? Surely that was impossible.

In the shadows of magic, however, there was so little that was impossible.

The Wasps intended to use the box. He was sure of it, irrationally, without being able to give a reason. This was no mere collector's toy. They *wanted* it. But how did one use it? What did one do with the Shadow Box? Holding it within his hands now, he realized that it had never been made with any *purpose*. It had never been made at all. No craftsman's hands had added that wealth of shifting detail. It had formed from the very death of the Darakyon, shaped itself out of hate and pain and failure.

Use it.

If the Wasps wished to use it, that meant it could be used. And the Wasps did not have it, because he held it in his hands. He, Achaeos, pawn of the Darakyon, he had reclaimed it for the forest and the ghosts, but why should he himself not use it? What blows could be struck with this relic, against the Empire?

It seemed to him that there was now another with them, there in Nivit's home. Some shadow-thing hidden from him, but lurking at the edge of his senses.

Use it.

His hands played over the box, gripping it, feeling the endlessly reiterated features. How else would one use a box?

He came to his senses suddenly: becoming aware of himself and what he was about to do. His mind was already issuing the countermand but, before he could recover his self-possession, his traitor hands had acted.

He opened the box.

⟨|⟩ ⟨|⟩ ⟨|⟩

Darkness came flooding out.

⟨|⟩ ⟨|⟩ ⟨|⟩

The walls were twisting, inward, downward, all knotted and thorny, and he was falling, drowning, a world opening about him . . .

⟨|⟩ ⟨|⟩ ⟨|⟩

Sef screamed, clutching at her head, but Gaved was bewildered, seeing nothing. Tisamon had leapt to his feet, claw ready on his hand . . .

⟨|⟩ ⟨|⟩ ⟨|⟩

The world was made of knotted, diseased trees, thorned, running awry with briars, leprous with fungi, and the space between the trees was darkness and shadows and yet more trees and he waited for the jump, the snap taking him back into Nivit's dingy little hut, but it did not happen.

Achaeos climbed to his feet, and saw his hands were empty and the box was gone.

No. I am within it.

The prison of the Darakyon, home of all the horrors that warped place could muster, and he was now inside it.

He turned all about, breath issuing swift and ragged, but he was alone, all alone . . .

Is this it? Am I here *now? Forever?*

"I am Achaeos, Seer of Tharn," he declared, choking on his own voice. "I demand that you acknowledge me."

We acknowledge you.

But this was not the great voice of the Darakyon, only the voice of the creature from his dream.

"Laetrimae!" He turned.

She was there, a Mantis-kinden maid possessed of their lean, angular beauty, and dressed now in the carapace-steel armour of centuries ago, looking fair and pale and terrible.

What have you done? She approached him, picking her way through tortured ground that writhed and contorted all around them. *You have opened the box. No other has ever dared to come here.*

"I am here." *I cannot admit weakness now, because she is Mantis, and she would kill me.* "I have followed the commands of the Darakyon. What would you have of me?"

She raised a hand, and he flinched, expecting thorns, but it was live, warm skin held against his cheek, and then she leant down and kissed him, briefly but passionately, on the lips, engaging his white eyes with her own.

You, little neophyte? she mocked. *We want nothing of you. You are not the one.*

And, despite himself, he let out a cry when the thorns and spines burst bloodily from her skin, ripping her apart, goring her through and through, the arcing, piercing and repiercing briars, and the jagged chitin that ripped through her armour and turned it to rust. And he heard—

"Achaeos!"

A voice from behind him. A real, live voice. Staggering back from Laetrimae, he turned to see Tynisa struggling toward him, brandishing her rapier in her hand. The sword gleamed with a green-white light, and he saw an answering gleam from deeper within the trees.

"Oh," he said slowly, because he had not appreciated the true scale of the problem.

"What in the wastes is going on?" Tynisa demanded. He looked back to Laetrimae, but the Mantis creature had gone, fading into smoke the moment he glanced away from her.

"I . . . may have made a mistake," he stuttered. She gaped at him and he recalled how she had been brought up by dull Beetle-kinden. She looked as though she was on the very brink of going mad.

"Achaeos, we were in Nivit's. We . . . *Where are we now?*"

"Calm. Be calm," he told her. Small help, as he sounded less than calm himself. Here now was the other gleaming light, striding out of the broken darkness: Tisamon with his claw blazing, his eyes locked on Achaeos.

"Magician, what have you done?" he asked. "Where have you brought us?"

"Can you not tell?" Achaeos asked of him. "You of all people? We are in the heart of the Darakyon, Tisamon. We are inside the Shadow Box."

Tisamon stopped, and Achaeos saw his throat work silently, his eyes widen. *He knows at least enough to be afraid.*

"Sef!" Achaeos called out. "Sef, come to us." Who else? Not Gaved, not Thalric, and Nivit's girl was out somewhere on business. "Nivit, are you there?"

"Help me!" It was Sef's voice, shrill with terror. Another Spider brought up by Beetles, Achaeos supposed.

"Here! Follow my voice! Come here!" he called out.

"Achaeos, how long are we going to be here?" Tynisa demanded of him.

He was glad that Sef appeared just then, stumbling and almost falling, until he caught her and set her on her feet. She promptly dropped to her knees, hugging herself, with eyes closed. He could not blame her.

"I . . . I need time to investigate our surroundings," he said, knowing his words were meaningless. *What if Gaved or someone plucks the box from my hands? Will we be wrenched out of here, or trapped for good?*

"Then get on with it!" Tynisa snapped at him, on the very edge of self-control. Tisamon put a hand on her shoulder.

"We are safe here," he said slowly. "We are safe from this place. You and I."

"And how do you know that?" she asked.

"Because this is *our* place, a Mantis place." He was looking into the coiling dark, stretching out his free hand, and for a second Achaeos saw Laetrimae there, just a glimmer of her, reaching back to him. *You are not the one*, she had said.

Tisamon?

"Achaeos, there's someone else out there," Tynisa hissed, and he looked, seeing only the suggestion of movement.

Has she seen Nivit? Or was it a . . . native?

"Nivit, is that . . . ?"

It was not Nivit. Achaeos felt the words dry up in his throat, seeing the newcomer approach so effortlessly. Gaunt and robed, it might have been a Moth Skryre, except that the gait and the build were all wrong—too tall, too thin, too pale.

A cadaverous face with bulging eyes that glared red in a world of green and black, Achaeos had never seen this man before but he remembered enough of his own people's lore to *know.* The recognition came as a blow, but he drew strength from it as well. Suddenly he was not just a lone seer in a hostile place, he was his whole kinden, its emissary to this ancient enemy.

"So," he said, "have I drawn you here as well—or is this the last hole your people have found to hide in?"

The newcomer's thin lips drew back, exposing needle-sharp teeth. Tisamon shifted uncomfortably, and Achaeos knew that he, too, must recognize this thing from folk stories.

"Oh, we are not gone at all," it said. "Hidden, but not quite gone, young Moth. We can hide more cunningly than your kind can ever search for us." One emaciated hand gestured at their surroundings. "Yet what a hiding place this would have made. No, I will not say that I have been drawn here, but merely accepted the invitation."

"What is your part in this?" Achaeos demanded.

"Must we be adversaries even here, even after so very long? Surely your kinden have realized how all we old powers are standing together now against the encroaching tide of progress and history. All the wars of the Days of Lore are long forgotten—by all save you and me. Who cares now about that fifty-year struggle with the Centipede-kinden who rose from beneath the earth? Who recalls the coup of the Assassin Bugs, and how it was turned aside? Who recounts the struggle for rulership between the Moth-kinden and the Mosquito-folk? None, save you and I."

Achaeos stared at him uncertainly.

"My name is Uctebri the Sarcad," the Mosquito told him. "My physical form is many leagues distant from you, so I am glad that your actions have allowed us to meet."

Sarcad. It was, he thought, their word for Skryre. A powerful magician, then? "I am Achaeos, seer of Tharn," he said. "I ask you again, what is your part in this?"

"I need the box, young Moth. I must have it."

"Then we are enemies, after all," Achaeos replied. He saw a brittle, sad smile on the Mosquito's face and realized that the man's words about the passing of so much history from the world had been quite sincere. "I do not hate you for your kinden. You are right, that is gone. I have the box, though, and I cannot give it to you."

"No," said Uctebri quietly, "you cannot. I am sorry for that."

"Achaeos," Tisamon said tensely. "Where is Tynisa? Where has my daughter gone?"

"Tynisa?" Achaeos looked round, but the Spider girl was nowhere to be seen. "I don't understand . . ."

The Mosquito was gone now, swallowed by the blackness. Was it all the time closing in? "Stay close by me," he said, feeling Sef clutch at his leg.

"Achaeos, something is wrong," Tisamon said, and a riveting pain lanced through the Moth, searing into his side and all the way through him. And suddenly he was falling . . . falling . . .

And then gone.

⁂

Tynisa snapped awake to see Thalric rushing toward her with a ragged cry. He vaulted some obstacle on the floor and she saw—actually saw—the crackle of his sting flower in his palm. She flung herself back and tripped over Nivit's low table. The flash of the sting seared over her head.

Her rapier was in her hand, as it had been in the dream. She bounded back up from the floor and lunged at him, and he twisted desperately to avoid her thrust.

I should have struck him. The blade was strangely sluggish in her hand. She tried to follow after him, feeling that perhaps this was still part of the dream, that maybe she had not awoken at all.

The blade of her sword was clotted with blood. Perhaps she had struck him after all, but she could see no wound on him even as he struggled away. He was shouting, though, shouting a name . . .

She saw movement behind her as Gaved tried to grab her. He got one arm about her throat, but she slammed her elbow into his face, catching him right in the jaw, and he reeled back. *Wasp traitor!* He and Thalric must have been in it together from the start, and more fool Sten for trusting them.

She tried to stab Gaved right in the face. Again the blade seemed heavy, lifeless in her grip, and it plunged past and into the wall. The twisted hilt smashed him across the jaw, though, and he fell back, stunned at least. The blade slid from the shoddy rotten wood of Nivit's shack and she turned on Thalric again.

"You've had this coming far too long!" she shouted at him, and something snapped in him, clearly something he had been holding back. A moment later he leapt at her, and her blade had only grazed his side before he slammed her to the floor with a grimace of rage. She punched him in the face, and he rammed her head back against the floorboards hard enough to make her vision blur, and then she dug her fingers deep into his side, where his wound was, as hard as she could, and he bellowed in pain and rolled off her.

She scrambled to her feet, but he already had one hand pointed at her.

"Die, you mad bitch!" he spat.

He lurched up on to one knee to shoot, but abruptly a puzzled expression spread across his face, and he plucked at something on his neck. A moment later he swayed, and then collapsed altogether.

Nivit stood in the doorway staring at her, a blowpipe to his lips.

She looked around to find Tisamon was slumped in one corner, while Sef was still sprawled where she had been sitting earlier. The two Wasps, of course, were both down, Gaved shaking his head groggily . . . and Achaeos was lying in a pool of spreading blood.

Just like the blood slicked on her blade.

And there was someone else, though she could only just see her. It was a bent old woman with red eyes, and something, some small thing, clasped in her hands.

She passed by Nivit on her way out, but it seemed as if the Skater did not notice her at all.

"Nivit," she called out, raising her sword, and she felt something sting her just above her eye.

"What?" She slapped at it awkwardly, her hand coming away with a tiny dart in it. "*Nivit?*"

Tynisa's world shook and swayed. The last thing she saw, before she collapsed, was Tisamon's eyes opening with a start, the Mantis leaping to his feet.

⁂

Sykore hurried away from Nivit's house as fast as she could, grasping the Shadow Box tightly to her, swathed by several layers of her robe. She dared not touch it directly. She dared not lose her purpose.

I was right there amongst them, she thought. The Spider girl had seen her, she knew, but then the Skater had pricked her with his dart. *I might have got hurt.* The mere thought of physical violence, of that glutted rapier darting toward her, made her shudder, momentarily unsteady on her feet. She would never take such risks again, but the prize had been too great and Uctebri's patronage too important.

They had nearly been too strong for her. She had been ready for the shift, but she had nearly become as trapped in the Shadow Box's little world as they had been. Uctebri's power, she knew, had helped free her, so that she could continue to act in the physical world while they were all stupefied. That had left only the Wasp-kinden, and it took no great skill to hide herself from those who never so much as suspected magic.

She had headed along the curve of the lake, looking for the swiftest way out of Jerez. Now she was bypassing the outlying hovels, out into the marshy grassland, lumpy and pitted through constant subsidence. She was well clear of the Lowlanders at least.

A great sigh of relief escaped her. She had not realized how much the possibility of harm had terrified her: her people's sense of self-preservation that routinely won out over common purpose or community. The Moth-kinden had always employed their Mantis guards to die for them, yet they had been willing to die themselves if it became ultimately necessary. Perhaps that was why they had triumphed, all those centuries ago.

She glanced down at the cloth-swathed object she was clutching, feeling its pull. She would hand it straight to Brodan and he would take it to his masters like the docile animal he was. He would feel nothing from it, however. To him it would be just a box.

"Turn," said a voice from behind her, and she did so, automatically, clutching the box to her and hissing in anger. There was a lean figure standing there with a metal blade jutting from his hand: the Mantis from the Moth's retinue. Her memory brought up the name "Tisamon."

She narrowed her eyes. "You are no magician, Mantis, so how did you get here?"

"Jerez is paved with mud and I need no magic to follow footsteps. I thought you would be Scyla, but you are not. Who, then, are you?"

"You do not wish to know," she told him. "Now leave me, Mantis. You do not dare test me."

"You have cast an enchantment over Tynisa," he told her flatly. She noticed that he was slowly inching closer.

"Why do you care what happens to a Spider?"

"She is my daughter," he replied. She saw his claw tilt back for the strike, and she thrust a sharp-nailed hand out toward him, seeing him flinch away automatically. She bared her teeth in a needled grin.

"So now you are here, but what will you do? I know your kind, Mantis. The Moth-kinden bred you well to serve them. But I am a magician, and you fear magic, do you not? And all the things it can do to you. You must know that to slay a magician is to bring a curse on you and all of yours."

"I have heard it said," he replied. He had stopped edging forward now and she knew she was right. A superstitious and ignorant race, the Mantids, for all their skill.

"Then leave here before I strike you down," she warned him. "Do you really think I shall stay my hand? Or will you dare to face me?"

"You are right of course," he said. "I shall not."

Her grin widened and just then a burning fist struck her in the small of the back, hammering her to the ground. She twisted round as she fell, still clutching the box to her, and saw a Wasp-kinden in a long coat landing to one side, a wisp of heat smoking from his hand.

They were coming for her. They were coming for the box.

Her strength was seeping away from her but she had one last trick, even though it was a mere apprentice's sleight. Concentrating only on the box, she summoned her powers before they had drained into the earth with her blood.

Looking up, she saw both Wasp and Mantis looming above her, the Wasp's sword poised about to stab. She spat at them defiantly, seeing the Mantis reel back. Then the blade drove into her.

⟨|⟩ ⟨|⟩ ⟨|⟩

Tisamon waited until the Mosquito was clearly dead—until Gaved had finished twisting his blade and pulled it out—before he reached for the box. He twitched the dead woman's voluminous sleeves aside. He had seen it there, the angular shape of it hidden in her grip. He had *felt* it there.

But it was gone. Her hands were crooked about its shape, but it was gone. He exchanged glances with Gaved, who could not understand. Swiftly the Wasp set to searching Sykore's body from head to toe, but Tisamon just stepped back, knowing that, by her magic, she had defeated them in the end.

❖ ❖ ❖

Nivit had sent for the best physician he knew, a grey-skinned creature named Doctor Mathonwy, who was seven foot tall, even with a pronounced hunchback, and had to bend double again just to get in through the door. He was now kneeling beside Achaeos, having just cut the Moth's blood-slicked robe away. Arranged all about him were bunches of herbs, a tiny brazier, some delicate bronze tools. The medicine he was performing was some strange mix of old and new.

Tynisa sat in one corner of the room, as though trying to push herself backward through the walls behind her. She stared at the prostrate Moth, biting her lip. Her sword lay discarded nearby. She did not want to touch it. She did not even look up as Tisamon returned.

He knelt down beside her, for a moment oddly awkward. "She is dead," he informed her, and when she made no response he continued, "The woman who enchanted you, she is dead."

"Does that help us?" Tynisa whispered. "Does that heal *him?*"

Tisamon grimaced. "You were not responsible. She had used her magic on you."

"I don't believe in magic." she spoke almost too softly for him to hear.

"Tynisa, you must. It is why we are here—"

"I don't believe it. I stabbed him. What will Che think? How could I do this to her?"

Tisamon shook his head, baffled. "But the magician herself is dead. I killed her."

"*That doesn't help!*" Tynisa almost spat at him. "Killing things . . . it's not the answer to everything, Tisamon. Is that your only way around any problem? To kill something?"

She saw his hurt, confused expression, and only then did she remember how he had dealt with the betrayal, as he had believed it, of her mother, his lover. He had gone to Helleron and hired out his blade, and killed people, even people who had nothing whatsoever to do with his pain. He had quenched his hurt in blood on a daily basis.

"Anyway, we've lost the cursed box," Gaved said tiredly. "I swear I searched everywhere, from here to where we found her, but there's nothing. She must have handed it on to someone."

"She sent it with her magic," Tisamon said.

"Whatever." The Wasp shrugged. "She might as well have done, since it's gone, and we've got no leads. And the Moth over there was the only one who seemed to be able to locate it."

Tynisa glared at him defensively but he was not accusing her, just thinking aloud.

"We have to get Achaeos out of here," she said. "We must get him to the *Maiden* and . . . away to Collegium. They have many good doctors in Collegium."

The spindly Doctor Mathonwy raised his hairless brows at that, but continued to tend to his patient.

"We've also attracted far too much attention," said Thalric. He was seated on Nivit's bed now, having tied some bandages about his freshly opened wound. The look he gave Tynisa was less than loving. "Up until now all the attention we merited was because we were also after this box. Now they'll be coming for *us*, so the girl's right: we should leave with the dawn."

Tisamon stared down at Tynisa's sword, and then bent forward to pick it up. Wordlessly he offered it to her.

"I don't want it," she said. Though he had cleaned it meticulously, in her eyes it was still reeking of Achaeos's blood.

"The sword is not to blame," Tisamon said softly.

"I don't care," she insisted. "I don't want it," she said.

"Consider this," he told her. "Achaeos could not move or defend himself when you struck. You are not so poor a swordswoman as to let such an open target live."

At last she looked at him, red-eyed. "What are you saying?"

"That the sword did not slay him. Remember the provenance of this blade. It is no mere steel: it is a weaponmaster's blade. It knew that you were not truly guiding it, not with your heart. If you had truly meant their deaths, then you would have slain them all: Achaeos, Nivit, the two Wasps. I have trained you, and I know that none of them could have stood against you had your heart desired to kill them. So take the sword. It has served you well."

"All delightful native colour, I'm sure," Thalric harshly interrupted, "but we have to be ready to leave." He stood up awkwardly just as Tisamon rounded on him.

For a moment the Mantis glared silently, but then he nodded. "You are correct. I shall find the Beetle, Allanbridge. We must get Achaeos back to Collegium or he will die."

The look that Doctor Mathonwy gave him suggested that this was more than just a possibility in any event.

◆ ◆ ◆

Brodan awoke in agony. Somehow he had fallen asleep, even here beside the dark lake. Now he was freezing, dew drenched, and his wounds had stiffened so he could barely move. He groaned in pain, tried flexing his limbs, to be rewarded with pain shooting down his back and into his side.

There was something unfamiliar in his hand. His fingers were locked about it hard enough for the object's irregular edges to dent his skin. He opened his eyes against the light of morning. It took some prying with the other hand to release his frozen grip.

It was the box. His breath caught as he saw it. He was holding the box. The very thing he had been so firmly instructed to recover.

That brief future composed of recrimination and punishment, which had been facing him like a looming wall, suddenly shattered, and behind it lay a sunny prospect of promotion and privilege, *because he had the box.*

With some effort, he rolled over onto his knees and then stood up unsteadily. He had to reach the garrison and secure transport immediately for the capital. Brodan was so invigorated by the discovery that he never paused to wonder what price others had paid, to bring the box to him.

ABOUT THE AUTHOR

ADRIAN TCHAIKOVSKY was born in Woodhall Spa, Lincolnshire, before heading off to Reading to study psychology and zoology. For reasons unclear even to himself he subsequently ended up practising law and has worked as a legal executive in both Reading and Leeds, where he now lives. Married, he is a keen live role-player and occasional amateur actor, has trained in stage fighting, and keeps no exotic or dangerous pets of any kind, possibly excepting his son.